LIBRA
Don DeLillo

PENGUIN BOOKS

PENGUIN BOOKS
Published by the Penguin Group
Penguin Books USA Inc.,
375 Hudson Street, New York, New York 10014, U.S.A.
Penguin Books Ltd, 27 Wrights Lane, London W8 5TZ, England
Penguin Books Australia Ltd, Ringwood, Victoria, Australia
Penguin Books Canada Ltd, 10 Alcorn Avenue,
Toronto, Ontario, Canada M4V 3B2
Penguin Books (N.Z.) Ltd, 182–190 Wairau Road,
Auckland 10, New Zealand

Penguin Books Ltd, Registered Offices:
Harmondsworth, Middlesex, England

First published in the United States of America by
Viking Penguin Inc., 1988
NAL/Penguin edition published 1989
Published in Penguin Books 1991

7   9   10   8   6

Portions of this book were published in *Esquire* magazine.

THE LIBRARY OF CONGRESS HAS CATALOGUED THE HARDCOVER AS FOLLOWS:
DeLillo, Don.
Libra.
I. Title.
PS3554.E4425L53   1988   813'.54   87-40649
ISBN 0-670-82317-1
ISBN 0 14 01.5604 6

Printed in the United States of America

To the boys at 607:
Tony, Dick and Ron

PART ONE

Happiness is not based on oneself, it does not consist of a small home, of taking and getting. Happiness is taking part in the struggle, where there is no borderline between one's own personal world, and the world in general.

LEE H. OSWALD
Letter to his brother

In the Bronx

This was the year he rode the subway to the ends of the city, two hundred miles of track. He liked to stand at the front of the first car, hands flat against the glass. The train smashed through the dark. People stood on local platforms staring nowhere, a look they'd been practicing for years. He kind of wondered, speeding past, who they really were. His body fluttered in the fastest stretches. They went so fast sometimes he thought they were on the edge of no-control. The noise was pitched to a level of pain he absorbed as a personal test. Another crazy-ass curve. There was so much iron in the sound of those curves he could almost taste it, like a toy you put in your mouth when you are little.

Workmen carried lanterns along adjacent tracks. He kept a watch for sewer rats. A tenth of a second was all it took to see a thing complete. Then the express stations, the creaky brakes, people bunched like refugees. They came wagging through the doors, banged against the rubber edges, inched their way in, were quickly pinned, looking out past the nearest heads into that practiced oblivion.

It had nothing to do with him. He was riding just to ride.

One forty-ninth, the Puerto Ricans. One twenty-fifth, the Negroes. At Forty-second Street, after a curve that held a scream right out to the edge, came the heaviest push of all, briefcases, shopping bags, school bags, blind people, pickpockets, drunks. It did not seem odd to him that the subway held more compelling things than the famous city above. There was nothing important out there, in the broad afternoon, that he could not find in purer form in these tunnels beneath the streets.

They watched TV, mother and son, in the basement room. She'd bought a tinted filter for their Motorola. The top third of the screen was permanently blue, the middle third was pink, the band across the bottom was a wavy green. He told her he'd played hooky again, ridden the trains out to Brooklyn, where a man wore a coat with a missing arm. Playing the hook, they called it here. Marguerite believed it was not so awful, missing a day now and then. The other kids ragged him all the time and he had problems keeping up, a turbulence running through him, the accepted fact of a fatherless boy. Like the time he waved a penknife at John Edward's bride. Not that Marguerite thought her daughter-in-law was worth getting into a famous feud about. She was not a person of high caliber and it was just an argument over whittling wood, over scraps of wood he'd whittled onto the floor of her apartment, where they were trying to be a family again. So there it was. They were not wanted anymore and they moved to the basement room in the Bronx, the kitchen and the bedroom and everything together, where blue heads spoke to them from the TV screen.

When it got cold they banged the pipes to let the super know. They had a right to decent heat.

She sat and listened to the boy's complaints. She couldn't fry him a platter of chops any time he wanted but she wasn't tight with the lunch money and even gave him extra for a funnybook or subway ride. All her life she'd had to deal with the injustice of these complaints. Edward walked out on her when she was pregnant with

John Edward because he didn't want to support a child. Robert dropped dead on her one steamy summer day on Alvar Street, in New Orleans, when she was carrying Lee, which meant she had to find work. Then there was grinning Mr. Ekdahl, the best, the only hope, an older man who earned nearly a thousand dollars a month, an engineer. But he committed cunning adulteries, which she finally caught him out at, recruiting a boy to deliver a fake telegram and then opening the door on a woman in a negligee. This didn't stop him from scheming a divorce that cheated her out of a decent settlement. Her life became a dwindling history of moving to cheaper places.

Lee saw a picture in the Daily News of Greeks diving off a pier for some sacred cross, downtown. Their priests have beards.

"Think I don't know what I'm supposed to be around here."

"I've been all day on my feet," she said.

"I'm the one you drag along."

"I never said any such."

"Think I like making my own dinner."

"I work. I work. Don't I work?"

"Barely finding food."

"I'm not a type that sits around boo-hoo."

Thursday nights he watched the crime shows. *Racket Squad*, *Dragnet*, etc. Beyond the barred window, snow driving slantwise through the streetlight. Northern cold and damp. She came home and told him they were moving again. She'd found three rooms on one hundred and something street, near the Bronx Zoo, which might be nice for a growing boy with an interest in animals.

"Natures spelled backwards," the TV said.

It was a railroad flat in a red-brick tenement, five stories, in a street of grim exhibits. A retarded boy about Lee's age walked around in a hippity-hop limp, carrying a live crab he'd stolen from the Italian market and pushing it in the faces of smaller kids. This was a routine sight. Rock fights were routine. Guys with zip guns they'd made in shop class were becoming routine. From his window one night he watched two boys put the grocery store cat in a burlap sack and swing the sack against a lamppost. He tried to time his movements against the rhythm of the street. Stay off the street from noon to one, three to five. Learn the alleys, use the dark. He rode the subways. He spent serious time at the zoo.

There were older men who did not sit on the stoop out front until they spread their handkerchiefs carefully on the gray stone.

His mother was short and slender, going gray now just a little. She liked to call herself petite in a joke she really meant. They watched each other eat. He taught himself to play chess, from a book, at the kitchen table. Nobody knew how hard it was for him to read. She bought figurines and knickknacks and talked on the subject of her life. He heard her footsteps, heard her key in the lock.

"Here is another notice," Marguerite said, "where they threaten a hearing. Have you been hiding these? They want a truancy hearing, which it says is the final notice. It states you haven't gone to school at all since we moved. Not one day. I don't know why it is I have to learn these things through the U.S. mails. It's a blow, it's a shock to my system."

"Why should I go to school? They don't want me there and I don't want to be there. It works out just right."

"They are going to crack down. It is not like home. They are going to bring us into court."

"I don't need help going into court. You just go to work like any other day."

"I'd have given the world to stay home and raise my children and you know it. This is a sore spot with me. Don't you forget, I'm the child of one parent myself. I know the meanness of the situation. I worked in shops back home where I was manager."

Here it comes. She would forget he was here. She would talk for two hours in the high piping tone of someone reading to a child. He watched the DuMont test pattern.

"I love my United States but I don't look forward to a courtroom situation, which is what happened with Mr. Ekdahl, accusing me of uncontrollable rages. They will point out that they have cautioned us officially. I will tell them I'm a person with no formal education who holds her own in good company and keeps a neat house. We are a military family. This is my defense."

The zoo was three blocks away. There were traces of ice along the fringes of the wildfowl pond. He walked down to the lion house, hands deep in his jacket pockets. No one there. The smell hit him full-on, a warmth and a force, the great carnivore reek of raw beef and animal fur and smoky piss.

When he heard the heavy doors open, the loud voices, he knew what to expect. Two kids from P.S. 44. A chunky kid named Scalzo in a pea coat and clacking shoes with a smaller, runny-nose comedian Lee knew only by his street name, which was Nicky Black. Here to pester the animals, create the routine disturbances that made up their days. He could almost feel their small joy as they spotted him, a little jump of muscle in the throat.

Scalzo's voice banged through the high chamber.

"They call your name every day in class. But what kind of name is Lee? That's a girl's name or what?"

"His name is Tex," Nicky Black said.

"He's a cowpoke," Scalzo said.

"You know what cowpokes do, don't you? Tell him, Tex."

"They poke the cows," Scalzo said.

Lee went out the north door, a faint smile on his face. He walked down the steps and around to the ornate cages of the birds of prey. He didn't mind fighting. He was willing to fight. He'd fought with the kid who threw rocks at his dog, fought and won, beat him good, whipped him, bloodied his nose. That was on Vermont Street, in Covington, when he had a dog. But this baiting was a torment. They would get on him, lose interest, circle back fitfully, picking away, scab-picking, digging down.

Scalzo drifted toward a group of older boys and girls huddled smoking around a bench. Lee heard someone say, "A two-tone Rocket Olds with wire wheels."

The king vulture sat on its perch, naked head and neck. There is a vulture that breaks ostrich eggs by hurling stones with its beak. Nicky Black was standing next to him. The name was always used in full, never just Nicky or Black.

"Playing the hook is one thing. I say all right. But you don't show your face in a month."

It sounded like a compliment.

"You shoot pool, Tex? What do you do, you're home all day. Pocket pool, right? Think fast."

He faked a punch to Lee's groin, drew back.

"But how come you live in the North? My brother was stationed in Fort Benning, Georgia. He says they have to put a pebble in their hand down south so they know left face from right face. This is true or what?"

He mock-sparred, wagging his head, breathing rapidly through his nose.

"My brother's in the Coast Guard," Lee told him. "That's why we're here. He's stationed in Ellis Island. Port security it's called."

"My brother's in Korea now."

"My other brother's in the Marines. They might send him to Korea. That's what I'm worried about."

"It's not the Koreans you have to worry about," Nicky Black said. "It's the fucking Chinese."

There was reverence in his voice, a small note of woe. He wore torn Keds and a field jacket about as skimpy as Lee's windbreaker. He was runty and snuffling and the left half of his face had a permanent grimace.

"I know where to get some sweet mickeys off the truck. We go roast them in the lot near Belmont. They have sweet mickeys in the South down there? I know where to get these books where you spin the pages fast, you see people screwing. The kid knows these things. The kid quits school the minute he's sixteen. I mean look out."

He blew a grain of tobacco from the tip of his tongue.

"The kid gets a job in construction. First thing, he buys ten shirts with Mr. B collars. He saves his money, before you know it he owns a car. He simonizes the car once a month. The car gets him laid. Who's better than the kid?"

Scalzo was the type that sauntered over, shoulders swinging. The taps on his shoes scraped lightly on the rough asphalt.

"But how come you never talk to me, Tex?"

"Let's hear you drawl," Nicky Black said.

"I say all right."

"Talk to Richie. He's talking nice."

"But let's hear you drawl. No shit. I been looking forward."

Lee smiled, started walking past the group hunched over the park bench, lighting cigarettes in the wind, the fifteen-year-old girls with bright lipstick, the guys in pegged pants with saddle stitching and pistol pockets. He walked up to the main court and took the path that led to the gate nearest his street.

Scalzo and Nicky Black were ten yards behind.

"Hey fruit."

"He sucks Clorets."

"Bad-breath kissing sweet in seconds."

"One and a two."

"I say all right."

"One two cha cha cha."

"He don't know dick."

"I mean look out."

"But how come he won't talk to me?"

"But what do we have to do?"

"Smoke a Fag-a-teeeer."

"Ex-treeeem-ly mild."

"I say all right."

"But talk to us."

"We're talking bad or what?"

"But say something."

"Think fast, Tex."

"I say all right."

At the gate a man in a lumber jacket and necktie asked him

his name. Lee said he didn't talk to Yankees. The man pointed to a spot on the pavement, meaning that's where you stand until we get this straight. Then he walked over to the other two boys, talked to them for a moment, gesturing toward Lee. Nicky Black said nothing. Scalzo shrugged. The man identified himself as a truant officer. Scalzo tugged at his crotch, looking the man right in the eye. Like so what, mister. Nicky Black did a little cold-day dance, hands in pockets, giving a buck-tooth grin.

Out on the street the man escorted Lee to a green-and-white squad car. Lee was impressed. There was a cop behind the wheel. He drove with one hand, keeping the hand that cupped a cigarette down between his knees.

Marguerite stayed up late watching the test pattern.

Lee purely loves animals so the zoo was a blessing but they sent him downtown to a building where the nut doctors pick at him twenty-four hours a day. Youth House. Puerto Ricans by the galore. He has to take showers in that jabber. John Edward tried to get him to talk to the nut doctor but Lee won't talk to John Edward ever since he opened the pocketknife on John Edward's bride. They have got him in an intake dormitory. They talk to him about is he a nail-biter. Does he have religious affiliation and whatnot? Is he disruptive in class? He doesn't know the slang, your honor. The place is full of New York–type boys. They see my son in Levis, with an accent. Well many boys wear Levis. What is strange about Levis? But they get on him about does he think he's Billy the Kid. This is a boy who played Monopoly with his brothers and had a normal report card when we lived with Mr. Ekdahl, on Eighth Avenue, in Fort Worth. It is a question of adjusting, judge. It was only a whittling knife and he did not actually cut her and now they don't talk, brothers. This is a boy who studies the lives of animals, the eating and sleeping habits of animals, animals in their burrows and caves. What is it called, lairs? He is advanced, your honor. I have said from early childhood he liked histories and maps. He knows uncanny things without the normal schooling. This boy slept in my bed out of lack of space until he was nearly eleven and we have lived the two of us in the meanest of small rooms when his brothers were in the orphans' home or the military academy or the Marines and the Coast Guard. Most boys think their daddy hung the moon. But the poor man just crashed to the lawn and that was the end of the only happy part of my adult life. It is Marguerite and Lee ever since. We are a mother and son. It has never been a question of neglect. They say he is truanting is the way they state it. They state to me he stays home all day to watch TV. They are talking about a court clinic. They are talking about the Protestant Big Brothers for working with. He already has big brothers. What does he need more brothers for? There is the Salvation Army that is mentioned. They take the wrappers off the candy bars I bring my son. They turn my pocketbook all out. This treatment is downgrading. It is not my fault if he dresses below the level. What is the fuss about? A boy playing hooky in Texas is not a criminal who is put away for study. They have made my boy a matter on the calendar. They expect me to ask their permission to go back home. We are not the common drifters they paint us out to be. How on God's earth, and I am a Christian, does a neglectful mother make such a decent home, which I am willing to show as evidence, with bright touches and not a thing out of place. I am not afraid to make food last. This is no disgrace, to cook up beans and cornbread and make it last. The tightfisted one was Mr. Ekdahl, on Granbury Road, in Benbrook, when the adulteries started. But I am the one accused of excesses and rages. I took back my name, your honor. Marguerite Claverie Oswald. We moved to Willing Street then, by the railroad tracks.

He did Human Figure Drawings, which were judged impoverished.

The psychologist found him to be in the upper range of Bright Normal Intelligence.

The social worker wrote, "Questioning elicited the information that he feels almost as if there is a veil between him and other people through which they cannot reach him, but he prefers this veil to remain intact."

The schoolteacher reported that he sailed paper planes around the room.

He returned to the seventh grade until classes ended. In summer dusk the girls lingered near the benches on Bronx Park South. Jewish girls, Italian girls in tight skirts, girls with ankle bracelets, their voices murmurous with the sound of boys' names, with song lyrics, little remarks he didn't always understand. They talked to him when he walked by, making him smile in his secret way.

Oh a woman with beer on her breath, on the bus coming home from the beach. He feels the tired salty sting in his eyes of a day in the sun and water.

"The trouble leaving you with my sister," Marguerite said, "she had too many children of her own. Plus the normal disputes of family. That meant I had to employ Mrs. Roach, on Pauline Street, when you were two. But I came home one day and saw she whipped you, raising welts on your legs, and we moved to Sherwood Forest Drive."

Heat entered the flat through the walls and windows, seeped down from the tar roof. Men on Sundays carried pastry in white boxes. An Italian was murdered in a candy store, shot five times, his brains dashing the wall near the comic-book rack. Kids trooped to the store from all around to see the traces of grayish spatter. His mother sold stockings in Manhattan.

A woman on the street, completely ordinary, maybe fifty years old, wearing glasses and a dark dress, handed him a leaflet at the foot of the El steps. *Save the Rosenbergs*, it said. He tried to give it back, thinking he would have to pay for it, but she'd already turned away. He walked home, hearing a lazy radio voice doing a ballgame. Plenty of room, folks. Come on out for the rest of this game and all of the second. It was a Sunday, Mother's Day, and he folded the leaflet neatly and put it in his pocket to save for later.

There is a world inside the world.

He rode the subway up to Inwood, out to Sheepshead Bay. There were serious men down there, rocking in the copper light. He saw chinamen, beggars, men who talked to God, men who lived on the trains, day and night, bruised, with matted hair, asleep in patient bundles on the wicker seats. He jumped the turnstiles once. He rode between cars, gripping the heavy chain. He felt the friction of the ride in his teeth. They went so fast sometimes. He liked the feeling they were on the edge. How do we know the motorman's not insane? It gave him a funny thrill. The wheels touched off showers of blue-white sparks, tremendous hissing bursts, on the edge of no-control. People crowded in, every shape face in the book of faces. They pushed through the doors, they hung from the porcelain straps. He was riding just to ride. The noise had a power and a human force. The dark had a power. He stood at the front of the first car, hands flat against the glass. The view down the tracks was a form of power. It was a secret and a power. The beams picked out secret things. The noise was pitched to a fury he located in the mind, a satisfying wave of rage and pain.

Never again in his short life, never in the world, would he feel this inner power, rising to a shriek, this secret force of the soul in the tunnels under New York.

17 April

Nicholas Branch sits in the book-filled room, the room of documents, the room of theories and dreams. He is in the fifteenth year of his labor and sometimes wonders if he is becoming bodiless. He knows he is getting old. There are times when he can't concentrate on the facts at hand and has to come back again and again to the page, the line, the fine-grained detail of a particular afternoon. He wanders in and out of these afternoons, the bright hot skies that give tone and depth to narrow data. He falls asleep sometimes, slumped in the chair, a hand curled on the broadloom rug. This is the room of growing old, the fireproof room, paper everywhere.

But he knows where everything is. From a stack of folders that reaches halfway up a wall, he smartly plucks the one he wants. The stacks are everywhere. The legal pads and cassette tapes are everywhere. The books fill tall shelves along three walls and cover the desk, a table and much of the floor. There is a massive file cabinet stuffed with documents so old and densely packed they may be ready to ignite spontaneously. Heat and light. There is no formal system to help him track the material in the room. He uses hand and eye, color and shape and memory, the configuration of suggestive things that link an object to its contents. He wakes up suddenly, wondering where he is.

Sometimes he looks around him, horrified by the weight of it all, the career of paper. He sits in the data-spew of hundreds of lives. There's no end in sight. When he needs something, a report or transcript, anything, any level of difficulty, he simply has to ask. The Curator is quick to respond, firm in his insistence on forwarding precisely the right document in an area of research marked by ambiguity and error, by political bias, systematic fantasy. But not just the right document, not just an obscure footnote from an open source. The Curator sends him material not seen by anyone outside the headquarters complex at Langley, material that includes the results of internal investigations, confidential files from the Agency's own Office of Security. Branch hasn't met the current Curator and doubts if he ever will. They talk on the telephone, terse as snowbirds but unfailingly polite, fellow bookmen after all.

Nicholas Branch in his glove-leather armchair is a retired senior analyst of the Central Intelligence Agency, hired on contract to write the secret history of the assassination of President Kennedy. Six point nine seconds of heat and light. Let's call a meeting to analyze the blur. Let's devote our lives to understanding this moment, separating the elements of each crowded second. We will build theories that gleam like jade idols, intriguing systems of assumption, four-faced, graceful. We will follow the bullet trajectories backwards to the lives that occupy the shadows, actual men who moan in their dreams. Elm Street. A woman wonders why she is sitting on the grass, bloodspray all around. Tenth Street. A witness leaves her shoes on the hood of a bleeding policeman's car. A strangeness, Branch feels, that is almost holy. There is much here that is holy, an aberration in the heartland of the real. Let's regain our grip on things.

He enters a date on the home computer the Agency has provided for the sake of convenient tracking. April 17, 1963. The names appear at once, with backgrounds, connections, locations. The bright hot skies. The shady street of handsome old homes framed in native oak.

American kitchens. This one has a breakfast nook, where a man named Walter Everett Jr. was sitting, thinking—Win, as he was called—lost to the morning noises collecting around him, a stir of the all-familiar, the heartbeat mosaic of every happy home, toast springing up, radio voices with their intimate and busy timbre, an optimistic buzz living in the ear. The Record-Chronicle was at his elbow, still fresh in its newsboy fold. Images wavered in the sunlit trim of appliances, something always moving, a brightness flying, so much to know in the world. He stirred the coffee, thought, stirred, sat in the wide light, spoon dangling now, a gentle and tentative man, it would be fair to say, based solely on appearance.

He was thinking about secrets. Why do we need them and what do they mean? His wife was reaching for the sugar.

He had important thoughts at breakfast. He had thoughts at lunch in his office in the Old Main Building. In the evening he sat on the porch, thinking. He believed it was a natural law that men with secrets tend to be drawn to each other, not because they want to share what they know but because they need the company of the like-minded, the fellow afflicted—a respite from the other life, from the eerie realness of living with people who do not keep secrets as a profession or duty, or a business fixed to one's existence.

Mary Frances watched him butter the toast. He held the edges of the slice in his left hand, moved the knife in systematic strokes, over and over. Was he trying to distribute the butter evenly? Or were there other, deeper requirements? It was sad to see him lost in small business, eternally buttering, turning routine into empty compulsion, without meaning or need.

She knew how to worry reasonably. She knew how to use the sound of her own voice to bring him back to what was safe and plain, among the breakfast dishes, on the tenth straight sunny day.

"One of the nicest things to watch? And I've never really noticed till we moved here? People coming out of church. Just gathering near the steps and talking. Isn't it one of the best things to watch?"

"You thought you'd find outlaws down here."

"I like it here. You're the one."

"Men swaggering into saloons. Thirsty from cattle drives."

"I mean churches anywhere. I just never paid attention before."

"I like to watch people come out of motels."

"No but I'm serious. There's something lovely about a church lawn or church steps with the service just ended and people slowly coming out and forming little groups. They look so nice."

"That's what I didn't like about Sundays when I was growing up. All the frumpy people in their starchy clothes. Depressed the hell out of me."

"What's wrong with frumpy? I like being a middle-aged frump."

"I didn't mean you."

He reached across the table and touched her arm as he always did when he thought he might have said something wrong or cut her off. Don't listen to what I say. Trust my hands, my touch.

"It's so comfortable," she said.

We tend to draw together to seek mutual solace for our disease. This is what he thought at the breakfast table in the sweet old house, turn-of-the-century, with the curved porch, the oak posts furled in trumpet vines. He had time to think, time to become an old man in aspic, in sculptured soap, quaint and white. It was not unusual for men in the clandestine service to retire at age fifty-one. A pension plan had been approved by some committee and a statement had been issued about the onerous and dangerous lives led by such people; the family problems; the transient nature of assignments. But Win Everett's retirement wasn't exactly voluntary. There was the business in Coral Gables. There were visits to the polygraph machine. And from three levels of specialists he heard the term "motivational exhaustion." Two were CIA psychiatrists, the other a cleared contact in the outside world, the place he found so eerie and real.

They called it semiretirement. A semantic kindness. They set him up in a teaching post here and paid him a retainer to recruit likely students as junior officer trainees. In a college for women, this was a broad comic thrust even Win could appreciate in a bitter and self-punishing way, as if he were still on their side, watching himself from a distance.

This is what we end up doing, he thought. Spying on ourselves. We are at the mercy of our own detachment. A thought for breakfast.

He folded the lightly toasted slice, ready at last to eat. In his ordinary body she saw the power of conviction. A lean and easy frame. A mild face, clear eyes, high and sad and mottled forehead. There was a burning faith in this man, a sense of cause. Mary Frances saw this more clearly than ever now that he'd been sent away from the councils and planning groups, the task forces, the secret training sites. Deprived of real duties, of contact with the men and events that informed his zeal, he was becoming all principle, all zeal. She was afraid he would turn into one of those men who make a saintliness of their resentment, shining through the years with a pure and tortured light. The radio said high seventies. God is alive and well in Texas.

Suzanne came in, hungry all over again, their six-year-old. She stood with her head propped against her daddy's arm, feet crossed in a certain way, half sullen, a routine bid for attention. She had her mother's matter-of-fact blondness, hair thick and wiry, her face paler than Mary Frances's, without the wind-roughened texture. Because they'd wanted a child but had given up hope, she was a sign of something unselfish in the world, some great-hearted force that could turn their smallness to admiring awe. Win gathered her in, allowing her to collapse dramatically. He fed her the rest of his toast and made slobbering sounds while she chewed, his gray eyes excited. Mary Frances listened to *Life Line* on KDNT, a commentary on the need for parents to be more vigilant in checking what their children read and watch and listen to.

"Danger everywhere," said the grim voice.

Win tapped his breast pocket for a cigarette. Suzanne hurried out, hearing the school bus. A silence fell, the first of the day's pauses, the first small exhaustion. Then Mary Frances in her Viyella robe began to remove things from the table, a series of light clear sounds hanging in the air, discreet as hand bells.

The two men sat in Win Everett's temporary office in the basement of the Old Main, under a weak and twitchy fluorescent light. Win was in shirtsleeves, smoking, eager to talk, surprised and a little dismayed at the high anticipation he felt, sharing news with a former colleague face to face.

Carpenters worked in the hallway, men with close-cropped hair and poky drawls, calling to each other under the steam ducts.

Laurence Parmenter leaned forward in his chair, a tall broad man in a blue oxford shirt and dark suit. He showed a vigor even in repose, his blond hair touched with silver at the sideburns, and he had the air of a man who wishes to conduct business, affably, over jokes and drinks. Win thought he was an impressive sort of fellow, self-assured, well connected, one of the men behind the crisp and scintillating coup in Guatemala in 1954, a collector of vintage wines, friend and fellow veteran of the Bay of Pigs.

"My God, they buried you."

"Texas Woman's University. Savor the name."

"What do you teach?"

"History and economics. Somebody in the DDP asked me to check out promising students for them. Foreign girls in particular. If there's a future prime minister here, the idea is we recruit her now, while she's still a virgin."

"Christamighty."

"First they hand me over to the psychiatrists," Win said. "Then they send me into exile. What country is this anyway?"

They both laughed.

"I say the name to myself all the time. I let it flow over me. I linger in its aura."

"Texas Woman's University," Parmenter whispered almost reverently.

Win sat nodding. He and Larry Parmenter had belonged to a group called SE Detailed, six military analysts and intelligence men. The group was one element in a four-stage committee set up to confront the problem of Castro's Cuba. The first stage, the Senior Study Effort, consisted of fourteen high officials, including presidential advisers, ranking military men, special assistants, undersecretaries, heads of intelligence. They met for an hour and a half. Then eleven men left the room, six men entered. The resulting group, called SE Augmented, met for two hours. Then seven men left, four men entered, including Everett and Parmenter. This was SE Detailed, a group that developed specific covert operations and then decided which members of SE Augmented ought to know about these plans. Those members in turn wondered whether the Senior Study Effort wanted to know what was going on in stage three. Chances are they didn't. When the meeting in stage three was over, five men left the room and three paramilitary officers entered to form Leader 4. Win Everett was the only man present at both the third and fourth stages.

"Could actually be worse," Parmenter said. "At least you're still in."

"I'd love to be out, completely, once and for all."

"And do what?"

"Start my own firm. Consult."

"On what, secret invasions?"

"That's one problem. I'm something of a tainted commodity. The other difficulty is I have precious little instinct for business ventures. I know how to teach. CIA has a picture of my prelapsarian soul in their files. They looked at it and sent me here."

"They kept you on. That's the point. They understand more deeply than you think they do."

"I'd love to be out forever. As long as I'm here, I still work for them, even though it's all a poor sick joke."

"They'll bring you back, Win."

"Do I want to be brought back? I don't like the kind of double-minded feeling I have about this thing. Despise them on the one hand; crave their love and understanding on the other."

Knowledge was a danger, ignorance a cherished asset. In many cases the DCI, the Director of Central Intelligence, was not to know important things. The less he knew, the more decisively he could function. It would impair his ability to tell the truth at an inquiry or a hearing, or in an Oval Office chat with the President, if he knew what they were doing in Leader 4, or even what they were talking about, or muttering in their sleep. The Joint Chiefs were not to know. The operational horrors were not for their ears. Details were a form of contamination. The Secretaries were to be insulated from knowing. They were happier not knowing, or knowing too late. The Deputy Secretaries were interested in drifts and tendencies. They expected to be misled. They counted on it. The Attorney General wasn't to know the queasy details. Just get results. Each level of the committee was designed to protect a higher level. There were complexities of speech. A man needed special experience and insight to work true meanings out of certain murky remarks. There were pauses and blank looks. Brilliant riddles floated up and down the echelons, to be pondered, solved, ignored. It had to be this way, Win admitted to himself. The men at his level were spawning secrets that quivered like reptile eggs. They were planning to poison Castro's cigars. They were designing cigars equipped with micro-explosives. They had a poison pen in the works. They were conspiring with organized-crime figures to send assassins to Havana, poisoners, snipers, saboteurs. They were testing a botulin toxin on monkeys. Fidel would be seized by cramps, vomiting and fits of coughing, just like the long-tailed primates, and horribly die. Have you ever seen a monkey coughing uncontrollably? Gruesome. They wanted to put fungus spores in his scuba suit. They were devising a sea shell that would explode when he went swimming.

The members of the committee would allow only generalities to carry upward. It was the President, of course, who was the final object of their protective instincts. They all knew that JFK wanted Castro cooling on a slab but they weren't allowed to let on to him that his guilty yearning was the business they'd charged themselves to carry out. The White House was to be the summit of unknowing. It was as if an unsullied leader redeemed some ancient truth which the others were forced to admire only in the abstract, owing to their mission in the convoluted world.

But there were even deeper shadows, strange and grave silences surrounding plans to invade the island. The President knew about this, of course—knew the broad contours, had a sense of the promised outcome. But the system still operated as an insulating muse. Let him see the softer tones. Shield him from responsibility. Secrets build their own networks, Win believed. The system would perpetuate itself in all its curious and obsessive webbings, its equivocations and patient riddles and levels of delusional thought, at least until the men were on the beach.

After the Bay of Pigs, nothing was the same. Win spent the spring of '61 traveling between Miami, Washington and Guatemala City to close out different segments of the operation, get drunk with station chiefs and advisers, try to explain to exile leaders what went wrong. It was the unraveling of the plot, the first weeks of a wreckage whose life span he seemed determined to prolong at the risk of his own well-being, as if he wanted to compensate for the half-measures that had brought about defeat. A new committee replaced the old, structured less cleverly, although many of the same men, to no one's shocked surprise, took chairs in the paneled room. The death of Fidel Castro was the small talk once more. But SE Detailed and Leader 4 would not take part. The groups were disbanded, their members marked not as failed plotters and operatives but as the Americans in the invasion array who had the deepest personal involvement in the exiles' cause. It was precisely the true believers who must be removed. Their contact with the exile leaders, their work in assembling and training the assault brigade, had made these men overresponsive to policy shifts, light-sensitive, unpredictable. All this was unspoken, of course. The groups simply disappeared and the members were given scattered duties unrelated to Castro's Cuba, the moonlit fixation in the emerald sea.

Interestingly, some of the men continued to meet.

"Will he find us?"

"I have a feeling he's already here," Win said.

"My plane leaves at five-twenty-five."

"He'll find us."

They sat at the lunch counter in Shraders Pharmacy on the courthouse square. Win stirred his coffee, thought, sat, stirred. Larry kept ducking in his seat to get a better look at the Denton County courthouse, a limestone building of mixed and vigorous character, with turrets, pediments, marble columns, pointed domes, roof balustrades, Second Empire pavilions.

"I look at these ornate old buildings in bustling town squares and I find them full of a hopefulness I think I cherish. Look at the thing. It's so imposing. Imagine a man at the turn of the century coming to a small Southwestern town and seeing a building like this. What stability and civic pride. It's an optimistic architecture. It expects the future to make as much sense as the past."

Win said nothing.

"I'm talking about the American past," Larry said, "as we naïvely think of it, which is the one kind of innocence I endorse."

The subject ostensibly was Cuba. They'd met several times in an apartment in Coral Gables, a place Parmenter had used to brief Cuban pilots on their way to Nicaragua. They talked about maintaining contacts in the exile community, setting up a network in the Castro government. They were five men who could not let go of Cuba. But they were also an outlawed group. This gave their meetings a self-referring character. Things turned inward. There was only one secret that mattered now and that was the group itself.

"Only be a minute," Win said.

They walked under a canopy and went into the long dark interior of the hardware store, a place of lost and reproachful beauty, with displays of frontier tools and ancient weighing machines, where Win often came to walk the two aisles like a tourist in waist-high ruins, expanded and sad. He had to remind himself it was only hardware. He bought a paint scraper and when they got back to Larry's rented car, parked off the square, they saw a figure in the front seat, passenger side, a broad-shouldered man in a loud sport shirt. This was T. J. Mackey, a cowboy type to Win's mind but probably the most adept of the men in Leader 4, a veteran field officer who'd trained exiles in assault weapons and supervised early phases of the landings.

Parmenter got behind the wheel, humming something that amused him. Win sat in the middle of the rear seat, giving directions. With Mackey here, the day took on purpose. T-Jay did not bring news of hirings and firings, the births of babies. He was one of the men the Cubans would follow without question. He was also the only man who'd refused to sign a letter of reprimand when the secret meetings in Coral Gables were monitored by the Office of Security. If a monumental canvas existed of the five grouped conspirators, a painting that showed them with knit brows and twisted torsos, darkly scheming men being confronted by crewcut security agents in khaki suits with natural shoulders, it might be titled "Light Entering the Cave of the Ungodly." Parmenter and two others signed letters of reprimand that were placed in their personnel files. Win signed a letter and also agreed to a technical interview, or polygraph exam. He signed a quit claim, stating that he was taking the test voluntarily. He signed a secrecy agreement, stating that he would talk to no one about the test. When he failed the polygraph, security men sealed his office, a small room with a blue door on the fourth floor of the Agency's new headquarters at Langley. In the office they found telephone notes and documents that seemed to indicate, amid the usual ambiguities, that Win Everett was putting people of his own into Zenith Technical Enterprises, the burgeoning Miami firm that provided cover for the CIA's new wave of operations against Cuba. It was a little too much. First he heads a group that ignores orders to disband. Then he runs a private operation inside the Agency's own vast and layered industry of anti-Castro activities. When Win took a second polygraph he sat at the desk apparatus sobbing, after three questions, the electrodes planted in his palm, the cuff around his bicep, the rubber tube traversing his chest. It was such an effort not to lie.

They drove south out of Denton into deep-green country. There were pastures abandoned to mesquite and juniper, places of sudden starkness, a burning glare, a single squat tree, burled and grim. The sky towered unbearably here.

Mackey sat with his right arm out the window, hanging down along the door. He showed no interest in the scenic details of the ride. They passed a Baptist church set on cinder blocks. He responded to remarks with a faint tilt of the head, a raised jaw, to show agreement or amusement.

Parmenter said, "There must be people in these old graveyards who came out on wagon trains. Circuit riders, Indian fighters. It's pretty country, Win. What the hell. Why not settle in, raise your little girl, sign up for the concert and drama series. The school's bound to have one. No, I mean it."

Eyes in the rearview mirror.

The psychiatrists were not unkind. But they'd made him aware of illness and disease. They carried disease with them. They were ill themselves. There were areas of their faces they'd neglected to shave carefully. He didn't have the heart to tell them. They were nice men but incomplete, or too complete. He saw the microscopic hairs so clearly. Motivational fatigue. The Agency was tolerant of such problems. The Agency understood. The truth was he hadn't placed agents in Zenith Technical Enterprises. His old team was already there, working with new case officers, prepared to run sea raids from secret bases in the Keys. But the evidence, thin, sketchy, incidental, was too far-reaching in principle to be convincingly denied by a man in his condition. It was easier to believe than to deny. They'd deciphered his notes, read his typewriter ribbons. Could he tell them he loved Cuba, knew the language and the literature? They had the contents of his burn bags. How could he make them see there was nothing to his scheme but the marginal notes of a diehard and fool?

He took off his jacket, folded it lengthwise and then top to bottom and dropped it on the seat next to him. He tapped his shirt pocket for a cigarette.

They went along a farm-to-market road and crossed the Old Alton Bridge, over Hickory Creek. Win indicated a right turn. They went down a red dirt road that ran a quarter of a mile under a thick canopy of post oaks and hickories. Woods on one side, pasture on the other. Larry eased the car to a stop alongside the rail fence. Win lit a cigarette, leaning forward from the middle of the seat. The two men up front sat with their heads tilted slightly toward him, although neither turned at any time to look back.

"When my daughter tells me a secret," Win said, "her hands get very busy. She takes my arm, grabs me by the shirt collar, pulls me close, pulls me into her life. She knows how intimate secrets are. She likes to tell me things before she goes to sleep. Secrets are an exalted state, almost a dream state. They're a way of arresting motion, stopping the world so we can see ourselves in it. This is why you're here. All I had to do was provide a place and time. You came without asking why. You didn't consider the risks to your careers, associating with Walter Everett Jr. after what's happened. You're here because there's something vitalizing in a secret. My little girl is generous with secrets. I wish she weren't, frankly. Don't secrets sustain her, keep her separate, make her self-aware? How can she know who she is if she gives away her secrets?"

The two men waited.

"The invasion failed because high officials didn't examine the basic assumptions. They got caught up in a spirit of compelling action. They were eager to accept other men's perceptions. There was safety in this. The plan was never clear. No one was ever responsible. Some of them knew a disaster was in the works. They let it ride. They put themselves out of reach. They wanted it over and done. There was pressure to get all those armed exiles out of Florida and into goddamn Cuba. I'm not sure anybody thought about what happens to them after we drop them off at the beach. That's where we came in. We were on the airfields or the ships or we were locked in barracks with the exile leaders. They had brothers and sons among the dead and there were armed American soldiers keeping them from leaving the barracks at Opa-Locka. What could

I tell those men? I felt like a messenger of plague and death. Then the long slow fall. I wanted to sanctify the failure, make it everlasting. If we couldn't have success, let's make the most of our failure. That's what we were doing at the end when we tried to keep things going. Just an empty exercise."

They waited. They were patient and attentive.

"The movement needs to be brought back to life. These operations the Agency is running out of the Keys are strictly pinpricks. We need an electrifying event. JFK is moving toward a settling of differences with Castro. On the one hand he believes the revolution is a disease that could spread through Latin America. On the other hand he's denouncing guerrilla raids and trying to get brigade members to join the U.S. Army, where someone can keep an eye on them. If we want a second invasion, a full-bore attempt this time, without restrictions or conditions, we have to do something soon. We have to move the Cuban matter past the edge of all these sweet maneuverings. We need an event that will excite and shock the exile community, the whole country. We know Cuban intelligence has people in Miami. We want to set up an event that will make it appear they have struck at the heart of our government. This is a time for high risks. I'm saying be done with half-measures, be done with evasion and delay."

A pickup came down the road and they rolled up their windows to keep the dust out. The driver gave a half-wave without taking his hand off the wheel. They waited for the dust to settle, then rolled down the windows. Win paused a moment before beginning to speak again.

"Some things we wait for all our lives without knowing it. Then it happens and we recognize at once who we are and how we are meant to proceed. This is the idea I've always wanted. I believe you'll sense it is right. It's the high risk we need. We need an electrifying event. You've been waiting for this every bit as much as I have. I believe that or I wouldn't have asked you to come here. We want to set up an attempt on the life of the President. We plan every step, design every incident leading up to the event. We put together a team, leave a dim trail. The evidence is ambiguous. But it points to the Cuban Intelligence Directorate. Inherent in the plan is a second set of clues, even more unclear, more intriguing. These point to the Agency's attempts to assassinate Castro. I am designing a plan that includes elements of both the American provocation and the Cuban reply. We do the whole thing with paper. Passports, drivers' licenses, address books. Our team of shooters disappears but the police find a trail. Mail-order forms, change-of-address cards, photographs. We script a person or persons out of ordinary pocket litter. Shots ring out, the country is shocked, aroused. The paper trail leads to paid agents who have disappeared in Venezuela, in Mexico. I am convinced this is what we have to do to get Cuba back. This plan has levels and variations I've only begun to explore but it is already, essentially, right. I feel its rightness. I know what scientists mean when they talk about elegant solutions. This plan speaks to something deep inside me. It has a powerful logic. I've felt it unfolding for weeks, like a dream whose meaning slowly becomes apparent. This is the condition we've always wanted to reach. It's the life-insight, the life-secret, and we have to extend it, guard it carefully, right up to the time we have shooters stationed on a rooftop or railroad bridge."

There was a silence. Then Parmenter said dryly, "We couldn't hit Castro. So let's hit Kennedy. I wonder if that's the hidden motive here."

"But we don't hit Kennedy. We miss him," Win said.

Mackey fed quarters into the public phone in the Esso station about a hundred miles from the Louisiana border. He was trying to reach a man named Guy Banister, a former FBI agent who ran a detective agency in New Orleans. Banister was a channel for CIA money supplied to the anti-Castro effort in the area. Mackey knew him in the period before the invasion, when Banister was shipping weapons and explosives to the exile forces. It was time to get in touch again.

The voice at the other end was not Banister's or his secretary's. It took Mackey a moment to place it correctly. David Ferrie. The investigator, bag man and spiritual adviser. Mackey put down the phone and walked across the windy plaza to his car.

David Ferrie made a face when he heard the click in his left ear. He had a tendency to wince. He winced all the time in front of mirrors when he pasted on his homemade eyebrows and mohair toupee. Ferrie suffered from a rare and horrific condition that had no cure. His body was one hundred percent bald. It looked like something pulled from the earth, a tuberous stem or fungus esteemed by gourmets. But he wasn't about to give in, grow despondent, sit in a dark room drinking Tastee Shakes and jerking off. He had some lively interests. A cure for cancer was one interest, almost a lifelong interest. He'd done research and written papers on the subject. He was interested in hypnotism and could put people into trances. Flying was a deep and abiding interest. Ferrie had been a senior pilot for Eastern Airlines before his disease made him bald and before his sexual sport with boys became a widely known fact that Eastern officials found disconcerting. He was interested in the communistic menace. Cuba was an interest.

Moments after he put down the phone, Ferrie was in the small room behind Guy Banister's office, making faces in the mirror as he adjusted the semicircular eyebrows. He was on his way to a shopping center in Jeff Parish where a model fallout shelter was on display. He wanted to check the dimensions, see what kind of supplies they had and how they were stored. He already had rubber bedsheets and a battery radio with CONELRAD frequencies clearly marked. He knew about a munitions bunker to the southwest that might be converted to an effective shelter, deep in the ground, isolated, with food and water for many months. It was heart-lifting in a way to think about the Bomb. How satisfying, he thought, to live alone in a hole. Not because he resembled a mutant form of life but just to eke out extra time while all hell thundered on the surface. He'd earned a reward for his unlucky life.

Laurence Parmenter drove toward Love Field in his rented Dodge Dart. He preferred to avoid thinking about Everett's plan for the time being. He listened to the radio, to an evangelist talking about retail prayer and wholesome prayer. Pray for yourself, pray for the world. Win was a bright man, dedicated, loyal to the cause, bright, very bright, but he'd suffered some kind of nervous collapse. Happens all the time. He seemed well now, alert, in full control, but an idea needs time to reveal its facets, its shifting lights and fires. Not that Larry meant to let the matter drag. He wanted Cuba back and the sooner the better. He had interests there. He had rights, claims, hidden financial involvement in a leasing company that had been working toward a huge land deal to facilitate oil drilling. This was before the plucky rebels came out of the hills.

He would begin to think about Everett's plan on the flight back to Washington. Sip a Beefeater martini, nibble salted nuts, pray for himself, pray for the world. A line from an old drinking song popped into his head. But where from? From Cairo, 1944, morale operations, Office of Strategic Services. Larry was part of the Groton-Yale-OSS network of so-called gentlemen spies, many of them now in important Agency positions. He was not old money, not quite elect, but still a member, ready to accede to the will of the leadership. They were the pure line, a natural extension of schoolboy societies, secret oaths and initiations, the body of assumptions common to young men of a certain discernible dash. He sang aloud, "Oh we are the jolly coverts, we lie and we spy till it hurts." He was trying to recall the next line when the first of the airport signs appeared.

On the radio a news announcer said that police were still keeping watch over Major General Edwin A. Walker's home and grounds following a gunman's attempt to kill the controversial right-wing figure one week earlier. There were no new leads in the case.

After dark the stillness falls, the hour of withdrawal, houses in shadow, the street a private place, a set of mysteries. Whatever we know about our neighbors is hushed and lulled by the deep repose. It becomes a form of intimacy, jasmine-scented, that deceives us into trustfulness.

Win was in the living room turning the pages of a book. This is what he did, according to his wife, instead of reading. Turned pages until there were no more. He wondered whether the two men realized he'd called them here specifically for April 17, the second anniversary of the Bay of Pigs. A thought for bedtime. He turned another page.

Upstairs Mary Frances was in bed. She worried about the worn-out rug, thought about breakfast, thought about lunch, tried not to be too foolishly proud of the renovated kitchen, large, handsome, efficient, with its frostless freezer and color-matched appliances, on the quiet street of oak and pecan trees, forty miles north of Dallas.

In New Orleans

A classmate, Robert Sproul, watched him cross the street. He carried his books over his shoulder, tied together in a green web belt with brass buckle. U.S. Marines. His shirt was torn along a seam. There was smeared blood at the corner of his mouth, a grassy bruise on his cheek. He came through the traffic and walked right past Robert, who hurried alongside, looking steadily at Lee to draw a comment.

They walked along North Rampart, on the edge of the Quarter, where a few iron-balconied homes still stood among the sheet-metal works and parking lots.

"Aren't you going to tell me what happened?"

"I don't know. What happened?"

"You're bleeding from the mouth is all."

"They didn't hurt me."

"Oh defiance. You're my hero, Lee."

"Keep walking."

"They made you bleed. It looks like they rubbed your face in it all right."

"They think I talk funny."

"They roughed you up because you talk funny? What's funny about the way you talk?"

"They think I talk like a Yankee."

He seemed to be grinning. It was just like Lee to grin when it made no sense, assuming it was a grin and not some squint-eyed tic or something. You couldn't always tell with him.

"We'll go to my house," Robert said. "We have eleven kinds of antiseptics."

Robert Sproul at fifteen resembled a miniature college sophomore. White bucks, chinos, a button-down shirt open at the collar. This was the second time he'd encountered Lee in the streets after he'd been knocked around by someone. Some boys had given him a pounding down by the ferry terminal after he'd ridden in the back of a bus with the Negroes. Whether out of ignorance or principle, Lee refused to say. This was also like him, to be a misplaced martyr and let you think he was just a fool, or exactly the reverse, as long as he knew the truth and you didn't.

It occurred to Robert that there was, as a matter of fact, a trace of Northern squawk in Lee's speech, although you could hardly blame him for it, knowing what you knew of his mixed history.

He spent serious time at the library. First he used the branch across the street from Warren Easton High School. It was a two-story building with a library for the blind downstairs, the regular room above. He sat cross-legged on the floor scanning titles for hours. He wanted books more advanced than the school texts, books that put him at a distance from his classmates, closed the world around him. They had their civics and home economics. He wanted subjects and ideas of historic scope, ideas that touched his life, his true life, the whirl of time inside him. He'd read pamphlets, he'd seen photographs in Life. Men in caps and worn jackets. Thick-bodied women with scarves on their heads. People of Russia, the other world, the secret that covers one-sixth of the land surface of the earth.

The branch was small and he began to use the main library

at Lee Circle. Corinthian columns, tall arched windows, a rank of four librarians at the desk on the right as you enter. He sat in the semicircular reading room. All kinds of people here, different classes and manners and ways of reading. Old men with their faces in the page, half asleep, here to escape whatever is out there. Old men crossing the room, men with bread crumbs in their pockets, foreigners, hobbling.

He found names in the catalogue that made him pause with a strange contained excitement. Names that were like whispers he'd been hearing for years, men of history and revolution. He found the books they wrote and the books written about them. Books wearing away at the edges. Books whose titles had disappeared from the spines, faded into time. Here was *Das Kapital*, three volumes with buckled spines and discolored pages, with underlinings, weird notes in an obsessive hand. He found mathematical formulas, sweeping theories of capital and labor. He found *The Communist Manifesto*. It was here in German and in English. Marx and Engels. The workers, the class struggle, the exploitation of wage labor. Here were biographies and thick histories. He learned that Trotsky had once lived, in exile, in a working-class area of the Bronx not far from the places Lee had lived with his mother.

Trotsky in the Bronx. But Trotsky was not his real name. Lenin's name was not really Lenin. Stalin's name was Dzhugashvili. Historic names, pen names, names of war, party names, revolutionary names. These were men who lived in isolation for long periods, lived close to death through long winters in exile or prison, feeling history in the room, waiting for the moment when it would surge through the walls, taking them with it. History was a force to these men, a presence in the room. They felt it and waited.

The books were struggles. He had to fight to make some elementary sense of what he read. But the books had come out of struggle. They had been struggles to write, struggles to live. It seemed fitting to Lee that the texts were often masses of dense theory, unyielding. The tougher the books, the more firmly he fixed a distance between himself and others.

He found enough that he could understand. He could see the capitalists, he could see the masses. They were right here, all around him, every day.

Marguerite browned flour in a heavy-bottomed pan. They watched each other eat. She was always right there, hands busy, eyes bright behind the dark-rimmed glasses. He could see the strain and aging in her face, the flesh going taut at the hairline, and he felt something between pity and contempt. They watched TV in the next room. Miniature willow baskets hung on the wall. Her skull was showing through.

"Lillian says I spoil you to a T. You think you own me, she says."

"I'm your son. You have to do what I want."

"I admit this, which I shouldn't say a word, but your brothers were a burden on my back. They demanded attention which it was not humanly possible to give. This is where the human element comes in. When I think of all the tragedies. Your daddy felt a pain in his arm, out mowing. The next thing I know."

"They're in the service to get away from you."

"When I think of being a grandparent who is denied affection. We ate red beans and rice on Mondays. I took you to Godchaux's in a stroller."

Ever since he could remember, they'd shared cramped spaces. It was the basic Oswald memory. He could smell the air she moved through, could smell her clothes hanging behind a door, a tropical mist of corsets and toilet water. He entered bathrooms in the full aura of her stink. He heard her mutter in her sleep, grinding the death's-head teeth. He knew what she would say, saw the gestures before she made them.

"I am entitled to better."

"So am I. I'm the one. I have rights," he said.

He helped her hang half-moon wall shelves. He would find a communist cell and become a member. This was a city with a hundred kinds of foreigners and ideas and influences. There were people who ran ads in the paper to seek favors of a patron saint. There were people who wore berets, who did not speak ten words of English. Down at the docks he saw oppressed workers unloading ninety-pound banana stems from Honduras. He would find a cell, be given tasks to prove himself.

"Lillian expects endless thanks. She lives off thank-yous and you're-welcomes."

"She thinks we're one jump up from handouts in the street."

"She thinks we're beholden," Marguerite said. "I was a popular child. I am willing to stand on the facts."

They'd lived with her sister Lillian on French Street. They took an apartment on St. Mary Street, eventually moving to a cheaper apartment in the same building. Then they moved to the Quarter.

He is a quiet and studious boy who demands his meals, like any boy.

"The Claveries were poor but not unhappy. We ate red beans and rice on Mondays. Just because she let us stay a few weeks, I know what she says behind my back. They talk and make up stories, which I am not surprised. They have hidden reasons they aren't telling for how they feel. They say I fly off too quick on the handle. I just can't get along, so-called. They never say it could be they're the ones at fault. They're the ones you can't reason with. She says I take one little word and make a difference out of it, which stands between us until we see each other on the street when it's 'Oh hello, how are you, come see us real soon.'"

"She thinks because she gives me money to rent a bike."

They lived in a three-story building in an alley that opened onto Canal Street, the dodging bodies and shopwindows glaring hot. The building had arched entranceways with decorative crests. That's what Marguerite liked most. It was otherwise a sad show. Lee had the bedroom, she took the studio couch.

In St. Louis Cemetery Number One he sees an old Negro snoring in his stocking feet, body propped against one of the oven vaults, the sun beating down on smashed amber glass.

They watched each other eat. He practiced chess moves at the kitchen table. She described houses and yards and furniture way back to the early decades of the century, in New Orleans, where she was raised, a happy child. He knew these things were important. He did not deny the value of what she said or the power of the images she carried with her. These were important things, family, money, the past, but they did not touch his real life, the inward-spinning self, and he let her voice fall through a hole in the air.

He sees a tough-looking Mexican or whatever he is suddenly strike a female pose outside a bar, getting a laugh from his friends.

He had his one-volume encyclopedia of the world, which his aunt Lillian said he read like a boy's novel of the sea. Kinetic energy. Grand Coulee Dam. He would join a communist cell. They would talk theory into the night. They would give him tasks to perform, night missions that required intelligence and stealth. He would wear dark clothes, cross rooftops in the rain.

How many people know a killdeer is a bird?

He got a letter from his brother Robert, his full brother, who was still in the Marines. He took a page out of his spiral notebook and replied at once, mainly answering questions. He liked his brother but was certain Robert didn't know who he was. It was the age-old family mystery. You don't know who I am. Robert was named for their father, Robert E. Lee Oswald. That's where his own name came from, Lee. His father was at the end of the Lakeview line, turning to chalk.

"I took you to Godchaux's to see the flag, the two of us. The war was on and we lived on Pauline Street and they hung a seven-story flag right down the front of Godchaux's, where I bought my light-gray suit which I am wearing in the photo with Mr. Ekdahl, which is shortly after our marriage. A seven-story American flag. This is when you caused a flurry with Mrs. Roach, throwing an iron toy."

He wanted to write a story about one of the people at the library for the blind. That was the only way to imagine their world.

Marguerite had blue eyes and dark lashes. She was a sales clerk and cashier, working near the hosiery shop she'd managed, about a dozen years earlier, on Canal Street, before they fired her. She could not add or subtract was the stated reason. Marguerite knew better, felt the vibrations, heard the whispers of nasty attitude, of grudge against the world, which wasn't as bad as the time she was fired from Lerner's in New York because they said she did not use deodorant. This was not true because she used a roll-on every day and if it didn't work the way it said on TV, why should she be singled out as a social misfit? New York was not behind the times in strange smells.

He did his homework at the kitchen table, questions only morons would want to answer. She woke him up for school by clapping her hands in the doorway, insistently, the fingers of one hand tapping the palm of the other. Something in him turned to murder at the sight of her, sometimes, in the street, coming toward him unexpectedly. He heard her footsteps, heard her key in the lock. The voice called out from the kitchen, the toilet flushed. He knew the inflections and the pauses, knew what she would say, word for word, before she spoke. She tapped her hands in the doorway. Rise and shine.

"It is evident," he read, "that the definition of capital-value invested in labor-power as circulating capital is a secondary one, obliterating its specific difference in the process of production."

He tried to talk politics with Robert Sproul's sister, mainly to say something. They played chess on a closed porch at the Sproul house. Robert sat nearby doing a term paper on the history of air power.

She was a year older than Lee, soft-skinned, blond, with a serious mouth. He had a feeling she tried not to look too pretty. There were girls like that, hiding behind a surface of neatness and reserve.

"Eisenhower gets off too easy," Lee was saying, "and I can give you a good example."

"I don't think you can but go ahead."

"It was Eisenhower and Nixon who killed the Rosenbergs. Guaranteed. They're the ones responsible."

"Well that's just you're daydreaming."

"Well no I'm not."

"There was a trial unless I'm sadly mistaken," she said.

"Ike is a well-known boob. He could have stopped the execution."

"Like a movie, I suppose?"

"Do you know who the Rosenbergs are, even?"

"I just said there was a trial."

"But the hidden factors, the things that don't get out."

She gave him a tight look. She was just the right height. Not too tall. He liked her air of restraint, the way she moved the pieces on the board, almost bashfully, giving no hint of the winning or losing involved. It made him feel animated and rash, a chess genius with dirty fingernails. There was a mother or father moving around inside the house.

"I read all about the Rosenbergs when I was in New York," he said. "They were railroaded to the chair. The idea was to make all communists look like traitors. Ike could have done something."

"He did do something. He played golf," Robert said.

"Now Senator Eastland's coming to New Orleans. You know why, don't you?"

"He's looking for you," Robert said. "He can't figure out how a boy in the Civil Air Patrol."

"He's looking for reds under the beds," Lee said.

"He's wondeiing how a clean-cut boy."

"The main thing is in communism that workers don't produce profits for the system."

"He's looking at your cute smile and he's just real upset. A teenage communist in the CAP."

Lee half enjoyed the ribbing. He looked at Robert's sister to get her reaction but her eyes were on the board. Well brought up. He saw her at the library. She was on the pep squad at school, the girl at the far end who went more or less unnoticed.

"What if they did spy? It's only because they believed communism is the best system. It's the system that doesn't exploit, so then you're strapped in the chair."

Lee was aware that the parent, whichever one it was, had moved to the edge of the open doorway. The parent was standing there, on the other side of the wall, listening.

"If you look at the name Trotsky in Russian, it looks totally different," he said to Robert Sproul's sister. "Plus here's something nobody knows. Stalin's name was Dzhugashvili. Stalin means man of iron."

"Man of steel," Robert said.

"Same thing."

"Dumb bunny."

"The whole thing is they lie to us about Russia. Russia is not what they say. In New York the communists don't hide. They're out on the street."

"Quick, Henry, the Flit," Robert said.

"First you produce profits for the system that exploits you."

"Kill it before it spreads."

"Then they're always trying to sell you something. Everything is based on forcing people to buy. If you can't buy what they're selling, you're a zero in the system."

"Well that's neither here nor there," the sister said.

"Where is it?" he asked her.

It was the father who appeared in the doorway, a tall man with a plaid blanket folded over one arm. He seemed to be looking for a horse. He spoke of homework and errands, he mumbled obscurely about family matters. The sister's relief was easy to see. It could be felt and measured. She slipped past her father and melted serenely into the dim interior.

The father walked with Lee to the front door and opened it as wide as it would go. They did not speak to each other. Lee walked home through the Quarter past hundreds of tourists and conventioneers who thronged in the light rain like people in a newsreel.

——————

He kept the Marxist books in his room, took them to the library for renewal, carried them back home. He let classmates read the titles if they were curious, just to see their silly faces crinkle up, but he didn't show the books to his mother. The books were private, like something you find and hide, some lucky piece that contains the secret of who you are. The books themselves were secret. Forbidden and hard to read. They altered the room, charged it with meaning. The drabness of his surroundings, his own shabby clothes were explained and transformed by these books. He saw himself as part of something vast and sweeping. He was the product of a sweeping history, he and his mother, locked into a process, a system of money and property that diminished their human worth every day, as if by scientific law. The books made him part of something. Something led up to his presence in this room, in this particular skin, and something would follow. Men in small rooms. Men reading and waiting, struggling with secret and feverish ideas. Trotsky's name was Bronstein. He would need a secret name. He would join a cell located in the old buildings near the docks. They would talk theory into the night. But they would act as well. Organize and agitate. He would move through the city in the rain, wearing dark clothes. It was just a question of finding a cell. There was no question they were here. Senator Eastland made it clear on TV. Underground reds in N'yorlenz.

In the meantime he read his brother's Marine Corps manual, to prepare for the day when he'd enlist.

There were two kids at school, in particular, before he quit, who called him Yankee all the time. Trailing him down the halls, calling across the lunchroom. He smiled and was ready to fight but they never made a realistic move.

The names on the order blanks excited him. Lisbon, Manila, Hong Kong. But soon the routine took hold and he realized the ships and cargoes and destinations had nothing to do with him. He was a runner. He carried paper to other forwarding companies and steamship lines or across the street to the U.S. Custom House, which looked like a temple of money, massive and gray, with tall granite columns. He was supposed to look eager and bright. People seemed to depend on his cheerfulness. The less important you are in an office, the more they expect the happy smile. He disappeared for hours at the movies. Or he sat in an unused office in a far corner of the third floor, where he spent serious time reading the Marine Corps manual.

He memorized the use of deadly force. He studied principles of close order drill and the use of ribbons and badges. He made unauthorized phone calls to Robert Sproul to read hair-raising passages about bayonet fighting. The whirl, the slash, the butt stroke. There was no end of things to quote from the manual. The book had been written just for him. He read deeply in the rules, impressed by the strictness and precision, by the stream of awesome details, weird, niggling, perfect.

Robert Sproul knew about a gun for sale, a bolt-action .22, a varmint gun, or we'll plink tin cans, and they went on Lee's lunch hour to a cheap hotel above the business district, among muffler shops and discount furniture, in the January chill. The lobby was like a passageway to a toilet. The rooms were on the second floor, above a boarded-up store with a sign reading Formal Rentals. Robert had the seller's room number but not his name. Supposedly he was an acquaintance of David Ferrie, an airline pilot and instructor in the Civil Air Patrol. Ferrie had commanded the unit Robert and Lee were enrolled in that summer, although Lee had attended only three sessions, just long enough to get the uniform.

The boys were surprised when Captain Ferrie himself opened the door. A man in his late thirties, sad-faced, friendly, standing in the doorway in a bathrobe and a pair of argyle socks reaching to his knees. He waved them into the room, looking carefully at Lee. The shades were drawn. There were clothes everywhere, Chinese food spilling out of white cartons, some bills and coins on the floor. The room stood in a kind of stupor, a time zone of its own.

"Boys, how nice. I was told to expect visitors. Alfredo is selling his gun, I understand. He claims he killed a man with that gun. Some gringo millionaire. Every Latin has killed a gringo in his daydreams. These are temporary quarters, you understand. Your flying ace is between assignments."

Ferrie sat in an armchair amid strewn clothing. Robert looked quickly at Lee. A strangulated grimace.

"Now let's see," Ferrie said. "Robert I know from our classes in the Eastern hangar at Lakefront. It seems a hundred years ago. But who's the shy one with the neat part in his hair?"

"I went a few times," Lee said, "but then I stopped."

"But you were there. I thought so. I was sure of it. In your uniform. A uniform makes all the difference. I know my boys. I never forget a cadet. Do you know Dennis Rumsey? Dennis is a cadet. He comes here after school. Do you know Warren Van Zandt, the fat boy? Warren's daddy has lung cancer bad."

"What about the rifle?" Robert said.

"It's around here somewhere. A Marlin bolt-action .22. It's clip-fed and you can have it real cheap because the firing pin's broken. Easy to fix. Take it to a welder, bang bang bang."

"Nobody mentioned broken," Robert said.

"They never do."

"Well I don't know, sir."

"Neither do I."

"If the rifle can't be fired as is."

"He'll weld an extension, bang bang."

"But this would mean an inconvenience."

"The pleasure may be worth it. Do you know guns? Guns are an interest of mine."

Robert shot a glance like let's get out of here. Something in the far corner seemed to be alive. Lee took a few steps in that direction. He was aware that some kind of well-intentioned look was pasted to his face, a smile not connected to things. There was a cage on the dresser with white mice running around inside.

He turned to Ferrie and said, "Mice."

"Isn't life fantastic?"

"What are they for?"

"Research. Here we are it's eleven years after the war, a new era, an age of hope, and we're no closer to ending the cancer plague than a thousand years ago. I've studied diseases all my life. Even as a boy I allotted my time. I knew what cancer was long before I heard the word. What's your name?"

"Lee."

"Allot your time, Lee."

Robert Sproul edged toward the door.

"Captain Ferrie, I think actually, sir."

"What?"

"I have to get going. I guess I'll take a rain check on the gun purchase."

"I've studied patterns of coincidence," Ferrie said to Lee. "Coincidence is a science waiting to be discovered. How patterns emerge outside the bounds of cause and effect. I studied geopolitics at Baldwin-Wallace before it was called geopolitics."

"Lee, are you coming?"

Lee wanted to leave but found himself just standing there grinning stupidly at Robert, who made a dumb face back at him and walked out, sort of tiptoed out. Maybe Lee thought it wasn't nice to leave abruptly. But in that case Robert was the one who should have stayed. He was the honor student, well brought up, who lived in a house with a closed porch amid azaleas, oaks and palms.

"Tell me about yourself," Ferrie said. "First, ignore the mess. The mess belongs mainly to Alfonso, Alfredo, whatever he's called. Anywhere he settles, even for a minute, you sense an air of criminal intent. Works on a tug out of Port Sulphur. A job that wouldn't interest a boy with intelligent eyes like yours. Tell me about your eyes."

Ferrie was deep in the armchair. At this angle, in the uncertain light, he resembled an eighty-year-old man, wide-eyed with fear. He was totally remote. Lee's sense of things was that he was one step ahead for having stayed, that Robert had bailed out too soon, that this business was too rich to be missed, and for the rest of his time here he experienced what was happening and at the same moment, although slightly apart, recounted it all for Robert. He had a little vision of himself. He saw himself narrating the story to Robert Sproul, relishing his own broad manner of description even as the moment was unfolding in the present, in the larger scheme, arms going like crazy, an animated cartoon, and he felt slightly superior in the telling. He'd stayed for the whole thing. What could be more squeamish and chicken-hearted than leaving too soon, thinking safety-first, home to your perfect family and plaid blanket, and then the thing turns out okay.

"If you allot your time, you can accomplish fantastic things. I learned Latin when I was your age. I stayed indoors and learned a dead language, for fear of being *noticed* out there, made to pay for being who I was."

He forgets I'm here.

"Cleveland," he said, making it sound like a lost civilization. "My father was a cop. I'm constantly haunted by the thought of cops, government cops, Feebees—the FBI. They're on you like the plague. Once you're in the files, they never leave you alone. They stick to you like cancer. Eternal."

This man is strange even to himself.

"What about the rifle?" Lee said. "Maybe I'll buy it. How much does he want for it?"

"He wants twenty-five dollars. But you give me fifteen. Because it's you, fifteen. You're one of my cadets. I look out for my boys. You wear a uniform, it makes all the difference. Look at me. I put on my captain's jacket, all this bleary shit just falls away. I become a captain for Eastern. I talk like a captain. I instill confidence in anxious travelers. I actually fly the goddamn plane."

He knows he's strange but can't help it.

"If I decide I'll buy it, how do I get it home?"

"How do you get it home is easy. You take it and wrap it in a blanket. You use that blanket right there. The hotel won't mind."

Added to everything else was the fact that he'd actually have the rifle. He'd emerge with the rifle. He'd be able to say he'd transported a rifle in a stolen blanket through the city of New Orleans. Ferrie watched the mice in the cage, made whistling sounds. All this built seamlessly into Lee's narration to Robert Sproul, the future inside the present, the little cartoon at the heart of events.

"The question is can you cure the disease before it kills you? Once you set out consciously to cure the disease, as I did even before I knew the word cancer, you run the risk of catching it. *Comprende?* Whatever you set your mind to, your personal total obsession, this is what kills you. Poetry kills you if you're a poet, and so on. People choose their death whether they know it or not."

"If we can find the .22 and wrap it up," Lee said, "I should probably be getting back."

"It'll be Carnival soon," David Ferrie told him. "Farewell, flesh."

He shouts for his meals. He hollers. I will be downstairs visiting with Myrtle Evans and we will hear him calling for his mother and I will jump right up and get upstairs to cook him his meal, like any boy.

Nobody knew what he knew. The whirl of time, the true life inside him. This was his leverage, his only control. He watched his mother browning flour, her hands rising sticky-white from the heavy-bottomed pan. He ran messages to steamship lines. He lay near sleep, falling into reverie, the powerful world of Oswald-hero, guns flashing in the dark. The reverie of control, perfection of rage, perfection of desire, the fantasy of night, rain-slick streets, the heightened shadows of men in dark coats, like men on movie posters. The dark had a power. The rain fell on empty streets. Always the men appeared, their long shadows bent behind them, then the rifle in his hands, the clip-fed Marlin, the idea of shooting for the gut, to draw out the dying.

There is a world inside the world. Stalin's party name was Koba. He would devise a secret name, find a cell in the buildings near the docks. He memorized a license number, the color and make of car. He checked out a book that contained police pictures of revolutionaries. Police picture, Trotsky, age nineteen. Police picture, Lenin, full face and profile. Richard Carlson as Herb Philbrick, ordinary citizen, member of the Communist Party, undercover agent for the FBI. She tapped her fingers on the palm of her hand. Rise and shine.

He saw a guy sitting backwards on a motorcycle, smoking a cigarette and looking into space, with tattoos running down one arm to the back of his hand.

The reverie of the girl in the plaid skirt. She lies back across the bed, her feet touching the floor. Brown-and-white saddle shoes, white socks, white blouse, the plaid skirt arranged four inches above the knees. The reverie of stillness, perfection of desire, perfection of control, her pale legs slightly parted, arms at her sides, eyes closed. He makes the picture come and go. It is what he knows about her, how he controls her, alone at night, watching her motionless on the bed, above the rain-slick streets. She is just the right height, thin-lipped, shy, stupid. He watches but is not there.

A dozen movies say the gut-shot man takes a long time dying.

Her hands rising sticky-white. She browned the flour in some fat until it was dark and muddy, the color she wanted her gravy to be. She added meat juices, onions, spices. They ate at the kitchen table. The sound of her mouth chewing the food. The noises in the street. She was always there, watching him, measuring their destiny in her mind. He had two existences, his own and the one she maintained for him. He couldn't get the .22 to fire. He showed it to a car mechanic, who kept it five weeks without looking at it. They had words over that. He was not afraid to stand up for his rights. In the end he sold the gun for ten dollars to Robert Oswald, who'd been mustered out of the Marines and who was always ready to do a favor, with or without acknowledgment, for his kid brother Lee.

Marguerite sat on the sofa watching TV.

It griped him to move to New York, which we traveled all the way in that 1948 Dodge, but that's where John Edward was stationed with his wife and baby and we are a family that has never been able to stay together. There are some women in this position who ignore history. But Lee has traveled with me and Mr. Ekdahl and he has traveled alone on a train from Fort Worth to New Orleans when he was eleven years old to visit my sister, a distance of some five hundred and twenty-five miles. Now, about does he live a healthy American life? I would answer as such, your honor, that there are many fine and well-to-do citizens living all around us but that the French Quarter has its vagrants and others. There are certain type bars, including we live over a pool hall, and there is business and gambling on the street. I would also state prostitutes by the galore. But in defense of a mother's position, he missed only nine days in his last term at Beauregard when I was working at Kreeger's, 800 and something Canal Street. His future and his dream is the United States Marines, which we bickered back and forth because he used a false affidavit to join but failed at this time. It is only a question of getting to age seventeen, although he has already left school, which he says is for good. This is a boy who grins while they are beating him up and waits for national news on TV. As far as his mother's place in his heart, he has worked as a messenger and office boy and bought me a thirty-five-dollar coat with his first pay and who gives over money to his mother for room and board and bought me a parakeet in a cage that came with a stand with a planter. It had ivy in the planter, it had the cage, it had the parakeet, it had a complete set of food for the parakeet. It is a question of adjusting, your honor, and he will make the effort every time. I cannot say enough how hard it is to raise boys without a father. I was sitting pretty in our American slang, managing Princess Hosiery, when Mr. Ekdahl proposed in the car. I made him wait a year and he was a Harvard man. I have always seemed to make a home against the odds. I have often been complimented on my appearance and my little bright touches here and there and now I am thinking we will go to Texas again to be with his brother Robert, to be a family again, in Fort Worth, so this boy can be with his brother. And I don't want to hear how I call the movers all the time. The point of our century is people move. I am a mother of three who sold needles and thread and yarn in her own shop in the front room of the house on Bartholomew Street, a frame house with a backyard, when Lee was a baby in a crib. I was a popular child, your honor. I was raised by a father with five other children to be happy and patriotic. I have made my best effort to raise my boy in this manner, regardless. Whatever is said by them, and they are at it all the time, he knows who has been his main support from the moment I took him home from the Old French Hospital on Orleans Avenue. I am not the looming mother of a boy's bad dreams.

George Gobel appeared on the screen, stubby, crewcut, with a wholesome smirk, right hand raised to the middle of his forehead in some kind of antic fraternal small-town salute.

Lee was in his room reading about the conversion of surplus value into capital, following the text with his index finger, word by word by word.

26 April

Pocket litter. Win Everett was at work devising a general shape, a life. He would script a gunman out of ordinary dog-eared paper, the contents of a wallet. Parmenter would contrive to get document blanks from the Records Branch. Mackey would find a model for the character Everett was in the process of creating. They wanted a name, a face, a bodily frame they might use to extend their fiction into the world. Everett had decided he wanted one figure to be slightly more visible than the others, a man the investigation might center on, someone who would be trailed and possibly apprehended. Three or four shooters would vanish completely, leaving scant traces of their affiliation. Spanish-speaking men, Mexican, Panamanian, trained specifically for this mission in Cuba. Then one other figure, one slightly clearer image, perhaps abandoned in his sniper's perch to find his own way out, to be trailed, found, possibly killed by the Secret Service, FBI or local police. Whatever protocol demands. This kind of man, a marksman, near anonymous, with minimal known history, the kind of man who surfaces in murky places, disappears, is arrested for some violent act, is released to drift again, to surface, to disappear. Mackey would find this man for Everett. They needed fingerprints, a handwriting sample, a photograph. Mackey would find the other shooters as well. We don't hit the President. We miss him. We want a spectacular miss.

Win sat alone on the porch. There was a glass of lemonade on a wicker table. Plants stood in tubs and window boxes, in terra-cotta pots on the steps. The brick walk was bordered in monkey grass. He waited for Mary Frances.

Of all the cities where the attempt might be made, Miami was the clear choice. Hundreds of exile factions lived there, conspired and squabbled, waited for another chance—*movimientos, juntas, uniones.* Win imagined how word would flash through the area, through all his old exile haunts, La Moderne Hotel, the offices of the Frente leadership. Miami had a resonance, an ardor. It was a city of open wounds, of explosive politics and feelings. This very inflammability, this Cuban heat and light, made him determined to keep the plan a secret from anti-Castro leaders.

Kennedy had been in Miami four months earlier to accept the brigade flag from survivors of the invasion, many just ransomed from Cuban prisons. This was the necessary cleansing of emotions. The failure was now openly acknowledged, commemorated before forty thousand people in a football stadium, all the repressed material sent in reconverted waves into Televisionland, where Everett had sat watching. He respected the President for going to Miami. He was surprised and touched when the President's wife spoke Spanish to brigade members. But the ceremony had not renewed the cause, the forceful devotion to a free Havana. He saw it now as pure public relations, the kind of gleaming imagery that marked every move the administration made.

The car pulled up and he went down the steps to help Mary Frances take the groceries inside. He gripped the heavy bags. A wind sprang from the east, an idea of rain, sudden, pervading the air. He saw himself go inside, a fellow on a quiet street doing ordinary things, unafraid of being watched.

He stood in the pantry and she handed things in to him. The

bulb had blown and he stood in the dimness putting objects on shelves. The faintly musty smell, the coolness of the small room, the familiar labels on jars and cans made him feel like an ancient and tired child, someone allowed to relive the simplest, the deepest times, moments that left a scar on the heart—not an evidence of some detailed pain but only of time itself, systemic, heavy with loss. He tried to register the idea of the burnt-out bulb so he wouldn't forget to replace it. He heard a shaking in the sky and thought of thunderstorms when he was a boy growing up in the country, the boy who tried not to seem smarter than his older brothers, seeing the light change, the landscape become serious, solemn. Everything ran with fear. It leapt out of the air into things and into children. Those smoky storms approaching. He used to stand in the pantry counting to fifty because that's when the thunder would stop.

"I have to pick up Suzanne."

"I'll finish this," he said.

"Don't you have a class?"

"Canceled."

"I want to stop at Penney's for a couple of things."

"We should all stop at Penney's."

"No but just some things I've been meaning to get. We won't be long."

"Penney's is home to us all."

"The light bulbs are stacked in the back stairway."

"She reads my mind. She remembers for me."

"I won't be long," she said.

Parmenter would tell him in advance if there were plans for JFK to return to Miami. Sooner or later the President would venture out with his train of attendants, protectors, handshakers and hacks, a city, a street where he'd be vulnerable. Everett was willing to wait a year for Miami. The message would be clearest there, a long-range attempt, high-angled, telescopic, without the pointless human mess some madman would create, walking out of a crowd with the family handgun.

He followed Mary Frances to the door.

He would not consider the plan a success if the uncovering of its successive layers did not reveal the CIA's schemes, his own schemes in some cases, to assassinate Fidel Castro. This was the little surprise he was keeping for the end. It was his personal contribution to an informed public. Let them see what goes on in the committee rooms and corner offices. The pocket litter, the gunman's effects, the sidetrackings and back alleys must allow investigators to learn that Kennedy wanted Castro dead, that plots were devised, approved at high levels, put into motion, and that Fidel or his senior aides decided to retaliate. This was the major subtext and moral lesson of Win Everett's plan.

The two men who shared a table in the Occidental Restaurant had certain physical similarities. Both were over six feet tall, expensively dressed, robust and athletic, men clearly at ease here, in the theater of the Kennedys, the capital city that measured itself to a certain kind of manliness, a confidence and promise, the grace to take the maximum dare.

Laurence Parmenter, perhaps five years the younger of the two, spoke in the slight whine of the educated Easterner, a way of drawing out syllables to express ironic self-regard.

The other man, George de Mohrenschildt, who lived in Dallas now, spoke English with a courtly foreign accent. He was not averse to being seen as the complete continental. This is what he was. A charming and worldly man able to converse fluently in Russian, English, French, Spanish, probably Togo as well, or whatever they spoke in Togoland. (Parmenter knew he had been there in 1958, posing as a stamp collector.) Larry liked the man. He'd known him for some years and was aware that George had been debriefed by the Agency after several trips abroad. But even though their business interests had overlapped once or twice, he wasn't sure quite what George's racket was.

"Then in May I go to Haiti," de Mohrenschildt said.

"Do I dare ask?"

"Ask, by all means. I'm going there to find oil for the Haitians. They're giving me a sisal plantation as a concession."

"Do they need help finding sisal?"

"I believe it grows aboveground."

They held their laughter.

"You turn up in interesting places, George."

Now they laughed, remembering the same thing, the time Parmenter walked into a dental clinic in a remote town near the CIA air base in southwest Guatemala where the Bay of Pigs was being rehearsed by Cuban pilots and American advisers. Sitting in the shabby waiting room, in an alligator shirt and madras shorts, was George de Mohrenschildt, also known as Jerzy Sergius von Mohrenschildt. He was on a walking tour of Central America, he said.

"That whole thing ended horribly," George said, "if I can actually say it has ended."

"I think you can say that."

"This administration still bullies Castro. It's ridiculous and unnecessary. I'll go even further. This whole administration revolves around the floating cinder of little communist Cuba. It's something of a joke, Larry, and I say this knowing which side of the Cuban fence you are on. Of course this is your job and I respect it."

"This *was* my job. I'm doing strictly support work now."

"I would like to believe the administration has no more designs on Cuba."

"Believe it, George. The missile crisis was resolved with the understanding that we wouldn't invade Cuba. Kennedy had the chance to get rid of Castro and he ends up guaranteeing the man's job. There is widespread lack of interest right now. Commitment to this issue is absolutely nil. The administration went from passionate and total dedication to an attitude of complete aloofness and indifference and they did it in goddamn record time."

"It's the American disease," George said with a warm smile.

De Mohrenschildt was a petroleum engineer by profession but didn't seem to spend much time at it. He was on his fourth wife, Larry knew, and they tended to be women from wealthy families.

But his marriages didn't explain his apparent association with Nazis in World War II, his apparent ties to Polish and French intelligence, his expulsion from Mexico, his apparent communist leanings when he was at the University of Texas, his Soviet contacts in Venezuela, the discrepancies in his stated history, his travels in West Africa, Central America, Yugoslavia and Cuba.

George had a tendency to be detained or shot at for sketching coastal installations in strategic areas.

But he knew Jackie Kennedy or her parents or someone in the family, and he spent time at the Racquet Club when he was in New York, and he was technically entitled to call himself a baron. It was part of George's attractiveness that he continually emerged from a different past.

"When do you leave Washington?"

"I go to New York tomorrow, then back to Dallas."

"I thought Dallas was Walker country," Larry said. "Who's taking potshots at the general?"

"He's a complete fascist degenerate, this man Walker. A very dangerous man with his racism, his anti-Castro crusades. This is what I mean about Cuba. Cuba stirs up the worst kind of American obsession. Here is a general who is relieved of his command for preaching right-wing politics, who leads a racist campaign in Mississippi, who is put in the loony bin, who settles down in Dallas where we see him in the papers every day with his John Birch Society nonsense and his Cuban tirades. Raw hate, Larry. Two men died in Mississippi because of Walker's provocations. He's a little Hitler plain and simple."

"You sound as though you'd like to take a crack at him yourself."

"I'm telling you, I wouldn't mind. As a matter of fact, I think I know who tried to kill him."

A waiter plunged after a dropped spoon.

"A boy I know in Dallas," George said. "I call him a boy. Maybe he's twenty-two, twenty-three. Now that I'm past fifty, they all look like boys and girls. But as long as the boys don't look like girls and vice versa."

"What got him interested in Walker?"

"The easy answer is politics. In 1959, an ex-Marine, what does he do? He defects to the Soviet Union. They send him to a factory in Minsk. Disillusionment sets in, of course, and back he comes. Naturally the Agency is interested. Domestic Contacts asks me to talk to the boy."

"A friendly debriefing."

"Exactly. I'm to take the fatherly approach. Find out what he saw, heard, smelled and tasted. It wasn't long before we started to like each other. In fact I think my own feelings about General Walker may have influenced Lee to take a shot at him."

"But you're not absolutely sure."

"Not absolutely."

"He hasn't said he did it."

"He hasn't said anything. But there were indications, certain signs, an atmosphere, you know? Plus a curious photograph he sent me. I'm frankly sorry he missed."

They returned to their food, their lunch. The voices and noise around them became apparent once more, a tide of excited news, a civilized clamor. George said something perfectly right about the wine, swirling it in the high-stemmed tulip glass. An attractive woman hurried toward a table, showing the happy exasperation that describes a journey through traffic snarls and personal dramas to some island of prosperous calm. There were times when Larry thought lunch in a superior restaurant was the highlight of Western man.

"You mentioned politics," he said. "How far left is this young friend of yours?"

"There is politics, there is emotion, there is psychology. I know him quite well but I wouldn't be completely honest if I said I could pin him down, pin him right to the spot. He may be a pure Marxist, the purest of believers. Or he may be an actor in real life. What I know with absolute certainty is that he's poor, he's dreadfully, grindingly poor. What's the expression I want?"

"Piss-poor."

"Exactly. He's married to a lovely, lovely girl. Really, Larry, one of those flawed Russian beauties. Innocent and frail. She speaks a lovely true Russian. Not Sovietized, you know? Her uncle is a colonel in the MVD."

Larry couldn't help laughing. It was all so curiously funny. It was rich, that's what it was. Everyone was a spook or dupe or asset, a double, courier, cutout or defector, or was related to one. We were all linked in a vast and rhythmic coincidence, a daisy chain of rumor, suspicion and secret wish. George was laughing too. A wonderful woodwind rumble. They looked at each other and laughed. They laughed in appreciation of the richness of life, the fabulous and appalling nature of human affairs, the good food and drink, the superior service, the wrecked careers, the whole teeming abscess of folly and regret. Larry felt flush and well fed, a little tipsy, all the right things. The Honduran ambassador said hello. A man from Pemex stopped to tell a richly filthy joke. It was a lovely lunch. It was great, rich, lovely and perfectly right.

Parmenter took the Agency shuttle bus back to Langley. Then he wrote a memo to the Office of Security requesting an expedite check on George de Mohrenschildt.

Somewhere in his room of theories, in some notebook or folder, Nicholas Branch has a roster of the dead. A printout of the names of witnesses, informers, investigators, people linked to Lee H. Oswald, people linked to Jack Ruby, all conveniently and suggestively dead. In 1979 a House select committee determined there was nothing statistically abnormal about the death rate among those who were connected in some way to the events of November 22. Branch accepts this as an actuarial fact. He is writing a history, not a study of the ways in which people succumb to paranoia. There is endless suggestiveness. Branch concedes this. There is the language of the manner of death. Shot in back of head. Died of cut throat. Shot in police station. Shot in motel. Shot by husband after one month marriage. Found hanging by toreador pants in jail cell. Killed by karate chop. It is the neon epic of Saturday night. And Branch wants to believe that's all it is. There is enough mystery in the facts as we know them, enough of conspiracy, coincidence, loose ends, dead ends, multiple interpretations. There is no need, he thinks, to invent the grand and masterful scheme, the plot that reaches flawlessly in a dozen directions.

Still, the cases do resonate, don't they? Mostly anonymous dead. Exotic dancers, taxi drivers, cigarette girls, lawyers of the shopworn sort with dandruff on their lapels. But through the years the violence has reached others as well, and with each new series of misadventures Branch sees again how the assassination sheds a powerful and lasting light, exposing patterns and links, revealing this man to have known that one, this death to have occurred in curious juxtaposition to that.

George de Mohrenschildt, the multinational man, a study in divided loyalties or in the irrelevance of loyalty, the man who befriended Oswald, dies in March 1977, in Palm Beach, of a blast through the mouth with a 20-gauge shotgun. Ruled a suicide.

One week later, in Miami Beach, police find the body of Carlos Prío Socarrás, former President of Cuba, millionaire gunrunner, linked by an informer to Jack Ruby. The body sits in a chair, a pistol nearby. Ruled a suicide.

David William Ferrie, the professional pilot, amateur researcher in cancer, anti-Castro militant, is found dead in his apartment in New Orleans in February 1967, five days after his name is linked in the press to the assassination of the President. Natural causes, says the coroner, but some people wonder how Ferrie had time to type a farewell note to a friend in the middle of a brain hemorrhage. ("Thus I die alone and unloved.") Among his possessions are three blank passports, a one-hundred-pound bomb, a number of rifles, bayonets and flare guns and a complete library of books and other materials, as of that date, on the Kennedy assassination.

Eladio del Valle, a friend of David Ferrie and head of the Free Cuba Committee, is found dead the same day, in a car in Miami, shot several times in the chest at point-blank range, his head split open by an ax. No arrests in the case.

The documents are stacked everywhere. Branch has homicide reports and autopsy diagrams. He has the results of spectographic tests on bullet fragments. He has reports by acoustical consultants and experts in blur analysis. He studies blurs himself, stooped over photos taken in Dealey Plaza by people who thought they were there to see the head of state come riding nicely by. He has a magnifier. He has detailed maps of photographers' lines of sight.

The Curator sends transcripts of closed committee hearings. He sends documents released under the Freedom of Information Act, other documents withheld from ordinary investigators or heavily censored. He sends new books all the time, each with a gleaming theory, supportable, assured. This is the room of theories, the room of growing old. Branch wonders if he ought to despair of ever getting to the end.

The FBI's papers on the assassination are here, one hundred and twenty-five thousand pages, no end of dread and woe. The Curator sends new material on Oswald's stay in Russia, gathered from a KGB defector (not the first such defector to offer a version of events). There is new material on Everett and Parmenter, on Ramón Benítez, Frank Vásquez. Data trickling down the years. Water dripping into his brain pan. There is 544 Camp Street in New Orleans, the most notorious address in the chronicles of the assassination. The building is long gone and the site is an urban renewal plaza now. The Curator sends recent photos and Branch understands that he must study them, although they do not pertain to the case. There are granite benches, brick paving, a piece of sculpture with a subsidized look about it, called "Out of There."

Branch must study everything. He is in too deep to be selective.

He sits under a lap robe and worries. The truth is he hasn't written all that much. He has extensive and overlapping notes—notes in three-foot drifts, all these years of notes. But of actual finished prose, there is precious little. It is impossible to stop assembling data. The stuff keeps coming. There are theories to evaluate, lives to ponder and mourn. No one at CIA has asked to see the work in progress. Not a chapter, a page, a word of it. Branch is on his second Curator, his sixth DCI. Since 1973, when he first set to work, he has seen Schlesinger, Colby, Bush, Turner, Casey and Webster occupy the Director's chair. Branch doesn't know whether these men were told that someone is writing a secret history of the assassination. Maybe no one knows except the Curator and two or three others in the Historical Intelligence Collection at CIA. Maybe it is the history no one will read.

T. J. Mackey stood across the street from the shabby three-story building where Guy Banister's detective agency was located. His light-brown hair was cut close and he wore a sport shirt and sunglasses, the shirt tight across his upper body. He had a way of clenching and unclenching his right fist. There was a bird tattooed there, in the webbing between thumb and index finger, and when he opened his fist the bird spread its blue wings.

He was watching someone on Camp Street, a rattled old woman, an outcast in a long coat and white ankle socks, one of the lost bodies of New Orleans this uneasy spring of 1963, already too hot, too heavy and wet. He was interested in the way she kept adjusting her pace as she walked down the street. She slowed down to let others get ahead of her. In a wary crouch she moved along the wall at number 544, swinging an arm out to wave people on. She wanted everybody up ahead, where she could see them all.

Mackey enjoyed this. He'd been in the city over a week now and had seen many a jumpy drunk but no one with this kind of paranoid wit.

Around were old warehouses and coffee-roasting plants, fifty-cent-a-night hotels. Over the original entranceway at 544, bricked up now, he could make out an inscription: Stevedores and Long-shoremens Building. He crossed the street and went in. The offices of Guy Banister Associates were on the second floor. Banister was at his desk, a tough and somber man in his sixties. Twenty years in the FBI, deputy superintendent of the New Orleans police, a member of the John Birch Society and the Minutemen. He opened a bottom drawer when Mackey walked in. Invitation to a drink. T-Jay waved it off and took a chair.

"You don't drink with me. You don't tell me where the hell you're staying."

"I leave tomorrow."

"Where to?"

"The Farm."

"Must be a great life, showing kids from Swarthmore how to break a chinaman's neck."

"It's an assignment."

"It's a fucking shame, that's what it is, T-Jay, a man like you, who risked his life. This Kennedy, he has things to answer for. First he launches an invasion without adequate air support, then he makes the movement pay for it. He's got people raiding our guerrilla bases, seizing arms shipments all over."

"What am I here for? You've had time, Guy."

"It's not that simple."

"You've got more guns than the Mexican army."

"There's priorities," Banister said. "It's looking like a busy summer we got coming."

"I'll need to see some money. Upkeep, monthly payments, a healthy severance."

"How many men?"

"Let's say several. Plus I may need a pilot."

"He'll walk in the door in ten minutes."

"Goddamn."

"Calm down."

"Not him."

"Never mind appearances or what he says for effect. Ferrie's a capable son of a bitch. He can fly a plane backwards. He has first-rate contacts. He does work for Carmine Latta's lawyer. He goes out to Latta's house and comes back with money in fucking duffel bags. It's all for the cause. He can lease a small plane, no questions asked, no records kept. Right now I've got him looking for a C-47 which I want to use to ship explosives out of here."

Banister opened the desk drawer again, took out a fifth of Early Times and reached back to snatch two coffee mugs from a shelf.

"I'm sending select items to one of our staging areas in the

Keys," he said. "Rifle grenades, land mines, dynamite, antitank guns, mortar shells. Listen to this: canisters of napalm."

Mackey noted the look in that silvery eye. Banister's rage toward the administration was partly a reaction to public life itself, to men who glow in the lens barrel of a camera. Kennedy magic, Kennedy charisma. His hatred had a size to it, a physical force. It was the thing that kept him going after career disappointments, bad health, a forced retirement. Mackey briefly met his eye. So many meanings crowded in, memories, sadnesses, convictions, lost Cuba, Cuba to come—a moment so humanly dense, rich in associations, such deep readings, the power of things unsaid, that T-Jay looked away. They were entertaining too many of the same thoughts.

"Where did you get the hardware?"

"A bunker in the woods. We put the key in the lock and there it was."

"Who arranged that?" Mackey said.

"It's a CIA weapons cache. Stuff never used at the Bay of Pigs. Which I assume you know."

"I don't know much these days."

"We have recruits coming in all the time. They want another crack at Fidel. We train them at a camp not far from here. We've had no problems up to now, knock fucking wood, which is something I personally see to, working it out with the feds. But this Kennedy, he's making all kinds of moves against us. Did you know he's got exile leaders restricted to Dade County? They can't travel out of the county. He's normalizing with Castro. He's dealing with the Soviets. They got a deal cooking. Cuba is guaranteed communist. From which Jack gets a second term unmolested by Moscow. He is interested in his own protection and security, which I believe he is correct in wishing to increase."

He poured the bourbon.

"What about the thing in Dallas," he said, "a couple of weeks ago?"

"The Walker shooting."

"Did they catch the nigger that did it?"

Mackey caught the sly tone of the older man's voice. Walker had been consuming news space like a movie star in a fever of insecurity. Being shot at over a backyard fence by a sniper on tiptoes, and missed, was just about the perfect payoff Mackey could imagine for a certain kind of fame. It reduced the man to the status of casual target for some gun-toting Mr. Magoo.

"Now, assuming I can come up with the rifles."

"Plus scopes."

"What do I do with them?"

"Hold them," Mackey said.

"Who are we talking about here?"

"Keep them absolutely secure and ready."

"What is the subject of this meeting? Because I have to know there's complete trust between us."

"You do know. Take my word. Or I wouldn't be here."

"Don't make me feel I'm getting too old for certain operations. This is my trade. There's only one subject for people like us."

Paint flakes on the desktop and floor, steel cabinets covered in dust. Inside the cabinets were Banister's intelligence records. He kept files on people who volunteered for the anti-Castro groups in the area. He kept microfilmed records of left-wing activity in Louisiana. He had the names of known communists. He had material supplied by the FBI on Castro agents and sympathizers. Mackey had seen handbooks on guerrilla tactics, back issues of a racist magazine Guy published. There were files on other organizations renting space at 544 Camp, past and present, including the Cuban Revolutionary Council, an alliance of anti-Castro groups put together by the CIA with Banister's help.

"People like us," he said to Mackey, "we have this dilemma we have to face. Serious men deprived of an outlet. Once we're pushed out, how do we retire to a chair on the lawn? Everyday lawful pursuits don't meet our special requirements." He laughed happily. "For twenty-some-odd years in the Bureau I lived in a special society that pretty much satisfied the most serious things in my nature. Secrets to trade and keep, certain dangers, an opportunity to function in tight spots, wave a gun in people's faces. That's a charmed society. If you've got criminal tendencies, and I'm not saying this is true of you or me, one of the places to make your mark is law enforcement." A short happy laugh. "How much of my manhood is watery puke? That's what I want to know. I was involved in the Dillinger case, earliest days of my career. Public enemy number one. Famous finish, got him coming out of a movie house in Chicago, sweltering night, the Biograph. I was with the Office of Naval Intelligence in the war, just like young Jack Kennedy." He took a swallow. "Spy work, undercover work, we invent a society where it's always wartime. The law has a little give."

He set the mug of bourbon to one side and ran his hand over the newspapers and files to find his cigarettes.

"In John Birch," he said, "we have a hundred thousand members. Way out of hand. Then there's General Ted Walker going on tour with the Reverend Billy James Hargis, coast to coast, in ten-gallon hats. The Minutemen are leaner, move close to the ground. But there's a fervor I don't trust. They're waiting for the Day. They've got their ammo clips hidden in the garage and they know the Day is fast approaching. They get their politics all mixed up with the second coming of Christ. I respect your methods, T-Jay. You want a unit that's small, tight and mobile. None of these bullshit mailing lists. You don't want theory and debate. Just impact. Two or three men to do serious things."

David Ferrie walked in wearing an undersized panama hat and a turtleneck shirt with a drooping collar. To Mackey, who'd met him once before, he had a look of sad apology, like a man who'd betrayed a public trust. (Banister claimed he was a defrocked priest.) He moved in a languid glide, loafers slapping.

He said to Banister, "Shouldn't be drinking this time of day."

"What do we have in the storeroom?"

Ferrie glanced at T-Jay.

"Some old, old Springfields. Thirty-aught-six. I mean old. We have M-1s, a whole raft of Yugoslav Mausers with markings stamped in Russian if that impresses you. We have some M-4s out by Lacombe. I burnt off a magazine only yesterday."

"Where do we keep our scopes?" Banister said.

"Most of the scopes and mounts are out at the camp. We have some extra-long target scopes stored here. Of course it depends on what you want to shoot. Hairy big game like Fidel, you want a wide field of view because he's always in motion. The fact is I used to admire Dr. Castro, secretly. A brief moment only. I wanted to fight by his side."

His voice was whispered, incredulous; something about the curious paths of his own life caused him endless surprise. The face itself was disbelieving, the stark pasted brows looped high over his pale eyes. Nothing he said could be separated from the eerie facts of his appearance, least of all, apparently, by Ferrie himself.

"Where would you park a light plane below the border?" Mackey said. "Figure you're leaving home in a hurry."

"I'd point her right on down to Matamoros. Below Brownsville. There's a field there. You want to go deeper into Mexico, you can play hopscotch on dry lakes. Avoid populated areas entirely."

"No offense. How old are you?"

"Forty-five. Perfect astronaut age. I'm the dark scary side of John Glenn. Great health except for the cancer eating at my brain."

"You'll die violently," Banister said.

"I want to believe it."

"A nacho stuck in your throat."

"I speak Spanish," Ferrie said, amazed to hear it.

He went into the small room behind the office, where Delphine Roberts was compiling one of the lists that someone in the firm was always gathering material for. Delphine was Banister's secretary and research aide, a nailed-down American, middle-aged, with airy spraywork hair.

"These are supposed to be runless stockings," she said.

"Everything is supposed to be something. But it never is. That's the nature of existence."

"I know. You studied philosophy where was it."

"Did you eat lunch?"

"I'm back on Metrecal."

"But you're a wisp, Delphine."

He turned on the little TV.

"Why do you think a Negro would want to be a communist?" she said, running a finger down the list. "Isn't it enough for them being colored? Why would they want a communistic tinge added on?"

"Are you saying why be greedy?"

"I'm saying don't they have enough trouble. Besides, if you're colored, you can't *be* anything else."

She worked at a Formica desk by the window. A cardboard shirt support was taped over a hole in the screen.

"I priced a bomb shelter last week," Ferrie told her.

"It's not the bombs coming out of the sky I worry about. The missile crisis came and went. It's the troops that will just appear one quiet morning, armies landing on the beaches, paratroops dropping through the clouds. Guy received a report that the Red Chinese are massing troops in Baja California."

"I have private torments, Delphine. They require something larger than an army."

They were watching *As the World Turns*. Ferrie sat in a folding chair with his legs crossed. He took off his hat and placed it on his right kneecap.

"I say to myself, I wonder why Delphine comes to this rat-trap office every day. A woman like her. With a background and so forth. A real pretty house on Coliseum Street. Social niceties, let's say. The DAR."

"This is the real work of the nation. What could I accomplish in the City Council or some ladies' group? Guy Banister is the vanguard of what is going on in this country, so far as actually making an impact. Recruiting, training, collecting information. I feel like this is a contribution I can make that I couldn't do in the normal ways, through committee work and so forth."

She glanced at Ferrie's faded red toupee, an object that resembled some windblown piece of street debris. She looked at the sloped forehead, the somewhat Roman profile, eagle-beaked, oddly impressive despite the man's overgrown ears, the clownish aspects of his appearance. In fact she'd seen the profile before she ever met Ferrie. There was a mug shot in Banister's files. It commemorated two arrests in 1961, in Jefferson Parish, for what were officially described as crimes against nature.

They watched TV.

"Dave, what do you believe in?"

"Everything. My own death most of all."

"Do you wish for it?"

"I feel it. I'm a walking sandwich board for cancer."

"But you talk about it so readily."

"What choice do I have?" he said.

On the screen two women commenced a dialogue in slow and measured movements, over coffee, with solemn pauses for hurt and angry looks. Delphine went back to her work, trying to listen past the TV set to the voices in the next room, the remote and private drone that fixed the limits of her afternoons.

"Why are homosexuals addicted to soap opera?" Ferrie said absently. "Because our lives are a vivid situation."

Delphine fell forward in bawdy laughter. Her upper body shot toward the desk, hands gripping the edges to steady her. She sat there rocking, a great and spacious amusement. David Ferrie was surprised. He didn't know he'd said something funny. He thought the remark was melancholy, sadly philosophical, a throwaway line for an aimless afternoon. Not that this was the first time Delphine had reacted so broadly to something he said. She considered his mildest comic remarks automatically outrageous. She had two kinds of laughter. Lewd and bawdy and abandoned, the required worldly response to Ferrie's sexual status, her sense of a kind of anal lore that informed the sources of his humor. Softer laughter for Banister, throaty, knowing, wanting to be led, rustling with complicities, little whispery places in her voice, a laughter you could not hear without knowing they were lovers.

"It's not just Kennedy himself," Banister was saying on the other side of the door. "It's what people see in him. It's the glowing picture we keep getting. He actually glows in most of his photographs. We're supposed to believe he's the hero of the age. Did you ever see a man in such a hurry to be great? He thinks he can make us a different kind of society. He's trying to engineer a shift. We're not smart enough for him. We're not mature, energetic, Harvard, world traveler, rich, handsome, lucky, witty. Perfect white teeth. It fucking grates on me just to look at him. Do you know what charisma means to me? It means he holds the secrets. The dangerous secrets used to be held outside the government. Plots, conspiracies, secrets of revolution, secrets of the end of the social order. Now it's the government that has a lock on the secrets that matter. All the danger is in the White House, from nuclear weapons on down. What's he plotting with Castro? What kind of back channel does he have working with the Soviets? He touches a phone and worlds shake. There's not the slightest doubt in my mind but that a movement exists in the executive branch of the government which is totally devoted to furthering the communist cause. Strip the man of his powerful secrets. Take his secrets and he's nothing."

Banister paused until Mackey's eyes shifted to meet his.

"I believe deeply there are forces in the air that compel men to act. Call it history or necessity or anything you like. What do you sense in the air? That's all I'm saying, T-Jay. Is there something riding in the air that you feel on your body, prickling your skin like warm sweat? Drink up, drink up. We'll have one more."

What passes in a glance.

That night Mackey sat in a small room across the street from a surgical-supply firm and two or three house trailers. Odds against a cool breeze about a thousand to one. The trailers were set in enclosures heaped with debris and guarded by bad-tempered dogs.

He sat by the window, in the dark, applying a pale lotion to the mosquito bites scattered across his ankles and the backs of his hands. It was going to be tough trying to sleep in this heat, without a fan, these little buzzing mothers closing in.

The rooming house was in an area where homes and junkyards

seemed to spawn each other. A rooster crowed every morning, amazing, only blocks from major thoroughfares.

Every room has a music of its own. He found himself listening intently at times, in strange rooms, after the traffic died, for some disturbance of tone, a nuance or flaw in the texture.

Getting weapons from Banister was less risky in the long run and a hell of a lot easier, short-term, than stealing them from the Farm. This was the covert training site the CIA operated in southeastern Virginia, five hundred wooded acres known to the outside world as a military base called Camp Peary. Mackey instructed trainees in light weapons there, college grads eager for careers in clandestine work. This was the Agency's way of letting him know where he stood for refusing to sign a letter of reprimand. He lived about ten miles off-post but during periods of special exercises he shared quarters with another instructor in an old wooden barracks partitioned into double rooms. They wore army fatigues and played brooding games of gin rummy, listening to dull rumbles from the sabotage site.

He poured the lotion on his fingers, then rubbed his fingers lightly over the bites. The bites continued to sting.

Everywhere he went, mosquitoes. He'd trained rebels in Sumatra and the commando units of CIA client armies in a number of piss-hole places. But he was not Agency for life. He could wait for them to drop him or beat them to it. He'd seen too many evasions and betrayals, fighting men encouraged and then abandoned for political reasons. They didn't call it the Company for nothing. It was set up to obscure the deeper responsibilities, the calls of blood trust that have to be answered. This was the only war story he knew, the only one there was or could be, and it always ended the same way, men stranded in the smoke of remote meditations.

He felt the heat beating in, midnight vibrations, the sirens down Canal, the growl of some solo drunk. A mosquito is a vector of disease. He clenched his right fist. The tattoo bird was an eagle, circa 1958, etched in a dark shop on one of Havana's *esquinas del pecado*, sin corners, where he was providing security in an Agency endeavor to supply funds to the movement of the rebel Fidel Castro, three years before the invasion.

Every room has a music that tells you things if you know how to listen.

Good men died because the administration delayed, pondering options to the end. To Mackey, aboard the CIA's lead ship, an old landing-craft carrier situated fifteen miles from Blue Beach, the operation began to resemble something surreal. As information became available, with data flowing across the radar screens and over the radios, with signals bounced off the clouds by a destroyer's twenty-four-inch lights, it seemed to him that something was running out of control. There was strange and flawed material out there, a deep distance full of illusions, deceptions, eerie perspectives.

The same ship used two different names.

Radio Swan, located on a tiny guano island, was broadcasting meaningless codes to pressure the Fidelist armed forces into mass defections. "The boy is in the yellow house." "The one-eyed fish are biting." All night the lonely babble sounded.

The seaweed in reconnaissance photos turned out to be coral reef that interfered with the landings.

Planes flew with insignia painted out and when pilots were finally allowed to reconnoiter inland they had to use Esso road maps to find their way.

Navy jets meant to link up with B-26s from Nicaragua arrived too early, or too late, because somebody mixed up the time zones.

Two ammunition ships appeared on radar, heading full-speed in the wrong direction, ignoring radio messages to return.

The DCI, Allen Dulles, was spending the weekend in Puerto Rico, delivering a speech to a civic group on the subject "The Communist Businessman Abroad."

There was a ten-minute mutiny on Mackey's ship.

"The sky is swollen with dark clouds." "The hawk swoops at dawn."

The second air strike, finally, was canceled.

He knew Everett believed the failure was more complex than

one scrubbed mission. A general misery of ideas and means. But Mackey insisted on a clear and simple reading. You can't surrender your rage and shame to these endless complications.

He had a wife somewhere. This was a complication to think back on. Two years of study, postwar, mining and metallurgy, with a wife to encourage him. He could barely picture her face. Paled and ballooned by drink. She was a paramilitary wife by then. She liked the movies. She liked to sit with her ass dipped down into the opening between the seat and the backrest, her feet up on the raised edge of the seat front, balanced like a serious toy, as the bullets flew. She had pretty hair, he seemed to recall, and drank in a methodical way, as if to forestall any complaint that she was out of control.

The scouting party came ashore before midnight. Mackey was the only American in the rubber raft and he wasn't supposed to be there. The raft skidded up the beach and one man vaulted into the water and ran alongside, scooping dense sand with both hands and muttering a prayer. They began marking the beach with landing lights for the troops waiting beyond the breakers in ancient pitching LCIs and born-again freighters. The place wasn't exactly deserted. Some people sat outside a bodega above the beach, old men talking. One of the scouts, wearing black trunks and a black sweatshirt, face smeared with galley soot, walked over to chat with them, carrying an automatic rifle. T-Jay wasn't armed. He couldn't be sure whether this was his way of letting the men know his role here was limited or whether he was feeling indestructible tonight. The sea tang was bracing. He saw an old Chevy near the bodega and got his chief scout Raymo to request the keys from one of the patrons as a gesture of welcome from those about to be liberated. He wanted to find out if the local militia camp was where the intelligence briefers said it was. The car was a '49 model with a picture pasted to the dashboard of a Cuban ballplayer in a Brooklyn Dodgers cap and shirt. They were an eighth of a mile down the stony road when a jeep appeared in the high beams, two heads bobbing in silhouette. T-Jay eased the car diagonally across the road. Raymo was out the door, saying something into the bursts from his submachine gun. Every other round was a tracer. Heat and light. When the magazine was empty, two dead militiamen sat in the vehicle, mouths open, the upholstery smoking. Raymo stood looking, his squat body immensely still. He was barefoot, in ridiculous checkered shorts, like a vacationing Minnesotan, a cartridge belt slung below his belly. They heard pistol fire from the beach and drove to the bodega in reverse. Someone said a scout had shot one of the old men over a careless remark. Near the body a cluster of people stood arguing. T-Jay walked down to the beach. Frogmen were in, helping rig the marker lights. He had his radioman tell the lead ship to send the brigade commanders ashore, send the troops ashore, get the goddamn thing going. Back near the road he saw a woman standing outside a straw hut, swatting the air around her. They were very near Zapata swamp, famous for mosquitoes.

He read the sign across the street. Discount on Lab Coats. There were voices around the corner, the particular ragged laughter of people leaving a bar. At daybreak the rooster would crow, the dogs would bark, like some tin-shack village in the Caribbean.

The memory was a series of still images, a film broken down to components. He couldn't quite make it continuous. He saw Raymo heaving open the car door, a stutter motion, each segment leaving a blur behind. The bursts from the surplus Thompson were the first shots fired at the Bay of Pigs. This made Raymo a figure of respect among his fellow prisoners during the twenty months they would spend in the fortress of La Cabaña listening to rifle reports from the moat, where the executions took place, each crisp volley followed by a precise echo, an afterclap, as the prisoners thought about the dog that lived in the moat, lapping up blood.

Finally the taxi stopped outside.

He went into the bathroom and ran cold water over his hands, trying to ease the sting where the lotion had failed. He'd contracted malaria during his Indonesian stint and felt the effects now and then, a sense that his body was a swamp. He went to the door and waited.

His wife cut him once, swinging a knife across the kitchen table and catching the left side of his jaw, after a night of who knows what. He never thought of her by name. He thought of her being somewhere very vague, in a room with curtains, never moving from the chair. This is what happens to loved ones who go away. We make them sit in a room forever.

The woman came in, wearing a hard tan, her skin smoked and cracked. She said she was Rhonda. She had heavy dark makeup that made him think of nights at the shore and gonorrhea.

"Casal said be nice to you."

"What do you think he meant by that?"

She smiled and unzipped her skirt. Casal was the bartender at the Habana, a waterfront dive that catered to merchant seamen, Cubans with a grudge and other floating bodies on the tide.

All night it sounded across the water. "Listen, my brothers, to the roar of the white typhoon." It was the grimmest, most godawful thing, to be ashamed of your country.

Win Everett was in pajamas looking at a two-day-old copy of the Daily Lass-O, the student newspaper at TWU. There were contests for yell leaders and twirlers. A nationwide search was under way for a typical coed. He sat in an armchair in a corner of the bedroom. He learned from the paper that the school's original name was the Texas Industrial Institute and College for the Education of White Girls of the State of Texas in the Arts and Sciences. He skipped the piece on JFK.

The phone rang downstairs. He heard Mary Frances walk into the kitchen and pick up the receiver. She came to the foot of the stairs and he dropped the newspaper, waiting to hear her call his name.

She watched him come down the stairs, looking nearly weightless in his pajamas, that softness of step he'd developed only lately, as if to show someone watching that he'd taken the path of self-effacement. They touched lightly as he moved past and she knew it meant they would make love on the fresh sheets with the window open and the smell of rain and dripping leaves still in the air.

Parmenter calling from a public booth. Win could hear traffic noises, excited air. He watched Mary Frances start upstairs, her hand leaving the carved newel and slipping along the handrail, barely touching.

"How do we proceed?"

"The phone is secure. They're not interested in me anymore. Besides, I've cleaned it."

A brief laugh. "You know how to do that?"

"I tinker in the basement," Win said.

"Do you know a man named George de Mohrenschildt?"

"No."

"Does odd jobs for Domestic Contacts. I find out he's also hooked to Army Intelligence. Cuba via Haiti. He's on the way to Haiti. It probably involves an arms deal. George comes across pro-Castro. I believe this is a genuine attachment. He thinks we've behaved rather badly. But the fact is, if my information is correct, he's working against Castro interests, or will be as soon as he gets to Haiti. In any case George doesn't concern us directly. He has a young friend, a kid he debriefed on behalf of the Agency. A defector who repented, more or less, after two years plus in the USSR. I got George to tell me his name and I've done some checking. There's a 201 file on the kid dating to December 1960."

"Did SR Division insert him?"

"The way we fake our own files, who knows for sure? There's no clear sign we put him into Russia. That's all I can tell you except for this. He spent some of his service time at a closed base in Japan. Atsugi. He was a radarman. Had access to data concerning U-2 flights. A nice house-present to give the Soviets when he went over. He married a Russian girl. Decided he wanted to come home. The young marrieds settled in Dallas, met George, spent evenings with the local émigrés, reminiscing. One night about two and a half weeks ago, according to George, our young man fired a shot into the night, aimed at the infamous head of Major General Edwin A. Walker, U.S. Army, resigned."

74 · Don DeLillo

A silence. Win listened to the dense rush of air in the earpiece, a city alive, horns blowing, cars streaming across the Potomac bridges.

"Could be a nice find, Larry."

"Don't make it sound like a three-room apartment. We could put him together. A far-left type. Work him in. Tie him to Cuban intelligence. Possibly even place him at the scene. If he thinks he's operating on the left, pro-Castro, pro-Soviet, whatever his special interest, we'll help him select a fantasy. There's never a dearth of reasons to shoot at the President."

"Tell Mackey. Give T-Jay the details. T-Jay will bring him in."

He always seemed to be going to bed. It was always bedtime. The day came and went and it was time to go to bed again.

He went around turning off lights, checking the front and back doors. He'd seen a U-2 once on a salt flat in Nevada. It looked like a child's idea of advanced reconnaissance. Freakish wingspan, basic body that looked unfinished, wingtips that folded over. But it had a jet engine under a glider frame and could climb at an angle steeper than forty-five degrees, soar to eighty-five thousand feet, its camera sweeping a path over a hundred miles wide. Dark lady of espionage, the Soviets called it. He checked to see that the oven was off. The last thing downstairs was the oven.

Mary Frances was in bed, waiting. A soft light glowed by the armchair. He felt the air on his body as he undressed. The night was full of new things, earth musk and wet bark and night jasmine, a scented freshness, a turning of the earth after rain. He pressed down slowly. The wind-burnt face and whitish brows. The perfumed tincture of her breasts. He would love her into death, into the secret sleep. Her head rolled on the pillow, eyes shut tight. He hid his face in the curve of her neck. The night was full of water moving, faint wet sounds, rainwater dripping through trees, water falling from eaves, running in downspouts, wet sounds of tires on asphalt, tires on a wet street. He raised up slightly, locked his hands in hers, fingers extended. Each pushed hard against the other. A charged fragrance. Hollow thunder in the distance. Water silent in grassy pools, running down leaf stems, collecting in the webbed centers of leaves, droplets, trembling drams, water on the leaves of the blackjack oak set near the house, a light spatter on the screen when the wind shifts. She was blond and white and pink, rough-textured, broader than he was and stronger-minded now, the stronger by far, and all she wanted for him was something safe and plain. He smelled light sweat, felt spittle reaching to his chin. Their hands pushed against each other, fingers tensed and shaking. He felt a rustling response in the sheets, her ass wagging, moisture in the white down at the sides of her mouth. He said her name and watched her eyes come open to that deep wondering of hers, that trust she placed in the ordinary mysteries. She was in the world as he could never be. She meant the world. He freed a hand and wiped away the spit. She said his name quickly, many times, like some cheerleader's sideline riff, and that was that was that.

Side by side, listening to the radio.

"I wonder," she said. "What do other people say to each other?"

"When?"

"Now. I want to know what people say. Maybe there are things we haven't thought of." Laughing at herself. "Things we ought to be saying."

"While having sex or afterward?"

"While having sex is not interesting. Moany-groany love talk. No, afterward, now."

"Do you think we've been saying the wrong things all these years?"

"Wouldn't you like to overhear? I don't want to watch other people. I want to listen."

"They talk about wanting a cigarette."

"Who was that on the phone?"

" 'Where are my cigarettes?' That's what they say."

"He wouldn't tell me his name."

"Larry Parmenter. You remember him. Somebody's house in Miami."

"Kind of just barely."

"Maybe three years ago."

"What did he want to talk about?"

"Curious lady."

"Some nights I need to be held. Tonight I'm a listener. So nice to lie in rumpled sheets and listen. Cover me with words. We're two gossipy bodies alone in the night. Tell me what you talked about."

"Very sexy stuff."

"Oh sure really."

"U-2 planes. The planes that spotted the missiles the Soviets were putting into Cuba. We used to call the photos pornography. The photo interpreters would gather to interpret. 'Let's see what kind of pornography we pulled in today.' Kennedy looked at the pictures in his bedroom as a matter of fact."

"Talk," she said.

"Spy planes, drone aircraft, satellites with cameras that can see from three hundred miles what you can see from a hundred feet. They see and they hear. Like ancient monks, you know, who recorded knowledge, wrote it painstakingly down. These systems collect and process. All the secret knowledge of the world."

"Isn't it one of the best things there is, feeling the air on your body on a night like this?"

"I'll tell you what it means, these orbiting sensors that can hear us in our beds. It means the end of loyalty. The more complex the systems, the less conviction in people. Conviction will be drained out of us. Devices will drain us, make us vague and pliant."

Years together, years of transience, cover operations, plausible denials, dead silences had given Mary Frances no reason to believe she would ever know exactly what kind of secrets Win was keeping at a given time, which meant there was something welcome in these moments of wordiness, in the shape and range of his meanders. She encouraged him to tell her whatever he could about subjects and developments close to his work, or simply things on his mind— encouraged him tacitly, creating receptive fields around him, stillnesses. A wifely labor as natural to her as choosing curtains. By now she was adept at discharging an air of shy curiosity and although there was no longer any real work for him to do, she still wanted to know, wanted badly to hear. But tonight it happened that she fell asleep, drifting lightly off, twisted in a bedsheet, one arm swept across his chest. He listened to the radio, a man preaching the gospel in a bright clear voice, a thrilling voice, youthful, assured. Yes yes yes yes. God is alive and well in Texas.

He would put someone together, build an identity, a skein of persuasion and habit, ever so subtle. He wanted a man with believable quirks. He would create a shadowed room, the gunman's room, which investigators would eventually find, exposing each fact to relentless scrutiny, following each friend, relative, casual acquaintance into his own roomful of shadows. We lead more interesting lives than we think. We are characters in plots, without the compression and numinous sheen. Our lives, examined carefully in all their affinities and links, abound with suggestive meaning, with themes and involute turnings we have not allowed ourselves to see completely. He would show the secret symmetries in a nondescript life.

An address book with ambiguous leads. Photographs expertly altered (or crudely altered). Letters, travel documents, counterfeit signatures, a history of false names. It would all require a massive decipherment, a conversion to plain text. He envisioned teams of linguists, photo analysts, fingerprint experts, handwriting experts, experts in hairs and fibers, smudges and blurs. Investigators building up chronologies. He would give them the makings of deep chronos, lead them to basement rooms in windy industrial slums, to lost towns in the Tropics.

He turned off the radio and slipped out from under her arm. He wanted a cigarette. He put on his pajamas and found two bent Winstons in his shirt pocket, on the armchair. He sat smoking, trying to read. The storm moved west in blue-white rattling streaks. T-Jay will bring him in. Win knew that the name Mackey was a pseudonym assigned by the Records Branch. Theodore J. MACKEY. Win had also used a false name through the years, standard practice for officers engaged in covert work. Mackey's name became enveloped in a certain favorable light, a legendary light, when exile leaders found out he had gone ashore with the scouts at Blue Beach. Once it was clear the invasion would fail, Mackey returned in a whaleboat and cruised the inlets with a megaphone, calling for and finding survivors. Win didn't know his real name.

He read the Daily Lass-O. He read that the school chucked its original name in 1905 to call itself the College of Industrial Arts, or CIA. He was too tired to appreciate the irony, or coincidence, or whatever it was. There were too many ironies and coincidences. A shrewd person would one day start a religion based on coincidence, if he hasn't already, and make a million. Yes yes yes yes. He looked around for an ashtray. He hadn't felt well for a long time now. Ever since whenever it was. He felt tired and forgetful. He had to talk to himself, inwardly, when he was driving the car, give simple commands, scold, to keep his concentration. He fumbled change at drug counters, buying kiddie soap in an aerosol can for his little girl. There were times when he could not bear to be alone in the house. The house was a terrible place when his wife and child were not there, when they were late coming home in the car. He imagined accidents all the time. A stunned wreck at the side of the road. The house grew dark around him.

It was all part of the long fall, the general sense that he was dying.

In Atsugi

The dark plane drifted down, sweeping out an arc of hazy sky to the east of the runway. It had a balsa-wood lightness, a wobbliness, uncommonly long-winged, and it came in over the power pylons that stretched through the rice fields and up into the hills and out of sight. A strange high sound whistled through the air, bringing people out of houses outside the base, men taking bowlegged stances to follow the line of descent—a sound like a gull-shriek endlessly prolonged, caroming through the deep caves set around the base, the kamikaze nests of the second war. Men appeared in barracks windows to catch a glimpse of the landing. A man stood outside the radar bubble watching with folded arms. Two men in utility caps paused outside the mess as the plane glided finally in over the fields and the barbed-wire fences, touching down lightly, its lop-eared wingtips sparking when they scraped the runway, cartoonishly, in the chalk blaze of noon.

"The son of a bitch climbs unbelievable."

"I know. I heard," Heindel said.

"But fast. It's gone before you know it. Never mind how high."

"I know how high."

"I was in the bubble," Reitmeyer said.

"Eighty thousand feet."

"The son of a bitch requests winds at eighty thousand feet."

"Which isn't supposed to be possible," Heindel said.

"I was plotting intercepts. I heard. The mystery man speaks."

The first marine, Donald Reitmeyer, had a large squared-off frame and a lazy amble that made him seem to be sinking into the ground. He watched the tractor approach to tow the plane to its remote hangar. The plane would be escorted, the hangar surrounded, by men with automatic weapons. Reitmeyer took off his cap and waved it at someone heading toward them across the fuming tarmac, a slightish man who walked with his head tilted and one shoulder drooping, the Marine who'd been watching from the radar hut when the plane came in.

"It's Ozzie. Looking like his usual self."

Heindel shouted, "Oswald, move it."

"More skosh," Reitmeyer called, using a familiar pidgin phrase.

"Show some life."

"Show some interest."

The three men walked toward the barracks.

"We know how high it goes, so the next question," Reitmeyer said, "is how far it goes and what does it do when it gets there."

"Deep into China," Oswald said.

"How do you know?"

"It's logic and common sense. Plus the Soviet Union."

"It's called a utility plane," Heindel said.

"It's a spy plane. It's called a U-2."

"How do you know?"

"Common knowledge, pretty much," Oswald said. "You hear things, and the things you don't hear you can find out easy enough. You know those buildings way past the hangars at the east end.

That's called the Joint Technical Advisory Group. Which is a phony name where the spies hide out."

"You're so fucking sure," Reitmeyer said.

"What do you think's there, dormitories for the wrestling team?"

"Well just shut up about it."

"I go to the briefings. I know what to shut up about."

"You see the armed guards, don't you?"

"That's my point, Reitmeyer. Nobody gets near this base without clearance."

"Well just try shutting up."

"Imagine flying over China," Heindel said. "The vastness of China."

"China's not so vast," Oswald said. "What about the Soviet Union, for vast?"

"How vast is it?"

"Someday I want to travel the length and breadth of it by train. Talk to everybody I meet. It's the idea of Russia that impresses me more than the physical size."

"What idea?" Reitmeyer said.

"Read a book."

"You always say read a book, like that's the answer to everything."

"Maybe it is."

"Maybe it isn't."

"Then how come I'm smarter than you are."

"You're also dumber," Reitmeyer said.

"He's not as dumb as an officer," Heindel said.

"Nobody's that dumb," Oswald said.

They called him Ozzie the Rabbit for his pursed lips and dimples and for his swiftness afoot, as they saw it, when there was a scuffle in the barracks or one of the bars off-base. He was five feet nine, blue-eyed, weighed a hundred and thirty-five, would soon be eighteen years old, had conduct and proficiency ratings that climbed for a while, then fell, then climbed and fell again, and his scores on the rifle range were inconsistent.

Heindel was known as Hidell, for no special reason.

He went to the movies and the library. Nobody knew the tough time he had reading simple English sentences. He could not always get a fixed picture of the word in front of him. Writing was even tougher. When he was tired it was all he could do to spell five straight words right, to spell a single small word without mixing up the letters.

It was a secret he'd never tell.

He had a liberty card, a gaudy Hawaiian shirt that made him feel like an intruder in his own skin, and a window seat on the train to Tokyo.

It was Reitmeyer who'd arranged the date, explaining to Lee that all he had to do was show up at the right time and place and flash his heartwarming American smile. A thousand forbidden pleasures would be his.

Welcome to JP—land of sliding doors and slant-eyed whores.

He walked invisibly through layers of chaos, twilight Tokyo. He walked for an hour, watching neon lights pinch through the traffic haze, with English words jumping out at him, TERRIFIC TERRIFIC, under the streetcar cables, past the noodle shops and bars. He saw Japanese girls walking hand in hand with U.S. servicemen, six doggie bakers and cooks by the look of them, all wearing jackets embroidered with dragons. It was 1957 but to Lee these men had the style of swaggering warriors, combat vets taking whatever drifted into meathook reach.

He walked through mazes of narrow streets mobbed with shoppers. He was remarkably calm. There was something about being off-base, away from his countrymen, out of America, that took the edge off his wariness, eased his rankled skin.

He checked the piece of paper with her name on it.

Lamps were lit along the alleyways. He saw a legless man with an accordion, his torso set on weird metal supports, like a Singer sewing machine—an ideogram sign flapping on his chest.

He found Mitsuko all right, a baby-face girl, sort of formless, wearing a skirt and white blouse and a handkerchief on her head, waiting by a sign that read SOLDIERS ACCESS, the rendezvous point as devised by Reitmeyer, on a street of cheap arcades.

She took him to a pachinko parlor, a long narrow room full of people pressed against upright machines. They were trying to maneuver a steel ball into a little hole. The machines made a factory din, like a stamping plant maybe. When she found a free machine, she pressed a lever that released the ball. This was the signal for nirvana or whatever they call the absolute state. She stared into the gray circle, watching the ball go round and round. People pushed through the room, students, old women in kimonos, men who looked educated, with high-paying jobs, all waiting for machines. They were three-deep in some places, patient in the noise and hanging smoke as if nothing hit upon the skin but the racing gray ball.

He checked the paper with her name.

Two hours later they were in a room with sliding panels and straw mats. Something told him the place wasn't hers. It looked imitation Japanese. A silk roll hung from the wall, except it probably wasn't silk. He caught a glimpse of a pinup calendar above a dressing table, some bars of Lifebuoy soap. She took off her open-toed shoes. It was a little hard to believe he was on the legendary verge of getting laid. The subject of a million words, noises, laughs and shouts in the sandlots and barracks of his experience. He felt a stillness, looking at his first naked girl, grown-up, outside a magazine. There was something serious about a woman nude. He felt different, serious, still. He was part of something streaming through the world. Then her hand was in his pants, matter-of-fact, like she was turning on a tap. He took off his clothes, folded the shirt with the windswept palms. The moment had been waiting to happen. The room had been here since the day he was born, waiting for him, just like this, to walk in the door. It was just a question of walking in the door, entering the stream of things.

Was he supposed to give her money? Reitmeyer hadn't said. He saw himself having sex with her. He was partly outside the scene. He had sex with her and monitored the scene, waiting for the pleasure to grip him, blow over him like surf, bend the trees. He thought about what was happening rather than saw it, although he saw it too.

He had a duty weekend coming up but was back in Tokyo the first possible chance. It turned out she took his money only to play pachinko. She was a pachinko fool, a total addict of the form, standing for hours in a raincoat that wasn't hers. He'd go out, come back, go out again, checking the strip joints and cowboy bars. He'd stand near the entrance and watch her play. People pressed into the room. Now and then somebody won a prize, a packet of leaf-shaped sweets. He watched her raise her right foot behind her, absently scratch the other ankle.

Strange days in the fabulous East.

This time she took him to a room in a large apartment block set near factories and oil-storage tanks. The air smelled of sulfur and tidal scum. He could see a river from the window but didn't know what it was called. She told him she was thirty-four years old. Strange days and nights. Some time after they were dressed again, a man came in, moving through the shadows, young, lean, familiar with the room, seeming to take Lee for granted, acting as if he knew everything Lee had ever said and done. He was looking for his raincoat.

Lee never understood the man's connection to Mitsuko. A brother, cousin, lover, a handler or protector of some kind, although not a pimp (if she didn't take money). Lee saw him several times over the next couple of weeks. He was an interesting guy, last name Konno, with wavy hair and dark glasses. He chain-smoked Lucky Strikes, knew American jazz, names that Lee was at a loss to identify. They talked politics. They drank beer and gin, which Lee brought to the room but only sipped to be polite. Konno's English was okay, better than rudimentary. He wore shabby clothes and shoes and a black silk scarf, always, outdoors and in.

The autumn damp took hold. Lamplight shimmered in networks of alleys crowded with wooden houses and shops. They'd taken away his American space. Not that it mattered. His space had been nothing but wandering, a lie that concealed small rooms, TV, his mother's voice never-ending. Louisiana, Texas were lies. They were aimless places that swirled around the cramped rooms where he always ended up. Here the smallness had meaning. The paper windows and box rooms, these were clear-minded states, forms of well-being.

Mitsuko took him into the land of *nūdo*. Billboards, photographs, leaflets, lamppost signs, nudes in booths and theaters, neon and paper nudes, models to be photographed, nudes arrayed in colored lights, strangely pale beneath the fake rose glow. Rain-slick streets like the streets in his reveries, movie shadows and dark-coated men, Mitsuko's little pouting mouth, her language of sighs and hints, reverie of stillness, perfection of desire, her legs slightly parted, arms at her sides.

She did none of the things Reitmeyer had said she'd do, and Ozzie didn't ask.

In the bubble he worked in a hot glow, marking intercept paths, checking the oscilloscope for traces of electron motion that represented air traffic within a given sector.

Through the all-night watches he engaged officers in conversation, asked them questions about world affairs. It turned out he knew more than they did. They didn't know the basic things. Names of leaders, types of political systems. The younger officers were the worst informed, Joe College types, which served to justify some old suspicion of his about the way things work.

A crackling voice requesting winds aloft at eighty thousand feet, a voice outside the dome of night, beyond the known limits.

There were bars and bar girls near the base but he preferred going to Tokyo, alone, where he visited Konno in the huge development near the factories. The coppery smog was so thick it obscured the setting sun. Konno smoked Luckies and talked about the struggle to exist. He worked only part-time, an elevator operator, because the country was awash in college graduates. Sometimes Mitsuko showed up and she and Ozzie made love to Thelonious Monk records, weird plinking and bonging blues, sort of Japanese come to think of it. Other times Konno took him to the Queen Bee, a nightclub with elaborate floor shows and gorgeous women drifting through the smoke like one hundred slit-skirt versions of a Howard Johnson's hostess. It occurred to Lee that he ought to wonder what an elevator man and a pfc. were doing in a place like this.

Konno would slouch in, taking off his raincoat and dragging it along the floor as they were led to a table in a platformed area above the tourists, the Japanese businessmen, American officers, contract pilots (recognizable by their drab short-sleeve shirts and fancy sunglasses, whatever the weather). Konno pocketed checks without seeming to pay and one night introduced Lee to a hostess named Tammy, a woman in a silver dress and shiny face paint.

Konno believed in riots.

Konno believed the U.S. had used germ warfare in Korea and was experimenting with a substance called lysergic acid here in Japan.

Life is hostile, he believed. The struggle is to merge your life with the greater tide of history.

To have true socialism, he said, we first establish capitalism, totally and heartlessly, and then destroy it by degrees, bury it in the sea.

He was a member of the Japanese-Soviet Friendship Society, the Japanese Peace Council, the Japan-China Cultural Exchange Association.

Foreign capital, foreign troops dominate modern Japan, he said.

All foreign troops are U.S. troops. Every Westerner is an American. Every American serves the cause of monopolistic capital.

Tammy took Lee to a Buddhist shrine.

One night at the Queen Bee, Konno announced that MACS-1, Lee's unit, would soon leave for the Philippines. This was news to the young Marine. He was beginning to like Japan. He liked coming to Tokyo. He counted on these discussions with Konno, who was able to argue Lee's own positions from a historic rather than a purely personal viewpoint, from the ashes, the rebuilt waste of a blasted landscape and economy.

Why were they shipping him out, now, of all times, when things were going well for a change, when he had things to look forward to, a woman, now and then, to crawl into bed with, people to talk to who did not see him as a figure in the shadows?

They went to the flat near the river. Konno paced the room, tugging at the ends of his silk scarf. He hinted there were others who knew about Pfc. Oswald and admired his political maturity. He said there were things that could be accomplished by people with similar ideas on world affairs, people situated in certain places, within easy reach of each other. He gave Lee a pistol, small and silver-plated, a derringer, a gift, modest, two-shot, and asked him to pick up some Luckies back at the base.

Reitmeyer tried to pick him up and turn him upside down, grabbing from behind, at the crotch and the shirt collar, basic aimless ballbreaking fun, but he messed it all up, ending with one hand gripping Ozzie's side pocket and the other in an armpit, with the victim more or less parallel to the ground, flailing for a door jamb. At first Ozzie reacted with good-natured yelping surprise, out for a midair swim; then, as Reitmeyer manhandled and yanked, refusing to see it wouldn't work, trying to cartwheel him halfway around, he complained in fierce whispers, with ultimatums and unfinished threats; then struggled hard to free himself, close to bursting into frustrated tears, a snared and wriggling kid, pink with rage; then, finally, and this brought forth a certain lurking satisfaction, familiar, falsehearted, awful, he went completely limp.

One night he wandered into a Tokyo bar that was either a queer hangout or some kind of kabuki show or maybe a little of both. The customers were all male and the hosts or hostesses—they looked increasingly like men as his eyes grew accustomed to the dark—wore bright kimonos and high swirling wigs, their mouths precisely painted, faces layered in chalk. Educational. Someone rustled nearby, a costumed man waiting to lead him to a table, but Ozzie walked quietly to the door, feeling watched, odd, peculiar, quaint. When he opened the door he saw a familiar figure in the street. It was a Marine from his unit, Heindel, just walking on by. Ozzie had a moment of small panic. He didn't want to be seen coming out of a place like this. They'd mop the barracks with him if word got out. They'd have a hog-wallow of gruesome fun. The oddball loner caught sneaking out of a swishy bar. He moved back into the dimness and ordered a beer, keeping an eye to the street. Hidell in a dark jacket with a pouncing tiger on the back. Ozzie drank his beer and got his bearings. The darkness was creepy. Whining music came from the walls.

He found a taxi and headed out to Konno's district. Chemical smoke pouring off the shipyards and factories. Skinhead kids on bikes shooting out of alleys, coming at a racing slant over the pot-holed streets.

Hidell means don't tell.

No one was home. He walked for miles, lost, before he found another cab. He went to the Queen Bee, greeted by a hostess whose sole duty was to bow to entering guests. Konno was alone at a table near the rear. They talked a long time. Girls in swimsuits passed across the stage, each throwing a hip toward the audience of businessmen and U.S. brass. It was a vast place, a noisy crowd. Konno was tired and hoarse, coming down with something. A silence at the table. Then Lee let it be known that he'd seen something interesting in Atsugi one day, a plane called a U-2.

He paused, measuring how he felt. Inside the bouncy music and applause, he occupied a pocket of calm. He was not connected to anything here and not quite connected to himself and he spoke less to Konno than to the person Konno would report to, someone out there, in the floating world, a collector of loose talk, a specialist who lived in the dark like the men with bright lips and spun-silk wigs.

He pointed out that the plane climbed right off the radarscopes.

He said it reached an altitude almost five miles above the known record. He suggested it was armed with amazing cameras and headed for hostile soil.

He barely noticed himself talking. That was the interesting part. The more he spoke, the more he felt he was softly split in two. It was all so remote he didn't think it mattered what he said. He never even looked at his companion. He sat in a white calm and let the sentences float. Konno studied him, listened, jittery, needing a shave, sniffing the nicotine on his fingers, a habit of his that seemed to imply there was never enough—enough of what you craved. Lee talked softly on. Ten thousand years of happiness, or whatever it means when they say *banzai*.

He let it be known that he'd figured out the U-2's rate of climb. He didn't say what it was but went into detail on other, minor matters, testing Konno's knowledge of technical things, lecturing a little, pointing out flaws in the base's security.

A man in a white tuxedo introduced the bathing beauties by name. Sincere applause. The two men went into the chill night. It was late and quiet and Lee pulled his windbreaker tight around him. Konno stood smoking, hunched away from the wind, knees bent, looking down an empty neon street.

Take the double-*e* from Lee.

Hide the double-*l* in Hidell.

Hidell means hide the *L*.

Don't tell.

White ideograms. Roman letters ticking in the dark. Konno said they were waiting for one of the hostesses, Tammy, and he looked a little dejected about it, maybe because he needed sleep. She came out a side exit wrapped in plastic rainwear including a hat and floppy booties, and seemed ready for some hard-earned relaxation. She thought she knew a pachinko parlor that might still be open. She wanted to play pachinko.

A radarman named Bushnell was climbing the exterior stairs of his barracks when he heard a sharp noise, a single hard rap, like a ruler striking a desk. On second thought, no, that wasn't it. More like a little popping sound, a two-inch firecracker maybe. Except that wasn't it either. That wasn't even close. Maybe just a slamming door actually.

He went inside and saw Ozzie sitting on a footlocker, alone in the squadbay, showing his funny smile. He had a little bitty pistol in his hand and there was a streak of blood across his left arm, above the elbow.

"I believe I shot myself," he said.

Bushnell studied the perfect little scene. He thought Ozzie's remark sounded historical and charming, right out of a movie or TV play.

"Where did you get the gun is what I'm thinking if I'm the duty officer and just happen to come around."

"Meanwhile would you do something?"

"What do you want me to do?"

"Get a corpsman would be fine with me."

"What's it doing? Is it bleeding? Looks like a shaving cut to me."

"There's a hole in my arm."

"You shave yet, Ozzie? I hear your mother shaves but you don't. What happens when they see the gun?"

"It was an accident."

"Bullshit. You should have used your .45."

"And blow my arm off."

"It's government issue, shitbird. What are you supposed to tell them, I found the gun on a sidewalk at high noon?"

"I did find it."

"Christ, Ozzie, you make me sick. You're sitting here all alone. What if I don't come in? You just sit and wait? If there's anything I don't respect, it's bad planning."

"Meanwhile I am shot."

"Well big fucking deal."

"I am bleeding, Bushnell."

"You deserve to bleed. You deserve to go white and fucking die. This is a stunt. It is just the oldest stunt in the world. How do you expect them to walk in here and say all right you're shot, Oswald, so you stay here and the rest of them have to ship their asses out to sea."

"Because I am shot. That's how I expect them to say it."

"Completely ignoring the fact you hit only flesh, which it looks like it to me. It's a court-martial offense, I guarantee, the minute they see a weapon that's not authorized."

"I took the gun out of the footlocker to turn it in when it went off."

"Tell us how small and cute it is."

"I am bleeding."

"You'll be hit with wrongful conduct, regardless. Same as if you had a riot gun."

"It went off when I dropped it. I picked it up off the floor, which at the time I felt dizzy and thought to myself I'm in a state of shock so I closed the footlocker in an attempt to sit down, which is how you found me."

"Don't tell me. Tell them, shitbird."

"Just get me a corpsman, Bushnell. Somebody has to treat me. I'm a wounded Marine."

DIAGNOSIS: WOUND, MISSILE, UPPER LEFT ARM
GUNSHOT, NO A OR N INVOLVEMENT #8255
1. Within command—work.
2. Patient dropped 45 caliber automatic, pistol discharged when it struck the floor, and missile struck patient in left arm causing the injury.

NARRATIVE SUMMARY:
This 18 year male accidentally shot himself in the left arm with a sidearm, reportedly of 22 caliber. Examination revealed the wound of entrance in the medial portion of the left upper arm, just above the elbow. There was no evidence of neurologic circulatory, or bony injury. The wound of entrance was allowed to heal and the missile was then excised through a separate incision two inches above the wound of

entry. The missile appeared to be a 22 slug. The wound healed well, and the patient was discharged to duty.

SURG: 10-5-57:   FOREIGN BODY, REMOVAL OF, FROM EXTREMITIES, LEFT UPPER ARM #926

Postcard #1. Aboard the USS *Terrell County* in the South China Sea. Ozzie sits on the afterdeck with Reitmeyer, counting the days of ghost maneuvers in the drenching heat, wondering if he'll ever see land again.

"What do you say I teach you to play chess?"

"Fuck you."

"It's for your own stupid good, Reitmeyer. Plus we have to pass the time somehow."

"Take a flying fuck at the moon."

"The best players in the world are generally Russian."

"Fuck them, in spades."

Men sit dazed in the streaming light.

Postcard #2. Corregidor, among the war ruins. John Wayne comes to visit the homesick leathernecks of MACS-1, interrupting work on a movie being shot somewhere in the Pacific. Ozzie has mess duty, he has mess duty all the time now, but he sneaks a look at the famous man eating lunch with a group of officers—roast beef and gravy that he has helped prepare. He wants to get close to John Wayne, say something authentic. He watches John Wayne talk and laugh. It's remarkable and startling to see the screen laugh repeated in life. It makes him feel good. The man is doubly real. He does not cheat or disappoint. When John Wayne laughs, Ozzie smiles, he lights up, he practically disappears in his own glow. Someone takes a photograph of John Wayne and the officers, and Ozzie wonders if he will show up in the background, in the passageway, grinning. It's time to get back to the galley but he watches John

Wayne a moment longer, thinking of the cattle drive in *Red River*, the great expectant moment when it starts. Stillness, nervous steers, horsemen in dawn light, the rim of hills, the deep sure voice of aging John Wayne, the voice with so many shades of feeling and reassurance, John Wayne resolutely to his adopted son: *"Take 'em to Missouri, Matt."* Then rearing mounts, trail hands yahooing, the music and rousing song, the honest stubbled faces (men he feels he knows), all the glory and dust of the great drive north.

He reads Walt Whitman in hospital ruins.

One thing about Konno. He never talked to Lee in a personal way. He seemed to be reciting, talking into a Dictaphone. There was no flexibility in his manner. He didn't see the individual.

One other thing. He was in over his head, technically speaking. He didn't know the terminology, all the phrases and labels in aviation electronics, high-altitude reconnaissance. An elevator operator. Ha ha.

Lee didn't let on that he'd wounded himself with the derringer Konno had supplied. First because the strategy had failed to keep him in Japan. Then, too, he didn't want Konno to know he'd been under his influence.

No talking.

You stand at attention until assigned.

You do not step on white paint at any time. Segments of the floor are painted white. Do not touch white. There are white lines running down passageways. Do not touch or cross these lines. Every urinal is situated behind a white line. You need permission to piss.

You take your beatings in the area between the chest and groin, so bruises won't show. This is tradition. Or a guard will put a bucket on your head and whack it with a truncheon.

If you are assigned a cell, your guard will hose out the cell while you are inside it.

There are special punishment facilities called the hole, the box, the cage—names with a vivid history familiar from the movies.

You never walk where there is room to run. You run to and from your storage box. You stop at every white line and wait for permission to cross. You run in the compound, your grub hoe held at port arms.

You are processed naked, holding your seabag above your head at arm's length, shouting *aye aye sir* and *no sir* at the slightest sound. You are permitted to lower the seabag to the back of your neck only when you bend over to allow them to check your anal cavity for printed matter, narcotics, alcoholic beverages, digging tools, TV sets, implements of self-destruction.

This was the brig in Atsugi, a large frame building with cement floors, a number of storerooms, offices and compartments, a turnkey's area and a large chicken-wire enclosure that contained twenty-one bunks. The enclosure was filled to capacity. New prisoners were lodged in six concrete cells located along a passageway marked with white lines. The cells were designed for single occupancy but summer was the season of misfits, runaways, violent drinkers, born losers, petty thieves, desperadoes, men of every manner of delicate temperament, and Oswald had a cellmate named Bobby Dupard, a slim sad-eyed Negro with a copper cast to his hair and skin.

Oswald, first in, got the stationary bunk. Dupard got a swayback cot and a mattress that was aglimmer with flat-bodied biting things— things you could crack between your fingernails and they'd break into two and become four and then eight, swarming back into their cottony nests to breed some more, so what was the point of even trying, according to Dupard.

They whispered to each other in the night.

"Are you saying when you kill them, they multiply?"

"I'm saying you can't kill them. Some things too small."

"Sleep on top of the blanket," Oswald told him.

"They get on through. They bore through."

"That's termites, that bore."

"Hey, Jim, I live with these things for years."

"Put the blanket on the floor. Sleep on the floor."

"Half the floor is white lines, like they foreseen. Which anyway the lice jump down on top of me."

A nearly bare place, simple objects, basic needs. Oswald's senses were fearfully keyed. He tasted iron on his tongue. He heard the voices from the chicken wire, guards grumbling like heavy dogs. When they hosed down the floor of the cell block he smelled the earth embedded in concrete—pebbles, gravel, slag and broken stone, all distantly mixed with ammonia, like contempt blended in.

Dupard was from Texas.

"Leads the nation in homicides," Oswald said.

"That's the place."

"Whereabouts?"

"Dallas."

"I'm from Fort Worth, off and on, myself."

"Neighbors. Ain't that something. How old is a kid like yourself?"

"Eighteen," Oswald told him.

"You a baby. They throw a baby into prison. How much time you bring with you?"

"Twenty-eight days."

"What's the charge?"

"First I accidentally shot myself in the arm, which they court-martialed me for, but suspended the sentence."

"If it's accidentally, what's their point?"

"They said I used an unregistered weapon. I had a private weapon."

"Which they never handed out."

"Which I found. But that doesn't matter in their eyes as long as the weapon is not registered."

"But they suspend the sentence, so then what?"

"Then there was a second court-martial."

"Sound like somebody push his luck."

"Based on an incident. That's all it was."

"I believe it."

"There's a sergeant, Rodriguez, that's been giving me mess duty all the time. Doesn't like me, which I guarantee it's mutual. So we had words more than once. I let him know how I felt about being singled out. He told me it's the court-martial that's keeping me out of the radar hut, plus general standards, which he's saying I don't dress or behave up to standards. I saw him at a local bar and went right over. I told him. I said get me off these menial jobs. We were standing jaw to jaw. He thought I'd say my piece and back off. But I stood right there. There were people pressing close. My mind was already working. Potential witnesses. I told him what I thought. That's all. I didn't wise off. I was simple and clear. I said I wanted fair treatment. I told him. I didn't bait him. He said I was baiting him. He said I wouldn't get him to fight. More trouble than it was worth. Lose him a stripe or something. Some guys egged us on. They told Rodriguez whip him good. But I wasn't trying to get him to fight. I was stating my case in the matter. He called me *maricón*. He whispered to me, *maricón*, with a little sweet smile. I told him I know what that means. I heard Puerto Ricans use those words. I know those words. He said he was no Puerto Rican. I told him don't use Puerto Rican words. It was heated then. They were all around us. Somebody shoved me and I spilled my beer all over Rodriguez. Accidentally spilled. I said you saw I was pushed. I told him. I didn't apologize or make an excuse. It wasn't my fault. There was shoving all around. I was only standing up for my military rights."

"Regulate the voice," Bobby whispered.

"So that was the second court-martial. But I defended myself this time. I questioned Rodriguez on the stand. I was proved not guilty of throwing my drink on him, which is technically an assault charge."

"How come here we are, having this talk?"

"They said I was guilty of a lesser charge. Wrongful use of provoking words to a staff noncommissioned officer. Article one seventeen. Bang."

"Slam the gate," Bobby said.

He wore faded utilities that still carried the imprint of long-gone sergeant stripes and he worked in the fields, clearing stones and burning trash. The guard wore a .45 and kept his gun side turned away from the prisoners. There was no talking or rest. They worked in the rain. There were great billowing rains that first week, rain in broad expanses, slow and lilting. Smoke drifted over the men, smelling of wet garbage, half burnt. Their useless work trailed them through the day. He thought there was a good chance he would go to OCS. He'd passed the qualifying exam for corporal before shipping out. He'd be in good shape if it wasn't for the shooting incident and the spilled-drink incident. He could still be in good shape. He was smart enough to make officer. That wasn't the issue. The issue was would they let him. He cut brush and cleared fields of heavy stones. The issue was would they rig the thing against him.

"I landed here like a dream," Dupard whispered that night. "I figure I'm already dead. It's just a question they shovel the dirt in my face."

"What did they charge you with?"

"There was a fire to my rack, which they accused me. But in my own mind I could like verbalize it either way. In other way of saying it, the evidence was weak."

"But you did it."

"It's not that easy to say. I could go either way and be convinced in my own mind."

"You're not sure you really wanted to do it. You were just thinking about doing it."

"I was like, Should I drop this cigarette?"

"It just seemed to happen while you were thinking it."

"Like it happened on its own."

"Did the rack go up?"

"Scorch some linen was all. Like you fall asleep a tenth of a second, smoking."

"Why did you want to start a fire?"

"It's a question of working it out in my own mind, the exact why I did it. Because the psychology is definitely there."

"Then what?"

"Mainly one thing. I deserted."

"Why?"

"Because I want to book on out of here," Bobby said. "I am not a Marine. Simple. They ought to see that and just call a halt. Because the longer it goes on, there's no chance I deal with this shit."

In the prison literature he'd read, Oswald was always coming across an artful old con who would advise the younger man, give him practical tips, talk in sweeping philosophical ways about the larger questions. Prison invited larger questions. It made you wish for an experienced perspective, for the knowledge of some grizzled figure with kind and tired eyes, a counselor, wise to the game. He wasn't sure what he had here in Bobby R. Dupard.

The next day he came back from a work detail and found two guards in the cell pummeling Dupard. They took their time. It looked like something else at first, an epileptic fit, a heart attack, but then he understood it was a beating. Bobby was on the deck trying to cover up and the two men took turns hitting him in the kidneys and ribs. One guard sat on Oswald's bunk, leaning way over to throw short lefts like a man trying to start an outboard. The other guard was down on one knee, biting his lip, pausing to aim his shots so they wouldn't catch Bobby's crossed arms. Bobby had a look on his face like this is bound to end someday. He was working hard to keep them unfulfilled.

They called him Brillo Head. He showed a little smile, as if only the spoken word might perk his interest. They went back to pounding.

Oswald stopped at the white line outside the cell. He thought if he stood absolutely still, looking vaguely right or vaguely left, waiting patiently for them to finish what they were doing so he could request permission to cross the line, they might be inclined to let him enter without a beating.

He hated the guards, secretly sided with them against some of the prisoners, thought they deserved what they got, the prisoners who were stupid and cruel. He felt his rancor constantly shift, felt secret satisfactions, hated the brig routine, despised the men who could not master it, although he knew it was contrived to defeat them all.

When a man was returned to his unit from the chicken-wire enclosure, a man from the cells took his place.

When a man in the chicken wire fouled up, he got a cell of his own, C-rats to eat, close and horrendous attention.

When a man from the cells fouled up, he was thrown in the hole, a junior-size cell with a dirt floor and a cat hole to crap in.

Because of the overcrowding, there was constant shifting of prisoners, many ceremonial occasions at white lines, inspections, friskings, shakedowns, foul-ups.

The night of the beating, Dupard had nothing to say, although Ozzie knew he was not asleep.

He tried to feel history in the cell. This was history out of George Orwell, the territory of no-choice. He could see how he'd been headed here since the day he was born. The brig was invented just for him. It was just another name for the stunted rooms where he'd spent his life.

He'd once told Reitmeyer that communism was the one true religion. He was speaking seriously but also for effect. He could enrage Reitmeyer by calling himself an atheist. Reitmeyer thought you had to be forty years old before you could claim that distinction. It was a position you had to earn through years of experience, like winning seniority in the Teamsters.

Maybe the brig was a kind of religion too. All prison. Something you carried with you all your life, a counterforce to politics and lies. This went deeper than anything they could tell you from the pulpit. It carried a truth no one could contradict. He'd been headed here from the start. Inevitable.

Trotsky in the Bronx, only blocks away.

Maybe what has to happen is that the individual must allow himself to be swept along, must find himself in the stream of no-choice, the single direction. This is what makes things inevitable. You use the restrictions and penalties they invent to make yourself stronger. History means to merge. The purpose of history is to climb out of your own skin. He knew what Trotsky had written, that revolution leads us out of the dark night of the isolated self. We live forever in history, outside ego and id. He wasn't sure he knew exactly what the id was but he knew it lay hidden in Hidell.

A naked bulb burning in the passageway. He watched Dupard in the shadows, sitting on the infested cot, showing an empty stare. His bony wrists dangled out of the faded shirt. He had a gangliness that made him seem sixteen, rompish and clumsy, but he moved well running—running in the compound, running to the head, eyeing those white lines. A long face, hangdog, sad-sack, and dusty hair, reddish brown. Eyes suspicious and hurt, quick to look away. Oswald lay still, aware of a drone in the block, a heaving breath, grimness, massive sleep. Dupard undressed, got under the blanket and began to masturbate, turned toward the wall. Oswald watched his top shoulder twitch. Then he turned to his own wall, closed his eyes, tried to will himself to sleep.

Hidell means don't tell.

The id is hell.

Jerkle and Hide in their little cell.

Oswald stood at the white line in front of the urinal. A guard moved alongside, peering in that inquisitive way, like what do we have here to pass the time.

Oswald requested permission to cross the line.

"I'm looking at your hairline, shitbird. What is supposed to be the length of the hair in the area of the nape of the neck?"

"Zero length."

"What do I see?"

"I don't know."

The guard pushed him stumbling across the line. When he turned to recross he looked directly in the man's face. A long-headed type, half intelligent, small bright eyes.

Oswald turned to face the urinal, requested permission to cross.

"I'm looking at your sideburns. What am I looking at?"

"My sideburns."

"The hair on your sideburns will not exceed what length when fully extended."

"One-eighth inch."

The guard extended the hair between his thumb and index finger, twisting for effect. Oswald let his head lean that way, not so much to ease the pain, which was mild, as to show he would not accept pain stoically in these circumstances. The guard released and then popped him in the head with the heel of his hand.

Oswald requested permission to cross the line.

"The length of the hair at the top of the head will not exceed how many inches maximum."

"Maximum three inches."

He waited for the guard to grab a handful.

"The fly of the trousers shall hang in what kind of line and shall not do what when they are what."

"The fly of the trousers shall hang in a vertical line and shall not gap when they are unzipped."

The guard reached around and grabbed him by the nuts.

"I know the type."

"Aye aye sir."

"I spot the type a mile away."

"Aye aye sir."

"The type that can't stand pain."

"Aye aye sir."

"The sniveling phony Marine."

A prisoner approached the second white line, requested permission to cross. The guard looked over, slowly. He let go of Oswald's crotch. It was raining again. He detached the billy club from his belt and approached the second prisoner.

"What's your name?"

"Nineteen."

"Don't you know the code, Nineteen?"

"I requested permission to cross the line."

"You didn't request permission to talk." The guard jabbed him lightly in the ribs. "Prisoners are silent. We observe the international rules of warfare in this head. This is my head. Nobody talks without my say-so."

He jabbed the prisoner with the billy club.

"Prisoners run silent. They fall to the deck silent when struck. Do you know how to fall, Nineteen?"

The guard jabbed twice, then three more times, harder, before Nineteen realized he was supposed to fall down, which he did, crumpling slowly, in careful stages. His right shoulder touched the white line. The guard kicked him back over.

"We observe the principles of night movement in this head. What is the first principle of night movement, Nineteen?"

"Run at night only in an emergency."

The guard swung the club without bothering to lean toward the prisoner, using a casual backhand stroke, grazing the man's elbow. The guard did not look at the man as he swung. This was one of the features of the local style.

The guard looked at Oswald.

"Why did I hit him?"

"He recited principle number two."

The guard swung the club, hitting the man in the shoulder.

"In this head we know our manual word for word," the guard told the crumpled man, standing with his back to him. "We say nothing in this head that does not come from the manual. We kill silent and with surprise."

Oswald needed desperately to piss.

"In the final assualt," said the guard, "it is the individual

Marine, with his rifle and his what, who closes with the enemy and destroys him."

"Bayonet," the prisoner said.

"A vigorous bayonet assault, executed by Marines eager to drive home cold steel, can do what, what, what."

Silence from the man on the deck. He tightened his fetal knot a second before the guard stepped back half a stride and swung the club in a wide arc, striking the knee this time. Oswald was eager to be called.

The guard looked at Oswald, who said at once, "A vigorous bayonet assault, executed by Marines eager to drive home cold steel, can strike terror in the ranks of the enemy."

The guard swung the club backwards once more, striking Nineteen on the arm. Oswald felt a slight satisfaction. The guard made a point of gazing into the distance as he struck his blows.

Oswald sensed the guard's interest shift his way. He was ready for the question.

"Principle number one."

"Get the blade into the enemy."

"Principle number two."

"Be ruthless, vicious and fast in your attack."

The guard took half a step, switched the billy to his left hand and swung it hard, striking Oswald's collarbone. He was genuinely surprised. He thought they'd reached an understanding. The blow knocked him back three steps and forced him to one knee. He'd thought he was through getting hit for the day.

"There are no right answers," the guard advised, looking into the distance.

Oswald got to his feet, approached the white line, stood staring at the urinal. He requested permission to cross.

"To execute the slash, do what."

"One, assume the guard position."

"Then what."

"Two, step forward fifteen inches with the left foot, keeping the right foot in place."

The guard swung the club, hitting him in the arm. He was sweaty with the need to piss, his upper body moist and chill.

"There are no right answers in this head. It is the stupidest arrogance to give an answer that you think is right."

The guard jabbed him in the ribs with the butt end of the stick. The other man, Nineteen, was still crumpled on the deck.

The guard swung the club, smashing Oswald on the upper back. The idea seemed to be why bother with questions. Oswald made a decision to let the piss come flowing out. It was an anger and a compensation. He felt it flow down his leg, knowing deep relief, deliverance, good health everywhere, long life to all.

The guard swung the club, hitting the side of Oswald's neck.

He put his hands over the back of his head, covering up. The last blow put the guard strangely on edge. He stood looking into the distance but was different from before, mouth hanging open, a dead spot in his eye, and Oswald knew they were all one word away from a private carnage of the type you hear about from time to time, nameless and undetailed.

He watched the puddle take shape on the floor, his arms crossed at the back of his head. He needed a moment to think.

He sighed deeply, stepping up to the white line. He looked straight ahead and lowered his hands slowly to his sides. It was his sense of things that if he moved slowly and openly and did not show terror, the guard would stand off. The guard's mental condition had to be taken into account. They were all here to see to it that the guard came through. Oswald believed that the man crumpled on the deck knew this as well as he did. He sensed the man's awareness of the moment. They had to let the moment cohere, build itself back to something they all recognized as a rainy Wednesday in Japan.

He stood at the white line and waited.

Dupard whispered in the dark.

"I definitely get the idea they want to send me home in a box.

The first minute I put on the green service coat, I look like I'm dead. It's a coffin suit for a fool. I seen it on the spot."

"I liked the uniform," Ozzie told him. "It was great how it looked. I was surprised how great I felt. I kept it cleaned and moth-proofed. I kept heavy objects out of the pockets. I looked in the mirror and said it's me."

"Nice joke. They told my mother. Get him in the service, Mrs. Dupard. The streets of America getting crazy by the day. Your boy is safe with us."

"That's what they told my mother."

"They sent me to JP to save me from West Dallas niggers. Believe this booshit? They put me behind bars so nobody slips off with my wallet and shoes."

"It's the whole huge system. We're a zero in the system."

"They give me their special attention. Better believe."

"They watch us all the time. It's like Big Brother in *Nineteen Eighty-four*. This isn't a book about the future. This is us, here and now."

"I used to read the Bible," Bobby said.

"I used to read the manual. I never looked at my schoolbooks but I read the Marine Corps manual."

"Make you a man."

"Then I found out what it's really all about. How to be a tool of the system. A workable part. It's the perfect capitalist handbook."

"Be a Marine."

"Orwell means the military mind. The police state is not Russia. It's wherever we have the mind that can think up manuals full of rules for killing."

"Where's this Stalin, dead?"

"Dead."

"I thought I heard that."

"But Eisenhower's not. Ike is our own Big Brother. Our commander in chief."

They lay in the dark, thinking.

Because of what they did to us. The way she had to work and

quit and take care of me and get fired and work and quit and pick up and leave. Let's pick up and leave. Scraping up pennies for the next move somewhere. Daily humiliations all her life. This is known as ground down by the system. Except she never questions that. It is only the local conditions. It is Mr. Ekdahl and his puny divorce settlement. It is the whispering behind her back. It is the neighbors with their Hotpoint washers and Ford Fairlane cars, which she competes against the only way she can.

"My boy Lee loves to read."

His mother never-ending.

Three days running, for no special reason, every meal was rabbit chow—lettuce, carrots, water.

Oswald ran past the chicken wire, turned into the cell block, stopped at the white line. Dupard was in the cell wearing skivvies and sitting on Oswald's rack. Dupard's mattress was smoldering. Oswald watched the pale smoke collect in the air. His cellmate just sat there, hangdog, thoughtful, picking at his feet.

"Bobby, how come?"

"You want your rack?"

"Stay there."

"We're not supposed to talk."

"You're only making things worse."

"I'm evicting lice, that's all. They're boring into my skin. Time to rid the premise, man."

"Did you ask for a new mattress?"

"I axed. They punch my face."

He was calm, a little sullen, mainly thoughtful and resigned.

"They'll only extend your time."

"In my own mind this is nothing to excite themselves. I don't feel like there's any guilt to be handed out whereby I'm punished. I'm fumigating these lice on out of here. In other way of saying it, it's like I'm doing their job for them."

"This is your second fire."

"Regulate the voice."

"Well I don't see the point of mattress fires, frankly."

"Stop talking, Ozzie. They kill your ass."

Two guards came down the passageway, brushed past Oswald and entered the cell. The fire was so insignificant they were able to delay getting water until after they'd spent five grim minutes pounding Dupard.

Oswald stood at the white line, looking away.

They moved him out to the chicken wire. Not only guards but fellow inmates, all those bodies to avoid, those eyes and inner melodies—terror, gloom, psycho violence. The trick inside the wire was to stay within your own zone, avoid eye contact, accidental touch, gestures of certain types, anything that might hint at a personality behind the drone unit. The only safety was in facelessness.

He developed a voice that guided him through the days. Forever, endless, identical. The brig was so unthinking it eventually drove out fear. He ran in the passageways, he ran in place. He scrubbed the brightwork in the head, squared away his area, made up his rack. The point of the brig was to clean the brig. He drew his bucket from the storeroom, stood at the white line. They'd built the brig just to keep it clean. It was where they put their white lines. Everything depended on the lines. The brig was the place where all the lines that were painted in the military mind were made bright and clean forever. Once he understood that, he knew he had their number.

He sat in the TV room watching reruns of Dick Clark's *American Bandstand*. Reitmeyer came in to shake his hand. Half a dozen other guys dropped by to ask about the brig. He wore his Hawaiian shirt, smirking a little, telling them he'd breezed right through. Great training for life in the U.S. Gives you that competitive edge. That's Ozzie for you, said his barracks-mates. That's the Rabbit, that's Bugs, and they drifted out one by one, leaving him to stare at the high-school boys and girls shuffling drowsily on a dance floor in Philadelphia.

Two weeks later he followed directions to a house in the Sanya district of Tokyo. He made his way through a ragpickers' village built with material scavenged from other parts of the city. Old women jogged through the alleys carrying empty bottles, broken chair legs, pieces of indefinable junk. Houses were shoulder-high, made of old packing crates and strips of sheet metal, the walls stuffed with cardboard and rags. There were lines of people selling blood at mobile units, people who seemed hollow-bodied, so small, in such collapse. It would never bottom out. No matter how far down you went into the world, there were distances still to go, worse things to see and experience. He made it a point not to hurry through the area. He wanted to see what was here.

He entered a tenement and looked in an open door to a flat where a young man was trying to fix a mimeograph machine. Konno had told him to go to the fourth floor but hadn't supplied an apartment number. The hallway was dark and rank. A child was wailing on one of the upper stories.

Hidell climbs the ancient creaking stairs.

On four, two more doors were open. Students milled inside the apartments, moved from one to the other. A young man looked at Ozzie, who was standing in the hallway, smiling, in his T-shirt and dusty jeans. The man smiled back and pointed to a door at the end of the hall. Oswald knocked and was told to enter. He saw a tatami mat and low table. A woman moved across the room. She was about fifty years old, with a moon face and pixie hairdo, wearing a light cotton kimono. She said her name was Dr. Braunfels. She taught German and Russian on a private basis to students at Tokyo University. She understood he was interested in learning Russian. He said he was, and waited. She sat cross-legged on the mat at the far side of the table. She asked him to take off his shoes. These were the nice little gestures that went with the setting.

She wore eye makeup that matched the pale-blue shade of the

kimono. He hadn't expected a European. It was encouraging, it was all to the good, it made his decision seem timely, fixed to favorable circumstances. She was probably important, an adviser to radical students and a recruiting officer or handler of agents. She gestured for him to sit facing her on the mat. She watched him assume the awkward position. They ate rice cakes wrapped in seaweed.

"And you are Oswald, Lee," she said finally, as if correcting an imbalance, adding the last stately note to some diplomatic exchange.

There were bamboo shades behind her, a screen to one side. The ceiling was low, a dark-toned wood. Small polished objects here and there. You were supposed to appreciate the near-bareness, the placement of things. Twigs in a vase on the lacquer table.

He told her he wanted to defect.

"I've been thinking this is the step to take, that I'll never be able to live in the U.S. I want a life like these students, political, working in the struggle. I'm not an innocent youth who thinks Russia is the land of his dreams. I look at this coldly in the light of right and wrong. I do think there is something unique about the Soviet Union that I wish to find out for myself. It's the great theory come to life. Before I was fifteen I began indoctrinating myself in the New Orleans library. I studied Marxist ideology. I could lift my head from a book and see the impoverishment of the masses right there in front of me, including my own mother in her struggle to raise three children against the odds. These socialist writings showed me the key to my environment. The material was correct in its thesis. Capitalism is beginning to die. It is taking desperate measures. There is hysteria in the air, like hating Negroes and communists. In the military I'm learning the full force of the system. There is something in the system that builds up hate. How would I live in America? I would have a choice of being a worker in a system I despise or going unemployed. Nobody knows how I feel about this. I'm sincere in my ideal that this is what I want to do. This is not something intangible. I'm ready to go through pain and hardship to leave my country forever."

That evening he sat alone at the Queen Bee, thinking he'd approached the main business too quickly. She did not seem happy to hear the news and she countered it with news of her own. His unit was shipping out for the latest hot spot, Formosa, in a couple of weeks. What she wanted him to do, for now, was put aside any thought of defecting and concentrate on getting access to classified documents and photographs. She spent some time discussing this. She talked about his job, not his life. She wanted tactical call signs, authentication codes, radio frequencies. She wanted spotter photos of U-2s.

There would be money for this, although she realized money was not his motive. She talked about a second meeting in Yamato, near the base, and gave him detailed directions. She spoke in a practiced way about procedures and craft, about the need for discipline, possibly referring to his rumpled street clothes and day-old stubble. She said she admired the Japanese because a man might spend a lifetime getting one thing right.

She had a full mouth and pudgy hands. There was a mock girlishness about her, several levels of something tricky and derisive. He told her he was serious about learning Russian.

At the Queen Bee he waited for Tammy to finish work and he spent the night with her in the flat she shared with two of her sisters. They had sex, more or less furtively, as the sisters watched TV. Curled in a corner of the room, unable to sleep, his head in the crook of his lover's arm, he thought of a number of things Dr. Braunfels didn't know. She didn't know he'd been on mess duty since the first court-martial. Mess duty, guard duty, a series of shit details—everything but gazing into radarscopes. She didn't know he'd lost his security clearance after the second court-martial. She didn't know there *was* a second court-martial, or a first for that matter, and she didn't know about the incidents that brought them about. One last thing she didn't know, and that was how far out on a limb he would have to go to snatch documents from a restricted area without clearance.

Seeing her smooth round face, doing her accented voice, he

said to himself in the dark, What kind of foul-up do we have here, Oswald Lee?

Back in Atsugi he went on a movie binge. He saw every movie twice, kept to himself, spent serious time at the base library, learning Russian verbs.

Ozzie thought, What if she's only interested in twisting me dry?

He met her in a flat above a bicycle shop. There was an open umbrella drying in the hall. She wore Western clothes, a raincoat over her shoulders. They shook hands like hospital roommates. She had that cropped uneven hair that was way too young and made him think she was undependable, a person who could not survive without double meanings, or saying one thing to mean the opposite.

"You are much greater value," she said, "going on with your duties, reporting to me at regular times. Go where they send you. Why not? We wish you to get ahead. You get ahead here, not in Moscow or Leningrad."

"What if I'm determined to go?"

"This is not the time for you."

"Couldn't they train me there, then send me back?"

"You are already back."

A little joke. He told her he had no documents. Documents would come, possibly, in the near future. It all depended. In the meantime he showed his good will by reporting the number and type of aircraft in his squadron and the squawk codes for aircraft entering and exiting the identification zone. He did not tell her everything he knew about the U-2. He told her a few technical things, studying her reaction to the terms. He told her there was talk around the base that the plane's cameras scanned through multiple apertures.

How wide a track?

He hated to say he didn't know. She asked the names of U-2 pilots. She wanted technical manuals, instruction sheets. He gave the impression that further information would be available in the normal course of things, depending.

He definitely wanted instruction in Russian. He'd brought along an English-Russian dictionary. The sight of it made Dr. Braunfels sink deeply into her raincoat. She told him never to do that again. She would bring whatever books were needed.

They sat at the table in dim light going over pronunciations. She seemed impressed by his efforts. If he was willing to keep studying on his own, without attracting attention, she would give him as much help as she could. She talked about the language for some time, seemingly against her better judgment, drawn by his earnest desire to learn.

Working with her, making the new sounds, watching her lips, repeating words and syllables, hearing his own flat voice take on texture and dimension, he could almost believe he was being remade on the spot, given an opening to some larger and deeper version of himself. The language had a size to it, a deep-reaching honesty. He thought she was a good teacher, firm and serious, and he felt a small true joy pass between them.

He said to her, "A thousand years from now, people will look in the history books and read where the lines were drawn and who made the right choice and who didn't. The dynamics of history favor the Soviet Union. This is totally obvious to someone coming of age in America with an open mind. Not that I ignore the values and traditions there. The fact is there's the potential of being attracted to the values. Everyone wants to love America. But how can an honest man forget what he sees in the daily give-and-take that's like a million little wars?"

Reitmeyer listened to the greetings, which were followed by a halting dialogue, with hand gestures, between his off-and-on buddy Oswald and a corporal named Yaroslavsky. He thought it was curious that a pair of U.S. Marines would turn up at muster every day chatting in Russian. It annoyed Reitmeyer. It definitely rubbed him the wrong way, the private joke they made of it all, laughing over certain phrases, calling each other comrade. They seemed to think this was hilarious. Seven, eight, nine days running. This half-ass foreign gibberish. Only in America, as the saying goes. Except this is Japan, he reminded himself, and every day is a strange day in the fabulous East.

He watched Tammy apply eyebrow pencil to her lips, a fad among teen-age girls in JP that year. She was younger than Mitsuko but not that young. Mitsuko had vanished into the floating world and it was possible Tammy would follow any time. She posed for him now in a fluffy blouse and toreador pants. It no longer made Ozzie feel self-conscious to be seen by other Marines with a woman who was put together so well. The guys in MACS-1 couldn't figure it out.

She took him to a place called the Loneliness Bar, where the hostesses wore swimsuits treated with a chemical substance. The idea was to strike a match on a girl's backside as she walked by your table. Four Negro GIs went apeshit striking matches on sleek bottoms. There were matches jutting from the knuckles of every hand. They hooted and laughed, could not contain their amazement. They were young Southern Negroes, awkward and spindly, with a likable slapstick manner, and they made him wonder what had happened to Bobby Dupard. It put a kind of doom on the evening. He sat drinking beer in the stink of all those blistered match-heads, explaining his past to Tammy in simple phrases. A night in the life of the Loneliness Bar.

Three days later he felt a stinging heat when he pissed. It burned inside. Two days after that he couldn't help noticing a thick discharge from the selfsame organ. He went to the head in the middle of the night to study the fluid, a dreadful yellowish drip. At the lab they took a series of smears and cultures, gave him nine hundred thousand units of penicillin, intramuscular, over a three-day period, and returned him to light duty.

Ozzie had the clap.

The pilot arrives in an ambulance, with armed guards. He wears a white helmet that is sealed to his airtight suit and he strides to the unmarked plane without delay. The ground crew and guards back off as the engine emits the high-pitched signal that always brings a few men slouching out of the radar shack to watch the black-bandit jet streak down the runway. It's over almost at once, the shrill sound rising, the strut-and-wheel devices keeping the long wings level until flying speed is reached. Then the plane is up, the pogos drop off, the men try to keep track of the fast steep climb, the brilliant leap into another skin. They scrunch up their faces, peering into the haze. But the object is already gone, part of the high quiet, the flat and seamless sky out there, leaving behind a string of soft drawled curses and murmurs of disbelief.

The pilot, sooner or later, whoever he is, whatever his base or his mission, thinks about the items stored in his seat pack. Water, field rations, flares, a first-aid kit; a hunting knife and pistol; a needle tipped with lethal shellfish toxin and concealed in a fake silver dollar. ("We'd just as soon they didn't get a chance to interrogate you guys, not that we think you'd breathe a word.") There is also the delicate charge of cyclonite that will pulverize the camera and electronic equipment an undetermined number of seconds after the pilot activates the timer and gets his feet into the stirrups of the ejection seat, should the remote possibility arise that any such maneuver is necessary. ("Now, you people understand the ejection seat can cause amputation of the limbs if things don't work just perfect, so maybe you ought to figure on slipping quietly over the side, like you don't want to wake the kids.") He can't help thinking, sooner or later, about the worst that could happen. A stall at extreme altitudes. Or an SA-2 missile just happens to detonate nearby, knocking out a stabilizer. ("Not that the bastards have the know-how to go that high.") Next thing he knows he is out in the stratosphere, sky-hiking with a pack on his back, and he tries to convince a somewhat dreamy hand to jerk the pull-ring. At fifteen thousand feet it happens automatically, *swat*, the orange plume streaming out of his shoulder blades. It becomes a matter of dignified descent. He comes floating down out of the endless pale, struck simultaneously by the beauty of the earth and a need to ask forgiveness. He is a stranger, in a mask, falling. People come into view, farm hands, children racing toward the spot where the wind will set him down. Their rough caps are tilted back. He is near enough to hear them calling, the words bounced and steered and elongated by the contours of the land. The land smells fresh. He is coming down to springtime in the Urals and he finds that this privileged vision of the earth is an inducement to truth. He wants to tell the truth. He wants to live another kind of life, outside secrecy and guilt and the pull of grave events. This is what the pilot thinks, rocking softly down to the tawny fields of a landscape so gentle and welcoming it might almost be home.

20 May

Laurence Parmenter booked a seat on the daily flight to the Farm, the CIA's secret training base in Virginia. The flight was operated under military cover and used mainly by Agency people with short-term business at the base.

The Farm was known officially by the cryptonym ISOLATION. The names of places and operations were a special language in the Agency. Parmenter was interested in the way this language constantly found a deeper level, a secret level where those outside the cadre could not gain access to it. It was possible to say that the closest brotherhood in the Agency was among those who kept the crypt lists, who devised the keys and digraphs and knew the true names of operations. Camp Peary was the Farm, and the Farm was ISOLATION, and ISOLATION probably had a deeper name somewhere, in a locked safe or some computer buried in the ground.

He showed his laminated badge to the MP at the gate. The badge was coded to reveal to the trained eye just how much clearance the owner had. After his letter of reprimand, Parmenter had been assigned to what was joshingly called the slave directorate, a support division of clandestine services, and he'd been issued a new badge with a diminished number of little red letters around the edges. His wife said, "How many letters do you have to lose before you disappear?"

T. J. Mackey was waiting at the gatehouse. He wore well-pressed fatigues and had the distant look of a doorman in a gold coat outside a new hotel. Basically he doesn't want his friends to see him.

He took Parmenter to the JOT area, where junior officer trainees received instruction in everything from the paramilitary arts to counterintelligence. They sat alone in one of four sections of bleacher seats that formed an amphitheater over a pit area. Two young men were grappling in the dust. An instructor circled them in a busy way, speaking a language Larry did not recognize.

"Things broke our way early," he said to Mackey, "but we've reached a static period."

"I've been in touch with Guy Banister."

"Camp Street."

"That's the one. He talked to the Dallas field office of the FBI about this Oswald. They finally got him an answer. He left Dallas April twenty-four or twenty-five."

"There's a Russian wife."

"Left Dallas May ten with their baby."

"Nobody knows where."

"That's right."

"Which leaves us groping."

"I thought you had a line of communication."

"George de Mohrenschildt. But he's in Haiti. Besides I don't want him to know how interested we are in Oswald."

"How interested are we?"

"He sounds right, politically and otherwise. Win wants a shooter with credentials. He's an ex-Marine. I managed to get access to his M-1 scorebook and other records."

"Can he shoot?"

"It's a little confusing. The more I study the records, the more

I think we need an interpreter. He was generally rated poor. But it looks like he did his best work the day he fired for qualification. He got a two-twelve rating that day, which makes him a sharp-shooter. Except they gave him a lower designation. So either the number is wrong or the designation is wrong."

"Or the kid cheated."

"There's something else we ought to discuss, although I told Win it seems way too soon. Accidental hits."

"You want a realistic-looking thing. That means multiple rounds flying from a number of directions."

"Win says hit the presidential limousine, hit the pavement, hit a Secret Service man. Just don't shoot anyone in the car."

"Hit a Secret Service man."

"Hit, don't kill."

"This isn't a controlled experiment," Mackey said.

"If at all possible, you try to wound one of the men in the follow-up car. The way these things work, there are two agents on each running board of the follow-up car. That's four dangling men. And the car is going about twelve miles an hour. And it's only five feet behind the presidential car, which makes it perfectly plausible, an agent taking a bullet meant for the President."

"Where do we do it?"

"Miami."

"Good enough."

"If at all possible, that's where Win says we do it."

"It ought to be Miami."

"Definitely."

"Agreed."

"Sooner or later the President will take a swing through Florida. All the political signs point that way."

Two more young men entered the pit. Mackey said they were South Vietnamese being trained for the secret police. Foreigners attending sessions at the Farm were known as black trainees. A few of them, on sensitive assignments, had been brought to the U.S. under conditions so secure, according to Mackey, that the men did not necessarily know what country they were in. Larry thought this was farfetched. Look at the damn trees, you know you're in Virginia. But he was careful to say nothing to T-Jay. T-Jay was not to be disputed on subjects central to his interests.

He told Parmenter he would stay in close touch with Guy Banister. Banister's detective agency was the Grand Central Station of the Cuban adventure. Every type renegade passed through. Guy would help them locate a substitute for this kid who'd disappeared. Someone rated expert with a rifle and scope. A shooter who could blast a finger off a dangling man.

When Parmenter was gone, T-Jay sat in the bleachers watching the Vietnamese bounce each other around. The hot new station was Saigon. It was the talk around the base. They were putting Cuba in a box, which was okay with him. Let them forget. Let them find a new excitement. It would make the moment in Miami all the more powerful.

Some hours later Mackey was in his trailer in the woods outside Williamsburg. Light beams floated through the trees and then he heard the ghetto clank of Raymo's '57 Bel Air. He opened the trailer door and watched them get out, two men showing the stiff weighted movements of long-distance drivers.

Mackey said, "Just in time for dinner except there isn't any." The words sounded abrupt and clean in the empty night.

"Maybe just a swallow. *Un buchito*," Raymo said. "We ate on the road."

The other man, Frank Vásquez, was occupied getting blankets and clothes out of the rear seat and then he backed out and stood erect and half turned, his hands occupied, and gave the door a rough shove with his hip and followed with a sweet kick, knocking it shut. Raymo, approaching the trailer, gave a little head-shake at the other man's treatment of the once-gorgeous car.

"Plenty of coffee," Mackey said. "Good to see you. How are things?"

"Good to see you. Long time. How are things?"

"Hello, T-Jay."

"Hello, Frank. I thought you were getting your teeth fixed."

"He never does it," Raymo said.

They embraced, pounding each other on the back, *abrazos*, absent-minded collisions.

"How are things?"

"Long time."

"Too long, my friend."

Standing by the trailer door exchanging nods, looks, half-sentences, everything so clearly shaped, their words sounding well made in the fine light air.

Mackey made room for their things in the trailer. Then they sat drinking coffee. Raymo was at the fold-out table, a thickset man with a wide mustache. He wore a black cowboy hat, black T-shirt, fatigue pants, combat boots. His lounging outfit. Mackey definitely wanted Raymo in on this. Raymo could not light a match, walk his dog, scratch his head without infusing the act with the single-minded energy of his rage. It was a consciousness they shared un-spokenly, Bahía de Cochinos, the Bay of Pigs, the Battle of Girón—whatever you wanted to call it. Even his stockiness, all that dense flesh, seeméd a form of energy and purpose. A flamingo was etched on his T-shirt. He was the one man T-Jay trusted completely.

"We spent part of April with the harvest."

"Picking oranges in central Florida," Frank said.

"We fill ten-box tubs. How many pounds you think that is?"

"He fell off the ladder," Frank said.

"I'm telling you, man, it's hard labor."

"Then what, we go to Live Oak near the Georgia border."

"We stack these huge bales of tobacco," Raymo said. "Like in huge sheets they're called. They work our ass, T-Jay."

Mackey knew they were working every job they could, night work, spare time, odd job, to save enough money to start a business, maybe a service station or small construction firm.

"Then my wife calls us from Miami," Frank said. "We drive up here right away."

Drive through Georgia and the Carolinas to hear what news

T-Jay has for them. It could only be a Cuban operation. Nothing else would make him get in touch with them and nothing else would bring them here.

Vásquez sat on the bunk bed. He had a thin sad face and would have seemed at ease in a cobbler's smock in some dark narrow shop on a fringe street of Little Havana. There were two rows of teeth in his lower jaw, or maybe one row haphazardly aligned, with zigzag patterns, teeth set at angles to each other. It made him look like a saint of the poor. A brother and a cousin lost at Red Beach, another brother allowed to die in a hunger strike at La Cabaña prison. Frank had been a schoolteacher in Cuba. Now, between jobs, he and Raymo drove to a training camp in the Everglades with the one weapon they owned between them, a so-called Cuban Winchester, put together from elements of three other rifles with handmade parts added on. They drilled with one of the groups out there, living in open huts made of eucalyptus logs and assorted vines. Raymo fired the rifle, swung from ropes, pissed in the tall grass. Frank did some target work but otherwise just hung around, the longtime silent buddy, dressed the way he always dressed, in oversized trousers and a sleeveless sepia shirt worn outside his pants.

Both men had been with Castro, originally, in the mountains.

"The wife and children, Frank? They're well?"

"Doing okay."

"Three kids, right? What about Raymo? The right woman doesn't show up?"

These were the only men Mackey could talk to like this, in extended ceremonial hellos, little arcs of family news and other details of being. It was the necessary foreground. He knew it was expected and he'd come to look forward to it. They had to say something to each other. There was only one subject among them and it did not adapt to easy chat.

All right. Mackey gave them some background on the operation. Extremely dedicated men were behind it. The idea was to galvanize the nation into full awareness of the danger of a communist Cuba. Dirección General de Inteligencia would be exposed as a criminal organization willing to take extreme action against important figures who opposed Castro.

He told them a shooting was in the works, designed to implicate the DGI. He wanted Frank and Raymo to be part of it and he supplied some operational details. High-powered rifles, elevated perches, a trail of planted evidence, someone to take the fall. There would be five hundred dollars a month for each of them, commencing now, and a nice payday when the job was done. The men behind the plan, he said, were respected Agency veterans, deep believers in a free Havana.

He did not mention Everett and Parmenter by name. He did not tell them who their target was or where the shooting would take place. He would let details drop, here and there, in time, as need dictated. The other thing he did not say was that they were supposed to miss.

The Parmenters lived in a stunted frame house at the edge of a brick sidewalk in Georgetown. The sidewalk bulged and rippled and the once-quaint house was slightly shabby now, a mousy relic no one noticed.

It was Beryl who'd wanted to live here. The corporate suburbs were not for them, she said. Guarded shoptalk over drinks and dinner with colleagues and their anxious wives. She wanted to live in town. Fanlights, wrought iron, leaded glass. The security of a small and darkish place with old familiar things lying about, with books, rugs, dust, a wine cellar for Larry, a tininess, an unnoticeability (if such a word exists). There was something about a long and low and open-space house with a lawn and a carport that made her feel spiritually afraid.

Larry paced the small rooms now, drink in hand, wearing an enormous striped robe. Beryl was at her writing desk clipping news items to send to friends. This was a passion she'd discovered recently like someone in middle life who finds she was born to show pedigreed dogs. Nothing that happened before has any meaning compared to this. A week's worth of newspapers sat on the desk. She sent clippings to everyone. There was suddenly so much to clip.

"Look at this, now. Am I angry or amused?"

She turned around to find her husband.

"Look at this, Larry. A folk singer named Bob Dylan is told by CBS he can't sing one of his songs on *The Ed Sullivan Show*. Too controversial."

"What's controversial about it?"

"It's called 'Talkin' John Birch Society Blues.' "

"Is he white or Negro? Because white boys shouldn't mess with the blues."

"But imagine forbidding him airtime."

"I'll try to get worked up about it. Give me ten minutes."

"I know the signs, old boy."

"What signs?"

"When you sweep through the house guzzling gin. I know exactly what it means. Nostalgic for Guatemala."

Some people thought Beryl had money. It was one of the false impressions that collected around her. What she actually had was a small picture-framing shop on Wisconsin Avenue, strictly a marginal income—lithographs, photographs, framing. Other people thought she was creative. One of the softer arts, quilt-making, water colors. She had a look and manner people took to be unconventional in a certain way, a kind of reclusiveness in a crowd. She wore soft clothes. She draped herself in casual layers, a smallish woman half buried in pastels. There was always the idea she was in quiet retirement from some fear or pain. She bought factory-outlet moccasins, never wore jewelry, kept snapshots of her mother in favorite books. People thought she was a canned-soup heiress who painted seascapes with birds. She ate soft food, spoke softly, with a slight huskiness, a sexiness. She was very sexy, at forty-seven. There was still that smoky little thing about her. The sexy swaying walk, the dark voice. She had a dry way of delivering friendly insults directly into people's chests. She walked softly swaying into a room and you could sense anticipation in the group. They began preparing their laughter before she said a word.

It was seen as a mark of the Parmenters' sophistication that she raked the Agency in mixed company while Larry looked on grinning.

Not that she didn't mean what she said.

"No. I am not making fun. I admire what you did in Guatemala. If not politically, then in other ways. It was practically bloodless. I certainly admire that."

"It was a textbook operation."

"Of course there would have been no need for an operation if the Guatemalans hadn't taken back all that land belonging to United Fruit."

"Is that what happened? Oh."

"I love the way you say textbook operation."

Yes. It was also the peak experience of Larry's career, centering on a radio station supposedly run by rebels from a jungle outpost in Guatemala. The broadcasts actually originated in a barn in Honduras and the messages were designed to put pressure on the leftist government and arouse anxiety in the people. Rumors, false battle reports, meaningless codes, inflammatory speeches, orders to nonexistent rebels. It was like a class project in the structure of reality. Parmenter wrote some of the broadcasts himself, going for vivid imagery, fields of rotting bodies, fighter pilots defecting with their planes. A real pilot tossed dynamite sticks out the window of his Cessna. A real bomb fell on a parade ground, sending up smoke in an ominous column. The government fell nine days after an invasion force of five thousand troops was said to be advancing on the capital. The force materialized then, several trucks and a crowded station wagon, about a hundred and fifty ragged recruits.

That was nine years ago. Larry became involved in proprietaries for a time, legally incorporated businesses actually financed and controlled by CIA. When the Agency wanted to do something interesting in Kurdistan or Yemen, it filed for incorporation in Delaware. It was during this period that he came into contact with a number of Agency assets who had important holdings in sensitive parts of the hemisphere. A man from United Fruit, a man from the Cuban-Venezuelan Oil Trust (it was George de Mohrenschildt as a matter of fact). Merchant banks, sugar companies, arms dealers.

A curious convergence of motives and holdings. Hotel interests here, gambling interests there. Men with vivid histories, sometimes including prison. He saw there was a natural kinship between business and intelligence work. And he realized that the companies he was helping set up as cover for Agency operations held potential for legitimate profits—and beyond that, for enormous personal gain.

Contact with wealthy and influential men was a bracing experience for someone who'd been brought up to believe in the American genius for making leaps to new levels of privilege. Being rich, he saw, was something you grew into. The Agency had huge collections of intelligence on banana republics and their leaders. Larry traded secrets for pieces of promising action. He spent time in Cuba, setting up transactions between the Batista government and interests in the U.S. He helped arrange mineral surveys, land-development deals, drilling contracts, casino franchises. He traveled to Oriente Province to learn the extent of the rebel threat to cane fields controlled by U.S. firms. The extent was considerable. When the American executives left their palm-shaded streets and large white houses, when the cooks and gardeners looked for new situations, when the company guards fled, when the local army post was overrun, Laurence Parmenter's fortune was still in the ground of the unexplored oil properties of Cuba.

"I admire that robe, Larry. You look like Orson Welles in deep focus."

He stood in the doorway smiling absently at the familiar flatness in her voice, not quite hearing what she said.

"On second thought I'll tell you what you look like. You look like one of those corrupt barons in *Ivan the Terrible*, got up deliciously in animal skins. Make me a drink so I can keep you company. We ought to keep each other company."

After the revolution came the plan to invade. He helped set up the Double-Chek Corporation, a front for the recruitment of pilot instructors. Gibraltar Steamship came next, a company whose nominal head was a former State Department officer and ex-president of United Fruit. Parmenter himself could not always tell where the Agency left off and the corporations began. There were men related by blood and by marriage; there were company directors who were former high-ranking intelligence officers; there were government advisers who were once company directors. It was a society he recognized as a better-working version of the larger world, where things have an almost dreamy sense of connection to each other. Here the plan was tighter. These were men who believed history was in their care.

Gibraltar Steamship provided cover for propaganda operations against Cuba. The device was Radio Swan, a transmitter stored in an oversized trailer on a remote island in the western Caribbean. Great Swan Island was the product of hundreds of years of bird droppings. There were three coconut palms, twenty-eight people. Lovely numbers, everyone agreed, pointing toward barrenness and isolation, the soul-testing elements of the trade. For the invasion Parmenter used the same broadcast techniques that had worked in Guatemala. Cryptic messages from spy movies of the forties. "Attention, Eduardo, the moon is red." Romantic imagery employing the names of local wildlife. "The barracuda sleeps at sundown." "The shark leaves a golden trail." Mackey would later tell Parmenter that in his LCI lying to off Blue Beach, this gibberish had the sound of a mind unraveling. It diminished the whole operation, made comic fucking opera of troops in combat.

When the messages were broadcast, Larry was in Washington at the Agency's invasion headquarters, a tempo building near the Lincoln Memorial. He was eating a soggy meal off a paper plate when news hit the control room that JFK would not approve air cover for the landings. The men did not accept it at first. Too unbelievably stupid and cruel. A colonel in golf togs walked through. The men shouted at superiors, damn near grew violent. Someone vomited lazily in a wastebasket, leaning over with his hands on his knees. Win Everett arrived from Miami, wrote out a letter of resignation, tore it up, flew back to Miami to be with exile leaders who were confined in a barracks at Opa-Locka so they would not leak word of the landings. It was the first major death watch in South Florida that week.

No one used the term textbook operation. Three days later

Radio Swan was still on the air, promising the abandoned troops in Zapata swamp that help was on the way. Larry slept on a cot in grubby clothes but made it a point to shave every day. Shaving had an impact on his morale and he needed all the help he could get. Several weeks earlier he'd borrowed heavily to buy stock in Francisco Sugar at depressed prices. Sugar was the word going round. There were stunning profits to be made, insiders said, once the plantations were back in U.S. control.

"People think we're the strangest marriage," Beryl said.

"Why should they? Who? What's strange about us?"

"Only everything."

"People think we're interesting. That's my impression."

"They think we're strange. We have nothing in common. We have no practical reason for being. We never even talk about practical things."

"We have no children. We're not parents. Parents talk about practical things. They have reasons to be practical."

"With or without children. Believe me. We're considered strange."

"I don't think we're strange. I think we're interesting."

"We're interesting in a way. But we're also strange. I'm the one they focus on. I'm the stranger of the two."

"I don't like conversations like this. I don't know how to have these conversations."

"They're probably not a good idea."

"So let's change the subject," he said.

"Although the fact of the matter is you're far stranger, love, than I could ever think of being."

"Strange how? I'm not strange. I don't like this at all."

"Strange like a man. Strange like someone I could never know the heart of, the truth of."

"This is thankfully outside my range."

"I don't think I could ever begin to imagine in years and years of living intimately with a man what it is like to be him."

"Funny. I thought women were the secret."

"No no no no no," she said softly, as if correcting a touchy child. "That's the wisdom handed down from man to boy, through the ages, a hundred generations of knowledge and experience. But it is just another Agency lie."

From the moment the CIA monitored a rebel broadcast on January 1, 1959, announcing that the tyrant Batista had fled the country at 2:00 A.M. and that Dr. Fidel Castro Ruz was the supreme leader of the Cuban revolution, from that moment to this, four and a half years later, as he stood in his striped robe mixing a drink for his wife, Larry Parmenter had been involved in one or another plot to get Cuba back. Soldiering on, Beryl said. She liked to remind him that he was not vindictive, had no strong political convictions, did not hate Castro or wish to see physical harm come to him. Larry was famous in fact for going to a costume party *as* Fidel Castro, with beard, cigar, khaki fatigues, about a month before the invasion. Seemed funny at the time.

One thing Larry didn't like at all. This was the kind of fellow he'd occasionally had to deal with in joint efforts to recover investments in Cuba. The gambling interests, the casinos and hotels, the men who bought off officials routinely, who sent a steady traffic of couriers with hefty satchels moving through the Bahamas to the International Credit Bank in Geneva—men who thought longingly of the millions they'd once skimmed from the gaming tables in Havana. He wanted nothing to do with those roly-poly wops.

Earlier that day a young man walked into the outer office at Guy Banister Associates in New Orleans. Delphine Roberts was at her desk typing a revised list of civil-rights organizations for Banister's files. The young man stood patiently waiting, in jeans with rolled cuffs, two days' stubble on his chin. Delphine stopped typing long enough to pat her teased hair, a nervous habit she was determined to overcome. Then she resumed her work, aware that the young man was studying a calendar on the wall in order to kid himself into thinking he was not being made to wait. She knew all the styles. She could type a complicated text and scrutinize a visitor at the same time. This visitor had a little smile that seemed to say, Here I am—just the fellow you've been waiting for.

"I would like to fill out an application for a position with the firm."

Delphine kept on typing.

"You have people who do undercover work, I believe, like mingle with students or go to political meetings. I am referring to collecting information. I want to apply to become an undercover agent. I have a verified alias. I have served in the armed forces. And I have lived abroad in a situation that gave me special depth into the communist mentality."

Delphine was not surprised. They had some thought-provoking individuals walking in unannounced at 544 Camp. This address tended to draw people from a colorful range of backgrounds.

She stopped typing long enough to give the young man an application. He said he had to get back to work at the coffee company around the corner but he would fill out the form and return it in the morning. Then he was gone.

David Ferrie came out of the small back room and said in his routine disbelieving whisper, "Who on earth was that?"

"He has a verified alias."

"Do we have forms for undercover agents?"

"No. It's just a normal form."

"Like height and weight."

"Whatever it says. I don't know."

"Like insanity in the family. Or give us the history of your disease."

"It says whatever you want it to say, Dave. I'm very, very busy."

"How can a person explain his disease on a printed form?"

David Ferrie went into Guy Banister's office, which was empty, and looked out the street-side window, trying to catch a glimpse of the young man whose voice he'd just been listening to. Had he caught something familiar in the tone? Would he be able to match a body to the voice? He looked at the swarm of people moving down the street. Dark folks aplenty, he thought. But no sign of the sweet-voiced boy who wants to be a spy.

In Fort Worth

Even coming back he was a military man. His father was a veteran. His brothers were in the service. My own brother was a navy man. We were a serviceman family. He sent me a regular allotment every month out of his pay and when he heard about my injury, which I said in a letter, he put in for a hardship discharge as I was disabled from work and trying for six months to collect on my claim. He was stationed in California then and they let him go early in order to help his mother. This is the injury of a candy jar falling off a shelf that four doctors have taken x-rays of my nose and face and there is travel time and carfare and the store is still holding tight to their cash. I am a disabled woman who can't collect. It is like the days of Mr. Ekdahl, a ten-thousand-dollar-a-year man with an expense account who fixed it so my welfare was ignored.

I am leaving out Lee had a beautiful voice and sang beautifully at age six in Covington, Louisiana. He sang a solo in the Lutheran church, "Silent Night," and that can be verified.

Now this boy comes home from the service and says he will work on a cargo ship and send money home to me. That was our only conversation over three days where he slept on a cot in the kitchen, which was the only place I had for him, plus he told me that he passed his high-school-level tests, Mother, which I don't know why you need this to lift crates on a boat. He was here only parts of three days before packing a bag and leaving. Then I received a letter postmarked New Orleans that he has booked passage on a ship to Europe. It is painful to accept, your honor. There is nothing in the letter that says cargo. There is nothing about he will work his way for a certain time until I have found a larger place for us to live. It is, "I have booked passage." It is, "My values are very different from Robert's or yours." It is, "I did not tell you about my plans because you could hardly be expected to understand."

It is the struggle hanging over my life that made him go away.

Postcard #3. Aboard the freighter SS *Marion Lykes* bound for Le Havre. The oddball loner has little to say to the three other passengers on the sixteen-day crossing. Gray seas, high swells, missed meals. He tells them he is going to school in Switzerland but doesn't mention the name of the institution or the course of study he plans to follow. He avoids a passenger's friendly attempts to take his picture. She is a nice enough lady whose husband is a lieutenant colonel, U.S. Army, retired. You'd think in the middle of the ocean he'd be able to sit on deck without answering questions from some clear-eyed military type. He talks least of all to the fourth passenger, his cabin mate, a boy just out of high school and on his way to France to study French. He is a Texas boy and just close enough to Lee outwardly to be the world's preferred version of the type.

It is like the shadow of his own life keeps falling across his path.

He watches them at dinner in the officers' mess and he thinks he knows why they look so satisfied with themselves. They have begun to feel the bond of being American. They almost glow with self-awareness, headed for foreign shores, surrounded and attended by a partly foreign and mainly dark-skinned crew, delighting in their own straightforward and affirmative ways, their democratic values, their moral strength, the way they hold their knife and fork, smiling over the glitter, and this is why he will not eat with them or share their conversation.

The spiral rind of a tangerine sits in a white saucer in front of him. He thinks of the nine months he spent at the Marine Corps Air Station at El Toro in California, after Japan. He continued his Russian studies, learned some Spanish (it was the time of Fidel Castro) and developed a neat little deception for the venture he was now engaged in.

At the base library he found a catalogue listing the names of colleges abroad. He scanned the list for obscure schools in certain locations, then wrote away for an application. Albert Schweitzer College. Churwalden, Switzerland. He needed to invent a reason to travel abroad because a Marine has two years in the reserve after active duty.

On the application form he listed under special interests: *Philosophy, Psychology, Ideology, Football, baseball, tennis, Stamp collecting.*

Vocational interest (if decided upon): *To be a short story writer on contemporary American life.*

In certain light the sea goes green, a slow dullish tumble he watches from the deck. When he goes below again he lies on his bunk, aware of the great slow creaking of the ship, like a mind stirring around him. Hawsers are ropes for mooring.

On the Albert Schweitzer application he made it a point to mention that after the term was completed he planned to attend the summer session of the University of Turku—Turku, Finland.

Hidell creeps closer to the East.

19 June

Mary Frances parked under an oak tree on the circular drive outside the College of Education Building, or Old Main. It pleased her that Win's office was in the oldest building on campus. The building pleased her with its arched entranceways and two-story columns. Denton had its hidden streets, its sense of languorous history, an old American stillness, wistful and unchanged, and these older traces too, older ideas and values scored in limestone and marble, in scroll ornaments atop a column or in the banknote details of a frieze. The Old Main, the county courthouse, the broad-fronted homes, the homes with deep shady porches, the trees, the streets named for trees—all this pleased her, made her think that happiness lived minute by minute in the things she saw and heard. Being happy was a small awareness, the sum of small awarenesses, day by day, minute by minute, and you knew it now, in the hair and skin as much as in the heart.

Suzanne sat next to her mother, arms at her sides, slim white legs pointed straight out, a show of mock obedience. They were not talking to each other.

You could be happy now. It did not have to be experienced in retrospect, as Win believed, as he liked to explain in his mild way, with the face he called a failed professor's tipped slightly right. It was not a slow-working glow or meditation. You could feel it now, collect it in the names of things around you, in chinaberry, oak and slippery elm. It pleased her to live here, after Miami, Havana, Mexico City, Guatemala City, temporary housing in southeast Virginia (ISOLATION), dusty tracts of identical homes near the Carolina coast (ISOLATION TROPIC).

They would go to the Steak House on South Locust for jumbo shrimp with salad, french fries and hot rolls and then Win would suggest an ice cream at Lane's.

Bright hot skies.

Silence in the car, on the burning lawns.

Suzanne was holding her breath.

In his basement office in the Old Main, Win Everett was on the phone with Parmenter.

"How does Mackey know all this if he hasn't made contact?"

"Whatever T-Jay knows comes out of Banister's office. Oswald confides in one of Banister's people."

"Go ahead."

"In January he orders a snub-nose .38 from a firm in Los Angeles. In March he sends away to Chicago for an Italian carbine with a sniper's scope."

"Armed and dangerous," Win said softly.

"Plus. Are you ready? He's handing out pro-Castro leaflets on the street. He was on the docks two or three days ago pushing leaflets at sailors off an aircraft carrier."

Everett looked into space.

"How does this fit in with the fact that he has the use of an office in the same building as Banister's detective agency, right above Banister's office, which is the damn pivot point of the anti-Castro crusade in Louisiana?"

"It doesn't fit in," Parmenter said.

"I'm glad you said that. I thought I might be missing something."

"All I know is what T-Jay tells me. As follows. The subject walks into Banister's office looking for an undercover job. Banister installs him in a broom closet upstairs. This little-bitty room becomes the New Orleans headquarters of the Fair Play for Cuba Committee. And the subject hits the streets in a white shirt and tie, handing out leaflets."

They talked about Oswald as the subject in the same way they referred to the President as Lancer, which was his Secret Service code name. Habit. One wants the least possible surface to which pain and regret might cling—anyone's, everyone's pain. A thought for late afternoon.

"Let me understand the sequence," Win said. "The subject leaves Dallas. He is gone, out of our lives, a promising part of our operation lost forever."

"Then he turns up in the one place we would never expect to find him."

"He turns up, out of nowhere, in New Orleans, in Guy Banister's office, looking for an undercover assignment. The same fellow who defected to the bloody Soviet Union, who used his mail-order rifle to take a shot at General Walker. Strolls right into the middle of the enemy camp."

"Mackey was supposed to ask Guy Banister to find a substitute for our boy. What happens? The original walks in off the street."

Everett searched his pockets for a cigarette.

"You've got to get close to the subject," he said.

"Oh no."

"Look, Larry."

"I don't want personal contact any more than you do, my friend. Give him to Mackey."

"Where is he?"

"Still at the Farm as far as I know."

"All right. Look. Get me a sample of the kid's handwriting."

"I'll talk to T-Jay right away."

The hallway was empty. Win climbed the stairs to the main floor. Nobody at the desk. He went outside. School year ended, slow-moving figures in the distance, summer students, maintenance men, and a lawn sprinkler sending out spray in overlapping arcs, all the lazy brightness of cobwebbed grass.

Before the murder attempt comes the provocation.

He'd devised a top-secret memo from the Deputy Director Plans to selected members of the Senior Study Effort, dated May 1961. It concerned the assassination of foreign leaders from a philosophical point of view. It also included a fragment from the psalmbook, not known to the outside world. *Terminate with extreme prejudice.* Parmenter was handling the actual production of the memo on a suitable typewriter and stationery.

Two. Through his contacts in Little Havana, Everett had planted a cryptic news item in an exile magazine published in New Jersey. The story, from an unnamed source, concerned an operation run in July 1961 by the Office of Naval Intelligence out of Guantánamo, the U.S. base near the eastern end of Cuba. The story was fabricated but the plan itself was real, involving the assassination of Fidel Castro and his brother Raúl. This news item would be found among the subject's effects after the failed attempt on the life of the President.

Three. He was working on a scheme involving telephone notes on pages of stationery used by the Technical Services Division. Doodles, phone numbers, abbreviations of the names of advanced poisons produced by a special unit of the division, known entertainingly as the Health Alteration Committee. A person following the sequence of phone numbers would be led along a serendipitous path with a number of ordinary stops (florist, supermarket) as well as the home of an exile leader in Miami, a motel in Key Biscayne known to be mob-run, a yacht moored at a Miami marina—living quarters of the CIA's chief of station.

He headed toward the car.

Local color, background, connections for investigators to ponder. He had other schemes, other documents, authentic, relating to attempts on Castro's life—attempts he'd personally been involved in at the planning stage. It would be up to Parmenter to get this reading matter, circuitously, into the hands of journalists, subcommittee members and anyone else who might bring them to light. Once people saw the attempt on the President as a Cuban response to repeated efforts of U.S. intelligence to murder Castro, we were all halfway home to getting the island back.

He saw them sitting in the car. He began to smile, shielding his eyes from the sun. He approached the front door on the passenger side. The wet grass looked spangled in the heat and glare. He tiptoed closer, smiling broadly, waiting for Suzanne to spot him.

Guy Banister sat alone in the Katz & Jammer Bar. He had his private spot at the near end, where the bar curves into the wall. He liked to sit with his back against the wall, looking out to the street, to the neon heads bobbing past the Falstaff sign in the high window.

His doctor told him don't drink. He drank. Don't smoke. He smoked. Give up the detective agency. He worked longer hours, compiled longer lists, shipped arms, stored munitions, ran a network of clean-cut boys who spied on local universities.

Dave Ferrie had this routine about a tumor growing on his brain. But it was Banister who had blackouts and dizzy spells, who sat at his desk and watched his hand start trembling, way out there, as if it belonged to someone else.

He was sixty-three years old, twenty years in the Bureau, a decorated agent drinking alone in a bar.

He carried a blue-steel Colt under his jacket, chambered for the .357 magnum cartridge. Guy sincerely believed the old reliable .38 special with standard police loads was simply not enough gun for the type of situation a man of his standing might run into any time of day or night. Amen. Beautiful auburn glitter at the bottom of the glass. He knocked back the last of the bourbon and watched the man come forward.

"We got him coming out of the Biograph in Chicago, July of '34, shot him dead in an alleyway three doors down from the theater."

"This is who are we talking about now," says the jug-eared barman.

"Mr. John Dillinger. This is who. Fill the fucking glass."

"Rocks or not?"

"Famous finish. Old Dillinger buffs could tell you what was playing at the movie house when we gunned him down."

"All right I'll bite."

"*Manhattan Melodrama* with Clark Gable."

The barman poured the drink, oblivious.

"Whenever there's a famous finish in the vicinity of a movie house, it behooves you to know what's playing."

"I don't doubt it, Mr. Banister."

"This is history with a fucking flourish."

He'd shipped munitions to the Keys for the bombing of refineries, for the Bay of Pigs. There was so much ordnance stored in his office he had to get Ferrie to take some home. Ferrie had land mines stacked in his kitchen. With dozens of factions angling for a second invasion, something had to happen soon. The government knew it. Raids and seizures were commonplace now. Things were turning upside down.

He saw the kid Oswald walk past the window on his way home from work at the William Reily Coffee Company. Another bobbing head in the great New Orleans current.

The hand starts trembling way out there. It has nothing to do with him.

He worked longer hours, compiled longer lists. He had researchers coming up with names all the time. He wanted lists of subversives, leftist professors, congressmen with dubious voting records. He wanted lists of niggers, nigger lovers, armed niggers, pregnant niggers, light-skinned niggers, niggers married to whites. You couldn't photograph a nigger. He'd never seen a picture of a nigger where you could make out the features. It's just a fact of nature they don't emit light.

The Times-Picayune was full of stories about the civil-rights program of JFK. You could photograph a Kennedy all right. That's what a Kennedy was for. The man with the secrets gives off the glow.

We gave away Eastern Europe. We gave away China. We gave away Cuba, just ninety miles off our coast. We're getting ready to give away Southeast Asia. We'll give away white America next. We'll give it to the Nee-groes. One thing Guy couldn't stand about these sit-ins and marches. When the goddamn whites get to singing. The whole occasion falls apart. It makes everyone feel bad.

He called the barman over.

"You know this Kennedy goes around with ten or fifteen people who look just like him. You know about that?"

"No."

"You never heard about that?"

"I never heard he had anybody."

"He has got them," Banister said.

"That look like him."

"He has got about fifteen. Whenever he goes anyplace, they go too. They're on constant fucking standby. You know why? Diversionary. Because he knows he's made a lot of people mad."

He was as old as the century, twenty years in the Bureau, a dignitary in the local police until he fired his gun into the ceiling of some tourist bar.

He finished his drink and got up to leave.

Public enemy number one. Sweltering night in July. We got him in an alley near the Biograph.

His office was next door to the bar but he did not use the Camp Street entrance, which was where they'd be waiting to blast him if and when the time came, now or later, day or night. He used the side entrance, on Lafayette, and trudged up the stairs to the second floor.

Delphine was at the desk in the outer office. She gave him a little prissy look that meant she knew he'd been drinking. With a mistress like this, he didn't need a wife.

"There's something I think you definitely ought to know," she said.

"Chances are I do know."

"Not this you don't."

He sat on the vinyl sofa that Ferrie said carried cancer agents and took his time shaking a cigarette out of the pack and lighting it. He had a Zippo he'd carried through the war that still worked perfect, with a whoosh and flare.

"It's about this Leon upstairs, whatever his name is, working in the vacant room."

"Oswald."

"I was up there after lunch trying to track down some files that just got up and walked off. There was no one in the office. Just small piles of handbills on a table. What do they say? Hands off Cuba. Fair Play for Cuba. This is pro-Castro material sitting on a table right over our heads."

Guy Banister gave a little twirl of the hand that held the cigarette.

"Go ahead, what else," he said, an amused light in his eye.

"This is no joke, Guy. There is inflammatory reading matter in that little office."

"Just you make sure those circulars don't get up and walk off in this direction. I don't want them down here. He has his work, we have ours. It amounts to the same thing."

"Then you know about it."

"We'll just see how it all works out."

"Well what do you know about *him*?"

"Not a hell of a lot, personally. He's working mainly with Ferrie. Ferrie recommended him. He's a David Ferrie project."

"I wonder what that means," Delphine said.

Banister smiled and got up. He put his cigarette in the ashtray on the desk. Then he stood behind Delphine's chair and massaged her shoulders and neck. On the desk was a recent issue of On Target, the newsletter of the Minutemen. A line in italics caught his eye. *Even now the crosshairs are centered on the back of your neck.*

Something in the air. There were forces in the air that men sense at the same point in history. You can feel it on your skin, in the tips of your fingers.

"What about the fellow who called early this morning?" Delphine said. "He sounded far away in more ways than one."

"Did you wire him fifty dollars?"

"Just like you said."

"One of Mackey's people. New to me. I told him how to contact T-Jay."

She put her hand to her hair, looking toward the smoked-glass panel on the office door.

"Do I get to see my G-man later tonight?"

He reached across her shoulder for his cigarette.

"I want you to start a file," he told her, "before you leave the office. Fair Play for Cuba. Give it a nice pink cover."

"What do I put in the file?"

"Once you start a file, Delphine, it's just a matter of time before the material comes pouring in. Notes, lists, photos, rumors. Every bit and piece and whisper in the world that doesn't have a life until someone comes along to collect it. It's all been waiting just for you."

Wayne Elko, an out-of-work pool cleaner, sat on a long bench in the waiting room at Union Station this chilly A.M. in Denver.

It occurred to Wayne that for some time now he was always arriving or departing. He was never anywhere you could actually call a place. He wasn't here and wasn't there. It was like a problem in philosophy.

Next to him on the bench was his khaki knapsack and an over-the-hill shopping bag from some A&P on the Coast. His life in material things he carried in these two weary pokes.

He was a long-chance man. This was a term from the real frontier a hundred years ago. For twenty dollars he'd roll your odometer back twenty thousand miles. Took about fifteen minutes.

For a hundred dollars he'd set a charge of plastique and blow the car into car heaven if your insurance needs were such. Except he'd probably do it free. Just for the science involved.

Early light collected at the tall arched windows. The benches were thirty feet long, with high backs, curved backs, nicely polished. Giant chandeliers hung above him. The waiting room was empty except for two or three station familiars, the two or three shadowy men he saw at every stop, living in the walls like lizards. The silence, the arched windows, the wooden benches and chandeliers made him think of church, a church you travel to on trains, coming out of the noise and steam to this high empty place where you could think your quietest thoughts.

He was asleep ten minutes on the bench when a cop bounced his nightstick off Wayne's raised knee. It made a sound like he was built of hollow wood. Welcome to the Rockies.

He got up, took his things, crossed the street and went immediately to sleep on the concrete loading-platform of a warehouse. This time it was trucks that got him up. He wandered an area of refrigerated warehouses with old dual-gauge tracks intersecting on the cobbled streets. At Twentieth and Blake he saw a man swabbing a garbage truck. They had a hundred wrecked cars behind barbed wire and a thousand specks of broken glass every square foot. It was the broken-glass district of Denver. At Twentieth and Larimer he saw some men with a stagger in their gait. Early-rising winos out for a stroll. Baptist Mission. Money to Loan. A guy with a Crazy Guggenheim hat came pitching down the street; might be Indian, Mexican, mix-blood or who knows what, muttering curses in some invented tongue. Made Wayne think of the faces in the Everglades and on No Name Key during his training with the Interpen brigade. All those guys who'd fought for Castro and then crossed over. Dark rage in every face. Fidel betrays the revolution.

He'd lived with a shifting population of rogue commandos in a boardinghouse on Southwest Fourth Street in Miami. They spent weeks at a time training in the mangrove swamps and went on forays along the Cuban coast in a thirty-five-foot launch, mainly to land agents and shoot at silhouettes. Otherwise they stayed close to the clapboard house, cleaning submachine guns in the backyard. Judo instructors, tugboat captains, homeless Cubans, ex-paratroopers like Wayne, mercenaries from wars nobody heard of, in West Africa or Malay. They were like guys straight out of Wayne's favorite movie, *Seven Samurai*, warriors without masters, willing to band together to save a village from marauders, to win back a country, only to see themselves betrayed in the end. First it was Navy jets making reconnaissance runs over No Name Key, snapping little pix of the muddy boys. Next it was five Interpen commandos picked up for vagrancy, courtesy of the Dade County sheriff. Then U.S. customs officers pounced, arresting a dozen men, including Wayne Elko in battle gear and a lampblacked face, just as they were setting out for Cuba in the twin-engine launch.

JFK had made his deal with the Soviets to leave Castro alone. Incredible. The same man Wayne would have voted for if he'd gotten around to registering. He believed in country, loyalty, mountains and streams. They were all tied together.

He found a telephone and made a collect call to the New Orleans number T. J. Mackey had given him about a year earlier. He told the woman at the other end he wished to speak to a Mr. Guy Banister.

"This is Wayne Elko calling. It seems like I have washed up in Denver, Colorado, tell T-Jay, and I am looking for a chance at some employment."

Win Everett was in his basement at home, hunched over the worktable. His tools and materials were set before him, mainly household things, small and cheap—cutting instruments, acetate overlays, glues and pastes, a soft eraser, a travel iron.

He felt marvelously alert, sure of himself, putting together a man with scissors and tape.

His gunman would emerge and vanish in a maze of false names. Investigators would find an application for a post-office box;

a certificate of service, U.S. Marine Corps; a Social Security card; a passport application; a driver's license; a stolen credit card and half a dozen other documents—in two or three different names, each leading to a trail that would end at the Cuban Intelligence Directorate.

He worked on a Diners Club card, removing the ink on the raised letters with a Q-tip doused in polyester resin. A radio on a shelf played soothing music. He pressed the card against the warm iron, heating it slowly to flatten the letters. Then he used a razor blade to level the remaining bumps and juts. He would eventually reheat the card and stamp a new name and number on its face with an addressograph plate.

He'd picked up a certain amount of sleazy tradecraft in his early years as an operations officer. Before that he'd taught in a series of small liberal-arts colleges in the Midwest, places like Franklin, in Indiana, where a perceptive colleague, affiliated somehow or other with CIA, recruited him for covert training. The idea seemed immediately right, a possible answer to the restlessness he'd felt working through his system, a sense that he needed to risk something important, challenge his moral complacencies, before he could see himself complete. Soon he was taking handy instruction in Flaps & Seals, or how to read other people's mail without letting them know about it, and remembering now and then those sleepy afternoons at little Franklin College. After some years in Havana and Central America, including duty as chief of station in Guatemala City, he was one of several men assigned to coordinate the training of a Cuban exile brigade. He was in a constant hurry after that. Underwater demolition in Puerto Rico and North Carolina, paratroop maneuvers outside Phoenix, teams to organize in Nicaragua, Miami, Key West.

He felt sharp now, better than he'd felt in some time, on top of things, alert.

The young man's address book would be next. A major project. Once he had a handwriting sample, Win would scratch onto those miniature pages enough trails, false trails, swarming life, lingering mystery, enough real and fabricated people to occupy investigators for months to come.

He unscrewed the top of the Elmer's Glue-All. He used his X-Acto knife to cut a new signature strip from a sheet of opaque paper. He checked the length and width of the strip against the bare space on the back of the credit card. Then he dribbled an even stream of glue over the paper and pressed it lightly on the card. He listened to the radio while the glue dried.

He was in a constant hurry then. Fort Gulick in the Canal Zone. Trax Base in Guatemala. Things were quieter now. He had time to turn the pages of all the books he'd been meaning to read.

After the address book came the false names. He looked forward to coming up with names. He removed excess glue from the back of the card with one of Suzanne's school erasers. Then he turned off the radio, turned off the light, climbed the old plank stairs.

His gunman would appear behind a strip of scenic gauze. You have to leave them with coincidence, lingering mystery. This is what makes it real.

He checked the front door. The days came and went. Bedtime again. Always bedtime now. He went around turning off lights, checked the back door, checked to see that the oven was off. This meant all was well.

Someday this operation would be studied at the highest levels of intelligence in Langley and the Pentagon.

He turned off the kitchen light. He began to climb the stairs, felt compelled to double-check the oven, although he was certain it was off. Astonish them. Create coincidence so bizarre they have to believe it. Create a loneliness that beats with violent desire. This kind of man. An arrest, a false name, a stolen credit card. Stalking a victim can be a way of organizing one's loneliness, making a network out of it, a fabric of connections. Desperate men give their solitude a purpose and a destiny.

The oven was off. He made an effort to register this fact. Then he went upstairs, hearing soft music on the bedroom radio.

This kind of man. A self-watcher, a man who lives in random

space. If the world is where we hide from ourselves, what do we do when the world is no longer accessible? We invent a false name, invent a destiny, purchase a firearm through the mail.

Lancer is going to Honolulu.

At one level he operated well. He felt alert, marvelously sharp, very much on top of things. The address book was next. We want a spectacular miss.

A voice on KDNT said that an eight-nation committee of the Organization of American States has charged Cuba with promoting Marxist subversion in our hemisphere. The island is a training center for agents. The government has begun a new phase of encouraging violence and unrest in Latin America.

He didn't need these reminders. He didn't need announcers telling him what Cuba had become. This was a silent struggle. He carried a silent rage and determination. He didn't want company. The more people who believed as he did, the less pure his anger. The country was noisy with fools who demeaned his anger.

He put on his pajamas. He seemed to be in pajamas all the time now. The day wasn't half done and it was time to go to bed again. Mary Frances was asleep. He switched off the radio, switched off the lamp. He spoke inwardly to whatever force was out there, whatever power ruled the sky, the endless hydrogen spirals, the region of all night, all souls. He said simply, Please let me sleep but not dream.

Dreams sent terrors you could not explain.

In Moscow

He opened his eyes to the large room. There were high walls, old plush chairs, a heavy rug with a stale odor hanging close. He got out of bed and walked to the window. Hurrying people, long lines for buses. He washed and shaved. He put on a white shirt, gray flannel trousers, the dark narrow tie, the tan cashmere sweater, and stood in his bare feet at the window once more. Muscovites, he thought. After a while he put on his socks and good shoes and the flannel suit coat. He looked in the gilt mirror. Then he sat in one of the old chairs in the lace-curtained room and crossed one leg carefully over the other. He was a man in history now.

Later he would print in his Historic Diary a summary of these days and of the weeks and months to follow. The lines, mainly in block letters, wander and slant across the page. The page is crowded with words, top to bottom, out to either edge, crossed-out words, smudged words, words that run together, attempted corrections and additions, lapses into script, a sense of breathlessness, with odd calm fragments.

He told his Intourist guide, a young woman named Rimma, that he wanted to apply for Soviet citizenship.

She is flabbergassed, but aggrees to help. Asks me about myself and my reasons for doing this. I explaine I am a communist, ect. She is politly sym. but uneasy now. She tries to be a friend to me. She feels sorry for me I am someth. new.

On his twentieth birthday, two days after his arrival, Rimma gave him a Dostoevsky novel, in Russian, and she wrote on a blank page: "Great congratulations! Let all your dreams come true!"

Things happened fast after that. He had no time to work out meanings, fall back on old attitudes and positions. The secret he'd carried through the Marine Corps for over a year, his plan to defect, was the most powerful knowledge in his life up to this point. Now, in the office of some bald-head official, he tried to explain what it meant to him to live in the Soviet Union, at the center of world struggle.

The man looked past Oswald to the closed door of his office.

"USSR is only great in literature," he said. "Go home, my friend, and take our good wishes with you."

He wasn't kidding either.

I am stunned I reiterate, he says he shall check and let me know.

They let him know the same day. The visa of Lee H. Oswald would expire at 8:00 P.M. He had two hours to leave the country. The police official who called with this news did not seem to know Oswald had talked to a passport official earlier in the day. Lee tried to explain that the first official had not given a deadline, had held out hope that his visa might be extended. He could not recall the man's name or the department he belonged to in the Ministry of Internal Affairs. He began to describe the man's office, his clothing. He felt a rush of desperation. The second official didn't know what he was talking about.

It was this blankness that caused his terror. No one could distinguish him from anyone else. There was some trick he hadn't mastered which might easily set things right. Other people knew what it was; he did not. Other people got along; he could not. He'd come so far on his own. Le Havre, Southampton, London, Helsinki—then by train across the Soviet border. He'd made plans, he'd engineered a new life, and now no one would take ten minutes to understand who he was. A zero in the system. He sat near the window looking at the open suitcase on the rack across the room, some of his things still unpacked.

I am shocked!! My dreams!

He was a foreigner here. There was no profit in discontent. He could not apply his bitterness. It was American-made and had no local standing. For the first time he realized what a dangerous thing he'd done, leaving his country. He struggled against this awareness. He hated knowing something he didn't want to know. He opened the door and looked into the hallway. The woman who handed out room keys sat at a small desk near the elevator. She turned to look at him. He went back inside.

7:00 P.M. I decide to end it. Soak rist in cold water to numb the pain.

He stood at the sink, left shirtsleeve rolled up. He stopped freezing his wrist long enough to prop a clean blade against the razor case. Warm water was running in the tub.

Hidell prepares to make his maker, ha ha.

Was there something funny about this? He didn't think so. They were always trying to get him to leave places he didn't want to leave. The cold water would numb the pain. That was step one. The warm water would make the blood flow easily. That was two. He would barely have to nick the skin. Gillette sponsors the World Series on TV—they use a talking parrot. He loosened his tie with his free hand.

My fondes dreams are shattered

He imagined Rimma coming at eight o'clock to find him dead. Hurried calls to officials at their homes. He watched the tub fill. Any reason why it had to be filled? He wasn't getting in, was he? Only plunging the cut wrist. Soviet officials call American officials. Always being the outsider, always having to adjust. He turned off the cold water, picked up the razor blade and sat on the floor next to the tub.

Then slash my left wrist.

But why was it funny? Why was he watching himself do it without a moan or cry? The first line of blood came seeping out, droplets running down in sequence from the careful slit. He wasn't here to escape personal pressures. He wasn't a guy with a problem marriage. He had solid convictions, practical experience in the world. He flopped his left arm over the rim of the tub.

somewhere, a violin plays, as I watch my life whirl away.

How do they measure cuts here, in centimeters? Hurried calls to Texas. It's me, Mother, lying in a pool of blood in the Hotel Berlin. He looked at the water going cloudy pink. I taught myself Berlitz. My Russian is still bad but I will work on it harder. I won't answer questions about my family but I will say this for publication. Emigration isn't easy. I don't recommend it to everyone. It means coming to a new country, always being the outsider, always having to adjust. I am not the total idealist. I have had a chance to watch the American military in action. If you've ever seen the naval base at Subic Bay, you know what I mean. Machines of war across the whole horizon. Foreign peoples exploited for profit. He closed his eyes after a while, rested his head on the rim of the tub. Go limp. Let them do what they want.

I think to myself, "How easy to die"

I would like to give my side of the story. I would like to give people in the United States something to think about. He knew where he was, could picture himself sitting on the tile floor, but felt a sense of distance from the scene.

and "A sweet death, (to violins)

Felt a sleepiness. A false calm. Something falsehearted. Felt like a child in the white tile world of cuts and Band-Aids and bathwater, a little dizzied by aromas and pungencies, fierce iodine biting in, Mr. Ekdahl's bay rum. There is a world inside the world. I've done all I can. Let others make the choices now. Felt time close down. Felt something mocking in the air as he slipped off the edge of the only known surface we can speak of, as ordinary men, bleeding, in warm water.

Ministry of Health of the USSR

EPICRISIS
Oct. 21   The patient was brought by ambulance into the Admission Ward of the Botkin Hospital and further referred to Bldg. No. 26. Incised wound of the first third of the left forearm with the intention to commit suicide. The wound is of linear character with sharp edges. Primary surgical treatment with 4 stitches and aseptic bandages. The patient arrived from the USA on Oct. 16 as a tourist. He graduated from a technical high school in radio technology and radio electronics. He has no parents. He insists that he does not want to return to the USA.

They put him in with the nut cases. Terrible food, soft eyes peering. Rimma kept him company and then helped get him transferred to the land of the normally ill. She took an unlabeled jar out of her coat and told him to sip the liquid slowly. Vodka with cucumber bits. To your health, she said.

After his discharge she took him to the visa-and-registration department. He talked to four officials about becoming a citizen. They'd never heard of him. They didn't know about his meetings with other officials. They told him it would be a while before they'd have an answer.

At his new hotel, the Metropole, he spent three days alone. This was the first of the silences Lee H. Oswald would enter during his two and a half years in the Soviet Union.

He walked the corridors past enormous paintings of Heroes of the Soviet. He took his key from the floor clerk, who wore her hair in braids. He smelled the varnish and tobacco.

In his room he sat in a fancy chair under a chandelier. He set his watch to the clock on the mantel. His watch, his ring, his money and his suitcase neatly packed had all been sent from the first hotel. Everything intact. Not a kopeck missing.

He sketched a rough street plan of Moscow in his notebook, Kremlin at the center.

His third day alone he ate only one meal. He stayed by the phone waiting for an official to call. He tried to read his Dostoevsky. He heard tourists go past his door talking about the sights, the beautiful subway stations, amazing bronze and marble sculpture. There was a statue at the end of the corridor. A nude, life-size. The language was hard. He thought he'd do better with his Dostoevsky.

Oct. 31. I catch a taxi, "American Embassy" I say.

The receptionist asked him to sign the tourist register. He told her he was here to dissolve his American citizenship. Oh. She led him into the consul's office. He selected an armchair to the left side of the desk. He crossed his legs, matter-of-fact.

"I am a Marxist," he began.

The consul adjusted his glasses.

"I know what you're going to say to me. 'Take some time to think it over.' 'Come back, we'll talk some more.' I'd like to say right now I'm ready to sign the legal papers giving up my citizenship."

The consul said the papers would take time to prepare. He had a look on his face like, Who are you?

"There are certain classified things I learned as a radar operator in the military, which I am saying as a Soviet citizen I would make known to them."

He believed he had the man's attention. He saw the whole scene in some future version. Three days alone. This convinced him he had to reach the point where there was no turning back. Stalin's name was Dzhugashvili. Kremlin means citadel.

I leave Embassy, elated at this showdown. I'm sure Russians will except me after this sign of my faith in them.

He stayed in his room, eating sparely, living on soup for a while, racked by dysentery, nearly two weeks alone, nearly broke, sitting in the plush chair, unshaven, in his button-down shirt and tie.

They moved him to another room, smaller, very plain, without a bath, and charged him only three dollars a day, as if they knew he could no longer afford the regular Intourist rate.

He wrote his name in Russian characters in his steno notebook.

Days of utter loneliness

The first snows fell. He spent eight hours a day studying Russian, serious time, using two self-teaching books. He took all meals in his room, owed money to the hotel, expected a visit from an assistant manager.

No one came.

He went to the visa-and-registration department. He told them about his visit to the U.S. embassy, his wish to become a citizen. They didn't seem to know what to do with him.

Out on the street a small boy figured him for American, asked for a stick of gum. Subzero cold. Broad-backed women shoveling snow. He was struck for the first time by the immensity of the secret that swirled around him. He was in the midst of a vast secret. Another mind, an endless space of snow and cold.

Lenin and Stalin lay together in an orange glow at the bottom of a stone stairway. It was one of the few sights he'd seen.

He was down to twenty-eight dollars.

He wrote in Russian in his notebook. *I have, he has, she has, you have, we have, they have.*

Two men came to his room before seven the next morning. He stood barefoot in his flannel trousers and pajama tops, studying their moves. He didn't think it was Grandfather Frost and his head elf. The room was theirs now. He wasn't sure how they'd taken it over so fast but he knew he felt like an intruder, some kind of bungling tourist. It was his fault they had to get up so early.

They weren't dressed like the officials he'd met. They weren't Intourist people or collectors of overdue bills. One of them wore a black car-coat and dark glasses like a gangster on the *Late Show*. The other guy was older, in snow boots, going quietly bald.

It was this second man who gestured for Oswald to sit on the bed. He said his name was Kirilenko.

Oswald said, "Lee H. Oswald."

The man nodded, smiling faintly. Then he sat in the chair, in his coat, facing Oswald, his right hand dangling between his knees.

Lee volunteered the following.

"My passport is with the U.S. embassy. I surrendered it to them as a sample of no longer wanting to be a citizen. As I told them flatly."

The man nodded one more time, eyelids falling shut.

"Do you know what organization I represent?"

Oswald gave a half-smile.

"Committee for State Security. We believe you've been trying to contact us in your own way. Not fully knowing how perhaps. You understand we're wary of all attempts to contact us. A nervous habit. With luck we'll get over it someday."

Kirilenko had light blue eyes, silvery stubble, the beginning of a sag to his lower jaw. He was stocky and wheezed a little. There was a slyness about him that Oswald took to be an aspect of friendliness. He seemed to be talking to himself half the time the way a middle-aged man might drift lightly through a dialogue with a child, to amuse himself as much as the boy or girl.

"Tell me. How do you feel?"

"Some diarrhea for a while."

Nodding. "Are you happy to be here? Or it was all a mistake. You want to go home."

"I feel fine now. Very happy. It's all cleared up."

"And you want to stay if this is what I understand."

"To be a citizen of your country."

"You have friends here."

"No one."

"There is your family in America."

"Just a mother."

"Do you love her?"

"I don't wish to ever contact her again."

"Sisters and brothers."

"They don't understand the reasons for my actions. Two brothers."

"A wife. You are married."

"No marriages, no children."

The man leaned still closer.

"Girlfriends. A young woman, you lie in bed and think of her."

"I left nothing behind. I had no quarrels with anyone."

"Tell me. Why did you cut your wrist?"

"Because of disappointment. They wouldn't let me stay."

Nodding. "Did you feel, in all seriousness, you were dying? I'm rather curious to know, personally."

"I wanted to let someone else decide. It was out of my hands."

Nodding, eyelids falling shut. "You have funds, or they will send funds from home?"

"I am down to almost nothing."

"Good warm clothes. You have boots?"

"It's a question of being allowed to stay. I'm ready to work. I have special training."

Kirilenko seemed to let that pass.

"Where would you work? Who would give you work?"

"I was hoping the state. I am willing to do whatever necessary. Work and study. I would like to study."

"Do you believe, I wonder, in God?"

"No."

Smiling. "Not even a little? For my personal information."

"I consider it total superstition. People build their lives around this falsehood."

"On your passport, why do I have the impression you crossed out the name of your hometown?"

"It's completely behind me was the reason for doing that. Plus I didn't want them contacting relatives. Which the press did anyway. But I didn't take their phone calls or answer their telegrams."

"Why did you tell your embassy you would reveal military secrets?"

"I wanted to make it so they had to accept my renouncing my citizenship."

"Did they accept?"

"They said it's a Saturday and they close early."

"Your unlucky day."

"They said, 'Come back and we'll do what we can.' "

"I think I'm enjoying this talk."

"I didn't give them the satisfaction of reappearing. I wrote them my position instead."

"And these secrets, which you've carried all this way."

"I was in Atsugi."

Nodding.

"Which is a closed base in Japan."

"We'll talk further. I wonder, though, if these secrets become completely useless once you announce your intention to reveal them."

This last remark was delivered directly to the other KGB man, who leaned against the window frame smoking. Kirilenko made it sound like a scholarly aside. He leaned close to Oswald once more.

"Tell me. The scar is healing well?"

"Yes."

"You can stand the cold? The cold isn't too ridiculous?"

"I'm getting used to it."

"The food. You eat the food they serve here? Not so bad, is it?"

"It's only the hospital food that wasn't good. Like any hospital."

He looked down to see if his pajamas were sticking out of his trousers. He was wearing his pajama bottoms under his suit pants because he'd hurried to answer the knock at the door.

"What about the Russian people? I'm personally curious to hear what you think of us."

Lee cleared his throat to answer the question. The question made him happy. He'd anticipated being asked, sooner or later, and had an answer more or less prepared. Kirilenko waited patiently, appearing to enjoy himself, as if he knew exactly what Oswald was thinking.

Oswald was thinking, This is a man I can trust completely.

Factory smoke hung fixed in the distance, tall streamers absolutely still in the iced blue sky. He rode with Kirilenko in the rear seat of a black Volga. The city was stunned, dream-white. He tried to figure out the direction they were taking by keeping an eye out for landmarks but after he spotted the main tower of Moscow University nothing looked familiar or recallable. He saw himself telling the story of this ride to someone who resembled Robert Sproul, his high-school friend in New Orleans.

It was Eisenhower and Nixon who killed the Rosenbergs.

The room was twelve by fifteen with an iron bed, an unpainted table and a chest of drawers in a curtained alcove. Down a dark hall was a washbasin and beyond that a toilet and small kitchen. Kirilenko said something to the other man, who left for a moment, returning with a squat chair, which he set by the table. They gave Oswald a questionnaire to fill out on his personal history, then another on his reasons for defecting, then another on his military service. He wrote all day, eagerly, going well beyond the scope of specific questions, scribbling in the margins and on the reverse side of every form. The chair was too low for the table and he wrote for extended periods standing up.

In the evening he had a short talk with Kirilenko. They talked about Hemingway. The older man was the one who sat on the bed this time, still in his bulky coat, remembering lines from Hemingway stories.

"Someday when I'm settled here and studying," Oswald said, "I want to write short stories on contemporary American life. I saw a lot. I kept silent and observed. What I saw in the U.S. plus my Marxist reading is what brought me here. I always thought of this country as my own."

"One day I would genuinely like to see Michigan. Purely because of Hemingway."

"The Michigan woods."

"When I read Hemingway I get hungry," Kirilenko said. "He doesn't have to write about food to make me hungry. It's the style that does it. I have a huge appetite when I read this man."

Oswald smiled at the idea.

"If he's a genius of anything, he's a genius of this. He writes about mud and death and he makes me hungry. You've never been to Michigan?"

"I went where I was told," Oswald said.

Kirilenko looked tired in the dim light. His boots were salt-stained. He stood up, pulling his muskrat cap out of his coat pocket and smacking it in the palm of the opposite hand.

"We have large subjects to cover," he said. "So: I would like you to call me Alek."

In the morning they talked about Atsugi. Oswald described a four-hour watch in the radar bubble. Alek wanted details, names of officers and enlisted men, the configuration of the room. He wanted procedures, terminology. Oswald explained how things worked. He talked about security measures, types of height-finder equipment. Alek took notes, looked out the window when his subject had trouble recalling something or seemed unsure of his facts.

Two men joined them to talk about the U-2. The weather plane, one of them called it, deadpan. They brought a stenographer with them. They wanted names of U-2 pilots, a description of the takeoff and landing. Not friendly types. The stenographer was an old man with a rosette in his lapel.

When Oswald didn't know the right answer he made one up or tried to vanish in excited syntax. Alek seemed to understand. They communicated outside the range of the other men, silently, without gestures or glances.

The name of a single pilot. The name of a mechanic or guard.

Deadpan fellows leaning toward him. He described times when the radar crew received requests for winds aloft at eighty thousand feet, ninety thousand feet. He described the voice from *out there*, dense, splintered, blown out, coming down to them like a sound separated into basic units, a lesson in physics or ghosts. They pressed him for facts, for names. Many more questions. Air speed, range, radar-jamming equipment. He hated to say he didn't know.

Alek said they would resume in the morning. Lee wanted a sign from him. How is it going? Will they let me stay, give me solid duties, allow me to study economics and political theory?

"I have a click in my knee when I bend," Kirilenko said. "What do you think, old age?"

There is time for everything, he seemed to mean. Time to recall the smallest moment, time to revise your story, time to change your mind. We are here to help you clarify the themes of your life.

They spent many days on Oswald's early experience in the military, many more days on the U-2 and Atsugi, dividing every compact topic into fractional details, then dividing these. They moved on finally to MACS-9, his radar unit in California.

Castro was exploding on the scene. Oswald had wanted to go to Cuba and train young recruits. He was a skilled technician and fighting man, sympathetic to Fidel.

He subscribed to a Russian-language newspaper and a socialist journal. He answered the guys in his quonset hut with *da* and *nyet*. It used to get them all worked up. They called him Oswaldovich.

He told Alek about the rumors he'd heard of a false defector program run by the Office of Naval Intelligence. They inserted agents into the Eastern Bloc, a select number of men posing as victims of the American system, lonely and impressionable, eager to adopt another kind of life.

This was precisely at the time he was taking steps to defect. The whole scheme was written with him in mind. He half expected to be approached by Naval Intelligence. It was easy to believe they knew about his pro-Soviet remarks and Russian-language newspaper. He would tell them he was trying to make contact in his own way. They'd train him intensively. He'd be a real defector posing as a false defector posing as a real defector. Ha ha.

Alek sat across the table shaking salted nuts in his fist. He said something about getting a TV set brought in. Oswald was surprised to hear that broadcasting started at six in the evening. It was one of the strangest things he'd heard since crossing the ocean.

The guard showed up. He showed up every evening before Alek left. Alek never introduced him, didn't seem to notice he was in the flat. The guard usually sat by the washbasin in the hall, his hat balanced on his knee.

There were things Oswald didn't tell Alek, like details of the MPS-16 radar system, just integrated into the network. He wanted to see how their friendship progressed. It occurred to him that the U.S. military might have to spend jillions to change the system anyhow, now that he'd crossed to the other side. How strangely easy to have a say over men and events.

The other thing he didn't tell Alek concerned the false defector program. When nobody contacted him, Ozzie decided to sign up for a foreign-language qualification test. Russian. Just to see if he'd get noticed.

His rating was P for poor throughout.

A doctor and nurse came to give him a physical. They listened to his heart, shined a light in his ears. They weighed and measured him and went away with samples of his urine and blood. Then three men arrived and took him to a concrete building about half an hour away. He walked into a modern apartment. They had him remove objects from his pockets. They sat him down in a chair that was attached to a console equipped with graph paper, pen recorders, dials, switches, etc. They told him to put his feet flat on the floor. Then they attached tubes and devices to the arms, chest and hands of Oswaldovich. One of the men sat facing him. Is your name such-and-such? Did you ever use another name or identity? Is your favorite color blue? Are you an agent of U.S. intelligence? Are you in secret contact with anyone in this country? Is your hair brown? Have you been sent here to assassinate some person or persons? Are you married? Are you homosexual? Do you smoke or drink?

Deadpan.

No sign of Alek. Oswald stood while they unplugged him from the console. He was lonely for his friend and had a sneaking suspicion he'd messed up the test something awful.

He told them Alek had promised TV.

Someone arrived with his belongings. He stayed in the new apartment for three days. They gave him intelligence tests, aptitude tests, personality profiles, tests in English and basic math, tests in the recognition of patterns and shapes.

He dreamed of walking into the house on Ewing Street, in Fort Worth, his hair sopping wet from a swim at the Y.

Lenin and Stalin in an orange glow. Caspian Sea, largest inland sea in the world, on the boundary between Europe and Asia. Kremlin means citadel.

He is telling the story of his stay in a guarded apartment somewhere in Moscow to a man in a suit and tie. Maybe it is Richard Carlson as Herb Philbrick on TV. *I Led Three Lives.* Maybe it is the man at the U.S. embassy, the second secretary or consul, whatever he is called, adjusting his glasses, listening with interest to the story of an ex-Marine who has infiltrated the Soviet intelligence apparatus as part of the U.S. Navy's false defector program.

Kirilenko stood on the parquet floor of his partitioned office in the First Section, Seventh Department, Second Chief Directorate at KGB headquarters, the Center, 2 Dzerzhinsky Square, a mass of elaborate stonework comprising an old main building, a postwar extension, a prison, Lubyanka, famous for exterminations, other, lesser buildings, and a courtyard visible through barred windows or screens of heavy-gauge mesh. He liked to think standing up.

The nice thing about the Center was the inexpensive caviar and salmon available in Building 12 across the square, and the J&B and Johnnie Walker at a dollar a bottle. The not-so-nice thing was the heavy sense of Stalinist terror. He also hated the chair they'd given him, a modern contour piece that looked ridiculous behind his old wooden desk.

All the more reason to stand. He kept his arms behind him, left hand clutching right forearm. He was thinking about the American boy, Lee H. Oswald. The lesson of Lee H. Oswald was that easy cases are never easy. It made him think of the classical axioms of his early training in geometry and arithmetic. Sad to learn that those self-evident truths, *necessary truths*, faltered so badly when subjected to rigorous examination. No plane surfaces here. We are living in curved space.

Alek liked the boy. Such naked aspiration in his eyes. He was trying to get a grip on the world. Facts, words, historic ideas. He struggled against his fate, yes, exactly, like someone in the social universe of Marx. He believed genuinely in high principles and aims even if he was not yet assured of a sense of perspective.

At twenty years old, all you know is that you're twenty. Everything else is a mist that swirls around this fact.

He slit his wrist to stay in Russia.

But idealists of course are unpredictable. They tend to be the ones who turn bitter overnight, deceived by lies they've told themselves. Men who defect for practical reasons are easier to manage and maintain. Money, sex, frustration, resentment, vanity. We understand and sympathize. We get close to the edge ourselves sometimes.

They'd been watching him since Helsinki, where he registered at the Torni Hotel, moved to the cheaper Klaus Kurki, applied for a visa at the Soviet consulate, told a clerk in passing that he was an ex-Marine highly qualified in radar and electronics.

A walk-in. But not so sure of himself. Not certain how to go about it.

They made it easy for him to get in, providing a visa in forty-eight hours.

In Moscow his Intourist guide, Rimma Shirokova, reported his choicest remarks to the Fourth Section of the Seventh Department, where they were passed on to Kirilenko. Alek waited, let the low officials mix things up, let the boy pace his room; had him moved to a cheaper room; waited, waited.

There were one hundred and thirty listening devices in the U.S. embassy. In his combination safe Alek had a transcript of Oswald's remarks about revealing military secrets. Through the efforts of a clerk in the consulate section he had a photograph of Oswald's passport as well as a copy of a confidential telegram sent from AmEmb Moscow to the Department of State concerning the young man's statement.

MAIN REASON "I AM MARXIST." ATTITUDE ARROGANT AGGRESSIVE.

An easy case that left Alek wondering about Oswald's procommunist career in the military. Didn't U.S. intelligence pick this up? Wouldn't they want to use his political sympathies to find out what they could about the people he contacted, about KGB recruitment methods, agent training? They would turn him when it suited their purpose. That's when he would tell them everything he'd learned, just as he was telling us.

Does Mother Russia want this boy? He was useful as a radar specialist at a U.S. base. What do we do with him here? Is it conceivable we might send him to the building on Kutuzovsky Prospekt, where he would be trained, genuinely educated, in Marx and Lenin, microphotography and secret writing, Russian and English, rebuilt so to speak, given a new identity, sent back to the West as an illegal?

That's what they all want, isn't it, these people who live in corners inside themselves, in blinds and hidey-holes? A second and safer identity. Teach us how to live, they say, as someone else.

The test results were in and only his urine got a passing grade. He tended toward emotional instability. Tended toward erratic behavior. Had some form of dyslexia or word-blindness. Scored fairly well in physical sciences, low in most other categories. The polygraph was more or less chaotic but then it almost always is. *Inconclusive owing to various factors.* Maybe the boy was scared.

An easy case—send him home—except that Alek had a quota. There was pressure to handle a certain number of recruitments, turn up beautiful information (or make it up yourself). The vital take was the U-2 data, which Alek did not wholly trust. Eighty thousand feet? Ninety thousand feet? Nothing flies that high. Fly to ninety thousand feet, you see the souls of the dead in rings of white light. The men who'd debriefed Oswald on the weather plane were officers of the GRU, military intelligence, and they hadn't officially pronounced on the data they'd been given. What could they say? If the boy was word-blind, couldn't he be number-blind as well?

Alek sat in the swooping chair.

A number of dangers cling to the slim figure of this Lee H. Oswald, an innocent who wanders into the outer rings of the Center, leaving thoughtful men to speculate. Are the Americans monitoring his progress? Would they let him fall into our arms if they thought he knew important things? Atsugi is a key base. There are reports from Hanna Braunfels, dredged from the files of the Seventh Department (Japan, India, etc.) of the First Chief Directorate. In a sense we have already gone too far with the boy, exposed too many of our methods. Despite all the tests and interviews, we may know less about him than he knows about us. In some office in the Pentagon, they are waiting to pick his brains.

Alek was paid to drive himself crazy.

One thing the tests confirmed. This was not agent material. You want self-command and mettle, a steadiness of will. This boy played Ping-Pong in his head. But Alek liked him and would arrange something decent. Has to be far from Moscow. A place where there are no foreign journalists, no chance to use him for propaganda. Give him a nice apartment, a well-paying job, a sweet subsidy in the name of the Red Cross—incentives to remain in this country. Alek had every reason to believe that Lee H. Oswald would eventually be given Soviet citizenship, become a genuine Marxist and contented worker, go to lectures and mass gymnastics, fit in, find his place in history, or geography, or whatever he was looking for. A true-blue Oswaldovich.

Still, he would recommend that surveillance be maintained, indefinitely, wherever the boy was sent.

Lee was not sure if this official was one of the men he'd seen before. There'd been so many, in the same dark suit.

The official told him he was not yet being considered for Soviet citizenship. Instead he was given Identity Document for Stateless Persons Number 311479. It was, anyway, a nice-looking piece of paper.

The official told him he was being sent to the city of Minsk.

The official pronounced the name with a devastating clarity, as if moved by a painful ringing in his teeth.

Oswald cracked a little joke. "Is that in Siberia?"

The official laughed, shook the American's hand, then clapped him hard between the shoulder blades and sent him out into the snow.

The next day the Red Cross gave him five thousand rubles, which just about knocked him flat.

One day later Lee H. Oswald, with a just-shaved look, set out by train for this place Minsk. Seven hours out of Moscow he caught twenty minutes' sleep on a wooden bunk with a rented mattress and pillow. Then he ate meat pie and drank tea and could not recall a meal that tasted better. The land was forested here, silent and white in the Russian dusk.

2 July

David Ferrie drove the Rambler south past chemical plants where waste gas flared yellow and red. Farther on he saw oystermen's shacks in the windy distances, set on stilts above the marsh grass. He reached a place called Wading Point, the country retreat of Carmine Latta. He went past the Dead End sign, past the No Trespassing sign, waved to three men conferring on a lawn, then turned onto a dirt road. Men were always conferring at Wading Point. He'd see them clustered at the door of one of the outbuildings or seated in a car on a rutted lane, four large men crowded into some nephew's VW, absorbed in serious talk.

The hunched bearing, the repetitive gestures, the set jaws and fixed regard, the economy of the group, the formal air of exclusion, bodies leaning inward toward a center.

Ferrie understood the *gestalt* of serious talks. He'd studied psychology through the mail with Italian masters. This was long before Eastern Airlines fired him for moral turpitude and for making false claims about a medical background. As if a degree could solve the riddle of Comrade Cancer. They took away his uniform for good.

He drove to an old lodge in the swampy bottoms where Carmine liked to relax with the boys. Four of the boys were roasting a goat on a spit outside the lodge, which was weathered past the point of rustic charm, with swallows' nests mud-stuck to the eaves. Ferrie parked in the shade and went inside. The white-haired man, bright-eyed, veined, ancient, was sitting on a sofa, drink in hand. He was frail and spotted, with the drawn and thievish look of a figure in a ducal portrait. There were times, entering his presence, when Ferrie experienced a deferential awe so complete that he found himself becoming part of the other man's consciousness, seeing the world, the room, the dynamics of power as Carmine Latta saw them.

Carmine ran the slots. Carmine had prostitutes from here to Bossier City, a place where you could get a social disease leaning on a lamppost. There were casinos, betting parlors, drug traffic. Carmine had a third of the Cuban dope before Castro. Now he had a shrimp fleet making deliveries from Central America. There was a billion dollars a year in total business. Carmine had motels, banks, juke boxes, vending machines, shipbuilding, oil leasing, sightseeing buses. There were state officials drinking bourbon sours in his box at the racetrack. The story was he funneled half a million cash to the Nixon campaign in September 1960. What the boys call a tremendous envelope.

"My friend David W. Ferrie. What's the W. for?"

"Wet my whistle," Ferrie said.

Carmine laughed and pointed at the liquor cabinet. The third man in the room was Tony Astorina, driver and bodyguard, oc-casional courier, known as Tony Push for obscure reasons. He and Carmine were reminiscing grimly about the Attorney General. Rob-ert Kennedy was an obsessive topic of conversation wherever Car-mine settled for ten minutes. Carmine had grudges. Ferrie could see the Bobby Kennedy grudge come to life in his eyes, a determined rage, but fine and precise, carefully formed, as if the lean old face held a delicate secret within it, one last and solemn calculation.

"So what I'm saying," Astorina said, "the whole thing goes back to Cuba. You look at everything today, the Justice Department, the pressure they're putting. If the boys took out Castro when they were supposed to, we wouldn't have a situation like this here."

"That's half true," Carmine said. "We would have leeway, with Cuba back in the firm. The value of Cuba, you use it to relieve pressure on the mainland. But the fact is nobody ever gave the Castro matter their full attention. We weren't very sincere."

They all laughed at that.

"Removing Castro was strictly a CIA daydream. The boys in Florida just strung them along. They were looking to keep the prosecutors off their back. They could always claim they were serving their country. And it worked. The CIA backed them up constantly."

"I still say everything goes back to Cuba."

"All right. But we're realistic people. We don't do tricks with mirrors and false bottoms. The styles don't match."

Ferrie wasn't surprised to hear them talking about delicate subjects in his presence. He did research on legal matters for Carmine and knew a great deal about his holdings and operations. He also knew the answers to some touchy questions.

Why did Carmine hate Bobby Kennedy in such a personal way, right down to the sound of his crackling Boston voice?

In early 1961 Carmine walks out of his modest house outside New Orleans and sees he is being followed by FBI. They tail his car, eat lunch at an adjoining table, photograph his movements to and from his office, above a movie theater in Gretna. It is the beginning of a campaign of total relentless surveillance carried out at the direction of the Attorney General. In March they go to Las Vegas with him, take his picture in hotels and casinos, come back with him, camp outside his house, photograph his family, the neighbors, the mailman, the boy who delivers groceries. In April they go to church with his wife and his niece, play with his great-granddaughter in a supermarket and shoot movies of his sister's funeral. It is Carmine's personal Bay of Pigs, coinciding in time with the better-publicized one. Although there is public ruckus here as well. Sightseers come to the street where he lives to watch the FBI watching Carmine. There are traffic jams, skirmishes with the boys. It goes on for close to a year. These men are in his face day and night. It is the systematic humiliation of a senior citizen in front of his family, his neighbors and his business associates. And that little Bobby son of a bitch is calling every shot.

Carmine said, "The CIA comes up with exotic poisons one after another. They all end up in the toilets of South Florida."

"But if we want to clip this Castro," Tony said.

"The word is feasible or not feasible. We don't go on fools' errands." He stared at the glass in his hand. "Then there's the other theory why Castro's still alive. One of our people in Florida made a deal with him."

Tony Astorina stood against the wall across the room. Ferrie saw in him the ruins of a certain kind of grace. He was one of those nervy sharp-dressing kids who wake up at age forty, ruefully handsome, with a wife, three babies and a liver condition, the adolescent luck and charm lost in mounting body fat. He'd worked his way from the floor of the gaming room at the Riviera in Havana. Ferrie thought he'd probably built some corpses in order to be standing where he was now.

Tony said, "Speaking of Cuba, a couple of weeks ago I dream I'm swimming on the Capri roof with Jack Ruby. The next day I'm on Bourbon Street, who do I fucking see? You talk about coincidence."

"We don't know what to call it, so we say coincidence. It goes deeper," Ferrie said. "You're a gambler. You get a feeling about a horse, a poker hand. There's a hidden principle. Every process contains its own outcome. Sometimes we tap in. We see it, we know. I used to run into Jack Ruby now and then. What was he doing in New Orleans?"

"Shopping for dancers. There's a girl at the Sho-Bar he's salivating."

"I was making leaflet runs in a light plane out of the Keys. A little while after Castro came in. I saw Ruby in Miami once or twice."

"Stop-offs," Tony said.

"He was running cash or arms or something."

"He was buying people out of Cuban jails."

Ferrie was drinking scotch and soda, same as Carmine. He was watching Carmine. They shook their glasses simultaneously, rattling the cubes. The old man's hands were long and thin. His ears were tufted with snowy hair. Ferrie smelled the roasting goat.

Tony Push said, "I remember I seen a picture six, seven months ago in a magazine. Anti-aircraft guns outside the Riviera. Dug in right in the street. Which comes a long way from what we had there. A whole city to pluck like a fruit."

"A whole country," Carmine said.

"It was fucking paradise, Havana, then. The casino was gold-leaf walls. I mean beautiful. We had beautiful chandeliers, women in diamonds and mink stoles. The dealers wore tuxedos. We had greeters at the door in tuxedos. Twenty-five thousand for a casino license, which is the steal of all time, plus twenty percent of the profits. Batista gets his envelope, everybody's happy. We let the Cubans turn the wheel. We did the blackjack and craps. What's it called, brocade, the fucking drapes. I like to see a room where the dealers wear a tux. Plus there's action all over town. Your cockfights, your jai alai. At the track you play roulette between races. I mean tell me where it went."

"Kennedy should have blown it up when he had the chance," Ferrie said.

"You blow up Cuba, you get the Russians."

"I've got my rubber bedsheets all ready. An eternity of canned food. I like the idea of living in shelters. You go in the woods and dig your personal latrine. The sewer system is a form of welfare state. It's a government funnel to the sea. I like to think of people being independent, digging latrines in the woods, in a million backyards. Each person is responsible for his own shit."

Carmine rocked on the sofa. The ice cubes rattled. Ferrie knew he could make Carmine laugh just about any time he wanted. He always knew the moment, always sensed the approach to take. This was because he shared the man's perceptions.

"One thing, I have to say it," Tony said. "I don't bear no feeling against the President one way or the other. It's this rat fink Bobby that's pushing too hard. I say all right. They have their job, we have ours. But he's making it like some personal program. He crosses the line."

"They both cross the line," Carmine said. "The President crossed the line when he put out the word he wanted Castro dead. Let me tell you something."

"What?"

"I want to tell you a little thing you should always remember. If somebody's giving you trouble, again, again, again, again, somebody with ambitions, somebody with a greed for territory, the first thing you consider is go right to the top."

"In other words you take action at the highest level."

"That's where they're letting it get out of hand."

"In other words you bypass."

"You clean out the number one position."

"In other words you arrange it so there's a new man at the top who gets the message and makes a change in the policy."

"You cut off the head, the tail doesn't wag."

David Ferrie loved a proverb. He loved the feeling of being swept into another man's aura. A power aura like Carmine's was a special state of awakening. The man was like a fairy-tale pope, able to look at you and change your life, say a word and change your life. Ferrie had devised a theology based on militant anticommunism. He was a sometime master of hypnotism. He studied languages, studied political theory, knew diseases intimately, had official records of his skill as a pilot. All this paled in the presence of a man like Carmine Latta.

Carmine had a battle column of lawyers with millions ready to spend against repeated government attacks. He had men working on conspiracy to defraud, obstruction of justice, perjury, a thousand pain-in-the-ass details. Carmine had Ferrie doing research on tax liens. He had state officials and bank presidents making personal pleas on his behalf. Carmine and the boys were the state's biggest industry. Carmine had finance companies, gas stations, truck dealerships, taxi fleets, bars, restaurants, housing subdivisions. Carmine had a man who washed his pocket money in Ivory liquid to keep it germ-free.

Now Ferrie followed Tony Astorina down a hall flanked by simple bedrooms. On the floor of the last room stood a tall canvas bag laced at the top. Ferrie could see the square bulges the stacks of money made. A gift from Carmine to the cause. Guy Banister saw to it that exile leaders knew who was providing cash for arms and ammunition. It was Latta's bid for gambling concessions after Castro fell.

Back in the living room Ferrie said, "I'll take it straight to Camp Street, Carmine. They'll be very happy, very grateful. All through the movement."

"We all look forward to the day," Carmine said softly. "We only want what's ours."

Ferrie believed there was a genius in the man. Carmine was born in the mid 1880s to an Italian father and Persian mother, at sea, under the sign of Taurus. This was a powerful blend of elements. Ferrie admired Taureans. They were generous people, steadfast and tolerant, with a gift for empire.

He carried the duffel bag to the car. He waved to the boys and drove out to the main road. Astrology is the language of the night sky, of starry aspect and position, the truth at the edge of human affairs.

Raymo furled the blue bandanna and tied it around the neck of his German shepherd. Stinking hot today. He had a room in a little stucco house bristling with TV antennas. It was not far from the stone house on Northwest Seventh Street where Castro had lived when he was in Miami, raising money, finding men for the revolution. Raymo stroked the animal's head, muttered into the silky ear. Then he put on the leash and followed the dog down the stairs.

He went south toward Calle Ocho, the main drag of Little

Havana. Dogs ran up to fences to yap at Capitán. A lot of killer dogs, a lot of cars with hood ornaments that were the only things worth saving. Old cars sinking into the tar. Dogs skidding sideways along the fences barking in the brilliant heat. Capitán plodded on, old and remote.

Raymo turned left on Calle Ocho. He walked past the jewelry shops, every bakery window with a pink-and-white wedding cake. A hundred men were crowded into a little corner park, playing dominoes and cards. Still plenty of time. He bought some fruit, stopped to talk to someone every half-block. It was busy on the street. Men stood in clusters, women moved from shop to shop. How the hell could you know, in an all-Cuban place, who were the spies for Fidel?

Up on Flagler Street, Wayne Elko slouched past the stumpy palms. He wore jump boots stained white by salt water and thought about stopping for a *cerveza* Schlitz. Not smart, Wayne. He'd been wandering Florida for nearly two weeks trying to find T-Jay. Spent three days as roustabout and barker with the Jerry Lepke Ten-in-One Carnival. They had a sword box, a ladder of swords, a fire-eater, a two-headed baby show and a snake girl with braces on her teeth. Called a dozen people he knew from the movement. Finally in Miami he received a message at Elliot Bernstein Chevrolet, where the assistant sales manager was an anti-Castro guerrilla who let him sleep in a used Impala.

Be on time, Wayne. He walked down to Calle Ocho and saw the man he was looking for, Ramón Benítez, standing at the designated corner with a doddering beast. He knew Raymo slightly from the days long gone when exiles used to practice close-order drill on front lawns, watched by sleepy children.

They shook hands, etc.

Wayne said to himself, Some tough hombre. Raymo led him a block and a half south. The Cuban façade faded into a version of suburban America. Sunny little stucco homes with postcard lawns. They went into a one-story house. The radio played in a back room. They came out a side entrance and sat at a wooden table in a small concrete enclosure with a statue of St. Barbara standing in the middle.

"This is Frank's house," Raymo said.

Hairy arms. One of those thick-bodied types you can't reach with the usual persuasion. There are only two or three things in the world he ever thinks about and he's made up his mind about each one. Wayne didn't know who Frank was.

"So there's still activity," he said. "There's this friend of mine who works in a Chevy dealership. He makes napalm in his basement with gasoline and baby soap. I sleep in a car in the lot. I'm the unofficial watchman."

"What T-Jay wants is just, like you stick around a couple of days."

"I've been looking for him."

"He's a pretty busy guy," Raymo said unconvincingly.

The dog lay throbbing in the shade.

Frank Vásquez showed up with a wife, two kids and some food. The wife and kids took a peek at the visitor. Wayne waited for someone to say, *"Mi casa es suya."* He got a little charge from the Old World graces. But they slipped back inside, leaving his smile hanging like a rag on a stick.

The three men ate a meal in the humming midday heat. Wayne could find out nothing of substance from the two Cubans. The smaller the talk, the clearer it became that something serious was in the works. The meal was so entrenched in seriousness, in that grave Latin manner and tact, that Wayne was outright convinced this was no mission to harass the Cuban coast as he'd done so many times with the boardinghouse commandos.

He told Raymo and Frank about the operations he'd been involved in. Many fabulous snafus. Squalls, Cuban gunboats, pursuit by police launches. He described how T-Jay had appeared out of nowhere—they didn't even know if he was Agency or not—to give them special training in weapons and night fighting. They needed every little extra they could get.

With Interpen, Wayne was still in the high-scream tempo of

his paratroop days. He was rounding out his youth. The business at hand gave every sign of being very different. A dark and somber plan. Just look at Frank Vásquez. Sad-eyed, long-faced, earnest, with little to say outside of what his family had suffered, which he narrated tersely, like a documentary of a war a hundred years ago.

It hit Wayne Elko with a flash and roar that this was like *Seven Samurai*. In which free-lance warriors are selected one at a time to carry out a dangerous mission. In which men outside society are called on to save a helpless people from destruction. Swinging those two-handed swords.

Win Everett sat in his office on the empty campus of Texas Woman's University. All that heat and light made him grateful for the gloom of the basement nook. Here he worked patiently on his bitterness, honing and refining. It was something he returned to periodically as if to some legend of his youth, a golden moment on a football field or frozen pond, some enterprise of such flawless proportions that he could forget it only at the risk of deep-reaching loss.

The office was a place to come to when Mary Frances and Suzanne were not at home. He didn't mind being alone here. It was a place to sit and think, searching for a grim justice in the very recollection of what they'd done to him—a place to refine and purify, to hone his sense of the past. The fluorescent light buzzed and flickered. When the room grew warm he took off his jacket, folded it neatly lengthwise, then over double, and dropped it softly on a cabinet.

It was no longer possible to hide from the fact that Lee Oswald existed independent of the plot.

T-Jay had picked the lock at 4907 Magazine Street in New Orleans. This became necessary when he learned there was no sample of the subject's handwriting at Guy Banister Associates. The files contained a single document, his job application, filled out in block letters and unsigned.

Lee H. Oswald was real all right. What Mackey learned about him in a brief tour of his apartment made Everett feel displaced. It produced a sensation of the eeriest panic, gave him a glimpse of the fiction he'd been devising, a fiction living prematurely in the world.

He already knew about the weapons. Mackey confirmed the weapons. A 38-caliber revolver. A bolt-action rifle with telescopic sight.

He knew about the leaflets. Oswald was handing out leaflets in the street. The headline was "Hands Off Cuba!"

There was Oswald's correspondence with the national director of the Fair Play for Cuba Committee.

There was socialist literature strewn about. Speeches by Fidel Castro. A booklet with a Castro quotation on the cover: "The Revolution Must Be a School of Unfettered Thought." Copies of the Militant and the Worker. A booklet, *The Coming American Revolution*. Another, *Ideology and Revolution*, by Jean-Paul Sartre. Books and pamphlets in Russian. Flash cards with Cyrillic characters. A stamp album. A twelve-page handwritten journal with the title "Historic Diary."

There was correspondence with the Socialist Workers Party.

A novel, *The Idiot*, in Russian.

There was a pamphlet titled *The Crime Against Cuba*. On the inside back cover Mackey found a stamped address: 544 Camp St.

There was a draft card in the name Lee H. Oswald. There was a draft card in the name Alek James Hidell.

There was a passport issued to Lee H. Oswald. A vaccination certificate stamped Dr. A. J. Hideel. A certificate of service, U.S. Marines, for Alek James Hidell.

There were forms filled out in the names Osborne, Leslie Oswald, Aleksei Oswald.

There was a membership card, Fair Play for Cuba Committee, New Orleans chapter. Lee H. Oswald is the member. A. J. Hidell is the chapter president. The signatures, according to Mackey, were not in the same hand.

A magazine photo of Castro was fixed to a wall with Scotch tape.

There was the room itself. Mackey had found most of these materials in a kind of storeroom off the living room. Small, dark, shabby, a desperate place, the gunman's perfect hutch, with roaches on display along the baseboards.

Everett had wanted only a handwriting sample, a photograph. With these he could begin to construct the illustrated history of his subject, starting with a false name. He'd looked forward to thinking up a name, just the right name, just the spoken texture of a drifter's time on earth.

Oswald had names. He had his own names. He had variations of names. He had forged documents. Why was Everett playing in his basement with scissors and paste? Oswald had his own copying method, his own implements of forgery. Mackey said he'd used a camera, an opaque pigment, retouched negatives, a typewriter, a rubber stamping kit.

He called the work sloppy. But Everett was not inclined to fault the boy on technicalities (Hidell, Hideel). The question was a larger one, obviously. What was he doing with all that fabricated paper, with a Minox camera buried at the back of a closet?

Everett flung both arms out briefly to free his shirt from his damp skin. He searched the room for cigarettes. It seemed there were more questions than actions these past days, and more bitterness than questions. The thing about bitterness is that you can work on it, purify the anguish and the rancor. It is an experience that holds out promise of perfection.

Lancer is back from Berlin.

It was coming back down to pure rancor, to this business of honing and refining. It was this business of how much they'd reduced his sense of worth. It was a question of measurement. It was a question of what they'd done to him. It was this business of sitting in his office in the Old Main and working on his rage.

The last thing Mackey saw, leaving the apartment, was a James Bond novel on a table by the door.

Nicholas Branch has unpublished state documents, polygraph reports, Dictabelt recordings from the police radio net on November 22. He has photo enhancements, floor plans, home movies, biographies, bibliographies, letters, rumors, mirages, dreams. This is the room of dreams, the room where it has taken him all these years to learn that his subject is not politics or violent crime but men in small rooms.

Is he one of them now? Frustrated, stuck, self-watching, looking for a means of connection, a way to break out. After Oswald, men in America are no longer required to lead lives of quiet desperation. You apply for a credit card, buy a handgun, travel through cities, suburbs and shopping malls, anonymous, anonymous, looking for a chance to take a shot at the first puffy empty famous face, just to let people know there is someone out there who reads the papers.

Branch is stuck all right. He has abandoned his life to understanding that moment in Dallas, the seven seconds that broke the back of the American century. He has his forensic pathology rundown, his neutron activation analysis. There is also the Warren Report, of course, with its twenty-six accompanying volumes of testimony and exhibits, its millions of words. Branch thinks this is the megaton novel James Joyce would have written if he'd moved to Iowa City and lived to be a hundred.

Everything is here. Baptismal records, report cards, postcards, divorce petitions, canceled checks, daily timesheets, tax returns, property lists, postoperative x-rays, photos of knotted string, thousands of pages of testimony, of voices droning in hearing rooms in old courthouse buildings, an incredible haul of human utterance. It lies so flat on the page, hangs so still in the lazy air, lost to syntax and other arrangement, that it resembles a kind of mind-spatter, a poetry of lives muddied and dripping in language.

Documents. There is Jack Ruby's mother's dental chart, dated January 15, 1938. There is a microphotograph of three strands of Lee H. Oswald's pubic hair. Elsewhere (everything in the Warren

Report is elsewhere) there is a detailed description of this hair. It is smooth, not knobby. The scales are medium-size. The root area is rather clear of pigment.

Branch doesn't know how to approach this kind of data. He wants to believe the hair belongs in the record. It is vital to his sense of responsible obsession that everything in his room warrants careful study. Everything belongs, everything adheres, the mutter of obscure witnesses, the photos of illegible documents and odd sad personal debris, things gathered up at a dying—old shoes, pajama tops, letters from Russia. It is all one thing, a ruined city of trivia where people feel real pain. This is the Joycean Book of America, remember—the novel in which nothing is left out.

Branch has long since forgiven the Warren Report for its failures. It is too valuable a document of human heartbreak and muddle to be scorned or dismissed. The twenty-six volumes haunt him. Men and women surface in FBI memos, are tracked for several pages, then disappear—waitresses, prostitutes, mind readers, motel managers, owners of rifle ranges. Their stories hang in time, spare, perfect in their way, unfinished.

RICHARD RHOADS and JAMES WOODARD got drunk one night and WOODARD said that he and JACK would run some guns to Cuba. JAMES WOODARD had a shotgun, a rifle and possibly one hand gun. He said that JACK had a lot more guns than he did. DOLORES stated that she did not see any guns in JACK'S possession. She stated that he had several boxes and trunks in his garage and ISABEL claimed they contained her furs, which had been ruined by mold, due to the high humidity in the area.

Photographs. Many are overexposed, light-blasted, with a faded quality beyond their age, suggesting things barely glimpsed despite the simple nature of the objects and the spare captions. *Curtain rods found on shelf in garage of Ruth Paine.* There they are. The picture shows no more or less. But Branch feels there is a loneliness, a strange desolation trapped here. Why do these photographs have a power to disturb him, make him sad? Flat, pale, washed in time, suspended outside the particularized gist of this or that era, arguing nothing, clarifying nothing, lonely. Can a photograph be lonely?

This sadness has him fixed to his chair, staring. He feels the souls of empty places, finds himself returning again and again to the pictures of the second-floor lunchroom in the Texas School Book Depository. Rooms, garages, streets were emptied out for the making of official pictures. Empty forever now, stuck in some picture limbo. He feels the souls of those who were there and left. He feels sadness in objects, in warehouse cartons and blood-soaked clothes. He breathes in loneliness. He feels the dead in his room.

W. Guy Banister, former special agent of the FBI, collector of anticommunist intelligence, is found dead in his home in New Orleans in June 1964, his monogrammed .357 Magnum in a drawer by the bed. Ruled a heart attack.

Frank Vásquez, the former schoolteacher who fought for and against Castro, is found dead in front of El Mundo Bestway, a supermarket on West Flagler Street in Miami, August 1966, shot three times in the head. Reports of a factional dispute among anti-Castro groups in the area. Reports of an argument in a social club earlier in the evening. No arrests in the case.

Ten years later, to the day, also in Miami, police find the decomposing body of John Roselli, born Filippo Sacco, an underworld figure who'd recently testified before a Senate committee investigating CIA-Mafia efforts to assassinate Castro. The body is floating in an oil drum in Dumbfoundling Bay, legs sawed off. No arrests in the case.

Branch sits staring.

The Agency is paying him at the GS level he'd reached at retirement, with periodic cost-of-living increases. They paid for the room he has added to his house, this room, the room of documents, of faded photographs. They paid to fireproof the room. They paid for the desktop computer he uses to scan biographical data. Branch is ill at ease billing them for office supplies and often submits a figure lower than the amount he has spent.

He eats most of his meals in the room, clearing a space on the desk, reading as he eats. He falls asleep in the chair, wakes up startled, afraid for a moment to move. Paper everywhere.

They sat in wooden bleachers in the early evening watching the old men play softball. The players wore short-sleeve white shirts, long white pants and dark bow ties, with baseball caps and white sneakers. It was the bow ties that made Raymo happy. He thought the ties were fantastic, a perfect yanqui touch.

Frank sat one row above him and slightly to the side, drinking an orangeade. He said, "I still think of the mountains."

"You still think of the mountains. Look at the first baseman. I bet anything he's seventy-five. He still does a dance around the bag."

But Raymo thought of the mountains too. He was with Castro in the movement of the 26th of July, the starved army of beards. Fidel was some kind of magical figure then. There was no doubt he carried a force, a myth. Tall, strong, long-haired, dripping filth; mixing theory and raw talk, appearing everywhere, explaining everything, asking questions of soldiers, peasants, even children. He made the revolution something people felt on their bodies. The ideas, the whistling words, they throbbed in all the senses. He was like Jesus in boots, preaching everywhere he went, withholding his identity from the campesinos until the time was dramatically right.

Frank said, "It was miserable because of the sickness and hunger, the rain. But also because I was never sure of my reasons. When I think of the mountains it's mainly my own confusion I recall. I was pulled in two directions. This made it hard for me."

It was true. Frank was always a bit of a *gusano*, with a sneaking admiration for Batista. Now they were all *gusanos*, anti-Castro worms, in the language of the left. But Frank was always half a worm, half a *batistiano*, even fighting for Fidel.

Castro liked to recall the earliest days of the insurrection, before Frank and Raymo went into the Sierra Maestra. Twelve men with eleven rifles. Raymo knows today it was not the 26th of July alone that overthrew the regime. From the first minute, Castro was inventing a convenient history of the revolution to advance his grab for power, to become the Maximum Leader.

The third baseman went into a crouch and bowed his arms wide. The old guy at the plate sent the ball on a line to left center and his teammates watched, half rising from the bench. The sun was in the palms behind the right-field fence.

Frank said, "I think of the mountains more than ever now."

"Because you're stupid, man."

"But I don't think of the invasion at all."

"Who wants to think about either one? Besides you were shipwrecked."

"Run aground. But still our confidence was unshaken."

"Stupid to the end. From the beach I saw the stern begin to sink."

"We still had hope," Frank said seriously.

"No wonder you think of the mountains. In the mountains we won."

Frank handed him the orange drink with a couple of swigs left. They watched the old men make a double play, more serious and alert than boys, mechanically correct at seventy, in bow ties. They recalled how Fidel used baseball terms when he talked about operations. We'll get them in a rundown. We'll shut the bastards out. They went down the steps and walked to the car. Capitán was sprawled in the back seat like a stolen coat.

Raymo drove his buddy home. Sure, Frank thinks of the mountains all the time. He spent twenty-three days in the mountains. He moaned every day for twenty-three days and when he finished his rosary of complaints he went back to teaching school. Teaching the children of men who cut cane for the sugar bosses, children who cleaned and packed cane without pay.

The building where Raymo lived was between the Miami River and the Orange Bowl. He parked the car, took the dog to the hydrant, then went inside. Stinking hot. The first thing he heard was the groan of traffic over the suspension bridge at Northwest Twelfth Avenue. It was a sound raised slightly above the natural tone of the world, the sound of someone thinking, alone in a room.

The troops of the regime were afraid of the cordillera. The mountains meant death to them. For Raymo there wasn't a chance in a million that he could die. He was untouchable in the Sierra, fat and rank, even during the last major offensive with repeated waves of napalm scorching the land and air. They were all untouchable in their minds. This was the point of being rebels.

He lay on the bed thinking.

The march to Havana took something like five days. They were greeted with the awe that heroes earn in books. Purify the country was the cry. Raymo watched a number of executions. These were the rapists and torture masters of the regime, drivers of nails into skulls. They were kindly asked to stand at the edge of a knee-deep ditch. They all ended differently, fell sideways, fell backwards, an arm flung wide, an arm tucked in, but all taken unawares, dying deeply surprised.

Then the communists appeared, entering the unions and rural committees. Castro gave them legal status. There were MiGs in crates waiting for Cuban pilots to learn how to fly them. Think in collective terms was the cry. The individual must disappear.

He talked about one revolution and gave us another. Certain areas were off-limits to Cubans. There were Russian and Czech technicians, Russian construction crews everywhere you looked. On highways, at night, students working against the new regime spotted flatbed trucks carrying long objects, canvas-shrouded, of a certain configuration. The joke was that palm trees were being sold on the black market. The cargo was the SA-2, the first of the Soviet missiles to reach Cuba. They were here to defend the heavens against high-altitude spy planes.

By this time Raymo was in La Cabaña prison, a veteran of the Bay of Pigs. Yes, like that, the bearded hero is a worm. The yard was flanked by ancient storerooms and magazines, barrel-vaulted galleries now used as cells, and he shared one of these with former

Castro guerrillas and Batista officers, with workers, radicals, union officials, student leaders, men who'd been tortured by the old regime and the new one, a perfect Cuban stew. The far end of his cell faced the moat, where executions took place. He waited for John F. Kennedy to get him out.

Some nights they'd hear ten executions. Once Raymo saw a slender man standing in the spotlight in front of the sandbags. He wore white shoes, a dark shirt and lariat tie, a nice-looking panama hat. They were in such a hurry to execute him they didn't even give him a set of prison grays, much less a hearing or trial. Raymo watched the hat go sailing off his head when they shot him. It went straight up in the air like a cartoon hat. The individual must disappear.

Another car hit the iron grillwork at the center of the bridge and that low groan went up.

He wanted to believe he was out of prison. A one-time fighter in the Sierra and Playa Girón, he was reduced to listening to endless arguments between Castro and Kennedy, arguments that determine where he lives, what he eats, who he talks to. In Oriente he was a skilled worker, a mechanic in a nickel-mining operation, American-owned, and this is where he learned about the movement of the 26th of July from students who spoke convincingly of wide injustice. Now he stands on ladders picking fruit and waiting for the maximum leaders to tell him where he goes next. They carry such a stain of greatness, both these men with their visions and heroic bearing. Each takes a turn as the other's shadow, his haunted dream. One buys what the other sells. Eleven hundred veterans of the assault brigade were released from prison after the U.S. paid fifty-three million dollars to the Castro government. Raymo stood on a sideline stripe in the Orange Bowl, three blocks from this stinking bed, and heard the renewed pledges, the second wave of emptiness. Six months had passed since then. He did not believe he'd been freed from anything. Training in the wild grass of the Everglades. This was the only time he felt free.

The thing he could not forget was the way the hat jumped

from the slim man's head. The heavy thudding surprise, the sudden insult. Even after you think you've seen all the ways violence can surprise a man, along comes something you never imagined. How much force do bullets have to exert if they can hit a man in the chest and make his hat fly four feet in the air, straight up? It was a lesson in the laws of motion and a reminder to all men that nothing is assured.

In Minsk

The plant was an eight-minute walk from his flat. He was a regulator first-class, which was another term for metalworker un-skilled. The plant covered twenty-five acres, employed five thousand people and turned out radios and TV sets.

On his first day he presented a handwritten autobiography to the plant director. "My parents are dead," he wrote. "I have no brothers or Sisters."

The director welcomed Citizen Oswald.

At eight sharp the duty orderly rang a bell. Grinding metal. Saws cutting through iron ingots. He hadn't realized such high-pitched fury went into the making of a radio.

Meetings all the time. A large picture of Lenin looked down on the workers. Fifteen meetings a month, all after work, plus compulsory daily gym.

He took girls to the opera and went sightseeing. There were a number of imposing structures in this industrial city, some of them a little funny, he thought. The trade-union building had a Greek temple façade but the figures carved into the frieze were a bricklayer, a surveyor, a woman shot-putter and a man in a double-breasted suit, with briefcase.

He ate fried cabbage in stand-up cafés.

Each autonomous republic is represented by eleven deputies in the Soviet of Nationalities of the Supreme Soviet. Soviet means council.

I am learning Russian quickly

In his fourth-floor apartment he had his own kitchen and bath. He slept on a sofa bed. There was a private balcony that overlooked a wide bend in the river that runs through Minsk. The fifth day of every month he got his Red Cross check.

He read on the balcony, wrote in Russian in his steno notebook. Thank you, he wrote. Neuter nouns ending in *o* take *a*. He wrote the lyrics of a popular song.

Church spires in the distance.

He had money to spend. He was someone interesting, an American, a stranger with a story. America was a rumor down the street, a gleaming place people didn't quite believe in, and they wanted to hear what he had to say.

Then on May 1, May Day, in the skies over Sverdlovsk in the Ural Mountains, the heart-shaking event took place.

The prisoner stood in a metal cage inside the elevator. Light-proof, soundproof. This was a form of naked awareness he didn't need right now. Irregular heartbeat. Right leg stinging. An exhaustion settling in over the raw headache, the whistling in his ears.

They marched him down a corridor. Four men, two in uniform. He sensed their grim satisfaction, something meritorious in the air, some old grievance righted at last. He was due to land, just about now, along a fjord in Norway.

They led him into a small room. Time to strip again. All afternoon they'd been telling him to take off his pressure suit, flight suit, long johns, stand still, bend over, give us a look, put on these pants, wear this shirt. Then they'd take him somewhere else and do it all over again.

He knew he was in Lubyanka now, right in downtown Moscow, the local political prison of the KGB. Maybe this was the last of the body searches.

They gave him another set of clothes, including a double-breasted suit three sizes too large, and took him to the interrogation room, where a dozen men sat waiting, three in uniform, two majors and a colonel. No tape recorder in sight. An interpreter sat next to the prisoner. A stenographer, who looked too old to record anything beyond name and nationality, sat at the end of the long table, a rosette in his lapel.

The prisoner nodded faintly at the array of somber faces. Men well established in state security. They seemed to regard him skeptically, although he hadn't said a word yet. Maybe they thought it was too good to be true, getting their hands on an American air pirate after four years of overflights in unmarked planes. The prisoner thought ahead to a lifetime of potatoes and cabbage soup. Maybe a short lifetime. They might shoot him in the courtyard, like a movie, to muffled drums.

Bright flash in the sky, the way the aircraft lurched forward like a car jolted in heavy traffic.

The long night of questions began. Name, nationality, type of aircraft, type of mission, altitude, altitude, altitude. The trouble with lies is trying to remember what you said so you can repeat it when they ask again. Mainly he told the truth. He wanted to tell the truth. He wanted these people to like him. A few shrewd lies in selected areas, if only he could be sure which areas were the ones he needed to protect. There had been no preparation for this. No one had told him what to say. He was only a pilot. This is what he tried to get across. He flew a certain route, flipped the mission switches. He was a civilian employee. He recorded instrument readings, drifted off course, corrected back. A boy from the Virginia hill country. Didn't smoke, drink or chew. Made a plane out of a cigar box for his fifth-grade teacher.

He told them he'd been flying at sixty-eight thousand feet.

Once they examined the wreckage, they would ask him about the destructor unit, which he hadn't activated because he thought it might detonate before he had time to leave the aircraft. Embarrassing. They would also ask him about the poison needle, which they'd confiscated in Sverdlovsk hours earlier. Yes, the prisoner felt a little sheepish. He was supposed to be dead. Some very important men would be mighty surprised when they learned he was still alive. They'd spent millions to make it convenient for him to die.

When the questions ended they gave him another set of clothes, took him to another room, signaled down with the pants, gave him an injection which he assumed would either help him sleep or make him tell the truth.

They marched him past the desk of the section supervisor into a two-tiered cell block. His cell was eight by fifteen with a solid oak door supported by steel bands. There was an iron bed, a small table and chair, a double-pane window reinforced with wire mesh. He was alone and could hear the Kremlin clock. Already word was beginning to spread of the missing U-2. Bodø, Incirlik, Peshawar, Wiesbaden, Langley, Washington, Camp David. This was exciting in a way. As he undressed for the fifth or sixth time this endless, weary and disconnected day, he noticed the peephole in the door.

The spin was upside down, nose of the aircraft pointing skyward, a little like a dream in which you're powerless to move.

The next day, instead of torturing him to get some answers they liked, they sent him on a tour of Moscow.

Aleksei Kirilenko was present for the second round of questions. A package of Laika filters sat on the table in front of him. There were ten men in the room. The questions rolled forth. The prisoner, called Francis Gary Powers, was sincerely telling the truth about half the time, just as sincerely lying the other half. So Alek estimated.

No, he had not flown over Soviet territory before.

No, the CIA had not given him a list of underground agents he could contact here.

No, he had never been stationed at Atsugi in Japan.

What about the plane?

Yes, the plane had once been based in Atsugi.

They'd given the prisoner a peasant haircut. It suited him well, Alek thought. He had a large square head, strong features, the worried look of a rustic crossing streets in the capital.

No, it did not occur to the prisoner that by violating Soviet frontiers he was endangering the upcoming summit conference.

The thinking in the Center was that Khrushchev would not reveal that Francis Gary Powers was alive and in custody until the American cover story was released in all its hopeful and pathetic variations. (An unarmed weather plane is missing somewhere near Lake Van in Turkey after the civilian pilot reported trouble with the oxygen system.) They would add or subtract details as need dictated. But they were counting on a dead man either way.

Then the Premier would mount the rostrum in the Great Hall, wearing a modest cluster of medals on the breast pocket of his business suit, and announce the interesting news, with photographs, with fitting gestures, his voice carrying in bursts over the delegates, Presidium members, diplomatic corps and international press.

Comrades, he would begin, I must let you in on a secret. The broad smile, the choppy gesturing hand. We have the pilot of the innocent weather plane you have all been hearing about. We have the wreckage of the plane. Shot down by our missiles two thousand kilometers inside Soviet territory. The shadow in the sky. Sent to photograph military and industrial sites. We have the camera and rolls of film. Waving the spy photos, making jokes about the air samples the plane had allegedly been sent to gather. Yes, yes, Francis Gary Powers is alive and kicking, safe and sound, despite the plane's destructor unit, despite the poison meant to end his life, and the pistol with silencer, and the long knife. Pausing to drink some water. Seven thousand rubles in Soviet currency. Did they send him all this way to exchange old rubles for new ones?

Laughter, applause.

Alek looked forward to the theater that Khrushchev would make of the U-2 affair. The summit was scheduled for Paris in two weeks. Eisenhower's moral leadership turns to shit.

But as the questions continued for hours, then days, he began to feel uneasy. The men in uniform, the GRU, kept coming back to the question of altitude. Didn't they know how high the plane was flying when they hit it? Had it been an accidental hit with a haywire missile? Had he taken the plane down to reignite the engine after a flameout? Is that how they hit it? There were rumors they hadn't hit it at all. Had the plane been sabotaged by the CIA to wreck the summit?

Francis Gary Powers repeatedly claimed he was at maximum altitude when he felt the impact and saw the flash. Sixty-eight thousand feet. It seemed the GRU thought he was lying. They believed U-2s went much higher and they knew Soviet missiles could not reach these altitudes.

Why would they believe the plane flew higher than the pilot contended?

Because Oswald told them? Surely they would have strong corroboration from other sources. In any case this affair tended to strengthen the boy's claim to authority. He'd evidently been right about the extreme altitude the plane could reach. He was also the one person in the USSR who had inside working knowledge of the U-2, who was American like Powers, who could measure his countryman's responses and telltale inflections, who could evaluate what he said about ground personnel, base security and so on.

Lee H. Oswald was taking shape in Kirilenko's mind as some kind of Chaplinesque figure, skating along the edges of vast and dangerous events.

Unknowing, partly knowing, knowing but not saying, the boy had a quality of trailing chaos behind him, causing disasters without seeing them happen, making riddles of his life and possibly fools of us all.

Alek had never been to the United States. Everything he'd

learned about the country made him wary of its impulsiveness, its shallow self-assurance. It is a nursery school of a culture, startled, dribbling, forgetful, compared to what we have here, the massive treasure of a history that endures in the souls of the people.

Cigarettes made him patriotic. He was smoking again after six years of nibbling tiny things.

At least Oswald looked American. Francis Gary Powers would eventually stand in the dock in the chandeliered courtroom of the Hall of Columns in his doltish haircut and ridiculous oversized clothes, or undersized clothes, looking like some woodchopper from the Balkans.

Citizen Oswald came to town wearing his dark tie, cashmere sweater and gray flannel suit. It was nice to be back in Moscow.

They led him into the room some minutes after the interrogation had begun. He sat against the wall, fifteen feet behind the prisoner, with a security man in plainclothes. He had a notepad and pencil.

The news, of course, was everywhere, dominating the press and the air waves. The U-2 was the biggest thing in years. A tremendous clamor of righteous Soviet voices, historic American lies, damaged relations. He listened to Francis Gary Powers trying to handle the questions of Roman Rudenko, who had been one of the chief prosecutors of Nazi war criminals at Nuremberg. He thought a prosecutor of Nazis was a slightly dramatic touch for someone like Francis Gary Powers. The prisoner sounded like an ordinary guy. A coal miner's son from some hollow in the boondocks. Paid to fly a plane.

For three solid hours of questions and answers, Oswald stared at the back of the head of Francis Gary Powers.

Then he went to the Chess Pavilion in Gorky Park to see a display of the plane's battered fuselage and tail section. The wings were mounted in the center of the room. The pilot's survival gear, personal effects and signed confession were in glass cases. There were photographs of the pilot under a sign reading POWERS FRANCIS GARY THE PILOT OF THE SHOT AMERICAN PLANE. The crowd was in a holiday mood. Oswald wondered if Powers played chess. It would be a nice gesture if Alek let him into the cell to play a game of chess with Francis Gary Powers.

His plainclothes escort took him back to Lubyanka. Alek and a uniformed guard led him into the cell block. The floor was carpeted. Powers' cell was on the lower level. The guard slid the cover off the spyhole on the door. Oswald looked into the cell. The prisoner sat at a small table, drawing lines on a piece of paper. Oswald thought he might be making a calendar. Men in small rooms, in isolation. A cell is the basic state. They put you in a room and lock the door. So simple it's a form of genius. This is the final size of all the forces around you. Eight by fifteen.

There was something gentle about Powers. He was the type Oswald could get along with in the barracks. He raised his head a moment and looked directly at the spyhole as if he sensed someone watching. Paid to fly a plane and incidentally to kill himself if the mission failed. Well we don't always follow orders, do we? Some orders require thought, ha ha. He wanted to call to the prisoner through the door, *You were right; good for you; disobey*. The prisoner wore a checked shirt buttoned to the top. He waved at a fly and returned to his piece of paper. He seemed to toil at those lines he was drawing. What is the Russian for firing squad?

Alek led Oswald to the interrogation room, where they sat alone in the faint stink of ground-out cigarettes.

"Now you've seen him as close as we can get you. Tell me. Does he look familiar?"

"No."

"Do you know him from Atsugi?"

"They wear helmets and faceplates. There are armed guards around them all the time. I never got a good look at a pilot."

"From the bars perhaps. The nightclubs."

"I don't recall him at all."

"Did you know they had flights from Peshawar?"

"Where is that?"

"Pakistan. Where this flight originated."

"No."

"Powers is telling us many lies. What do you think?"

"He's confused. I think he's mainly truthful. He wants to survive."

"He says sixty-eight thousand feet, maximum altitude. You say eighty thousand, ninety thousand."

"I could be wrong."

"I don't think you're wrong."

"I could definitely be mistaken."

"You sounded very sure. You described the pilot's voice. There is reason to believe you were correct."

"Eighty is pretty damn high. Maybe I thought I heard eighty but it was sixty-eight. I think Powers is telling the truth, based on the type fellow he seems to be."

"What type is that?"

"Basically honest and sincere. Cooperating to the best of his ability. What will happen to him?"

"Too early to say."

"Will they put him on trial?"

"This is almost certain."

"Will they execute him?"

"I don't know."

"He'll get the firing squad, won't he?"

"This is not correct to assume."

"That's the way it's done, isn't it? They shoot them here."

Smiling. "Not so much anymore."

"Let me talk to him."

"Not a good idea."

"I could lecture him on the virtues of life in the Soviet Union. Making radios for the masses."

"The masses need radios so they won't be masses anymore."

"I have an idea I've been thinking." He paused to assemble the dramatic words. "I want to go to Patrice Lumumba Friendship University."

"A wonderful place no doubt. But it happens to be in Moscow

and I don't think this is the right time for you to live here."

"Alek, how do I get ahead? I want to study. The plant is dull and regimented. Always go to meetings, always read the propaganda. Everything is the same. Everything tastes the same. The newspapers say the same things."

"All right, this much. We will think about further schooling for Lee H. Oswald."

"I will wait to hear from you. I depend on it."

"Tell me, personally, for my own enlightenment, is Francis Gary Powers a typical American?"

It occurred to Oswald that everyone called the prisoner by his full name. The Soviet press, local TV, the BBC, the Voice of America, the interrogators, etc. Once you did something notorious, they tagged you with an extra name, a middle name that was ordinarily never used. You were officially marked, a chapter in the imagination of the state. Francis Gary Powers. In just these few days the name had taken on a resonance, a sense of fateful event. It already sounded historic.

"I would say a hardworking, sincere, honest fellow has found himself in a position where he is being crushed by the pressure exerted from opposite directions. That makes him typical, I guess."

He spoke these words in Russian and saw that Alek was impressed.

From the Historic Diary.

The coming of Fall, my dread of a new Russian winter, are mellowed in splendid golds and reds of fall in Belorussia plums peaches appricots and cherrys abound for these last fall weeks I am a healthy brown color and stuffed with fresh fruit.

my 21st birthday see's Rosa, Pavil, Ella at a small party at my place Ella a very attractive Russian Jew I have been going walking with lately, works at the radio factory also.

Finds the approach of winter now. A growing lonliness overtakes
me in spite of my conquest of Ennatachina a girl from Riga

New Years I spend at home of Ella Germain. I think I'm in
love with her. She has refused my more dishonourable advanis

After a pleasent handin-hand walk to the local cinima we
come home, standing on the doorstep I propose's She hesitates
than refuses, my love is real but she has none for me. (I am
too stunned too think!) I am misarable!

He talked to his friends about Cuba, surprised to find they
weren't passionate on the subject. Cuba was a situation he could
easily get heated about and it was steady news in the English-
language Worker, on local radio and the BBC. Mikoyan signs a
trade pact with Che Guevara. Russia sends heavy arms. Ike breaks
diplomatic relations.

Chocolate was expensive. These people had a vicious sweet
tooth. Always a crowd at the local confectionery. Life was small
things. Chocolate, a record player, a meal at the automat.

His friends had trouble with his name. They didn't feel comfortable saying Lee. It sounded Chinese or just didn't fit right on
the tongue.

He told them to call him Alek.

Postcard #4. Washington, D.C. It is January 21, 1961, the
day after the inauguration of John F. Kennedy, and Marguerite
Oswald is in Union Station looking for a telephone. She has just
traveled three days and two nights on a train from Fort Worth,
borrowing on an insurance policy to pay for the ticket, wiping out
her bank account to buy a pair of shoes, traveling all this way *sitting
up*—not enough cash for a roomette in the sleeping car. This is an
angry, tired and frustrated woman. Letters to her congressman un-
answered. Phone calls to the local office of the FBI unreturned.
Telegrams to the State Department. Letters and calls to the Inter-

national Rescue Committee. The State Department talks to the International Rescue Committee but nobody wants to talk to her. Is it really so strange that she uses the word conspiracy? She is only trying to analyze a whole condensed program of things that are not correct.

The White House switchboard tells her the President is in conference.

She throws another coin down the slot.

The State Department switchboard says Secretary Rusk is not available right now but anything they could do for her, etc. etc. The operator is a Negro woman and Marguerite used to live in a mixed neighborhood of Negroes and whites on Philip Street in New Orleans when she was growing up, and played with Negroes, and lived next door to a lovely Negro family, so she finally gets connected, after a lot of back and forth, to a man who seems to be talking from an office instead of a switchboard. There is a silence around him and he says he is an aide and asks her politely what the trouble is.

"I have come to town about a son of mine who is lost in Russia."

She tells the man she is not the sobbing-mother type but the fact is she is getting over a sickness and she doesn't know whether her son is living or dead. He is somewhere abroad working as an agent of our American government. He has the right to make his own decisions, she says, but there is a good chance he has become stranded by his government and cannot get out.

The man says the Weather has predicted a terrible snowstorm and they have orders to leave early.

Marguerite is wary of conspiracy.

She says into the phone, "I cannot survive in this world unless I know I have my American way of life and can start from the very beginning. I have to work into this, starting from the time he was determined at age sixteen about joining the Marines, which we bickered back and forth, living in the French part of town."

She says, "He read Robert's manual day and night. He knew

Robert's manual by heart. And now he is unheard from in over a year, which I am convinced is not completely of his doing, however agents operate overseas. I am here to demand the substance of where he is."

The man at the State Department says they are all leaving the office due to this predicted storm. It is apparently bearing down. The Weather says it could hit any time.

Marina loved hearing English spoken. It was exciting, an adventure of a sort. She hadn't even known there was an American in Minsk. This was something fairly remarkable. The thing that people felt about America never went away.

She danced with Alek on the vast floor of the Palace of Culture. He was polite and neatly dressed, told her how pretty she was in her brocade dress and upswept hair. He spoke English to some of the other boys but only Russian to her, of course. She'd rarely heard English, didn't know a word except song lyrics, Tarzan, Spam.

Marina herself had arrived in Minsk like snow off the roof, her uncle Ilya said. She was illegitimate, she was an orphan, she was drawn to people who were different. Ilya told the American she had breezes in her brain.

She saw Alek often. They seemed to shine together at the center of things. They made things theirs. A certain bench in the park, near the chess players, ordinary things, not unusual in any way. They fell in love the way anyone does. They were from different worlds, totally different cultures, but they were brought together by fate, Marina believed. Her heart began to beat in a different way.

They flattered each other, made each other seem unique and marvelous. It is the lie everyone accepts about being nineteen, which was Marina's age when she met this unexpected man.

She threw over Anatoly, who looked like an actor in the movies, and she threw over Sasha, who was wonderful in every way and therefore not for her.

Alek had a small lovely flat and listened to Tchaikovsky on the phonograph. He took Marina boating on Youth Lake. They were the same as anyone, completely ordinary, saying what people say. Every fact about their lives was precious. Marina's weight at birth was a little over two pounds. Alek was in awe of this fact. It was a private charm, something about her to hold dear. He gestured with his hands, trying to find a shape for two pounds of precious life. Her eyes were blue. Her childhood name was Spichka, or Matchstick, for her spare frame and her tendency to flare up, to speak in abrupt excited phrases. These things they told each other were like stories in a book that changes every day, giving their love a quality of never ending.

He told her his mother was dead.

They talked about everything, the sun and the moon, a fly on a pane of glass. He hid in doorways when the cold wind blew. There was a killer wind that blew along the river.

They were marked by fate to be married and they went to the registry office, with spring coming on, only six weeks after they'd met. Alek brought her a cluster of early narcissus and she wore a short white gown with a grass-blade pattern. That night he thanked her sweetly for being a virgin.

She came home from work in the hospital pharmacy to find him doing the laundry or mopping the floor. He would not let her wash his work clothes. He was ashamed of the grime and sweat and did not like thinking of himself as a factory hand, a manual laborer, slotted to do a certain eternal task.

He tuned in the Voice of America every night at ten.

They had matching scars on their arms, his left arm, her right, both scars near the elbow, the same size and shape. A sense of destiny, or mirrored fate. He told her he'd been wounded in action, in Indonesia, in an operation against the communists. He would say nothing to her about the other scar, the one on his wrist.

He was an orphan like her, an outsider, which was all to the good, but beyond that she was not sure who Alek really was. She saw him from a slight distance, it seemed. He was never fully there. He was the other person, the one she lived with, the American who told her he was twenty-four years old but who turned out, on their wedding day, when she saw the marriage stamp in his residence permit, to be only twenty-one.

It was some weeks later that she learned his mother was not dead.

Some of the boys from the plant told Marina that he was a good enough fellow but always kept to himself, always the loner, not really part of things, not at all like a Russian in temperament and feeling—not straight from the heart, in other words.

The day they were married Castro won the Lenin Peace Prize. This was two weeks after the Bay of Pigs.

He wrote in Spanish in his notebook the numbers one to seventeen, leaving out five and six.

"The other girls I knew here, why did they want to go out with me, just like you?"

"I don't know," she said.

"Because I'm American. That's the funny thing. I left my country out of protest against the conditions there and now I'm the all-American boy to everyone. Except I'll tell you this. When I wanted to marry that girl from the factory, Ella, she turned me down flat for the same reason she went out with me in the first place. I'm an American. Sooner or later I'd be arrested as a spy, she said. Her family thinks I'm a spy. She probably thinks I'm a spy. It's the state of fear of ordinary life in Russia. I saw her the other day. Fat as a barrel now."

Interesting, Marina thought, how much writing he seems to do on those large new pads. What are those photographs he keeps on the top shelf of the closet, behind the suitcases? What is this pencil sketch that looks like a ground plan of the radio factory?

He told her he was writing his impressions of Russia.

And what is that thing on the wall, the little fixture near the sofa bed that seems to have no earthly use? Is someone listening to what we say?

Even now, after Stalin, she wasn't sure who to trust. Her own uncle Ilya was a colonel in the MVD. In his uniform he was like a painted hero of the Great Patriotic War. Alek wanted her to find out everything she could about Ilya's rank, his salary, his duties. She knew his position had something to do with the timber industry. A sensitive post but not at all related to spies or counterspies. He was Head of Timber or something similar. That was her impression.

Alek told her to find out more. It was for the sketches he was writing of Russia.

Sometimes Alek rented a boat alone and let it drift along the river past their building. He would shout her name, call repeatedly into the wind until she appeared on the balcony to wave. His return wave was like a child's, a deep and excited delight. He seemed in his little boat to say, "Look at us, a miracle, so true and sure."

Two years earlier, on a vacation trip to Minsk when she lived in Leningrad, Marina had noticed a handsome apartment house with balconies overlooking the river. One terrace was bright with flowers and she'd imagined how lovely it would be to live there. She was certain this was the balcony she stood on now, hers and Alek's, waving, as the boat moved slowly past.

Destiny is larger than facts or events. It is something to believe in outside the ordinary borders of the senses, with God so distant from our lives.

Some people don't believe in God but they color eggs at Easter just to change the pattern of their days.

Postcard #5. A foldout number. "Scenes of Minsk." Oswald is photographed at the Victory Monument, the Palace of Culture, Stalin Square. He is a cheerful enough subject, smiling squarely at the camera, but in fact there is little to be happy about right now.

His application to study at the Patrice Lumumba University of the Friendship of Nations has been turned down. He takes the news hard. It makes him feel small and worthless. The Chief of Student Welcoming writes that the school was created exclusively for youths of the underprivileged countries of Asia, Africa and Latin America. Lee wonders how they can think he is privileged. It is part of the general stupidity about life in the U.S.

What else? Well, he has written to the U.S. embassy in Moscow to ask for his passport back. He's a little nervous about this, considering he dumped the passport in their lap, practically forced them to take it, and then said some things he wishes he hadn't about military secrets. Would they want to prosecute him if he returned?

What else? There's this funny little device on the wall of his flat and it's not a socket, a light switch or a thing to hang a picture from. Not only that. He keeps seeing a car marked "Driving School" going up and down his street. Maybe his street is the site of the final exam, he thinks, except there is never a student in the car.

He believes they are watching him because they think he is a false defector sent by the Office of Naval Intelligence. He easily sees the possibility that ONI is waiting to get him out of here so he can tell them what he's learned.

He *knows* someone is intercepting his mail because right after he wrote to the U.S. embassy, his monthly payments from the so-called Red Cross suddenly disappeared, cutting his income in half. He took the money in the first place because he was hungry and broke and there was snow on the ground in Moscow. He didn't want to think about the true source of the funds. They were paying him for defecting, for answering questions about his military service. Now that he wants to go home, the money stops coming.

No sign of Alek. Not a word. Total silence.

Maybe this is all Alek. It is everything Alek. It is get the goods on him. It is pin him to the wall when all I want to do is study.

I still hadn't told my wife of my desire to return to US.

His friend Erich introduces him to some Cuban students and he likes talking to them, likes exchanging complaints about the dreariness of Minsk. The Cubans have a talent and a flair. There is an integrity in the Cuban cause, he believes. It is an underdog effort. Here, people use the party to get ahead. The party is an instrument of material gain.

He is photographed one more time, wearing dark glasses.

Near his building was a five-hundred-foot radio tower enclosed in barbed wire and patrolled by armed guards with the usual snarling dogs. Not far away were two smaller structures, just as well guarded. These were jamming towers, designed to interfere with high-frequency broadcasts from Munich and other Western cities.

He saw himself writing this story for Life or Look, the tale of an ex-Marine who has penetrated the heart of the Soviet Union, observing everyday life, seeing how fear rules the country. Chocolate is four times more expensive than in the U.S. No choice, however small, is left to the discretion of the individual.

He has taken photographs of the airport, the polytechnic institute and an army office building, just to have, to save for later.

"A strange sight indeed," he would write, "is the picture of the local party man delivering a political sermon to a group of robust simple working men who through some strange process have been turned to stone. Turned to stone all except the hard faced communists with roving eyes looking for any bonus-making catch of inattentiveness on the part of any worker."

He saw himself in the reception room at Life or Look, his manuscript in a leather folder in his lap. What is it called, morocco?

He got his friend Erich to give him lessons in German.

When Marina told him she was pregnant he thought his life made sense at last. A father took part. He had a place, an obligation. This woman was bringing him the kind of luck he never figured on. Marina Prusakova, herself born two months premature, weighing two pounds, from Archangel on the White Sea, halfway round the world from New Orleans. He took her face in his hands. Fair-haired wispy girl. Full mouth, high neck, blue-eyed flower girl, his slender pale narcissus. Let the child look like her, even that little sulky curl of the mouth, her eyes showing fire when she is angry.

He danced her around the room, promised to take better care of her than anyone ever had. She would be the baby until the real baby came.

He told her the stores in America were incredibly well stocked, full of amazing choices. Whatever a baby needed, all you had to do was find the nearest department store. Whole departments for babies. Whole stores, babies only. You've never seen such toys.

He was home first, washing the breakfast dishes. He heard her climb the last flight, getting slower every day. She had ice cream and halvah in a bag.

"They're getting ready to make Stalin disappear," she said. "I walked past the square and it's roped off."

"They'll have to use dynamite."

"They'll drag him down with chains."

She put the food away and sat at the kitchen table, behind him, lighting up a cigarette.

"It's way too big," he told her. "They'll have to blow it up."

"Too many Stalinists still around. I think they'll knock him down with chains and drag him off under cover of dark. So no one knows until it's too late."

"They already know. The square's roped off. Put out that cigarette please."

"I am doing much, much less these days."

"No good for baby. No, no, no," he said.

"I don't do so much, Alek."

"You hide them all around. I find cigarettes in every corner. Very bad for baby."

"I do less and less now. Two cigarettes today. What about the visas?"

"I went all over. The ministries, the departments, a total runaround. They are hopeless people, Marina. They read my mail, so I complain to my brother in my letters about their hopeless bureaucracy."

"You are writing to him and to them. Two letters for the price of one."

"We're saving a fortune," he said.

"Where is Texas actually?"

He washed the coffeepot in tepid water.

"It's where General Walker lives. The head of all the ultra-right hate groups in America. The Worker had a headline today. GENERAL WALKER BIDS FOR FUHRER ROLE. He resigned his army command so he won't have any military restraints when he tries to lead a far-right takeover."

"Should I learn English now?"

"Later, when we get there."

These days and nights were a revelation to him. He was a domestic soul, happy in the home, a householder who did the dishes, chatted with his wife about the wallpaper. It was wonderful to discover this. He had a chance to avoid the sure ruin. It seemed so safe in these small rooms with Marina near him to talk to and touch, to make this Russia seem less vast and secret. So many angers waned as he sat under a lamp reading, reading politics and economics, his wife always near, in a loose dress, pregnant, with streetlights shining on the river.

That night they heard the rumble in their sleep. Two, three, four hollow booms, like some power in the sky, deep-rolling across the night. He lay still, eyes open now, waiting for her to speak, knowing what she would say, word for word.

"What is it, Alek, thunder?"

He heard the last slow rumble.

"They're blowing up the statue of your leader."

Tishkevich, the personnel chief, told Citizen Oswald that his performance as a regulator was unsatisfactory. He was not displaying initiative. He was reacting in an oversensitive manner to helpful remarks from the foreman. He was careless in his work.

He said he was writing a report. He would state all these things and would add that Citizen Oswald takes no part in the social life of the shop.

No trace of Alek. No word. Not a single sign he even knew Oswald was alive.

His mother found him. She wrote a letter telling him that the Marine Corps had given him a dishonorable discharge.

He wrote to his brother to ask whether the government might be planning to take action against him.

He wrote to the U.S. embassy to ask for a government loan so he and his family could travel to America.

He wrote to his mother to ask her to file an affidavit of support on Marina's behalf.

He wrote to Senator John Tower of Texas and to the International Rescue Committee.

The whole process of paperwork channels, endless twisting systems, documents in triplicate—an anxious labor for him to decipher these forms and fill them out.

He was writing to John B. Connally Jr. because he thought that Connally was Secretary of the Navy. He was actually the Governor of Texas.

Marina walked in, carrying the paperback Dr. Spock a friend of hers had sent from England. She sat next to him and he translated passages into Russian. She told him that giving birth is a woman's secret, like something that happens on the ocean floor, in dim light and silent water, the one mystery no one can solve even when we know the biology involved.

Dr. Spock wrote, "Don't be afraid of your baby. Your baby is born to be a reasonable, friendly human being."

Marina looked at him when he translated these lines. She seemed to be asking for the first time, What kind of place is America?

He went back to his letter. Could he tell the Secretary that he was a false defector? He wanted to repair the damage done to him and his family. He knew his rights. He wanted his honorable discharge reinstated. But could he tell the Secretary, the way his mail was constantly intercepted, that he'd been sent by Naval Intelligence to live in the USSR as an ordinary worker, observing the system, photographing areas of strategic value and making note of the details of everyday life?

He saw himself sitting next to a tasseled flag in the Secretary's office, talking to the Secretary, a square-jawed man with honest eyes, a friendly type Texan.

Dawn. Marina wakes me. Its her time.

The experience had a form, a sense of tradition and generation, like his own father standing in a dimly lit hallway waiting for word of a son. Word of Robert Oswald. The second son would not be born until the father was two months dead.

He wrote at once to Robert.

> Well, I have a daughter, June Marina Oswald, 6 lbs. 2 oz., born Feb. 15, 1962 at 10. am. How about that?!
> But then you have a head start on me, although I'll try to catch up. Ha-Ha.
> How are things at your end? I heard over the voice of america that they released Powers the U2 spy plane fellow. Thats big news where you are I suppose. He seemed to be a nice, bright american-type fellow, when I saw him in Moscow.

He put another coat of paint on the secondhand crib while Marina was in the hospital. He dusted and scrubbed the whole flat, did the laundry, ironed her blouses and skirts. In the end the bureaucrats insisted that the baby's middle name must be the same as the father's first. He moved the crib to his side of the bed and slept every night only inches from June Lee.

Stateless, word-blind, still a little desperate, he got up in the middle of a spring night and wrote the Historic Diary.

He wrote it in two sittings, breaking for coffee at 4:00 A.M. He wanted to explain himself to posterity. People would read these words someday and understand the fears and aspirations of a man who only wanted to see for myself what socialism was like.

It was his goodbye to Russia. It signified the official end of a major era in his life. It validated the experience, as the writing of any history brings a persuasion and form to events.

Even as he printed the words, he imagined people reading them, people moved by his loneliness and disappointment, even by his wretched spelling, the childish mess of composition. Let them see the struggle and humiliation, the effort he had to exert to write a simple sentence. The pages were crowded, smudged, urgent, a true picture of his state of mind, of his rage and frustration, knowing a thing but not able to record it properly.

He went back to the first day, fall of 1959, jumping right in, writing in a child's high fever in which half-waking dreams, dreams with runny colors, can seem a state of purer knowledge. He felt little charges of excitement when he set to work on his suicide attempt in the voice of Hidell, theatrical, self-mocking. It was the true voice of that episode. He'd heard it then, watching his own fishy blood mix into the bath water (*somewhere, a violin plays*) and he was quick to use it now, sweating in his pajamas at the kitchen table.

Always the pain, the chaos of composition. He could not find order in the field of little symbols. They were in the hazy distance. He could not clearly see the picture that is called a word. A word is also a picture of a word. He saw spaces, incomplete features, and tried to guess at the rest.

He made wild tries at phonetic spelling. But the language tricked him with its inconsistencies. He watched sentences deteriorate, powerless to make them right. The nature of things was to be elusive. Things slipped through his perceptions. He could not get a grip on the runaway world.

Limits everywhere. In every direction he came up against his own incompleteness. Cramped, fumbling, deficient. He knew things. It wasn't that he didn't know.

He stood on the balcony with his coffee. The breeze made his wet pajamas stick to his body. An N on its side becomes a Z.

Even in the rush of filling these pages, he was careful to leave out certain things that could be used in legal argument against his return to the U.S. Yes, the diary was self-serving to a degree but still the basic truth, he believed. The panic was real, the voice of disappointment and loss.

He knew there were discrepancies, messed-up dates. No one could expect him to get the dates right after all this time, no one cared about the dates, no one is reading this for names and dates and spellings.

Let them see the struggle.

He believed religiously that his life would turn in such a way that people would one day study the Historic Diary for clues to the heart and mind of the man who wrote it.

"It will be terrible, Alek, breathing the air of Russia for the last time."

"Your friends already envy you."

"I'll be unbearably sad at the train station. Our good friends standing on the platform. No one will believe I'm actually going. My uncle and aunt will be so unhappy. 'Marinochka, it's like a trip into space.' I can't bear to think about it."

"They'll weep with envy, I bet."

"I want them to throw flowers when our train pulls out. White narcissus petals floating down. The air must be full of flowers."

She imagined ahead. The train station, the border, the ship. But that was as far as she could go. There was nothing collecting in her mind that looked like a picture of a home.

Her husband sat at the kitchen table, writing.

He wrote "The Kollective," a painstaking essay of more than forty handwritten pages on life in Russia, life in Minsk, the hard-fisted discipline of the radio plant. He compiled statistics and asked Marina a hundred questions about food prices, customs, etc. He wanted to examine the subject of control, the Communist Party's domination of every aspect of Soviet life.

He wrote "The New Era," a brief account of the destruction of the Stalin monument in Minsk.

He made notes for an essay on "the murder of history"—the terrible march of Soviet communism. Deportations, mass exterminations, the prostitution of art and culture, "the purposeful curtailment of diet in the consumer slighted population of Russia."

Marina cried, leaving Minsk. A man at the train station stood watching, half hidden in the crowd. She saw him briefly through the window. Was it her former boyfriend Anatoly, with the unruly blond hair, who'd once proposed to her, whose kisses made her reel, or was it the KGB?

When their train approached the Polish border, Lee took his diary pages, his essay pages, all his notes, and began stuffing them in his pants and shirt. He had pages nestled ridiculously in his crotch. Two Soviet customs men came aboard and Marina drew their attention to the baby. The agents gave their luggage a quick look and wished them good fortune.

Aboard the SS *Maasdam* he kept on writing. Rotterdam to New York. He wrote speeches he might one day deliver as a man who'd lived for extended periods under the capitalist and communist systems.

He wrote a forward to "The Kollective."

He wrote a sketch titled "About the Author." The author is the son of an insurance man whose early death "left a far mean streak of indepence brought on by negleck."

The women on the ship were American and European, up-to-date, carefully tailored. Marina seemed a girl in their company, small, shabby-looking, lugging a baby swaddled Russian-style in bands of linen. She sat in their third-class stateroom. Except for mealtimes she was almost always there.

"Should I learn English now?" she said.

Early morning, June 13—June, his daughter's name—he stood on deck and watched the south rim of Manhattan appear at the edge of the sea, an arc of broad buildings crowded in the mist. He was seeing what Leon Trotsky saw near the end of his second foreign exile, 1917, the skyline of the New World. All the time he was in Russia he'd barely thought of Trotsky. But now he could feel the man's spirit. Trotsky was the seeker of asylum. Thrown out of Europe. Hounded by secret police. Crossing the ocean to Wall Street on a rusty Spanish steamer.

Lee was worried that the police would be waiting for him on the Hoboken docks. Here comes the defector with his beggar wife and beggar child. He had answers ready for them, two sets of answers he'd drafted and memorized in the ship's library. If he sensed he could get by as an innocent traveler, those were the answers he'd give, friendly and nonpolitical. But if the authorities were hostile, if they tried to put him on the defensive, if they had information about his activities in Moscow, he was prepared to be defiant and scornful. He would make an issue of his right to certain beliefs. Stand up to them, mock them, look right in their squeezed policemen's eyes and tell them who you are.

A tugboat moved through the harbor dawn, and bridges emerged, piers, highway lights along the Hudson.

If they could only make it to Texas, things would be all right.

PART TWO

Somebody will have to piece me
together. . . .

JACK RUBY
Testimony

15 July

The woman knew some ways to disappear. You could be alone in a room with her and forget she was there. She fell into stillness, faded into things around her. T-Jay liked to imagine this was a skill she'd been refining for years.

He stood at the window eating grapes from a paper bag torn open down the side. Norfolk was a foreign city. It was where trainees from the Farm came to practice the dark arts. Break-ins, dead drops, surveillance exercises, audio penetrations. Newport News and Richmond were also designated foreign. Baltimore was foreign off and on. But T-Jay wasn't here to supervise a break-in and grade the fellows on technique.

She sat on the bed dealing two hands of five-card draw and playing both hands. She was Formosan, she said, and looked young enough to be a war orphan in a public service ad. This was his third visit to the narrow room. She wore a T-shirt stenciled USS Dickson, which he hadn't noticed her putting on. Her nakedness was unstriking, so natural it seemed involuntary. He could easily believe she lived that way.

He watched her crash a magazine against the wall, trying to bat a horsefly. Seconds later he forgot her again.

The thing that hovers over every secret is betrayal. Sooner or later someone reaches the point where he wants to tell what he knows. Mackey didn't trust Parmenter. There were a thousand career officers like Parmenter. Their strongest conviction is lunch. He didn't trust Frank Vásquez. Frank had spied on fellow exiles at Mackey's direction in the months before the invasion. Frank was hard to figure. He had the heart of a *chivato*, a bleating little goat-face spy, but he was also quietly determined once he had an object in mind. Mackey didn't trust David Ferrie. Ferrie knew that weapons for the operation were being supplied by Guy Banister. He probably also knew that Banister had offered to channel cash from the New Orleans rackets to maintain the team of shooters. The larger the secret, the less safe it was with someone like Ferrie. There were others who would have to be recruited. Eventually one of them would reach the point. He knew how they thought, these men who float through plots devised by others. They want to give themselves away, in whispers, to someone standing in the shadows.

He drew a chair up to the bed and played one of the poker hands. Why did he have the feeling he was spoiling her fun? She had short chopped hair and narrow hips and a casual, almost dismissive manner, a kind of body slang that T-Jay took to be her free adaptation of the local style. She walked like a girl shooting a cart down a supermarket aisle.

"I ought to teach you gin rummy. It's a better game for two to play."

"Why, you coming back?"

"I might."

"You might not."

"I might not."

"So why do I learn?" she said.

He liked the idea that whores were profound. He was respectful of whores. They were quick in their perceptions—it was a quick business—and he sometimes had the feeling they could tell him things about himself that he'd missed completely. They had access to the starker facts. This made him wary and respectful.

She took his right hand and placed it against hers, palms touching. He didn't get the point at first. Then he realized she was comparing the size of their hands. The difference made her laugh.

"What's funny?"

She told him his hand was funny.

"Why mine? Why not yours?" he said. "If the difference is great, maybe you're the funny one, not me."

"You're the funny one," Lu Wan said.

She matched left hands now and fell sideways to the bed laughing. Maybe she thought they were two different species. One of them was exotic and it wasn't her.

The beer was warm now. He shook the bottle and looked at her.

"Stores close," she said.

It was Everett who'd made the leap. Everett took the once-bold idea of assassinating Castro and turned it over in his mind, finding it unworkable and crude. He struck a countermeasure that made better sense on every level. It was original, spare and clean. The man we really want is JFK. Mackey gave him every credit. Everett was a complex and passionate man who could think economically. All over Langley and Miami they were still formulating plans to hit Fidel. It was an industry like wood pulp or shoes. Everett had seen the logic in staying home. The idea had power and second sight. Of course Everett did not plan to shoot Kennedy in the strict sense. Only to lay down fire in the street. He wanted a surgical miss.

The second leap was Mackey's. He made it after hearing Everett's plan, driving alone toward the Louisiana border, his sunglasses on the dash in the softfall of evening light, two years to the day after Pigs. They had to take it one more step. Everett's obsession was scattered in technique. The plan grew too twisty and deep. Everett wanted mazes that extended to infinity. The plan was anxious, self-absorbed. It lacked the full heat of feeling. They had to take it all the way. It was a revelation to him that in the moment he saw what had to be done, feeling the crash of air on the hood of the car, he felt the oddest goddamn sympathy for President Jack.

There was fruit juice in the refrigerator. He drank some and handed her the bottle. She wiped her mouth with her hand, then drank and wiped her mouth again. A ship's horn sounded on the river. He took the bottle and put it down and she slipped out of the T-shirt. He put a knee to the edge of the bed, watching her pass imperceptibly into a second skin. All trace of personality was gone. He'd never known a woman who phased so completely into her body. She had a body that could reshape itself, roll itself into a straw ball, make sex a little mystery of sun-glint and shadow. He had a hand on the bedpost. They were screwing on top of a magazine and the pages stuck to her, rattling hard.

In stages, through a marriage, a career of sorts as a roving paramilitary, a fall from official grace, he had become a man with no fixed address. To a certain way of thinking, this was the stuff of paramount despair. He was getting on to forty, loose in the world, nothing to show for the time and risk. Yet here he was, starting up his car for the long drive south and feeling a curious edge of contentment, feeling charged with advantage. He had Jack Kennedy's picture stuck in his mind and nobody even knew he was out here, a man they used to pay to teach other men the fundamentals of deadly force.

Win Everett was in his daughter's room listening to her read from a book of stories with pop-up figures. Mary Frances left these story sessions to him. She was impatient with Suzanne's actressy moods and thought the child ought to be learning to read, not deliver lines. Win followed every word. His face changed as the girl's did, shifting through emotions and roles.

It was uncanny how these tales affected him, gave him a sense of what it was like to be a child again. He found he could lose himself in the sound of her voice. He searched her face, believing he could see what she saw, line by line, in the grave and fateful progress of a tale. His eyes went bright. He felt a joy so strong it might be measured in the language of angelic orders, of powers and dominations. They were alone in a room that was itself alone, a room that hung above the world.

Later he sat downstairs turning the pages of a magazine. He knew he'd become remote from the cutting edge of the operation. He used Parmenter to talk to Mackey. They both used Mackey to find out what was going on at 544 Camp Street. He was wary of Oswald. He only wanted to know selective things. He was putting too much distance between himself and the others. Did he expect his themes to develop in the field through otherworldly means? He was making the same mistakes the Senior Study Effort had made before the Cuban invasion. He didn't know if he could pull himself out. He half wanted to lose control. He wanted a way out of fear and premonition.

Plots carry their own logic. There is a tendency of plots to move toward death. He believed that the idea of death is woven into the nature of every plot. A narrative plot no less than a conspiracy of armed men. The tighter the plot of a story, the more likely it will come to death. A plot in fiction, he believed, is the way we localize the force of the death outside the book, play it off, contain it. The ancients staged mock battles to parallel the tempests in nature and reduce their fear of gods who warred across the sky. He worried about the deathward logic of his plot. He'd already made it clear that he wanted the shooters to hit a Secret Service man, wound him superficially. But it wasn't a misdirected round, an accidental killing, that made him afraid. There was something more insidious. He had a foreboding that the plot would move to a limit, develop a logical end.

Lancer is going to Miami.

Mary Frances moved past the doorway. Then she ran water in the kitchen. He heard her looking for something on the back stairway. He heard the kitchen radio. He waited for her to pass by the porch window with the watering can. It was an old metal can, gray and dented, and he waited to hear her walk across the porch. He listened carefully. She was still in the kitchen. That was all right.

As long as he knew where she was. She had to be close and he had to know where she was. Those were the two inner rules.

He heard an old familiar voice on the kitchen radio, some voice from the old days of radio, couldn't quite recall the man's name, but famous and familiar, with laughter in the background, and he sat very still as if to draw out the moment, struck by the complex emotion carried on a voice from another era, tender and shattering, a three-line joke that brings back everything.

He turned another page.

There was no date set for the President's trip. But it is definitely going to happen, said Parmenter. He wants to go to Florida because the state voted Republican in 1960 and because the whole South is pissing blood over his civil-rights program. Cape Canaveral, Tampa, Miami. There'll be a motorcade in Miami.

Mary Frances was in the doorway wearing rubber gloves, a scrub brush in her hand.

"Something odd lately? I don't know."

"What?" he said.

"Suzanne? Although it's probably nothing."

"It's not like you."

"Worry over nothing."

"She's all right. She's fine. She's a healthy child."

"With a morbid streak."

"What do you mean?"

"I don't know. Lately she seems."

"What?"

"She's always going off with Missy Tyler. They practically hide from me at times. I don't know, it's just, I think she's so preoccupied lately, so *inner,* and I wonder if there's something unhealthy there."

"Missy's the skinny little redhead."

"Adopted. They hide in corners and whisper solemnly. There's a kind of mood that descends whenever Missy's here. Very sort of haunted-house. Awestruck. Something walks the halls. I get the feeling it's me. I'm a very suspicious presence in this house. The girls hush up when they hear me coming."

"They have their own world. She's dreamy," he said.

"She listens to a Dallas disc jockey named the Weird Beard."

"What does he play?"

"It's not what he plays. He plays top forty. It's what he says between records."

"Example."

"Impossible to duplicate. He just like, here I am, on and on. It's a completely other language. But she is fixed to the radio."

"Inka dinka dink."

"I know. It's not like me. Most of my worrying makes sense."

"She read to me for forty minutes nonstop and it was remarkable, remarkable."

" 'Please, Daddy, I want to read some more.' "

"Are you handling plutonium with those gloves?"

" 'Daddy, Daddy, please.' "

He went upstairs, moving slowly in his light and silent way. Miami has an impact, a resonance. City of exiles, unhealed wounds. The President wants a motorcade because the polls show he is losing popularity by the minute. Appear among the multitudes in his long blue Lincoln, men on motorcycles to trim the crowds, men in sunglasses dangling from the sides of the follow-up car. Lancer stands to wave. It is necessary to wing a bystander or Secret Service man in order to validate our credentials. This is how we show them it is real. Plots. The ancients shared in nature by echoing the violence of a windstorm or thunder squall. To share in nature is the oldest human trick. A thought for bedtime.

The watering can was gritty metal with an ugly snub spout.

He found Suzanne awake when he looked inside. There was a cloth-and-vinyl toy at the end of the bed, a football player they'd named Willie Wonder, with padded shoulders and polished chino pants. Win turned the key at Willie's back and sent him on a broken-field run the length of the bed. He broadcast the run in an urgent voice, described missed tackles and downfield blocks, added the roar of the crowd, became the official who signaled touchdown when the toy spun backwards into a pillow. Suzanne showed a pleasure that seemed to start at her feet and creep up her body and into her eyes, making them large and bright.

If he could only keep surprising her, she would have a reason to love him forever.

Mackey drove across a drawbridge over the Miami River. The tires wailed on the iron grid. A white sloop moved upriver in the dark, a little mystery of grace and stealth. Two blocks south of the bridge he saw the first *Volveremos* bumper sticker. Empty streets. His hands sticking to the wheel.

He parked on a sidestreet and walked around the corner to a vast car lot. It took him ten minutes to find Wayne Elko stupidly sprawled in the back seat of a red Impala. The top was down and Wayne was gazing into the night.

"How did I get in here so easy?"

"T-Jay."

"You're the watchman, I hear."

"Where'd you come from?"

"I drove nearly a thousand miles just to see you, Wayne."

"I about gave you up."

Mackey leaned against the car and looked off toward the street as if the sight of the bedraggled Wayne Elko, in bare feet, with clothes and other possessions strewn about, was a little too bleak to take in right now.

"I saw Raymo and what's-his-name. I spent time with them training in the Glades, man. There is Alpha 66 people infesting the Glades. We trained with them a little bit. I never turned my back except to pee."

"Alpha won't bother us. I have long-time contacts in Alpha."

"Are you Agency, T-Jay, or what?"

"Not no more, Bubba. Sold my peewee trailer for small change and here I am. What do they call us, retirees?"

"We train with real shit weapons."

"Weapons are coming."

"The stars are fucking fantastic. I love the Glades for the clear nights. It's a whole other world out there. See those hawks zoom.

I wouldn't mind going out again. My back's messed up from sleeping in the car."

"We have a friendly source of funds will come through for you soon."

"When I was with Interpen, we had hotel and casino money."

"We have a fellow in New Orleans."

Mackey didn't trust Guy Banister. Guy was past it now, a once able man who'd grown fierce and unsteady in his hatreds. He was delivering money and weapons but would not support the operation blindly. Mackey would have to tell him who the target was or else invent a target. Either way he risked betrayal. Guy was deep in causes and affiliations. He had influence in a dozen directions. It was not reasonable to expect a man like that to sit and watch the event unfold. He'd want to take an active hand. He'd set loose forces that would threaten the self-contained system Mackey wanted to create.

He didn't trust Wayne Elko. Not that Wayne would knowingly turn. It was a question of temperament, unpredictability. Wayne had a gift for the celebrated fuck-up. He also had a nature that went violent in a flash. There was something a little viperish about him. He drawled and rambled and looked sleepy-eyed, stroking his lean jaw, then suddenly took offense. He was a man who took offense in a serious way. Scraggly and lank. Those ripe eyes bulging. An idea of himself as born to the warrior class. Mackey was sure he could get Wayne to do just about anything he wanted, just so long as it challenged his sense of limits.

"We did a certain amount of small arms in the Glades," he said to T-Jay now. "They had me using a pistol on a stationary target. I'm making the mental leap this is what you told them you want."

Wayne's assignment wouldn't take him anywhere near President Jack. He would be working strictly short-range. It was a matter of fitting the man to the nature of the task. He was the intimate killer type.

In Fort Worth

She wore shorts like any housewife in America. She thought she was in a dream at first, walking on the street in bare legs, with her hair cut short, looking in shopwindows. She saw things you could not buy in Russia if you had unlimited wealth, if you had money spilling out of your closets. She knew she hadn't lived in the world long enough to make comparisons, and Russia suffered terribly in the war, but it was impossible to see all this furniture, these racks and racks of clothing without being struck by amazement.

They had very little money, practically no money. But Marina was happy just to walk the aisles of the Safeway near Robert's house. The packages of frozen food. The colors and abundance.

Lee got angry one night, coming back from a day of looking for work. He told her she was becoming an American in record-breaking time.

They were like people anywhere, people starting life a second time. If they quarreled it was only because he had a different nature in America and that was the only way he could love.

Neon was a revelation, those gay lights in windows and over movie marquees.

One evening they walked past a department store, just out strolling, and Marina looked at a television set in the window and saw the most remarkable thing, something so strange she had to stop and stare, grab hard at Lee. It was the world gone inside out. There they were gaping back at themselves from the TV screen. She was on television. Lee was on television, standing next to her, holding Junie in his arms. Marina looked at them in life, then looked at the screen. She saw Lee hoist the baby on his shoulder, with people passing in the background. She turned and looked at the people, checking to see if they were the same as the ones in the window. They had to be the same but she was compelled to look. She didn't know anything like this could ever happen. She walked out of the picture and then came back. She looked at Lee and June in the window, then turned to see them on the sidewalk. She kept looking from the window to the sidewalk. She kept walking out of the picture and coming back. She was amazed every time she saw herself return.

Lee stood in front of Robert's house and watched his mother approach. She looked shorter, rounder, her hair gone gray and worn in a bun. She was working as a practical nurse and showed up in uniform, all white, with dark-rimmed glasses and the little bent hat that nurses wear. It was the official uniform of motherhood and she looked like the angel of terror and memory sweeping down from the sky.

She embraced him crying. She held his face in her hands and looked into his eyes. She searched for her lost son in the tapered jaw and thinning hair. All this love and pain confused him. This blood depth of feeling. He felt a struggling pity and regret.

She was writing a book, she said, about his defection.

One day they were living with Robert, the next day with his mother. He didn't know how it happened. She took an apartment large enough for all of them, although she had to sleep in the living room. It was like growing up with her all over again, the bed in the living room, and one night they stayed up late, mother and son, after Marina and the baby were asleep.

"She doesn't look somehow Russian to me."

"She is Russian, Mother."

"Well I think she is beautiful."

"She admires you. She says the place is so clean and neat. She likes your soft hair, she says. But no book, Mother."

"I went to see President Kennedy. I have done my research. I had a lot of extenuating circumstances because of your defection."

"Mother, you are not going to write a book."

"It is my life as I was forced to live it because of not knowing if you were alive or dead. I can write what's mine, Lee."

"She has relatives there that would be jeopardized."

"Jeopardized. But you have given a public stenographer ten dollars to type pages for your own book."

"That is a different book."

"It is Russia and the evils of that system."

"It is a different book. 'The Kollective.' It deals with living conditions and working conditions. I will change people's names to protect them. Don't think we don't appreciate that you have bought clothes for the baby and that you're cooking and feeding us, so forth."

"It was the ten dollars I gave you that you gave that woman for the typing."

"It is a book of observations, Mother. I owe money to the State Department for getting me home. Robert paid our airfare from New York. I am only looking for ways to pay back my debts."

"I have a right to my book," she said. "The President was not available at that time but I spoke to figures in the government during a snowstorm who made promises that they would look into the matter."

"It is only an article, not a book. I am having notes typed for an article. It is so many pages."

"How many pages did she type?"

"Ten pages. That's all I had money for."

"A dollar a page I call a rooking."

"I smuggled those notes next to my skin right out of Russia."

"Marina watched a daytime movie with Gregory Peck with me sitting right here and she knew Gregory Peck."

"So what, he is well known everywhere."

"We have to use the dictionary to talk."

"Little by little she'll get the hang."

"I think she knows more than she's letting on," his mother said.

He found a job as a sheet-metal worker, drudge and grime and long hours and low pay. They left his mother's and moved to their own place, one-half of a matchstick bungalow, furnished, across the street from a truck lot and loading docks. This was the shipping and receiving entrance of a huge Montgomery Ward operation. Marina went to the retail store. She walked the aisles. She told Lee about the cool smooth musical interior.

All the homes on their street were bungalows. Everybody called it Mercedes Street. The lease for the apartment said Mercedes Street. Lee's map of Fort Worth said Mercedes Street. But the sign on a pole at the corner said Mercedes Avenue.

He sat on the concrete steps out front, next to a baby yucca, reading Russian magazines.

His mother came with a high chair. She came with dishes. Lee told her he didn't want anyone's charity. She came with a parakeet in a cage. It was the same bird in the same cage he had given her in New Orleans when he worked as a messenger.

It is the shadow of his prior life that keeps appearing.

"No more," he told Marina. "You keep the door closed."

"How can I do that to your mother? She is kind to us."

"Keep the door closed. Or she'll move in on us. Absolutely keep her out. She comes with a camera to take pictures of our baby."

"She is the grandmother."

"It is the first phase to moving in."

"It is a picture, Alek."

"This is how she insinuates. This is conniving her way into our house."

"You don't want her coming around but at the same time you try to take advantage of her at every chance."

"That's what mothers are for."

"This is a cruel thing."

"I'm only kidding and don't call me Alek anymore. This is not Alek country. June is not Junka. People will think you don't know your own family by their right names."

"It doesn't sound like kidding when you raise your voice to her."

"You have to learn American kidding. It's how we talk to each other."

"All your life she worked very hard."

"She told you with the dictionary. You and Mamochka."

"I know this. It's very obvious to me."

"Very obvious is only half the story."

"What's the other half?"

He hit her in the face. An open-hand smash that sent her walking backwards to the stove. She stood there with her head tucked against her left shoulder, one hand raised in blank surprise.

A man spoke to him from the other side of the screen door. Lee looked at his bloated face peering in above the set of credentials he held under his chin. Freitag, Donald. Federal Bureau of Investigation. Dark eyes and five o'clock shadow. They agreed to talk in his car.

There was another man in the car, an Agent Mooney. Agent Freitag sat in the front seat with Mooney. Lee sat in back, leaving the rear door open. He thought of a word, Feebees, for FBI. It was dinnertime and sweltering.

"What this is, we want to know about your period of time in

the Soviet Union," Agent Freitag said. "And being back here, who has contacted you at any time that we should know about."

"So if I have something sensitive I know about, they would want to hear it."

"That's correct."

"I assemble ventilators. This is not a sensitive industry."

"You would be surprised how many people link the name Oswald to turncoat and traitor."

"Let me state I was never approached or volunteered to Soviet officials any information about my experiences while a member of the armed forces."

"Why did you travel to the Soviet Union?"

"I don't wish to relive the past. I just went."

"That's a long way to just go."

"I don't have to explain."

"Are you a member of the Communist Party of the United States?"

"No."

Agent Mooney took notes.

"Are you willing to talk to us hooked up to a polygraph?"

"No. Who told you where to find me?"

"It wasn't hard."

"But who told you?"

"We talked to your brother."

"He told you where I live."

"That's correct," Freitag said with some satisfaction. There was a line of beady glisten above his lip.

"Am I being put under surveillance?"

"Would I tell you if you were?"

"Because I was watched in Russia."

"I thought everyone was watched in Russia."

Agent Mooney laughed quietly, his head bobbing.

"My wife is holding dinner," Lee said.

"How is it you were able to get your wife out? They don't let people out just by asking."

"I made no arrangements with them to do anything."

They covered several subjects. Then Freitag made a faint gesture to his partner, who put away his pen and notebook. There was a pause, a clear change in mood.

"What we are mainly concerned, if there are suspicious circumstances to inform us immediately of any contact."

"You're saying let you know."

"We are asking cooperation if individuals along the lines of Marxist or communist."

"I want to know if I'm being recruited as an informer."

"We are asking cooperation."

"So if someone contacts me."

"That's right."

"I will inform the Bureau."

"That's correct."

Lee said he would think about the matter. He got out of the car and closed the door. He glanced at the license plate as he walked behind the car on his way across the street and into the house. He wrote the license-plate number in his notebook along with Agent Freitag's name. Then he looked up the Fort Worth FBI office in the phone directory and wrote that number in his book beneath the agent's name and the license plate, just to have for the record, to build up the record.

Marina called him in to dinner.

He sat in a corner of the large room and watched them talk and eat. Their conversation had a munching sound. They milled and dodged, Russians, Estonians, Lithuanians, Georgians, Armenians. It was an evening with the émigré colony, some of the twenty or thirty families in the Dallas–Fort Worth area, English-speaking, Russian-speaking, French-speaking, constantly comparing backgrounds and education. Baby June was in his lap.

Marina always looked her prettiest on these evenings. People gathered round, prodding her for news. She was recently arrived, of course, and some of them had come here decades ago, thirty years, forty years some of them. Her pure Russian impressed the old guard. She was small and frail. They pictured Soviet women as hammer-throwers, brawny six-footers who work in brick factories. She stood smoking, sipping wine. She wore the clothes they gave her. They gave her dresses and stockings, comfortable shoes. He had his book he could not afford to get typed sitting in a closet in a Carrollton Clasp envelope, notes on scraps of paper, brown bag paper, and they are giving her dental work and stockings. Everything is measured in money. They spend their lives collecting material things and call it politics.

He watched them shake hands and embrace. They complained to Marina that he did not give them a human hello. They thought he was a Soviet spy. Anyone back from Russia who did not share their beliefs was a spy for the Soviet. Their beliefs were Cadillacs and air conditioners.

They gave him shirts which he returned.

A few of them came to his house now and then to take Marina to the dentist or supermarket. Show her how to shop. Here is the baby food. Here is the Swiss cheese. He kept his library books on a small table near the door where they would have to notice as they entered and left. There were books on Lenin and Trotsky plus the Militant and the Worker. Show them who he is. They didn't want to hear what he had to say about Russia unless it was bad. They closed in on the bad.

George came and sat next to him. The only one he could talk to was George de Mohrenschildt. A tall man, warm-spirited and assured, with a relish for conversation and a voice that surrounds you like a calm day.

"You know, Lee, you have told me practically nothing about Minsk."

"It's not an interesting place."

"It's interesting to me, you know, because I lived there as a child. My father was a marshal of nobility of Minsk Province in the czarist days. Not that I cling to this nonsense. But I am Baltic nobility, which some of my wives adored."

"Minsk, we had to get on line sometimes to buy vegetables."

"You prefer Texas?"

"I don't prefer Texas. Marina prefers Texas."

"Do you want me to tell you what Dallas is? It's the city that proves that God is really dead. Look at these people, wonderful people actually, most of them, but they come by choice to this bleak empty right-wing milieu. It's the local politics they find so congenial. Anticommunist this, anticommunist that. All right they have suffered, some of them, in one way or another, sometimes horribly. You know how I feel about Marxism. I will tell you frankly the word Marxism is very boring to me. It is very hard for me to find a word or subject more boring than this. But you and I know the Soviet Union is a going concern. We accept this and accept the realities. To the old guard there is no such place. It doesn't exist. A blank on the map."

George was in his fifties, still dark-haired, broad across the chest, an oil geologist or engineer, something like that. Lee liked to switch from English to Russian and back again, talking to George. He could take the older man's kidding and teasing and even his advice. George gave advice without making you feel he wanted a week of thank-yous.

"Marina says you have written some notes or something about Minsk. Something, I don't know what she said, impressions of the city."

"Everything I learned at the radio plant plus the whole structure of how they work and live."

A woman picked up June and made the same noises that Marina's relatives used to make, shaking the baby and gabbling at her.

George said, "You know, I am sitting and looking at this wonderful child and I am saying to myself, I can't help it but she looks just like Khrushchev. She is a baby Khrushchev with a big round head, a bald head, little narrow eyes."

"Kennedy would be better, for looks."

"I admire Kennedy. I think this man is very good for the country."

"Jacqueline, for looks."

"And his wife. And Jacqueline too. I knew her on Long Island when she was a girl. Very lovely child. Although he is quite a libertine with the women, this particular President, I understand. Not that I consider this a flaw. I am the last to say. But I'll tell you about some women. They will love you for your weaknesses. They will love you precisely for your flaws. This means trouble, my friend."

Lee found the child back in his arms. He said, "What Kennedy is doing for civil rights is the most important thing. He started off badly with the Bay of Pigs disaster. But I think he learned."

"He changed."

"I saw American Negro athletes get the greatest glory for their country and then they went back home."

"It's a humiliation to me," George said, "that I am sitting in a room with not a single Negro here."

"To face blind hatred and discrimination."

"Kennedy is trying to make the shift. Painfully slow but he's doing it. It's humiliating to me that I can't befriend a Negro without consequences among my friends or in my profession. I live in University Park. We are incorporated, a township. If a Negro family tries to move in, the township buys the house at two or three times its value. The family disappears, goodbye, like magic."

"Look at the anti-Kennedy feeling here."

"Poisonous. Young Dallas matrons tell the most vicious jokes. Their eyes light up in the strangest way. It's clear to me they want him dead."

George went across the room to embrace an elderly man and woman. Lee found himself smiling at the scene. He watched people steer through the room, holding plates of food before them. A man offered Marina a cigarette from a black-and-white case. Lee had his collection. He'd written to an obscure press in New York for a twenty-five-cent booklet called *The Teachings of Leon Trotsky*. Back comes a letter saying it's out of print. At least they sent a letter. He saved their letters. The point is they are out there and willing to reply. He was starting a collection of documents.

She would never refuse a cigarette.

He planned to write to the Socialist Workers Party for information about their aims and policies. Trotsky is the pure form. It was satisfying to send away and get this obscure stuff in the mail. It was a channel to sympathetic souls, a secret and a power. It gave him a breadth and reach beyond the life of the bungalow and the welding company.

She is the type that doesn't refuse. It is thrilling to her to be given things. She will take your cigarettes, money, paper clips, postage stamps, whatever you want to give her. There is a certain woman that glows at the smallest gift.

Trotsky's name was Bronstein.

Half a bungalow on an unpaved street. He slept next to his Junie, fanning her with a magazine in the middle of the night.

When George came back he did a curious thing. He moved his chair around and sat facing Lee, with his back to the room. He had a hanky folded to a point in his breast pocket. His tie was brown.

"Now, what I am talking about is having you show me these notes of yours, whatever condition they are in, because it is Minsk and I am interested."

"It is also the system. The whole sense of historic ideas being corrupted by the system."

"Good, wonderful, you must let me see."

"It isn't all typed yet," Lee said.

"Typed. I will have it typed. Please, this is the least of your worries."

"It's called 'The Kollective.' I did serious research. I read journals and analyzed the whole economy."

"Is there anything else? Because I would like to see anything at all from that period. Observations of the most innocent type. What people wear. Show me everything."

"Why?"

"Okay I will tell you why. It is really very simple. In recent years I have been approached a number of times about my travels abroad. It is strictly routine. In other words you went to such-and-such, Mr. de Mohrenschildt, and we'd like to know what did you see, who did you meet, what is the layout of the factory you toured and so on. It is routine intelligence that thousands of travelers every year say okay this is what I saw. It is called the Domestic Contacts Division and there is a man who asked me to talk to you strictly low-key, friendly, of the CIA, and this is what I am doing. He is a good fellow, reasonable fellow, so on. I am always traveling, I am always coming back, and when I come back there is Mr. Collings on my doorstep and we have a chat, low-key, with drinks. I have written things on my trips which I give him willingly and I have given things to the State Department because this is my philosophy, Lee, that I must take on the coloration, let us say, of the place where I am living and earning my income at the particular time. A country is like a business to me. I move from one to another as opportunity dictates. I will learn Croatian in Yugoslavia. I will learn the French patois as the Haitians speak it. This is how I survive as someone who has come through a revolution and a world war and so on. I am always willing to cooperate. I take on the coloration. It is my message to them that I am not the enemy. A necessary gesture. I am not in the market to be persecuted. In other words here is my itinerary, here are my notes, here are my impressions. Let's have a drink and be friends."

"It isn't all typed."

"Please, I have my consulting firm, you know, with paper, pencils and a girl who types. I will give you a copy, of course, plus the original notes."

"You will also give a copy to Mr. Collings."

"This is understood. They collect and analyze. It can be helpful to someone in your position if you cooperate. Let's face it, you are in a cramped position. If I am a Mr. Collings and I see cooperation from an individual who can use and appreciate a better-paying job, then I am inclined to make a call. This happens all the time."

Lee bounced the child on his knee to quiet her down.

"Also, George, I would like to publish 'The Kollective.' "

"I would advise you no. I would say no, this is not right for you at this time. Let us look at the work. Then we discuss publication. You will be compensated one way or another, I guarantee this. These people have a thousand ways. They reach across the world. It's amazing. How do you think you re-entered this country? When a person defects, his name is put on the FBI's watch list. There is a lookout card that is prepared in such cases. But they returned your passport. They let Marina in. They gave you a loan and let you in."

"They were keeping an eye all that time."

"They're still keeping an eye. You're an interesting individual. I'm sure they would very much like to learn about your contacts in the Soviet Union. We'll have a nice talk, you and I, in private somewhere, without the baby listening in."

George laughed. They both laughed.

First Freitag and his partner, now this man Collings. They were swarming all over him like ants on a melon rind.

He looked at Marina. She was standing slightly curled, listening carefully to someone. Even in the heat and smoke she looked wind-scrubbed and fresh. Never love me for my weaknesses, he wanted to say. Never take the blame for me. Never think it is your fault when I am the one. I am always the one.

He slapped her on the side of the head and she took half a swing at him. He sat down and opened a magazine. She could tell he was turning the pages without really looking. She wanted something to throw. She grabbed a sheet of paper and crumpled it up and threw it at him. It bounced off his arm but he didn't react. She went to the table and ate some of her dinner, looking at him. She stared hard. She wanted to make him uncomfortable, make it hard for him to read. She felt stupid, throwing a piece of paper.

"No cigarettes," he said. "I do not want you smoking. That is period, forever."

"If I want to smoke once in a while."

"No good for baby. Very, very bad. You could not fill my bathtub? It is too much to come home, for me to expect a warm bath is ready, after a day of noise and sweat."

"I don't smoke too much. It is reasonable, what I smoke."

"Lazy, lazy girl."

"I make dinner. I scrub on my knees."

"I scrub on my knees," he said.

He flung the magazine sidearm, whipped it hard against the wall. The baby started in to cry. He got up and walked over to Marina.

"I scrub on my knees," he said.

He hit her in the face. She sat in the chair, with leftover food in her plate.

"I scrub on my knees."

She covered up. He hit her again. Then he went back to his chair and picked up a book. She took the plate of leftovers to the sink and left it there without scraping the food into the little pail. She left it there for him to clean. He would do it too. There was always something lying around after a fight that he would carefully clean.

"You tell those Russians how we live our lives, about our sex, our private lives."

"This is how friends communicate," she said.

"Everything is public for you."

"I trust friends, that they understand how things are. Who else do I talk to? I need these friends."

"You don't need to tell our private life. I don't want them coming here. Keep them out."

"I must keep your mother out. I must keep my friends out."

"My own brother told the FBI."

"It's no secret where we live. What did he tell? People know where we live. We can't hide where we live."

He read the book. She turned on the tap and watched water swirl into the drain. The baby was crying.

"You like your wine," he said, not really talking to her.

"Teach me English."

"You wait for them to refill your wine."

"I never loved you. I took pity on a foreigner."

"Meanwhile cigarettes."

"I tell my friends how you hit me. He doesn't hit so hard. It's just that I have soft skin. That's why they see the marks."

She was standing at the sink with her back to the room. She heard him get up and come toward her. She picked up a sponge and began cleaning the edges of the sink. He hit her in the side of the face. He stood there a moment, deciding whether one was enough. Then he went and sat down and she wet the sponge and worked a stain out of the countertop.

They were unloading across the street. She heard truck engines, men's voices. She had another bite of leftovers and cleaned the windowsill behind the sink.

"I tell them he is careful of my well-being. He hits very lightly. It's only my fair skin that makes it look so bad."

He came over and started pummeling her on both arms. She turned off the tap. He hit her high on the arms, using open hands.

"I tell them it isn't his fault if I bruise so easily."

She put her hands to the sides of her head for protection. He kept hitting her on the upper arms like some kid's game of slap-the-arm. He hit in rhythm, hitting with the right hand, then the left. He worked quietly behind her, one and a-two, breathing through his nose. She could feel the labor of his concentration.

She lay in the dark and thought of the paper she'd crumpled and thrown. It was lesson number seven. An elderly man in the Russian colony sent her pages in the mail to improve her English. At the top of the first page he wrote in large, large letters, in Russian, *My name is Marina*. She was supposed to write the English words below. Lesson number two, *I live in Fort Worth*. Lesson number three, *We buy groceries on Tuesday*. Each lesson had its own page. She mailed him the finished pages and he corrected them and mailed them back, with new lessons for her to work on. Now lesson seven was crumpled and he would wonder how it happened.

Lee came out of the bathroom and got into bed. She felt how he carefully eased into bed so he wouldn't disturb her if she was asleep. She was facing away from him, of course.

She thought of Holland again. This was a recent thing, out of nowhere, thinking of Holland, of their train journey across Europe and her surprise at seeing Dutch villages and hearing church bells ring. It is the cleanest country in the world, unbelievably clean, with cozy houses and spotless streets and fences in the meadows that are perfectly straight.

She didn't want her baby sucking nervous milk.

She thought they would have a life that was not unusual in any way. Simple moments adding up. They had matching scars on the arm, which meant they were marked by fate to meet and fall in love.

She thought of walking the aisles of Montgomery Ward. She went in out of the heat to piped-in music and little ringing bells. The floors were polished. The aisles were immensely long, bordered with cosmetics in display cases and counters full of shiny handbags, with dresses spreading into other rooms. Fragrances drifting everywhere.

He wanted to go to college at night and take courses in politics and economics. But there was the need to make a living which interfered.

She saw him from a distance even when he was hitting her. He was never fully there.

Mamochka bought her modest shorts, pleated, with deep pockets. This was a difference of opinion.

She knew he was trying to sense if she was awake. He was on the verge of saying something or leaning over to touch. He would probably touch, rise on an elbow and touch her on the hip with his hand curled soft. She felt his desire like an airstream in the dark. It was absolutely there. He was waiting, thinking if this was the time. His own wife and he had to think.

She thought of Holland again.

She thought of landing in New York. One night in a hotel in the middle of cascading neon. Rivers and lakes of neon.

He is someone you see from a distance.

Fragrances. The floors remarkably clean. She stood in an area with TVs stacked everywhere. She watched TV half the morning, five different programs side by side. She walked the aisles. It was cool and peaceful. Nobody talked to you unless you asked a question or made a purchase and she didn't have the means of doing either.

He went out to find food and she was alone with the baby in New York, an old hotel, and she took a washcloth and cleaned the grime off the venetian blinds.

She sensed he was going to touch, he was making up his mind to touch, after the beating, after everything they'd said.

They were brought together by fate but she wasn't sure who he really was. Sharing the bathroom she wasn't sure. Making love she didn't know who he was.

When she learned English he would be less distant. It was absolutely true.

We buy groceries on Tuesday.

They made love, when they did, in a tender way, full of honest forgiving.

There is a broadsheet plastered crookedly to a wall near their bungalow.

THE VATICAN IS THE WHORE OF REVELATION.
Lee translates for Marina.

Marguerite was calm. She stood at the ironing board running the iron over her uniform blouse. She faced the living room, which had a sofa with a mound of bright pillows, two comfortable chairs, a writing desk and TV set and a decorative stand with ivy twisting out of a long pot. She ironed the uniform every chance, keeping it crisp and fresh. She worked in other people's homes, by word of mouth, some of the best homes in Fort Worth, taking care of babies of the rich.

And I mentioned to the woman that it is two weeks to Lee's birthday and he doesn't have work clothes, so she said, "Mrs. Oswald, what build is he?" And I told her. And he was about the same build as her husband. And she got out the work clothes her husband didn't want, some worn-out pairs of pants, she wanted me to pay, for ten dollars. Here is a woman, she knows I make a hard living, she knows they are a young couple starting a home in a new country. This is being rich in Fort Worth, asking payment from a nurse for used clothing. I am calm about it today, your honor, but this to me is very strong in my mind, that here is another instance of a troubled situation. Because from the very first day I looked in his face and saw a different boy. And I was like, What have they done to my boy over there? Because his skin was not fair and smooth as previous. Because his face was drawn, a tint of sand to a tint of ash gray. Because his hair was kinky out of nowhere. Because his hair was coming out, which he says himself, from a full head of hair to badly thinning in front that you could practically see his scalp. We had him bend his head down, Robert and I, to where we could actually look at the top of his head in a bright light. Judge, this is a family where the men have always displayed full heads of hair and he is still a boy. He said it is the cold of Russia. I thought to myself it is shock treatments. This is my conclusion, his being an agent of our government and lost for a year. There are many ways this figures out, remembering the incident where we sat watching the television in my apartment on West Seventh Street after she came home with a cancan petticoat and some hose that Lee bought with a few dollars from Robert and me, and we sat watching the television and she said to me, "Mama, it is Gregory Peck," and I looked at the movie and it was Gregory Peck sitting on a horse. Now, about my suspicions does a foreign girl know movie stars? I think it is frankly something to examine. I know I have not traveled abroad but when I think of Minsk and the frozen cold, where are the movie magazines in this city? Where are the theaters that show our American West? I am a person who plunges straight into things and this is an incident that shows the character of what I am trying to bring out. Who is this girl and what is she doing here? Is this girl trained to know more than she lets on? I try to talk to Lee about is he happy, does she run a proper household, because there are a lot of Russian friends who are established, with cars and homes, that have publicly interfered. They could not see this Russian girl do without. She pictured America in her mind and these people seem to think she should not be disappointed. I am calm about it today but I am the one who bought her a little longer shorts. The Lord would know me for a liar if I said I stopped bringing things after he told me to stop, but it was only the shorts and the parakeet, and the parakeet was just to give a touch of color because it was bright green, to color up a home in a new country.

He freed the parakeet. He opened the cage and let it go. The boy who adored animals, judge.

But about the shorts it is, "No, Mama, I no like." And I said, "Marina, you are a married woman and it is proper for you to have a little longer shorts than the younger girls." But it is, "No, Mama, this no good." And I am strongly saying that this girl was not home. And this man was working. And I saw myself that this man came home and didn't have any supper in front of him. This couple does not have a maid to give this workingman his supper. We are a family that has struggled to stay together. His daddy collected insurance premiums right up to the moment he went down on the lawn, mowing the lawn in a raging heat. It is Marguerite and Lee ever since.

A family expects you to be one thing when you're another. They twist you out of shape. You have a brother with a good job and a nice wife and nice kids and they want you to be a person they will recognize. And a mother in a white uniform who grips your arms and weeps. You are trapped in their minds. They shape and hammer you. Going away is what you do to see yourself plain.

It was a Sunday and he stood in the empty lobby of the Republic National Bank Building in Dallas. Tan marble everywhere. He was waiting for George de Mohrenschildt. This was the second time he was meeting George. He wore a clean white shirt and the ready-made trousers of rough material he'd bought at the state-run store in Minsk.

George had a handful of keys. He jiggled them in greeting and walked to the elevators. They rode to sixteen and went down deserted corridors. The air was heavy and dense, with a carpet smell, a closeness. George was in tennis shorts and a shirt with an alligator emblem. He had a nice-size office with diplomas on the wall.

"You've been reading about this nut-case general."

"I know about him since Russia," Lee said.

"He's getting involved in Cuba now. Sit down. I have your papers."

"He's only reflecting the feelings of what most people think. What Walker says and does, this is white America."

"There are missiles poised to demolish us all and we have to open the newspaper and see this man."

"It is Mississippi, it is Cuba, it is wherever he sees the opportunity."

"He is making a switch to Cuba. He will jump into the Cuba thing. Wait and see."

"They are asking questions about my mail," Lee said.

"What do you mean?"

"A postal inspector talked to my landlord about the type mail I get."

"What type mail?"

"What some people would say subversive."

"Why do you read this material? It is totally boring material. I know this material without reading a word. It is the definition of boring."

"They are coming at me from a number of angles," Lee said, breathing a little laugh through his nose.

George gave him a copy of the material that had been typed since their last talk. He returned the original handwritten pages, page fragments, random notes, autobiographical notes, notes for speeches.

"I'm not disappointed, Lee. This is solid work, the main essay in particular. I think it is definitely a prospect that you move here to Dallas with a new job, something more suited. You'll come to my house. You'll be nearby, for easy visits. I'll tell you the most interesting thing about the house where I live. It is less than two miles from the house of General Walker."

George stuck out his index finger and raised his thumb.

The door opened and a tall man with cropped gray hair walked in. He was very tan and wore a tan suit with a blue shirt and he had to be Marion Collings. George introduced them. Collings had the spare build, the leanness and fitness of an older man who wants you to know he is determined to outlive you.

George left.

"This essay you've written," Collings said. "Very impressive, very thorough. I appreciate the fact you've allowed us to see it. You picked up things only a trained observer ordinarily spots. Many interesting facts about the radio plant and the workers. Well organized, a nice grasp of social interplay. I would say a good beginning. We have something solid to start us out."

"I told George just about everything I remember that I didn't put in 'The Kollective.' "

"Yes, George and I have had our sit-down. I would say the major omission is glaring enough."

"Which is?"

"Lee, if I may, it is not even remotely conceivable that you spent over two and a half years as a defector in the Soviet Union and remained free of contact with the KGB."

"I had an interview with Internal Affairs, MVD, as final clearance for my departure."

"Who cleared your entry? You applied for a visa in Helsinki and had it in two days. Normally a week is what it takes. We happen to know the Soviet consul in Helsinki at that time was a KGB officer."

"You may know it but I didn't. They're all over the place. That doesn't mean I was doing any business. I went there to seek a better life."

"Lee, if I may, once we saw that you wanted out of there, we helped smooth the way. You're an interesting fellow. You've lived in the heart of the USSR for a long period. We want to have a relationship. We're very pragmatic people. We don't care what sort of affair you carried on with the Second Chief Directorate. You had a romance, you broke up. Fine. Happens all the time. Supply some details is all we're looking for. We're not the FBI. We don't pursue with a vengeance, or apprehend and prosecute. We want a relationship. A give-and-take, okay?"

"Is the FBI watching me?"

"I wouldn't know," Collings said. "How would I know a thing like that?"

It was as if he'd been asked the melting point of titanium.

"Look, it's simple. We want to know how you were handled. Who you saw, where you saw them, what they said. We don't have to get into it right this minute. We purposely waited some weeks to debrief you. We want to be careful not to crowd you. We understand defection, disillusionment, mental pressures. This piece of writing you've done shows that you know exactly what kind of material is worth recording. Understand, we're not asking for confessions or apologies. That's not our agenda."

He sat on the edge of George's desk.

"A fact is innocent until someone wants it. Then it becomes intelligence. We're sitting in a forty-story building that has an exterior of lightweight embossed aluminum. So what? Well, these dullish facts can mean a lot to certain individuals at certain times. An old man eating a peach is intelligence if it's August and the place is the Ukraine and you're a tourist with a camera. I can get you a Minox incidentally, any time. There's still a place for human intelligence. George, for example. George gives us material that we promptly analyze and disseminate to other agencies."

Lee said nothing.

"May I call you Lee?"

"All right."

"Lee, you have no high-school diploma, only a so-called equiv-alency. You have no college degree. You have an undesirable discharge. You have almost three years in the USSR, which is either a gap in your employment record or it is three years in the USSR. Take your pick. Now, all I have to do is make a call and you'll have a job with a firm here in Dallas that does very interesting work, classified work, where you'll start low but have a chance to learn a serious trade."

Marion Collings stood by the desk, well tanned, sincerely and correctly tanned, so trim and fit he could snap his fingers and knock a picture off the wall.

"It's a job I guarantee you are suited for and you'll be working there in a matter of days. Okay. Just tell me what to do."

Minox is the world-famous spy camera. Hidell has seen the name in books.

He walked through empty downtown Dallas, empty Sunday in the heat and light. He felt the loneliness he always hated to admit to, a vaster isolation than Russia, stranger dreams, a dead white glare burning down. He wanted to carry himself with a clear sense of role, make a move one time that was not disappointed. He walked in the shadows of insurance towers and bank buildings. He thought the only end to isolation was to reach the point where he was no longer separated from the true struggles that went on around him. The name we give this point is history.

12 August

Brenda Jean Sensibaugh, known professionally as Baby LeGrand, sat at the vanity in the dressing room of the Carousel Club, putting flesh-tone ointment on a pimple near her mouth. The narrow table was crowded with hairbrushes, coffee cups, thermos bottles, makeup kits, eight-by-ten glossies, sprays and foams, boxes of Kleenex, and it extended the length of the room, supporting four unframed mirrors. Brenda wore a bathrobe belonging to her sister.

Life Line was on KRLD, a patriotic show where they hiss at federal spending.

To get the ointment on right, Brenda had to stick her tongue against the side of her mouth, bulging the face, and this made it hard to talk. She was talking to the girl at the next mirror, Lynette Batistone, who looked barely out of high school.

"He might let you have an advance," Brenda said. "Only make sure he's in a good mood when you ask."

"I heard about his advances," Lynette said.

"This is just Jack. It's not, he doesn't expect results in other words. Who all'd you talk to, honey?"

"Molly Bright was saying."

"Never mind Molly. The thing of Jack is, he gets personal with words. This is the windbag of the world talking. But it's not like you have to fight your way out of the club."

"From what I hear. But this is strictly, you know."

"What?"

"He threatens his girls with, 'Dumb cunt,' like, 'I'll throw you down the fucking stairs.' "

"Honey, all right, this is not a bookkeeping firm. What's a little language?"

"He gets screaming fits all the time," Lynette said.

"He will not put a hand on your body."

"Molly Bright offered she would fill in for Blaze and what happens, there's this pandemonium."

"You want to quote Molly. Let me say about Molly. If bullshit was music, she'd be a brass band. You need the money bad, go tell Jack. Just be sure to mention groceries. He reacts to anything concerning food."

Lynette was in costume, a cowgirl outfit with a riding crop and long-barreled pistol. Brenda thought the girl had talent but not an ounce of taste. What she did was not even striptease. She was doing the dirty dog basically, with added little struts and touches.

"They told me in New Orleans this Jack is up and coming."

"He owns another club."

"He owns another club. I heard that."

"The Vegas," Brenda said. "But I don't know about up and coming. I have to think on that a little."

"What are these dogs I keep seeing?"

"He has dogs he calls his family. They live at the club except for one he takes home."

"This is in case of protection."

"I don't know what he's got to protect here but just us strippers."

"I gotta go wee," Lynette said.

"The other thing of Jack is, he'll ask you if he's queer. 'Do you think I'm queer, Lynette?' 'Do I look like I'm queer to you?'

'Serious, tell me, do I strike you as queer from your experience?' I guarantee he will ask these questions. 'How surprised would you be if someone told you I'm a queer?' 'Do I talk the way a queer might talk if he's trying to hide it, or what?' "

"What am I supposed to tell him?" Lynette said.

"Doesn't make the slightest little difference. This is just Jack."

Jack Ruby came in off Commerce Street, paunchy, balding, bearish in the chest and shoulders, fifty-two years old, carrying three thousand dollars in cash, a loaded revolver, a vial of Preludins and a summons from small-claims court for passing a bad check in a department store.

He walked into the dressing room.

"Quiet," he told Brenda. "I want to hear this."

They listened to *Life Line* on the radio. It was a commentary on heroism and how it has fallen into disuse.

Jack sat at the second mirror, his head lowered for maximum listening.

The announcer said, "In America, not so long ago, thirty-five bright young university students in a history class were asked to identify Guadalcanal. Less than one-third of them had ever heard of it. Three thousand years of military history tell no story more splendid than the blazing heroism on Guadalcanal, every bit of it American, as truly American as the log-cabin frontier and the open range. But nobody hears it now. United Nations Day gets a hundred times the publicity."

Jack was wearing a dark suit, white shirt and white silk tie, and he carried the snap-brim fedora that put him into focus, gave him sharpness and direction, like a detective on assignment.

"I love this stuff," he said. "I get welled up something tremendous when they talk about our country. You should have seen me when FDR died, when they announced on the radio, I was in uniform crying like a baby. Where is this Randi Ryder of mine?"

"Taking a pee."

"Is she torrid or what? I don't know what to do. I'm afraid they'll take my license."

"This is striptease," Brenda said.

"She was a big draw on Bourbon Street. But this is, I don't know, they might think she goes too far, popping her G-string like that."

"She is after publicity, Jack."

"I could make her wear a different little doohickey there."

"She would snap it and pop it whatever."

"Dallas draws the line at pussy hair. She could get me closed down."

"She is awful young to me."

"That's part of the draw. The competition's breathing down my back."

"Is that why you're paying her more than us?"

Jack leaned away, incredulous.

"Do I know this?" he said. "When did this come out?"

"You are paying Lynette like double."

"Brenda, I swear this sounds like something I never heard of. I am claiming I am nowhere on this."

"You pay extra, then you complain she'll close you down."

"I give her the margin so she'll draw. I need the draw very bad."

"You have this big thing built up in your mind that the competition is trying to put you out of business. They're just the competition, making a living like the rest of us."

"Fuck you, Brenda, okay."

"Same back, Mr. Ruby."

"I'm only the owner of this establishment and I have to sit here."

"That is exactly right."

"I have to listen."

"They have nothing better to do than get Jack. When Jack is the biggest conniver and sharpie of all."

"Hand me a Kleenex," he said.

"I also have to say. Now that I'm started. You're always off somewhere in your mind. Carrying on your own conversation. You don't listen to people."

"You don't know how deep they're digging me."

"That's why there is all this yelling all night long in this place."

"I have my dogs and I."

"Which you're very welcome."

"You should know my early life, Brenda, which I'm still obsessed. My mother, this is the God-honest truth, I swear to God, she spent thirty years of her life claiming there was a fishbone stuck in her throat. We listened to her constantly. Doctors, clinics, they searched for years with instruments. Finally she had an operation. There was nothing caught in her throat, absolutely, guaranteed. She comes home from the hospital. The fishbone is there."

"Well this is just a woman and a mother."

"So help me, thirty years, my brothers and sisters, never mind. And that's the least of it. I'm just showing you some idea. My father was the drunk of all time. But I don't care anymore what they did to each other or to me. I'm not a person who maintains a malice. I feel only love and respect for those people because they suffered in this world. So forget it, I don't care, go away."

"You never married, Jack, but how come."

"I'm a sloven in my heart."

"Personal-appearance-wise, you dress and groom."

"In my heart, Brenda. There's a chaos that's enormous."

They heard the MC telling jokes out on the stage. Jack leaned toward the radio and listened some more.

"I love the patriotic feeling I get, hearing this stuff. I am one hundred percent in my feeling for this country. What else do I trust? My own voice goes creepy at times. I can't control the inner voice. There are pressures unbelievable."

"Everybody gets pressure. We get pressure. You work us seven days a week."

"I'm about halfway out of it in common terms."

"Why don't you marry your Randi Ryder? She'll straighten out your life."

"She's a famous lay in New Orleans but she won't do anything unnatural."

Somebody shouted around the corner. Visitor for Jack. He touched Brenda on the shoulder and went out of the room. It was six paces to his office, where Jack Karlinsky was sitting on the sofa with one of the dogs.

"This is my dachshund Sheba," Jack Ruby said. "Get down, baby."

Jack Karlinsky was in his sixties, an investment counselor who had no office, no business phone, no employees and no clients. At his twenty-room house outside Dallas, a Coast Guard fog light played over the grounds all night long.

"I want to know did you hear."

"Be calm, Jack. That's why I'm here. To discuss terms."

"There are people who'll speak for me out of long association. I talk to Tony Astorina on the phone."

"I know you have connections," Karlinsky said. "But this is not the same as so-and-so is *connected*."

"What is Cuba, nothing?"

"I understand full well you took some trips for people."

"This is when Cuba was popular in the press."

"You did some things for the Bureau too," Karlinsky said.

"Where is this? Is this something I'm just hearing?"

"Please. You volunteered your services to the FBI in March 1959. They opened a file."

"Jack, you know as well as I."

"Potential criminal informant. You informed a little bit here, a little bit there."

"This is for my own protection in case something is held against me, so I can say look."

"Jack, it means nothing to me personally. I appreciate you are known in New Orleans, you are known in Dallas. You are a constant face in Dallas."

"I have associations going back to the old Chicago days which

I am prouder of than anything in my life, Newberry Street, Morgan Street, the pushcarts, the gangs."

"We all love the old Chicago stories. What do you think I was born here? Nobody is born in Dallas. We all carry the old Chicago thing, and the street life, and the scrappy days. But we are speaking here about a very sizable loan and the boys are naturally picky who gets the use of their capital."

Jack went through his desk drawers.

"Look, I can show you notices of tax liens, rejections of compromise offers. They're all over me about excise taxes. I am getting killed, Jack. They have history sheets on me this thick. I keep running in to pay cash in trickles. Two hundred dollars, two hundred and fifty dollars. In other words to show them some concern. But it's like a kid on an errand. I am in for over forty-four thousand dollars to the IRS alone and on top of that there is this union that wants me to ease up on the hours of the girls, there is this competition next door that is killing me with amateur nights and there is this girl from New Orleans that's gonna close me down for popping her G-string."

Jack Karlinsky had an invisible laugh. You heard it down in his throat but didn't see anything in his face that resembled mirth. He wore a sport coat over a turtleneck shirt and smoked a panatela. Jack checked out the shoes and haircut. He admitted left and right he was still learning how to live.

"I am telling my lawyer to settle eight cents on the dollar."

"Jack, they will tell you."

"I know."

"This is not a proposal they are drooling to accept."

"So I have to resolve in my own mind."

"You have to resolve in your own mind who you want to owe this money to. It is not found money. I have structured a deal here that I am not looking to pull in five points a week like the neighborhood loanshark. We are talking about a forty-thousand-dollar loan. We are speaking in a range of one thousand dollars a week vigorish."

"Which is ninety-two thousand total after one year."

"Or you keep paying the vig."

"Till my balls drop off."

"This is correct, Jack."

"Just to say. What if I can't pay one week?"

"One week, they will let it ride. They don't want to pop you on the head, Jack. They let it ride."

"Two, three weeks."

"The procedure you would do here is take out a second loan. This is not a good idea because you would pay the vig on one amount while they are actually giving you a lesser amount. Frankly, do you want my advice?"

"What?"

"Frankly, don't take the loan. You can't make a vig like that with your kind of operation that you're running here. You will fall deep into the pit."

"It's my pit, Jack."

"It's your pit but it's not your money."

"What happens, just saying, if I miss five weeks, six weeks?"

"If you are bled totally dry and white, they will simply stop the clock. Which is, pay the principal, forget the interest. In other words this fellow is known to us and we will settle for a piece of his business plus the original sum. They don't want to blow up the building."

"But they will grab my business."

"This is the ballfield you're playing on."

"What if I can't pay the principal?"

"Jack, this is what I'm telling you. I'm saying explore other avenues."

"A bank would make a credit check. They won't give me ten cents."

"Think of friends, relatives. Take a partner into the business."

"I can't work with other people. I already have backers. My sister manages the Vegas for me. We fight all the time."

"You strike me a little unreasonable. You have to grasp a major point. You are not outfit, Jack. Understand *connected*."

The drums were going out front.

"All right. Say this. I am willing to go for five hundred a week interest over one year when the convention business will pick up by then."

"I structured a serious deal here."

"Jack, take it to them and tell them. Mention I talk to Tony Push all the time. He has the reputation he's very close to Carmine Latta."

"Carmine is not in loanshark in a big way."

"I am only saying make a statement that I am known to Tony Astorina."

Karlinsky looked at him. A silent countdown. Then he said he would do whatever Jack asked. He had a deep, smooth and reasonable voice, gone hollow now, and a house with a giant search-light, and a perfect turquoise pool, and four daughters and a son, and Jack Ruby wondered if this is what it takes to look invincible.

They shook hands in the doorway and then the older man stepped back into the office, briefly, as if he had a happy secret to reveal.

"The jacket is mohair. Look."

Then they walked to the head of the narrow stairway that led down to the street. They shook hands again. The saxophone was blatting. Jack took a Preludin with a glass of water at the bar for a favorable future outlook. Then he walked among the tables to min-gle with the crowd. What is the point of running a club if you can't do that?

Dinner at home was a quiet affair with harpsichord concertos on the stereo and conversation coming in small runs. Beryl watched her husband raise the wineglass to his lips. Larry didn't drink his wine. He chewed it. To savor the tonality—the dryness, or the wetness. This is how we build a civilization, he liked to say. We chew our wine.

"You don't look happy," she said. "You haven't looked happy

in a while. I want you to feel good again. Say something funny."

"You're the funny one."

"I am always the funny one, the strange one, the tiny one. I want you to assume one of these thankless roles."

They ate in silence for some moments.

"Remember the missile flap?" he said. "It's about ten months now since U-2 planes photographed offensive missiles in Cuba. Guess what? They've come up with something new."

"Do I want to know what it is?"

"A Soviet surveying team has found a major oil field. And it's precisely the area where I'd arranged drilling contracts. I saw the photos last week and they were so detailed I could recognize the terrain. I was there. I stood right there. I visited the fields. We did mineral surveys. There was serious money behind us."

"Your oil. Your field."

"Ours. And better ours than the goddamn Russians. You know what they'll do to that island. Drain the living blood out of it."

"I don't doubt it. But it's hard sometimes to live with a man who never, never, never lets go."

"This is damn right I don't let go."

They let it drop for a while. She got up and turned over the record. It was raining hard and she caught a glimpse of someone running in the street.

"Let me explain about obsessions," he said.

"Oh yes please."

"I take a sweeping view of the subject."

"God yes."

"It's the job of an intelligence service to resolve a nation's obsessions. Cuba is a fixed idea. It is prickly in a way Russia is not. More unresolved. More damaging to the psyche. And this is our job, to remove the psychic threat, to learn so much about Castro, decipher his intentions, undermine his institutions to such a degree that he loses the power to shape the way we think, to shape the way we sleep at night."

"Maybe what I don't understand is why Cuba. Do I know the

first thing about this island? Is it West Indian, is it Spanish, is it white, is it black, is it mulatto, is it Latin American, is it Creole, is it Chinese? Why do we think it belongs to us?"

"It's not a question of belongs to us. It's a question of something working beautifully, of private investment being given the chance to help a country rise in the world, and Cuba was rising in distribution, manufacturing, literacy, social services, and any high-school student can make a solid case that the flaws and excesses of the Batista regime could have been contained without a revolution and certainly without a march into the communist camp."

They fell silent again. The power of his feelings made her want to pause. There weren't many things he believed in strongly. She felt a shrinking in herself, the old pathetic readiness to give in quietly. But what was there to fight about? She didn't know the subject. She saw the world in news clippings and picture captions, the world becoming bizarre, the world it is best to see in one-column strips that you send to friends. Refuge only in irony. If her aim was to go unnoticed, then why fight?

"Things are looking better in some areas," he said. "There are things I'm not unhappy about at all. I am making something of a professional comeback. There is talk of moving me to the Office of Finance. There is a field unit in Buenos Aires. This is not to be discussed, of course. I'll work in money markets, making sure we have foreign currencies on hand for certain operations."

"Is this a plum, Buenos Aires?"

"I don't know where it stands in the fruit-and-vegetable kingdom. It is just goddamn good of them to give me this chance. The Agency understands. It's amazing really how deeply they understand. This is why some of us see the Agency in a way that has nothing to do with jobs or institutions or governments. We are goddamn grateful for their understanding and trust. The Agency is always willing to consider a man in a new light. This is the nature of the business. There are shadows, there are new lights. The deeper the ambiguity, the more we believe, the more we trust, the more we band together."

It was remarkable how often he talked to her about these things. The Agency was the one subject in his life that could never be exhausted. Central Intelligence. Beryl saw it as the best organized church in the Christian world, a mission to collect and store everything that everyone has ever said and then reduce it to a microdot and call it God. She needed to live in small dusty rooms, layered safely in, out of the reach of dizzying things, of heat and light and strange spaces, and Larry needed the great sheltering nave of the Agency. He believed that nothing can be finally known that involves human motive and need. There is always another level, another secret, a way in which the heart breeds a deception so mysterious and complex it can only be taken for a deeper kind of truth.

There were anemones in a bud vase on the table. The phone rang and Beryl went to her desk in the living room to answer. It was a man named Thomas Stainback. She knew from the tone of voice that it was a call Larry would take upstairs. She simply stood in the doorway. When he saw her, he got up from the table. She waited for him to climb the stairs to the guest room and pick up the phone and then she put the receiver down softly and went in to drink her coffee.

Parmenter said, "I'm here," and waited for Everett to ask the first question on the list.

"What do we know about schedule?"

"It looks like mid-November."

"That gives us time. I'm anxious to hear what Mackey is doing."

"He knows we've got Miami. I haven't told him when."

"Tell him right away."

"I can't find him," Parmenter said.

A pause on the other end.

"Is he reassigned?"

"I did some very delicate checking. He's not at the Farm or anywhere else he might logically be. There is no trace. It's beginning to look like he just submerged for a time."

"It's a reassignment," Everett said.

"I looked into it, Win. I was extremely goddamn thorough.

He is not in a cover situation. He is supposed to be training JOTs and he isn't."

"Does it mean he's out? We can't operate without Mackey."

"He's setting up. That's all. He'll get in touch."

"He can't just walk away."

"He'll get in touch. You know the man is solid."

"I've had a foreboding," Everett said.

"He's setting up. I'll get in my car one morning and find him sitting there. He wants this to happen as much as we do."

"I've had a feeling these past weeks that something isn't right."

"Everything is right. The city, the time, the preparations. The man is absolutely solid."

"I believe in the power of premonitions."

Larry put down the phone. Downstairs he found Beryl at the table with the newspaper, her coffee and a pair of scissors. Pages were spread over the wineglasses and dinner plates.

He'd stopped commenting on this oddness of hers. She said the news clippings she sent to friends were a perfectly reasonable way to correspond. There were a thousand things to clip and they all said something about the way she felt. He watched her read and cut. She wore half-glasses and worked the scissors grimly. She believed these were personal forms of expression. She believed no message she could send a friend was more intimate and telling than a story in the paper about a violent act, a crazed man, a bombed Negro home, a Buddhist monk who sets himself on fire. Because these are the things that tell us how we live.

Baby LeGrand stood at the end of the runway, knees bent, hands locked behind her neck, the drummer going boom to the jolt of her pelvis, and she scanned the club meantime, making out shapes beneath the tinted lights, whole lives that she could diagram in seconds, oh sailors and college boys, just the usual, plus a waitress taking setups to the hard drinkers, a kid in a skimpy outfit that makes her titties bulge. She ran a sash between her legs and waved it slow-motion through the baby spot. She eyed the table of off-duty cops drinking their cut-rate beer. She saw the odd-job boy taking Polaroids of the customers which Jack will present as gifts. These are men in suit and tie, on business in the city, and men who come with dates to do the twist between sets. Brenda knows the twist crowd. She likes the younger cops if they are blue-eyed. She knows the smallest tomato stain on the narrowest tie because the only food is pizza from up the street, which somebody sticks in the warmer. Meantime the drummer's picking up the beat and a sailor says go go go. She drags the sash through the smoke and dust, scans the bar for the lowlife types that Jack drags in off the street, sad sacks and drifters he feels sorry for. And there is the gambling element or whatever they are, the vending-machine and Sicilian element, men of sharp practices, standing frozen at the back of the club. It's the whole Carousel in a five-second glimpse, plus the tourists from Topeka. They are saying go go go. They are crying for a garment. They want the piece of silk that passed between her legs. They are here to bathe in the flesh of the sleepwalking girl, the girl who wakes up naked in a throbbing crowd. This is how it always seems to Baby L. She is having a private fit in the middle of the night, like she is demonized, and wakes up naked in a different dream, where strange men are clutching at her body. Does anybody here know the stupid truth? She wants to be a real-estate agent who drives people around in a station wagon that is painted like wood. An award-winning realtor in a fern-green suit. But she is humping a spotlight in front of a crowd, flinging sweat from her belly and thighs, and the tassels on her pasties are swishing to the beat.

She did her trademark twirl of the breasts, one breast spinning clockwise, the other counter, and quickly disappeared.

Then she showered and wrapped herself in a towel and sat in the dressing room, smoking. This was the time when a cigarette was the purest pleasure known.

Lynette was in street clothes sitting at the next mirror. She had her head in a copy of Look.

"If I had the slightest sense," Brenda told her, "I'd get what

I'm owed and just scram. I have a seven-year old and a four-year old and I am half the time too tired to say hello."

Lynette turned a page. She said, "I will tell you this Bobby Kennedy is right up my alley. Bobby is the one who could make me crazy. He has got this little hard gleam. Ten minutes with Bobby, I am out of my head."

"He doesn't do a thing for me."

"He could drive me into wah wah land."

"Where is that, Lynette?"

"He has got this little meanness in the eye but he doesn't really know it like?"

"I think he knows it," Brenda said. "Give me his brother any day. Jack would be better in bed. I like a lover with some shoulder to him. I stay away from these rabbity types."

"Bobby's an athalete."

"The President is mature to handle a woman like us. Not that I'm ready to settle down with the man."

"You need one of those bouffant hairdos like Jackie."

"I need more than that."

"You got the knockers, Brenda."

"Tit tit tit. This is my Achilles heel you're pointing out. Too much talent up front. It means a bunch of trouble."

"What's he do anyway, the Attorney General?"

"Are you kidding? He's the top cop."

"Top cop or top cock?"

"Same difference," Brenda said.

There was some kind of commotion out front. They could hear a few voices and a glass or bottle breaking. Lynette turned a page.

"Do you believe what they say about tell a person exactly when you were born, to the hour and the minute, and they can figure out everything about you?"

"I smell a fish, to quote a maxim," Brenda said.

The disturbance, whatever it was, grew louder. You feel these things in the walls. Brenda put on her robe and went to the end of the hall and looked out. Between the bar and the entranceway there was a flurry of bodies and arms, maybe four guys including Jack who were physically propelling a man who looked like he combed his hair with firecrackers. It now developed that Jack wanted to throw the man down the stairs. The others were trying to prevent this as extreme. Brenda waited until the odd-job boy lost his place in the moving knot of people and came off to the side, shaking a hand that may have been bitten.

"What is it?" Brenda said.

"This guy like grab-assed one of the waitresses. You know, felt her going by."

"Do we kill people for this?"

"You know Jack when it comes to abusing the girls. He about flipped sky-high."

Jack wrestled the man away from the others and the two of them went quick-walking down the narrow stairs, actually out of control, banging off the handrail, almost pitching forward to the street.

The bar crowd went after, hurrying down single-file and loud. Brenda took a deep drag on the cigarette and went back to finish her talk.

Out on the street Jack knocked the guy down. He went after him with his feet, kicking in a fastidious way as if trying to shake dog matter off his shoe. The guy skittered away and ran down the street, breaking through a line of people in front of the club next door, where an amateur strip night was going on. Jack went after him, followed by five or six others from the Carousel. The man was much faster but turned halfway down the block and was ready to fight. It made no sense to anyone and only got Jack madder. Jack charged into him swinging. The sheer bulk and force of the attack knocked the guy down. Jack kicked at him twice and the guy grabbed Jack's ankle and twisted him down to the pavement in slow motion. Then he started crawling toward a parking sign. Jack was on his knees and grabbed the guy's leg to keep him from reaching the signpost. Someone from the bar crowd tried to break Jack's grip, speaking soothingly to Jack. The guy kept struggling toward the sign. This was the clear meaning of what was going on. If he could only reach the sign. Two men from the bar crowd broke the fighters apart but Jack got in two kicks at the guy's ribs. The guy stood up, eyes averted. His pants were somehow unbuckled. Jack punched him hard in the head over the shoulders of the men between them and the guy walked out in the middle of the street and stood there, making the cars go around him. He fixed his clothes. He stood out there in traffic. He would not look at the men on the sidewalk, their chests pumping from the run and scuffle.

Jack went back down the street. When he reached the line of people outside the other club, he started shaking hands and giving out cards with the Carousel name and hours. Then he got into his white Olds and drove off to clear his head.

Jack's car was a movable slum. His dogs had chewed up the seat covers and mats. They'd eaten the stuffing inside the rear seat, exposing the springs. There were paw marks on the windows. There were eight empty liquor cartons tilted and wedged across the rear seat. He had jars of diet food rolling across the floor when he stopped or turned. He had a couple of hundred dollars on top of the dashboard, folded in butcher wrap stained with lamb-chop blood. There were extra Preludins in the glove compartment plus a bathing cap, a number of unpaid tickets, a number of address books, some loose condoms, a set of brass knuckles and a TV Guide.

He tuned in KLIF, looking for a disc jockey called the Weird Beard. He needed a familiar voice to calm him down.

He drove around downtown Dallas. It happens a few times where I have to pummel one of these guys who causes trouble in the club. Once they get you cowered to that extent, you are physically doomed. He felt his jacket for the .38, which was tucked into a Merchants State Bank moneybag along with three thousand dollars in recent receipts tightly rolled in pink rubber bands.

It was the talk with Jack Karlinsky that probably got him inflamed with the guy who put his hand on what's-her-name. He had to get the money. He had no other source. There were debts and harassments in every direction. Even with forty thousand dollars in his hands tomorrow, the problems were not solved. He had to get the business built up. He had this union thing with the girls. He had an extortionist of long standing on the West Coast who'd already turned down his request for a loan and now Karlinsky was leaning the same way.

So the jacket is mohair. You should have bought two. One to shit on; one to cover it up.

He had a deal going where you put a token in a machine and it washes your car. His brother Sam sold one of his two washaterias and was looking with interest at this machine. It would never happen but it could. He'd tried different things with different brothers, from selling salt and pepper shakers to nice-looking busts of FDR. He sold costume jewelry, sewing machine attachments and cures for arthritis from Chicago to San Francisco.

Thirty years with a fishbone in her throat.

Weird Beard said, "I know what you think. You think I'm making it up. I'm not making it up. If it gets from me to you, it's true. We are for real, kids. And this is the question I want to leave with you tonight. Who is for real and who is sent to take notes? You're out there in the depths of the night, listening in secret, and the reason you're listening in secret is because you don't know who to trust except me. We're the only ones who aren't them. This narrow little radio band is a route to the troot. I'm not making it up. There are only two things in the world. Things that are true. And things that are truer than true. We need this little private alley where we can meet. Because this is Big D, which stands for Don't be Dissimilar. Am I coming in all right? Is my signal clear? We're the sneaky little secret they're trying to uncover. Do you think I'm making it up? I'm not making it up. Weird Beard says, Eat your cereal with a fork. Do your homework in the dark. And trust your radio before you trust your mother."

Jack had no idea what the guy was saying. He squeezed a Preludin down his throat. It takes away your procrastination about what you want to do next.

He drove to the Ritz Delicatessen and parked outside. He opened the trunk and threw in the moneybag with the gun and heavy cash so he wouldn't forget to do it later. The trunk was a little overflowing with barbells, weights, a summer suit, a can of paint, a roll of toilet paper, dog toys and dog biscuits, a holster for his gun, a golf shoe with a dollar bill in it and about a hundred glossies of Randi Ryder that he'd brought back from New Orleans. You might as well call it my life because it's not any neater at home.

He walked into the Ritz and ordered everything with extra mustard and extra mayonnaise, a dozen sandwiches. Roast beef, corned beef, sliced turkey, tongue, dill pickles, cole slaw, relish, potato salad, black-cherry soda, ginger ale, etc. He told the man to give these sandwiches special handling because they were going to police headquarters.

He got back in the car. These cops of ours deserve the best because they put their lives on the line every time they walk out the door. This is a homicidal town. Bam. He had to remember to go back to the club later to get his dachshund Sheba and clear the register and grab his hat. He didn't like being without his hat because the balding head is here for all to see. He took scalp treatments that he felt were doing some good although he doubted it.

He drove to the Police and Courts Building, feeling a sharp sting in his left knee and hiking up his pants leg as he drove. A nice ripe gash. A street fight takes up your attention to the point where you don't know you're bleeding for an hour. He drove with his left pants leg raised above the knee. No responsible party would finance him because he gave away drinks to nobodies and brought in people and dogs off the street. He got out of the car, lowered his pants leg and went into the old part of the building, walking between the tall columns.

He took the elevator to three, holding the carton with the food and drinks, thinking that if he doesn't do something soon he will be running a business out of his pants pockets forever, if they let him run it at all, if they don't turn him into a nothing person completely. He got off the elevator and went down the corridor to the juvenile bureau. He felt blood seeping into his shoe. But just seeing these men in uniform, clean shaven, he wanted to say it is the proudest feeling of my life being a friend of the police in the most pro-American city anywhere in the world.

His rabbi told him many times, "Don't be so emotional."

In Dallas

Lee Oswald sat in Sleight's Speed Wash at midnight, waiting for his clothes to dry and reading H. G. Wells. One other customer was in the place, an obese and scary-looking man who wore slippers cut open near the front to give his swollen feet some room. The air had a sour reek. Lee was slumped over volume one of *The Outline of History*, biting the skin of his thumb, the book spread open in his lap.

He was living apart, off and on, from Marina and Baby June.

The night attendant came around, a lanky Negro saying in a kind of singsong, "Closing time, closing time, y'all go home." He carried somebody's sheets in a red mesh basket.

The other customer got up and went to a dryer to collect his things. Lee sat reading, folded over the book, chewing a knuckle now. The customer hobbled out.

About three minutes passed. The dryer with Lee's clothes stopped running. He sat with his head in the book. He knew the attendant was shooting him a very level look from fifteen feet. He turned a page and read toward the end of the chapter, which was at the bottom of the facing page. He read slowly, concentrating hard to get the meaning, the small raw truth inside those syllables.

"Hey, Jim. You are wearing me thin, okay."

The Greeks and the Persians. He looked up. The attendant had a droopy lower lip, a rust-tone complexion with a spatter of freckles across the cheekbones, those dangling hands, and Lee thought Japan before he was able to supply a name or set of circumstances. In an instant he knew. This was Bobby Dupard, his cellmate in the brig in Atsugi.

It took him a while to get Dupard to remember who he was. Bobby stared hard, taking in Oswald's hair, receding on the left side, where the part was; taking in the haggard look, the three-day stubble, the shirt with a popped seam near the collar; taking in a lot actually, four years plus of manhood and exile and hard times. Ozzie the Rabbit. Remembrance entered Dupard's face in a complicated way.

"What it is, I don't look real close at whites no more. So it takes me a while to pin down the individual I'm basically talking to."

They didn't talk about Japan. They talked about West Dallas, where Bobby lived with his sister and her three small kids in a project of hundreds of buildings stretched in barracks formation between the Trinity River and Singleton Boulevard. They called it a housing park. Fenced in, isolated from the city, with ripped-out plumbing set on the mud lawns. Bobby worked at the speed wash from seven to midnight six days a week. Twice a week he took a course in mechanical drawing at Crozier Technical High School downtown. Sometimes he worked a noon-to-four shift as a mixer in a bakery, a fill-in for the sick and the missing. He went home in clothes dusted white. His mother was dead now. His father lived in another part of the project. Bobby wasn't sure where. From the 52 bus he saw his old man all the time sitting in front of an auto-wrecker service sipping malt liquor from a can. Big Cat brand. Bobby knew his father would not recognize him if he walked over and said hello. His father would talk to him the same way he talked to everyone, explaining his conversations with the Lord.

That was West Dallas. Smoke from the lead smelter. Staccato lives.

Bobby had a trace of wispy chin hair now. His eyes had lost their quicksilver fear. He looked at Lee from an angle, cool and fixed, with a slow nod of the head to measure remarks.

Lee explained that he was living underground. He'd left his last job without a word. He'd disappeared from his last address. He had a post-office box. His brother didn't know what part of Dallas he was in. His mother thought he was still in Fort Worth. His wife was living with friends of hers due to misunderstandings. He was working for a graphic-arts firm. He didn't explain the occasional classified nature of the work. He said nothing about Marion Collings. Collings, through George de Mohrenschildt, was pressing him for details of his contacts with the security apparatus in the USSR. He was avoiding Collings. He was avoiding the postal authorities. He was hiding from the Feebees. He was using false addresses on every form he filled out. He was making posters after hours on the job and sending them to the Socialist Workers Party. He had a spy camera stashed in a seabag at the bottom of his closet.

He didn't explain about Marina and how much he missed her and needed her and how it made him angry, knowing this, trying to fight this off, another sneaking awareness he could not fight off.

Forget Japan. Bobby talked about the South, about the police dogs and fire-bombings, the integration of Ole Miss. It was a daily event just about, the TV footage of segregationist rage, crowds of Negro marchers bending to the charge of riot police, toppled in sudden clusters. Demonstrators smashed in the face, hit with rocks. Someone falls, those white boys move in kicking. Cops gripping those billy clubs, one hand at each end, twisting hard. Look at their eyes. Look at those firemen come jumping off the trucks. They turn on those hoses and it's like a wrath from out of hell that sends everybody spinning.

All over the project there were makeshift barbecue pits, fifty-five-gallon oil drums cut in half horizontally and set belly-down on metal legs—smoke rising, hoses shooting water on TV.

The clothes tumbled in a dozen Loadstar dryers.

Bobby said, "I believe the whole system works to make the black man humble down. Follow the penny hustle, drink the cheap wine. This is what they got planned out for us. I'll tell you where I'm at, Ozzie. When I read crime news in the paper, I look at the names to figure out was the perpetrator black or white. Some names just black. I check them over close. I say, Go brother. Say, Do it to them. Because what edge do we have asides hating?"

He said, "I'm not looking to wear the white man out with my ability to suffer."

He said, "I'm trying to learn a trade to keep me sane."

They stayed in the speed wash talking until 2:00 A.M. Two nights later they talked again while Bobby loaded machines and folded clothes for the drop-off customers. The next day Lee punched out a little early and met Bobby downtown outside his drafting class and they took a bus to the Oak Cliff section, where the speed wash was located and where Lee was living in an area of rooming houses and rusted car hulks sitting in long weeds. They shared a box of donuts and talked some more. Later that night Lee walked six blocks to the speed wash from his flat on Elsbeth Street and they talked until closing time, talked politics and race and Cuba while the machines turned and the night stragglers threw fistfuls of clothes into the churning soap.

Next day they had an idea. Let's put a bullet in General Walker's head.

Marina stood arm-rocking little June. He'd cleaned the place for her return. He was happy to see her. He took the baby and spoke his fake Japanese, wagging his head. It made them all laugh.

He began to study bus schedules. The Preston Hollow bus, the 36, stopped a block and a half from the general's house. He walked past the house, which was set back from the street and very near to Turtle Creek, a lushness of cottonwoods and elms, a deep quiet. Just walking down the street made him feel untouchable. He memorized the license-plate number of a car at the head of the driveway and wrote it in his notebook. He kept a notebook of travel times, distances and other observations.

She asked him if he would teach her English now.

He sent $29.95 to Seaport Traders for a 38-caliber revolver with a shortened barrel. It was made by Smith & Wesson and known as the two-inch Commando. He used the name A. J. Hidell on the order form and entered his address as Box 2915, Dallas, Texas.

The next day he went to typing class. It was his first day there and he sat in the last row, talked to no one, studied the keyboard on his machine. It was like Chinese. He inserted paper, placed his fingers on the keys, trying to understand why the letters were positioned the way they were. It was a picture of his humiliation. Nine dollars to enroll. George had told him if he could type he'd get a better job someday.

It was the very end of January in '63.

He stood in the darkroom with another trainee, Dale Fitzke, a cripple. Dale wore a high shoe. He walked in a kind of tick-tock motion and had a soft clean face, incredibly smooth, that made him look about twelve years old.

They stood shoulder to shoulder by the developing trays. People moved in and out, squeezing behind them. There were dim red lights that made the room look radioactive.

"What kind of person are you?" Dale said. "I am sort of weird in my family. They have finally stopped expecting great things."

"What do they expect?"

"They are holding their breath, sexually. What do you like best about the darkroom? It's the way my room used to look when I had a fever. Childhood fevers were the best times. I had tremendous high fevers. What kind of feeling do you get about this company?"

"I like it here. The work is interesting by comparison to some."

"Because I get the feeling these various and sundry tasks are not the only things going on around here. For example. Do you want to hear an example?"

"Like what?" Lee said.

"They told me to stay away from the worktables in the type-setting area. Not allowed. No lookee."

"You can look. No one will stop you. I look all the time."

"So do I," Dale said with a jump in his voice. "I'll tell you what I see if you tell me what you see."

"They have lists of names for the Army Map Service."

"What kinds of names?"

"Place names."

"That's what I see too. They set the names in type on three-inch strips of paper."

"Some of the names are in Cyrillic letters. Which I know in Russian. For maps of Soviet targets."

They were both whispering.

"I'll tell you what I overheard," Dale said, "if you promise not to tell anyone. The maps are made from photographs. The photographs are the really secret things. They come from U-2s."

The light was an eerie neon rouge.

"Isn't that a neat thing to know? I love being in a position where I can exchange fascinating stuff with someone. Like you tell me, I tell you. U-2s. When I first heard this stuff, around Eisenhower, I thought they were saying you-toos, like there's me-too and you-too."

It was a Saturday and they were getting time and a half. Lee put in for Saturdays whenever possible because he knew this job was doomed the minute Marion Collings gave the word.

"Do you like the people here?" Dale said. "I saw you with that Russian magazine you were reading. There's been a little comment. The people here are friendly up to a point. Not that it matters to me, what anyone reads. Do you remember what it was like, being under the blankets, sweating, as a kid? A fever is a secret thing. It's like falling down a hole where no one can follow but there's no terror or pain because you don't even feel like yourself. I love huddling in sweat."

"I had an ear operation when I was little. I still remember the dreams after they put on the mask."

"I had *four* operations! I *loved* going under!"

Dale was gesturing in the glow, with fluid dripping off his hands into the tray.

"What kind of mind do you have, Lee? One day I heard my mother say, 'He'll never be brilliant, Tom.' She was talking to Tom, my brother. I have used that sentence at dinner a hundred thousand times."

The mysterious U-2. It followed him from Japan to Russia and now it was here in Dallas. He remembered how it came to earth, sweet-falling, almost feathery, dependent on winds, sailing on winds. That was how it seemed. And the pilot's voice coming down to them in fragments, with the growl and fuzz of a blown speaker. He heard that voice sometimes on the edge of a shaky sleep.

Dale Fitzke said, "I'll listen for things, you listen for things. Then we'll meet here and talk some more."

His typing class was at Crozier, the same school where Dupard was taking a course, and they met in an empty classroom whenever they could work out the timing. They talked strategy and philosophy, waiting for the gun to arrive in the mail.

Bobby said, "You think it's some coincidence this Walker come to live in Dallas? Get off, man. He is here because the fury and the hate is here. This is the city he made up in his mind."

"Did you see today's paper? He's going out of town on a speaking tour. Twenty-nine cities. He won't be back till April."

"What's he doing, the kill-a-nigger tour?"

"Operation Midnight Ride. The dangers of communism here and abroad. It's going to be pure Cuba. He loves to hit at Cuba. If we have to wait till April, let's make it worthwhile. We get him on the seventeenth. The second anniversary of the Bay of Pigs."

"Who is the shooter?"

"I am," Oswald said.

"You sure about that."

"I am the one that does it."

"If it's the seventeenth, I have to see if there's class."

"What do you mean?"

"It's a question do I want to cut class."

"I will need an accomplice, Bobby. This is not just walk in and shoot him. The house is located in such a way. There's an alley. We may need a car."

"I can get a car. I can always borrow a car. I don't know about dependable running. Just so we put him on the ground. That man got to taste some blood."

"They have a phrase they use in Russian for assassinations that involve blood being spilled. *Mokrie dela*. Which is wet affairs. Like the ice pick they used on Trotsky."

"Just so we do it to him," Bobby said.

They moved to Neely Street, nearby, another furnished apartment, two rooms in a frame house with a concrete porch and a balcony with sagging posts. They could put out flowerpots and pretend it's Minsk. There was a small additional room, the size of a walk-in closet, where Lee could work on his notebook and keep his correspondence and other writings.

They moved their belongings in Junie's stroller. They made six or seven trips, dishes, baby things, letters from Russia. Lee made the last trip alone, pushing the stroller west on Neely wearing most of the clothes he owned, to save another trip.

The little room could be entered from the living room and from the staircase outside their flat. Both doors could be locked from inside. It was like an airtight compartment, part of the building but also separate from it. He called the room his study. He squeezed a lamp table and chair in there and set to work on his notes for the death of the general.

He began taking photographs of Walker's house. He had a box camera he carried in a paper bag on the bus back and forth. He photographed the lattice fence behind the house, the alleyway that extended from the parking lot of the Mormon church to Avondale Street. He took some pictures of the railroad tracks where he could hide the gun if necessary.

There is a world inside the world.

He made detailed notes on the location of windows at the rear of the house. He studied maps of Dallas. He put the finishing touches on the false documents he'd made after hours at work. When the Hidell gun arrived at the post office, he'd have Hidell identification to claim the package. He did the typing for the documents on his machine at school.

He felt good about having Dupard behind him. Downtrodden. Dupard was the force of history, the show of a solid front against the far-right surge.

He used Hidell again, March 12, sending a money order for $21.45 to Klein's Sporting Goods in Chicago for a 6.5-millimeter Italian military rifle, the Mannlicher-Carcano, equipped with a four-power scope.

The rain fell on empty streets.

What a sense of destiny he had, locked in the miniature room, creating a design, a network of connections. It was a second existence, the private world floating out to three dimensions.

He went to a gun shop and bought an ammunition clip that would fit the Mannlicher, so he could fire up to seven rounds before reloading.

Rain-slick streets. He walked to the speed wash and talked excitedly with Dupard about the logic of a long-range shot, given the layout of the house and grounds. Then he let himself back into the study and no one even knew he'd been gone.

He stood barefoot in the living room in his pajamas, working the bolt. He jerked the handle, brought the bolt rearward, then drove it forward, jerking the handle down. He turned up the handle, drew the bolt back, drove it forward, jerking the handle down. He turned toward the mirror over the sofa. He jerked the bolt handle, drew the bolt back, then drove it forward, jerking the handle down.

Marina was out at the store. Junie sat in the high chair near the window, rolling a marble back and forth across the tray.

There was a yard behind the house, a small dirt enclosure with a couple of forsythia shrubs. A clothesline ran parallel to the back fence and Marina stood there hanging diapers. The ground-floor tenants were away.

Ten minutes passed. Lee came down the exterior wooden steps. He carried the rifle in one hand, a couple of magazines in the other. He wore a black pullover shirt, short-sleeve, and a pair of dark chinos. The revolver was snug on his hip.

Marina watched him set the rifle against the stairway and climb back up. He returned seconds later with his box camera, an Imperial Reflex he'd bought cheap in Japan.

"Why do you want to do this?" she said. "If we are seen by a neighbor."

"It's for Junie, to remember me by."

"Does she want her father in a picture with guns? I don't know how to take a picture."

"You hold the camera at your waist."

"I've never taken a picture in my life."

"No matter what. I want you to keep a print for my little girl."

"Dressed all black. It's foolish, Lee. Who are you hunting with that gun? The forces of evil? I want to laugh. It's stupid. It impresses no one. It's pure and simple show."

He posed in a corner of the yard, the rifle in his right hand, muzzle up, butt end pressing on his waist, just inches from the holstered .38. The magazines, the Militant and the Worker, were in his left hand, fanned like playing cards.

She snapped the shutter.

He posed one more time, the rifle in his left hand now, the

magazines held under his chin with the word Militant visible above the fold, his shadow trailing to the wooden gate and his thin smile carried forward by light and time into the frame of official memory.

Lee stood in a corner of the Gulf station on North Beckley, eight-thirty sharp, the stink of gasoline hanging low in the night. It was ninety-nine degrees. It was record-breaking heat for this date. He had a military slicker draped over his left shoulder and held a half-finished Coke in his right hand, drawn from the machine nearby, just as a reason to be here.

He kept his eye on a tan Ford turning slowly into the station and coming to a stop near the service area. It looked like a 1950 model, thereabouts. He watched Dupard get out and stand by the open door, peering. Bobby wore light-blue coveralls and a little round cap, with the words American Bakery embroidered across his shirtfront and a heavy dusting of flour on his face and clothes, whiting his eyebrows and the backs of his hands.

Lee walked toward the car, his left arm stiff beneath the slicker, the rifle held parallel to his body with the butt wedged in his armpit. They did not speak until the car was on the street, headed north, the rifle on the floor behind the seat.

"But how come, Bobby?"

"What?"

"You're in work clothes."

"I had a chance to make some overtime, which I'm forced to accept it if I'm not doing no laundry tonight."

"Am I keeping you from the laundry? Is that what this is all about?"

"I'm just saying. The chance came up. I squeezed in four extra hours."

"You can be identified. This is not a night you want to stand out."

"Nobody sees shit. We go in quick and dark. Where's the handgun?"

Lee took the .38 out of his belt and put it on the seat between them.

"Did you get the bullets?" he said.

"Totally," Dupard said. "I got fifteen bullets I bought right off the street from some school kid. They're like two different-make bullets but they're .38 specials, so I don't foresee no problem."

"I don't foresee using them. It's just in case."

At the first red light Bobby swung out the cylinder of the gun and took six cartridges from the breast pocket of his uniform. He inserted them in the chambers.

"I'll tell you a good sign," Lee said. "I order the handgun in January, I order the rifle in March. Both guns arrive the same day. My wife would say it's fate."

"What did you tell her about tonight?"

"She thinks I'm at typing class. I dropped out of typing class two weeks ago. I got fired from my job last Saturday was my last day."

"I dread getting fired, man."

"They said my work wasn't exact. It had to happen. Just like tonight has to happen. They'll know about this in Havana. Before midnight the news will reach Fidel."

They crossed the Trinity River on the Commerce Street viaduct.

"What I seen, that rifle looks like war surplus. How do you know it shoots?"

"I wrapped it in my raincoat and took it on the Love Field bus. Then I went down to the river bottom out west of the freeway where there's an area that people test-fire their guns. It's like a war in ordinary daylight."

"That sling, that strap, like it comes off a tenor sax."

"It fits all right. Everything works. Everything fits. I planned this thing with care. I had to go to six gun shops before I found ammo for this type carbine."

"It's bearing on my mind that the general has to die."

"I hit him the first shot," Lee said softly.

"I need to stop feeling bad all the time."

"It's a clear shot to every window."

"I want him on the ground."

"Less than forty yards," Lee said.

"For Mississippi, for John Birch, for the KKK, for every fucking thing."

Bobby looked a little smoky-eyed. They were quiet for a while. The heat came washing through the windows. They headed up Stemmons to Oak Lawn Avenue.

Lee said, "We turn left off Avondale into an alley that runs about two hundred and fifty feet to a church parking lot. We go slow. I get out near the end of the alley. You keep going and turn right into the church driveway. There'll be a service in progress. You're like a latecoming Mormon. You stop and wait. Cut your lights. I aim the rifle through the lattice fence at the back of Walker's house. I have a clear line of fire. You sit and wait. I see a picture of him now. He likes a well-lighted house. He sits in his study at night."

He had a thirty-nine-week subscription to Time. He imagined the backyard photograph in Time. The Castro partisan with his guns and subversive journals. He imagined the cover of Time, a picture seen across the socialist world. The man who shot the fascist general. A friend of the revolution.

"They'll appreciate in Havana that we did it April seventeen," Lee said. "Two years to the day. The invasion was the thing that produced a General Walker, more than any other event."

They turned onto Avondale. He realized Bobby was staring, eyebrows white with flour.

"Seventeen. What seventeen?" Dupard said.

"It's Wednesday, isn't it?"

"This here is April *ten*."

Ted Walker was at the desk in his office, a fifty-three-year-old bachelor who looks like anybody's next-door neighbor, tallish, with jutting brows, flesh going a little slack in the jaw and neck, body slightly stooped, the neighbor who is stern with children, doing his taxes now.

It is the biggest joke in America. General Walker does his taxes.

He was used to talking about himself in the third person. He talked to the press about the Walker case, the attempts to silence Walker. It is only natural, his sense of a public self, when you consider the close and pulsating attention he received in the local press where he ran neck and neck last October with the Cuban missile crisis. It was President Jack who said about the Morning News, "I'm sure the people of Dallas are glad when afternoon rolls around."

The aging ladies love their Ted. They are the last true believers. He mutters the poem of their missing lives.

A cigarette burned in the ashtray. He sat with his back to the window, totaling figures on a scratch pad, taxes, doing his taxes, like any fool and dupe of the Real Control Apparatus. Letters from the true believers were stacked in a basket to his right. The Christian Crusade women, the John Birch men, the semiretired, the wrathful, the betrayed, the ones who keep coming up empty. They had intimate knowledge of the Control Apparatus. It wasn't just politics from afar. It wasn't just the deals of the sellout specialists and softliners, the weak sisters, the no-win policymakers. The Apparatus paralyzed not only our armed forces but our individual lives, frustrating every normal American ambition, infiltrating our minds and bodies with fluoridation, with the creeping fever of trade unions and the left-wing press and the income tax, every modern sickness that saps the nation's will to resist the enemy advance.

The Red Chinese are massing below the California border. There are confirmed reports.

This is the man, ladies and gentlemen, who climbed the base of the Confederate monument in Oxford, Miss., to rally thousands against the integration of the university. The man who so-called led an insurrection, wearing his proud gray Stetson. Oh it was something. Four hundred federal marshals, five hundred state and local police, helicopters, jeeps, fire engines, three thousand National Guardsmen, tear gas blowing through the streets, burning cars, rocks flying everywhere, and birdshot, and sniper fire, two men dead, countless wounded, a couple of hundred arrested, military trucks full of regular army, sixteen thousand combat troops massed against a few thousand students and country boys and patriots of the South, and here is the object and source and cause of the whole thing, one gloomy nigger with a hanky in his face to keep the tear gas from making him cry.

Bring your flag, your tent and your skillet.

That's the main thing Ted actually said. Like a Boy Scout saga, a couple of days in the wholesome outdoors.

To his left was another basket, this one filled with news stories clipped by an aide. Here is Ted filing for election in the Democratic race for governor, a primary in which the Control Apparatus will see to it that he finishes sixth out of six candidates, which is dead last by any reckoning. Here he is with dear mother Charlotte outside a hearing room in Oxford with the leaves rustling down from the sweet gums and maples. This is when they tried to justify putting him in a mental ward with a bunch of gap-tooth idiots. The Apparatus in its grimmest stage, right out of the communist handbook, trying to put a decorated vet in the rubber room. This is what the general is up against, ladies and gentlemen, fellow patriots, loyal Birchers, members of the White Citizens Council, Boy Scouts, Christians, Mother dear.

In the Old Senate Caucus Room they asked him to name the members of the Real Control Apparatus. This is like naming particles in the air, naming molecules or cells. The Apparatus is precisely what we can't see or name. We can't measure it, gentlemen, or take its photograph. It is the mystery we can't get hold of, the plot we can't uncover. This doesn't mean there are no plotters. They are elected officials of our government, Cabinet members, philanthropists, men who know each other by secret signs, who work in the shadows to control our lives.

But he didn't say these things. He mumbled and groaned in the crowded room, then punched a reporter in the face.

I sometimes am confused. We are dealing with tragedies of speech, tragedies of the human body. There are forces we can't comprehend.

He put out one cigarette, lit another. He got tired early now. It was a lingering effect of Operation Midnight Ride, the series of one-night stands in Louisville, Nashville, Amarillo, his journey to arouse the heartland, to get them to listen, St. Louis, Indianapolis, etc., and he was still recovering. Beatniks came to picket, the most godawful bunch of Castro look-alikes anybody ever saw.

It is time to go down and liquidate the scourge which has descended on the island of Cuba.

It tired him and got to him, plain wore him out. Those deadly hotel rooms where he was never more totally alone and bare of comfort. I sometimes am confused and lost, ready to give in to lonely despair, tired of shuffling and dodging what I know and feel. Think of those uncombed boys in baggy jeans, sign-carriers, who shout dirty words into the night. They are soft beneath the drifting Cuban hair. Hotels. This is where the switch takes place, where he is a stranger who mind-wanders into the midst of the other side, only following what he's always felt.

Some people think a nigra is a sunburnt white.

He had a better time when he was running in the Texas primary. The crowds were rollicking. They were chanting and singing crowds, hopeful people, not the worn souls of Midnight Ride. He scratched out numbers, added up tax dollars, but what he thought about were flags waving in halls across the whole damn state, the draped bunting, the clear American voices calling out a song.

> Put on your Pro Blue bonnet
> With the Lone Star upon it
> And we'll put Ted Walker on the way

Was that a firecracker? He turned to the window, standing in the same motion, but slowly, giving the matter some thought. Kids throwing firecrackers around? Did we put the screen back in? The screen was in, he saw, and the window was shut. All the windows were shut because the air conditioner was on. He moved out of the light and something caught his eye. There was a hole in the wall about the size of a half-dollar. He was trying to get it straight. He looked at the window again and the glass had radial streaks in it near the crosspiece of the wooden frame. He moved farther out of the light. His cigarette burning in the ashtray. He went upstairs and got his revolver. He came down quickly. He went out the back door and stood in the dimness with the gun, stood looking, dead still, feeling the heat like a wall of air. Then he went back inside and called the police. That's when he noticed bits of glass and wood in the hair on his right forearm, just below the rolled-up sleeve, and there were grainy fragments mixed in, bright as sand, a residue he believed were slivers of the copper jacket of a high-velocity bullet.

He was not half surprised. They have been plotting for a long time, every element in the Control Apparatus, planning and scheming carefully to keep Walker quiet. This is what shooting people does.

He got a pair of tweezers, sat in his easy chair and began picking metal out of his arm while he waited for the police to arrive.

Marina was worried about Lee. In the morning he told her he'd lost his job. He blamed it on the FBI. He said they'd probably come around the shop and asked questions about him. Now he was late coming home. Coming home from what? He said he had typing class but the class ended at a quarter past seven, three hours ago, and besides it was a Wednesday and there was no class on Wednesday.

He wanted her to go back to the USSR. He could not support a wife and child in America. He made her write to the Soviet embassy in Washington. Would they pay for the return of a Russian citizen and her baby girl?

She was pregnant again, which is the way destiny sometimes intervenes.

At least they had a balcony where June could crawl around in the fresh air. When they separated, after Fort Worth, she stayed with half a dozen different families, some nights with this one, then over to that one. It was beating on her nerves, all that moving around. One night Lee stayed with her in one of the Russian homes. There was a full refrigerator and an electric can opener. Two telephones. They made love with the TV on.

He told the landlady on Elsbeth Street she was a Czech.

He hit her once in front of people because the zipper on the side of her skirt was partly open. In front of people.

Holland was unbelievably clean. It was her dream country, with trim houses and spotless little children.

There were bargain stores in Oak Cliff. She went in out of the heat and walked the aisles. She went to shoe stores and stores called army-navy. She bought this, rejected that, mentally, walking the narrow aisles.

Maybe they would all go back to Russia, although she didn't want to. Maybe they would move to New Orleans. He was talking about New Orleans, his hometown, a port city like Archangel, where she grew up.

He did most of the housework and gave her breakfast in bed on Sunday. She was shameless when it came to sleeping late. People gave her things and he insulted them.

He took the bus to a place called the Field of Love, where he practiced shooting his rifle. They argued about this. He hit her and she threw something at him and he hit her again with a closed hand, making her bleed from the nose.

We buy groceries on Tuesday.

It was one more misfortune on her head, this lost job of his. But the pattern of a life can't be seen in fleeting days or weeks. Maybe it was their destiny to live in a port city, to feel the sea breeze and glimpse the tender promise ahead.

He'd never been so late. Something told her to look in his study. She found a note in Russian on the small table he used as a desk. There were eleven points listed by number, with certain words underlined.

She read quickly, in a blur.

He told her not to worry about the rent. He'd paid the rent on the second. He'd paid the water and gas. He told her to send newspaper clippings (if there was anything about him in the papers) to the Soviet embassy. He said the embassy would come to her aid once they knew everything. He said the Red Cross would help her. He told her money was due from work. Go to the bank and cash the check. He asked her to hold on to his personal papers. But throw out his clothes or give them away.

Number eleven was, If I am alive and taken prisoner, the city jail is located at the end of the bridge we always cross when we go downtown.

She stood a moment in the small room. Then she moved softly to the kitchen, where she folded the note and hid it in a Russian volume called *The Book of Useful Advice*.

Lee was back at the Gulf station drinking another Coke, his shirt sticking to him. He edged closer to the office, where a radio was playing. He figured it wouldn't take long before a report came in. Every time a song ended and someone on the radio started to speak, he moved a little closer to the office door, listening for urgent words, for *shot, dead, dying*, that excitement riding high in the chest when there is news of important violence. Both weapons were in the car, with the green slicker, about three miles away by now, somewhere in the West Dallas ghetto. He'd get them in a day or two, or when it was safe.

He took a deep swallow, then let the bottle dangle between his index and middle fingers. Things were slow. Two men in grease suits talked inside the office. The room was brightly lit, with stacked cans of motor oil, a sexy wall calendar. Lee moved closer. He tried to look like an idler on some weedy edge of town.

Late. The cars stopped coming. There was nothing on the radio but rock 'n' roll. He finished the Coke, put the bottle in the case of empties and walked home in the head-splitting heat.

George de Mohrenschildt listened to the car radio, changing stations often. He was trying to get some fresh news on the Walker affair. The attempt fascinated him. Evidently it was the nearest of misses. The bullet changed course when it nicked the window frame. The police weren't saying much else. It was frustrating. He was hungry for developments. He didn't want the episode to slip into oblivion.

He drove the Galaxie convertible into Oak Cliff. Next to him on the seat was a big pink rabbit for Baby June.

He hadn't seen Lee for some time. Lee undoubtedly felt used and badly handled and abandoned. All the sad words in the beggar's dictionary. But it was his own fault. All he had to do was talk to Collings, man to man. George half admired his resistance. There was a purity of sorts. But it was boring too.

There was a new abandonment in the works. George was going to Haiti and he knew Lee would feel that the one man who took an interest in him was scramming out the door. George wanted to open up the country of Haiti. He knew the number-one banker there, which meant many things were possible. Oil surveying, resorts, holding companies. There was also a weapons shipment in the works, deep deep in the dark. Front companies were rising out of desk drawers. There were numbered bank accounts, untraceable ship charters. A fellow at the Pentagon wanted George to help provide cover for an anti-Castro operation centered in Haiti.

He found Neely Street. He thought about people spending their lives in a place like this. Lee sat in this hole reading obscure economics, mumbo-jumbo theory of the left. It was sad, interesting, boring, stupid. It was also infuriating. It hadn't occurred to George that seeing where Lee and Marina lived would make him angry. There was something serious and unsettling about this kind of squalor. Everything was rickety, makeshift, slanting. Everything slanted. It was repellent, not much better than a slum in Port-au-Prince, and George realized he could never again be amused by Lee, by the boy with the odd past and the out-of-place manner.

Marina and Lee came to the door. George said to Lee in his biggest voice, "So my friend. How come you missed that son of a bitch?"

He waited for the sure laugh. But they retreated to the living room. There was a shrinking in the air. Obviously the joke was not so funny in this household.

He handed over the Easter bunny and told them he was going to Haiti, long-term business, let's keep in touch.

He watched Lee's face change. He felt bad about that. He was leaving the boy without someone to go to with his ideas and his troubles. Marina went to the kitchen to make tea and George talked in her general direction about his vision of Haiti. Hotels, casinos, hydroelectric plants, food-processing plants. Lee sat on the sofa. His peculiar smile appeared, the little smirk that made George think of a comedian in a silent film with the screen going dark around his head.

"So someone finally smiles. It's a very delayed reaction. I walk in the door with a joke, no one makes a sound. I think I'm in the valley of lost souls. Now I see a smile peeping out. What is so amusing? Please. Inform me."

"I sent you a picture," Lee said.

"What picture?"

"It's the kind of picture a person looks at and maybe he understands something he didn't understand before."

"Sounds mysterious," George said.

"Maybe he sees the truth about someone."

Driving home George thought about the heavy schedule of appointments he had in New York and Washington, preparing the way for various aspects of the Haitian venture. He had the Bureau of Mines, Lehman Trading, Chase Manhattan, Manufacturers Hanover Trust, the Pentagon, the ICA, the CIA. The last in fact was strictly social, lunch with an old Agency friend, Larry Parmenter, a Bay of Pigs character but otherwise decent and amusing, a chap who knew his wines.

He sat at his desk opening and reading three days of mail. He came to the envelope addressed by Lee Oswald. Just a snapshot inside. It showed Lee dressed in black, holding a rifle in one hand, some newspapers in the other. Am I interested or bored, thought George. He looked at the reverse side. It was inscribed *To my friend George from Lee Oswald*.

George checked the postmark on the envelope. April 9. One day before the attempt on General Walker.

He looked at the second inscription. This was in Russian, clearly in Marina's handwriting and evidently written without Lee's knowledge, sneaked in before he sealed and mailed the envelope— a private message from the wife of the poseur to the sophisticated older friend.

Hunter of fascists—ha ha ha!!!

6 September

Wayne Elko sat at the window of a shotgun shack in the bayous west of New Orleans. There was no glass in the windows, just dusty plastic stripping, and he looked at three blurry men taking target practice in a mixed stand of cypress and willow.

There were other shacks in the area, here and there, used by weekenders who came out frogging and crawfishing.

Early mist. The gunfire sounded small and distant, little pop-gun compressions in the heavy air.

David Ferrie, a magnetic presence, a humorous master of games, was shooting at tin cans with a .22.

The swag-belly Cuban, Raymo, had a modified Winchester he liked to break down and reassemble, running a patch through the bore, sandpapering the stock.

The third man, named Leon, worked the bolt on an ancient carbine; sighted, fired, worked the bolt.

This was a new and hastily assembled camp, Ferrie explained, which is why the lack of creature comforts. The regular setup was at Lacombe, nearer New Orleans, where a number of anti-Castro factions had trained in guerrilla tactics until federal agents raided, grabbing a huge store of dynamite and bomb casings. This project would be kept small and restricted. Speak to no one. Respect the environment. Wait for the moment.

Wayne thought these were rules that verged on mystical.

He knew they weren't here just to fire weapons. T-Jay wanted them sequestered. Raymo and Wayne especially. The business was sorting itself out and he wanted his shooters wrapped tight, where he could find them.

Wayne stood outside wearing Levis, his bare chest pale and veined. He was growing his hair down over his neck, a rat's tail he painstakingly braided. He went barefoot over the moist ground. There was a storm hanging close, a stillness and metallic light, pressure building. The bird noise was fretful and spooked.

Frank Vásquez was back in the Everglades spying on Alpha 66.

The others stood talking by a fallen tree. Wayne wore a hunting knife in a leather sheath clipped to his belt, just for the general look of it. Ferrie smiled at the sight of his bare feet.

"Here is a man who has no fear."

"I never understand about people and snakes," Wayne said. "Like what harm do they intend? They never touch me. I've had incidents with snakes where they never touch me."

"It's not they touch you," Raymo said. "It's stepping on them. Not seeing where you step."

"Copperhead," Leon said.

"I have the primitive fear," Ferrie said. "All my fears are primitive. It's the limbic system of the brain. I've got a million years of terror stored up in there."

He wore a crushed sun hat, the expressive brows like clown paint over his eyes. He handed Wayne the rifle. They watched him walk to the lopsided dock and climb into the skiff. His car was parked on a dirt road about half a mile downstream and the skiff was the only way in and out.

They took turns firing at a silhouette target that was the one-time property of the FBI. Then they went up to the long shack for something to eat.

The first drops of rain hit the sheeting, well spaced and heavy. They sat around the table and talked about jobs, odd jobs, seasonal jobs. Wayne told them about his pool-skimming days in California. Leon described a radio plant somewhere, lathes and grinding machines, floor awash in oil, the workers' hands stained black. Raymo talked about the hands of cane-cutters, seamed with cuts, sticky and black from the juice.

This was the first time Wayne had heard Leon say more than two words. He didn't know where Leon fit in, except it was obvious he was some kind of special component with his own little twist or spin. He came and he went, carrying the Italian carbine. The others seemed to leave some space around him, like he was holy or diseased.

They talked about prisons they'd been in.

"I used to believe the great thing of Castro was the time he spent in prison," Raymo said. "He went to prison in Cuba and Mexico both. I used to say this is the man's honor and strength. He comes out of prison with authority if he is sent there for his beliefs. It is completely different in Castro's own prisons. We came out of La Cabaña with anger and disgust. We were the worms of the CIA."

"They sent me to prison in the military," Leon said.

"What for?"

"Politics. Just like Fidel. I spent a night in jail in New Orleans a month ago. Politics."

"I sat in a lockup for three days," Wayne said. "Our launch was intercepted about ten minutes out of the Keys. Violating the neutrality act. It was T-Jay that got us out. He fixed it somehow. The charges were dropped nicey-nicey."

Raymo said, "Castro spent fourteen months in an isolation cell. He read Karl Marx. He read every Russian. He told us he read twelve hours a day. He read in the dark. Always studying, always analyzing. Years later I saw the executions of men who fought by his side in the mountains."

"It's clear in history," Leon said, "that a man has to go to prison for his beliefs. It's a necessary stage in the evolution of any movement that cuts against the system. Eventually he merges his beliefs in the actual struggle."

"I thought about it a lot," Raymo said, "and I'll tell you my beliefs. I believed in the United States of America. The country that could do no wrong. It was bigger than anything, bigger than God. With the great U.S. behind us, how could we lose? They told us, they told us, they promise, they repeat and repeat. We have the full backing of the military. We went to the beaches thinking they would support us with air, with navy. Impossible we could lose. We are backed by the great U.S. What happens? We find ourselves in the swamps, lost and hungry, we are eating tree bark by this time, and the radio is saying, 'Attention, brigade, the owl is hooting in the barn.' "

He looked from one face to the other, laughing.

" 'Tomorrow, my brothers, the crippled child climbs the hill.' "

They were all laughing.

"They disarmed us and fastened our hands in one big looping chain and put us in troop trucks to go to the nearest militia camp and there's a plane passing right overhead and I call out, I tell our men, 'Don't shoot, boys, it's one of ours.' "

His eyes were fierce and happy. He looked from Leon to Wayne and back, laughing cockeyed, hitting the table hard. The tin plates jumped. When they were quiet again he looked at his home fries and eggs for two full minutes. He brushed his mustache with an index finger, then began to eat.

"We are actually eating tree bark," he said again, without the wild-eyed glee this time, chewing his food slowly.

Later they saw T-Jay coming through the downpour, a wavy windblown rain. Behind him the trees were leaning. He had a duffel bag on his right shoulder and another under his left arm. Inside he worked the bags open. There were two leather cases in one bag, a single case in the other. Each case was lined in billiard cloth and fitted with a pair of high-powered rifles. The men hefted the guns, mumbling, and passed them hand to hand. The window sheeting billowed and snapped.

"Scopes are in the car," T-Jay said.

They sat and talked about the guns. Wayne believed there was friendship in guns. This might or might not be a paradox. His experience in life and in the movies told him that peace can wear away the bonds of friendship. This was the lesson of the samurai. Action is truth, and truth falters when combat ends and the villagers are free to go back to their planting. Again we survive, again we lose, says a character in *Seven Samurai*.

T-Jay had water still running down his face. He sat in a puddle. He had his right elbow on the table, arm up, and kept clenching and unclenching his fist. He was more talkative than Wayne had ever known him. Raymo was talkative. The guns were a language and a memory. Wayne happened to catch some sideline dialogue between T-Jay and Leon. To the effect that Leon would not be using one of the new rifles. To the effect that he would be using the Mannlicher he'd come into camp with. It was clear this was mutually agreed.

The wind was battering the shack. They talked for hours, telling funny and bloody stories. Wayne felt sweet and light as Jesus on a moonbeam.

Frank Vásquez was on the road in Mississippi driving Raymo's Bel Air *decrépito*. Driving was not natural to him. He was literal-minded about speed limits and grew tense when road signs appeared, not always understanding the symbols and fearing he would enter upon misfortune. He'd had car trouble twice since Miami. He'd taken wrong roads twice. He spent a night in a motel where a fight broke out in the parking lot among four or five men, their feet crunching on the gravel, breath coming heavy, a woman crying in a white convertible, somewhere near Pensacola.

He was not used to being out here in the U.S., away from Spanish-speaking people, without Raymo by his side.

He had news for T-Jay. Alpha was planning a major operation. Miami, November. At first he could not guess the nature of the mission but it had to be unique if it involved an American city and not some Cuban port or refinery.

Frank had spent two and a half weeks in Alpha's camp off Highway 41 along with men from other groups and factions, running obstacle courses through the slash pines. One day he was approached by Alpha's secretary-general. This man wanted Mackey to take part in an operation that would go a long way toward paying back the failure of Playa Girón. Mackey was held in highest esteem. The mission leaders believed he should have a hand in this action.

No place or date was mentioned. Frank gleaned these things from the general run of talk. The fellowship oppressed him. He hated the drilling and shooting. The leaders of Alpha wore sunglasses, combat boots, berets, half-serious beards. If these men were so violently anti-Castro, why did they want to look like Che Guevara?

He remembered what Raymo had told him, that after a battle in the Sierra here comes Che on a mud-spattered mule to talk to the captured troops. What is the first thing they do? They ask for his autograph. This is when everyone knew Batista was finished.

Frank thought of the mountains, the dense green cover, smoke rolling down from the heights, vanishing at a certain altitude, rolling down. The rain was total. They lived in camouflaged barracks and sometimes in mud and he thought about the idea he was fighting for. Full dignity for the people of Cuba. Justice for the hungry and forgotten. He knew from the first day he would not remain. He was not a rebel in body or spirit. He had an ordinary nature.

His mother, the author of his days, welcomed him back with a sad laugh.

Frank taught grades one to six, often at the same time, in a school at the edge of the company town. The company was United Fruit and he had two brothers who were foremen in the cane fields and lived with their wives and kids, each family in a ten-by-ten room in a row of ten rooms built back to back with ten other rooms, all set in one long building constructed on five-foot stilts. The cane-cutters and their families lived under the building in squat hovels made of cardboard and sacking.

One could not help noticing that the American executives of La United lived in well-staffed and graceful homes on streets lined with coconut palms. Frank blamed the government, not the company. He expected his brothers to get out of the fields and become skilled workers in the vast mill. La United was not blind to the notion of ambition. From mill workers they could advance to office staff or engineering. They could get two rooms each in a house on a street that was lighted at night. Americans respected those who worked efficiently, who got things done. A man could conceivably get ahead.

Then the rebels came, his former comrades, to burn the cane fields. This was consistent with Cuban history. Whoever rises in revolt, the first thing they do is burn the sugar cane. It is a statement about economic dependence and foreign control. Frank watched the fields burn and knew there were communists behind it. He'd feared this all along. There's more to it, there's something we don't know about. The fires cut and jumped through the canebrakes. The private police of La United were long gone.

In Havana he stood in line with hundreds of others at the curbside outside the U.S. embassy, waiting to apply for a visa. And now he was on the road near the Louisiana border, driving into thunderheads.

On his fourth day with Castro he shot a government scout, aiming through a telescopic sight. It was uncanny. You press a button and a man drops dead a hundred meters away. It seemed hollow and remote, falsifying everything. It was a trick of the lenses. The man is an accurate picture. Then he is upside down. Then he is right side up. You shoot at a series of images conveyed to you through a metal tube. The force of a death should be enormous but how can you know what kind of man you've killed or who was the braver and stronger if you have to peer through layers of glass that deliver the image but obscure the meaning of the act? War has a conscience or it's ordinary murder.

Frank knew what Alpha was planning to do. He thought and he thought and it had to be that. Once he learned the President was going to Miami, there was nothing else to believe.

His brothers also fled Castro, later, dangerously, floating to Key West on an oil-drum raft. They went back in boats as well, one killed in the fighting on the beaches, one captured and taken to the fortress prison, where he was allowed to die quietly of starvation, his form of public prayer, a demonstration against the beatings and executions.

Fervent men, exiles, fighters against communism took off from the Keys in Cessnas and Piper Comanches to drop incendiary devices on the sugar cane of Cuba. The fields were burning again.

Here on the road in the Deep South he saw something that showed how strangely and completely a hatred for this President reached into certain parts of the culture, into daily lives. During the first long day of driving he'd wandered into Georgia by mistake and passed a drive-in theater where they were showing a movie about young Kennedy the war hero. It was called *PT 109* and under the title on the signboard there was a special incentive: *See how the Japs almost got Kennedy*.

It scared him all right, the signs he saw on the road in the U.S. Here was Louisiana in heavy rain. He would tell T-Jay everything he'd seen and heard with Alpha 66 in the Glades. The conclusion wasn't hard to draw, that Kennedy was the object of the mission.

Something in his heart longed for this murder, even though he knew it was a sin.

The Curator sends autopsy photos of Oswald. Nicholas Branch feels obliged to study them, although he doesn't know what he can possibly learn here. There are the open eyes, the large wound in the left side, the two ridges of heavy stitching that meet beneath the clavicle and descend in one line to the genital area, forming the letter Y. The left eye is swiveled toward the camera, watching.

The Curator sends the results of ballistics tests carried out on human skulls and goat carcasses, on blocks of gelatin mixed with horsemeat. There are photographs of skulls with the right cranial portion blown away. There are bullet-shattered goat heads in close-up. Branch studies a picture of a gelatin-tissue model "dressed" like the President. It is pure modernist sculpture, a block of gelatin layered in suit and shirt material with a strip of undershirt showing, bullet-smoked. There are documents concerning exit velocities. There is a picture of a human skull filled with gelatin and covered with goatskin to simulate a scalp.

The Curator sends FBI memos concerning the President's brain, which has been missing from the National Archives for over twenty years.

He sends an actual warped bullet that has been fired for test purposes through the wrist of a seated cadaver. We are on another level here, Branch thinks. Beyond documents now. They want me to *touch* and *smell*.

He doesn't know why they are sending him this particular grisly material after all these years. Shattered bone and horror. That's all it means to him. There is nothing to understand, no insights to be had from these pictures and statistics, from this melancholy bullet with its nose leveled and spread like a penny left on trolley tracks. (How old he is.) The bloody goat heads seem to mock him. He begins to think this is the point. They are rubbing his face in the blood and gunk. They are mocking him. They are saying in effect, "Here, look, these are the true images. This is your history. Here is a blown-out skull for you to ponder. Here is lead penetrating bone."

They are saying, "Look, touch, this is the true nature of the event. Not your beautiful ambiguities, your lives of the major players, your compassions and sadnesses. Not your roomful of theories, your museum of contradictory facts. There are no contradictions here. Your history is simple. See, the man on the slab. The open eye staring. The goat head oozing rudimentary matter."

They are saying, "This is what it looks like to get shot."

How can Branch forget the contradictions and discrepancies? These are the soul of the wayward tale. One of the first documents he examined was the medical report on Pfc. Oswald's self-inflicted gunshot wound. In one sentence the weapon is described as 45-caliber. In the next sentence it is 22-caliber. Facts are lonely things. Branch has seen how a pathos comes to cling to the firmest fact.

Oswald's eyes are gray, they are blue, they are brown. He is five feet nine, five feet ten, five feet eleven. He is right-handed, he is left-handed. He drives a car, he does not. He is a crack shot and a dud. Branch has support for all these propositions in eyewitness testimony and commission exhibits.

Oswald even looks like different people from one photograph to the next. He is solid, frail, thin-lipped, broad-featured, extroverted, shy and bank-clerkish, all, with the columned neck of a fullback. He looks like everybody. In two photos taken in the military he is a grim killer and a baby-face hero. In another photo he sits in profile with a group of fellow Marines on a rattan mat under palm trees. Four or five men face the camera. They all look like Oswald. Branch thinks they look more like Oswald than the figure in profile, officially identified as him.

The Oswald shadings, the multiple images, the split perceptions—eye color, weapons caliber—these seem a foreboding of what is to come. The endless fact-rubble of the investigations. How many shots, how many gunmen, how many directions? Powerful events breed their own network of inconsistencies. The simple facts elude authentication. How many wounds on the President's body? What is the size and shape of the wounds? The multiple Oswald reappears. Isn't that *him* in a photograph of a crowd of people on the front steps of the Book Depository just as the shooting begins? A startling likeness, Branch concedes. He concedes everything. He questions everything, including the basic suppositions we make about our world of light and shadow, solid objects and ordinary sounds, and our ability to measure such things, to determine weight, mass and direction, to see things as they are, recall them clearly, be able to say what happened.

He takes refuge in his notes. The notes are becoming an end in themselves. Branch has decided it is premature to make a serious effort to turn these notes into coherent history. Maybe it will always be premature. Because the data keeps coming. Because new lives enter the record all the time. The past is changing as he writes.

Every name takes him on a map tour of the Dallas labyrinth.

Jack Ruby was born Jacob Rubenstein. He adopted the middle name Leon to honor the memory of a friend, Leon Cooke, shot to death in a labor dispute.

There are several versions of George de Mohrenschildt's name. He sometimes used the alias Philip Harbin.

Carmine Latta was born Carmelo Rosario Lattanzi.

Walter Everett used the cover name Thomas R. Stainback during his years in clandestine work.

Lee Oswald used about a dozen names including the backward-running O. H. Lee and the peculiar D. F. Drictal. He employed the latter in the blank space for Witness when he filled out an order form for the revolver he purchased through the mail. Branch has toiled over the inner structure of D. F. Drictal for many an hour. He feels like a child with alphabet blocks, trying to make a pretty word, and he has managed to find fragments of the names Fidel, Castro, Oswald and Dupard. It may be that D. F. Drictal is the strained merging of written and living characters, of words and politics, a witness to the decision to assassinate General Walker. Branch wonders whether Oswald registered the fact that the general's first name and middle initial match those of Edwin A. Ekdahl, young Lee's stepfather for a time and the man Marguerite Oswald never stopped blaming.

The Dallas disc jockey known as Weird Beard was Russell Lee Moore, who also used the name Russ Knight.

The man calling himself Aleksei Kirilenko, a KGB cover name, was in fact Sergei Broda, according to records supplied by the Curator.

After repeated requests, Branch has learned from the Curator that Theodore J. Mackey, known as T-Jay, was born Joseph Michael Horniak and was last seen in Norfolk, Virginia, January 1964, in the company of a suspected prostitute, possibly of Asian extraction, name unknown.

Mackey sat in the car listening to Frank Vásquez. Frank was excited and tired. He said everything three times and quoted Alpha leaders completely, precisely and with gestures. The two men were surrounded by swamp night, the car sitting downstream from the shack, lights off, the banjo frogs getting up a racket.

Frank's judgment was that Alpha planned to kill the President. He seemed to think Mackey would have trouble believing this. But it was easy to believe. Mackey believed everything these days including how simple it was for Frank to walk into Alpha's camp and out again, carrying every kind of rumor and news.

Alpha was not known for shyness or tight security. They held press conferences to announce their raids on Cuban installations and Soviet freighters. Once they invited a Life photographer on a raid, ten men in two boats. A storm ruined the mission and the pictures but Life did a story anyway. Brave boys of Alpha. South Florida was full of Alpha members, uncounted, devout, screaming in their teeth.

"And this is what you also planned, all this time, T-Jay, to get Kennedy?"

"It's just his time has come."

"I don't think we kill an American president so easy. Miami, they'll have extra protection. This is not like walking into some little capital city, walking into the palace, buying off some bodyguards with a few dollars."

"The barrier is down, Frank. When Jack sent out word to get Castro, he put himself in a world of blood and pain. Nobody told him he had to live there. He made the choice with his brother Bobby. So it's Jack's own idea we're guided by. And once an idea hits."

"Not that I don't wish to see it happen."

"Oh I think it will."

"Someone has to pay for Cuba."

"You and I demand it, Frank."

"And it will point to Castro. They will say here is the source. He sent the men."

"This is what we're looking for. But even so, if all the gears don't mesh, at least we have our man. Someone has to die. It is very much a part of our thinking that Jack is the one."

"This is like Alpha. Someone has to die, they say."

"They can't contain it anymore."

"Do we go in with them?"

"I say why not, Frank."

"Do you trust them to run it?"

"They cross the water to blow up Russian shipping. What the hell. This is a man in an open car."

Frank needed to get some sleep.

"Who's in the camp?" he said.

"Raymo and Wayne and a visitor. You don't say too much to him. Smile nice, shake hands."

Oswald wanted his path to be tracked and his name to be known. He had private designs, a hero's safe haven in Cuba. He wanted to use the rifle that could be traced to him through the transparent Hidell. Mackey was cautious. The kid had a dizzying history and he was playing some kind of mirror game with Ferrie in New Orleans. Left is right and right is left. But he continued to fit the outline that Everett had devised six months earlier. There were the homemade documents, the socialist literature, the weapons and false names. He was one element of the original plan that still made sense.

Mackey trained the headlights on the skiff. Frank climbed in and switched on the deer lamp and the boat moved quietly through the duckweed and past the sunken trees.

Mackey sat in the dark again.

Some of Alpha's boldest operations were run by elements hidden in the Agency. Alpha had CIA mentors. These were men Mackey wasn't even close to knowing. They weren't necessarily known to the leaders of Alpha. A case officer would show up to provide money and to advise on sabotage missions. He would limit his contacts to one or two men in Alpha. They would not know his real name or his position in the Agency. There's always something they aren't letting you know. Alpha was run like a dream clinic. The Agency worked up a vision, then got Alpha to make it come true.

Too many people, too many levels of plotting. Mackey had to safeguard the attempt not only from Alpha but from Everett and Parmenter. They might decide to expose the plan now that he'd removed himself from contact, leaving them to their hieroglyphics. Then Banister and Ferrie and the men dealing out the cash. He had to protect the attempt, make it safe from betrayal.

He waved a hand at the persistent hum that jumped around his ear. A mosquito is a vector of disease. He got out of the car and listened. Something felt strange. Then he heard a vast rustling in the trees, coming louder with the wind. It took him some time to realize it was only water tapping on the leaves, rainwater stirred by the wind and falling leaf to leaf, everywhere around him.

His own car was parked next to Raymo's. It was a three-hour drive to New Orleans, where he would talk to Banister about Alpha 66. Let everyone know. Let everyone tell everyone.

Mackey would put every effort into Miami. He would put men and weapons into Miami. Agree to a joint operation with Alpha. Do the groundwork. Get people and money moving. Eighteen November in Miami. He would build a Miami façade.

In New Orleans

The first thing he did was take a bus to the end of the Lakeview line to see his father's grave. The keeper helped him find the stone. He stood there in the heat and light, searching for a way to feel. He pictured a man in a gray suit, a collector for Metropolitan Life. Then his mind wandered through a hundred local scenes. Oh bike-riding in City Park. Seafood dinners at Aunt Lillian's every Friday when he was eleven, after he took the train alone from Texas. He hid in the back room reading funnybooks while his cousins fought and played.

A man in a gray suit who tips his hat to women.

In Exchange Alley there was a Negro hunkered on the curb looking in the side mirror of a parked car as he shaved, his mug and his brush on the pavement next to him.

Lee looked up Oswald in the phone book, tracking lost relations.

Lee looked for work. He lied on all his job applications. He lied needlessly and to a purpose. He made up past addresses, made up references and past employment, invented job qualifications, wrote down names of companies that didn't exist and companies that did, although he'd never worked for them.

An interviewer noted on a card: *Suit. Tie. Polite.*

Marina sat in a chair on the screened-in side porch. She held Lee's half-finished glass of Dr Pepper. It was nearly midnight and still wet and hot and awful. This was their home now, three rooms in a frame house with a little bit of gingerbread up top and some weedy vegetation at the front and side.

Lee was out there somewhere with the garbage. They couldn't afford a garbage can so he slipped out three nights a week to stuff their garbage in other people's containers. He went out wearing basketball shorts from his childhood or the childhood of one of his brothers, no top, and sneaked along the 4900 block of Magazine Street looking for a can to stuff the trash.

She watched him come back now, walking up the neighbor's driveway, which was how you reached the entrance to their part of the house. He came onto the porch and took the glass from her hand. TV voices traveled across the backyards and driveways.

"I am sitting here thinking he doesn't love me anymore."

"Papa loves his wife and child."

"He thinks I am binding him like a rope or chain. His attitude is I bind him. He has the high-flying world of his ideas. If only he didn't have a wife to hold him back, how perfect everything would be."

"We're here to start over," he said.

"I am thinking he wants me to go back to Russia. This is what he means by starting over."

"Russia is one idea. I've also been working on the idea I could hijack a plane, take a plane and go to Cuba and then you'll come with June to live there."

"First you shoot at a man."

"We may not be finished with him."

"I am finished with him."

"There's a travel ban to Cuba."

"And you are finished with him. Leaving me a note."

"Little Cuba needs trained soldiers and advisers."

"Scaring me to death. Now you want to steal an airplane. Who will fly it?"

"Stupid. The pilot. I kidnap it, I hijack it. It's a flight to Miami and I take my revolver and go in the flight cabin. It's called the flight cabin."

"Who is stupid? Which one of us?"

"My snub-nose revolver. My two-inch Commando."

She had to laugh at that.

"I stick up the plane and tell them to drop me in Havana."

They both laughed. They took turns drinking the warm soda pop. Then he went around with the spray can squirting roaches. Marina stood in the doorway watching. They had roaches in large numbers, really extraordinary numbers. She told him he would never kill a roach with the cheap spray he bought. She followed him into the kitchen, telling him that roaches drink these cheaper sprays and have babies. She watched him spray the baseboards carefully, with strict precision, so he wouldn't waste a drop.

The next evening he took her to the French Quarter and they rode the streetcar home. Tourists glanced at the Russian-speaking couple. Exotic New Orleans.

They made love on the small bed in the closed room. He had the feeling she wanted more, more of something, more of body, money, things, excitement, and he knew it in the technicalities of the act, in the breathing minutes, mysteriously.

He was paid a dollar fifty an hour to grease coffee machines. The maintenance man complained that he couldn't read Lee's notations in the greasing log. He complained that he couldn't find Lee, that he had to go through the building top to bottom looking for him. Lee stuck out his index finger and raised his thumb, holding the pose for a moment. Then he dropped the thumb and went "Pow."

The main library at Lee Circle was gone. He had to ask people where the new one was located. He walked north and then east and when he found the building he took a placard out of a manila envelope and unfolded it. The placard had a hole at either end with a string going through. He stood in front of the library with the placard strung around his neck and started handing out pamphlets he'd been receiving in the mail from the Fair Play for Cuba Committee.

He wore a short-sleeve white shirt and dark tie. He'd written in crayon on the placard: *Viva Fidel*.

About a minute and a half later the Feebees pounced. A man came sauntering up showing the grin of a long-lost pal. His name was Agent Bateman.

"Seriously. I'm not here to arrest or harass you. Let's find a place to sit and talk."

They went to a sorry-looking diner near the Trailways station. It was late afternoon, a Saturday, and nobody was in the place. They sat at the counter and spent some time reading the bill of fare on the wall. Agent Bateman was probably younger than he looked at first glance, a man with a longish head, balding, like a high-school coach and science teacher in a TV series.

The only thing slick about him was his shoes, which were shined into the fourth dimension.

"We have you in our files at the field office here. I'm the fellow who keeps an eye."

"You handle my file."

"Ever since your defection. Queries come in, due to you were born here."

"I like the high old ceilings and the live oaks."

"Is that why you're back?"

"They talked to me once before. An Agent Freitag."

"That was Fort Worth. I am New Orleans."

"My Russian period is over. That was long ago. Why can't I just live my life without someone coming around, coming around?"

"I have the theory, Hey, there's nothing in the world that's harder to do than live a straightforward life. I go so far to say there's no such thing."

"What do you want?" Lee said.

"Right now? A grilled-cheese sandwich with crisp bacon, which is impossible to get because they grill everything together and the cheese gets done before the bacon. It's a law of physics. So you get pale bubbly bacon. I know about your correspondence with Fair Play for Cuba in New York and the Socialist Workers Party and so on. Routine mail intercepts. I could spend about four hours a day making your life miserable. Visit your place of work. Put out lead sheets to have you and your wife and your relatives interviewed and reinterviewed to the end of recorded time."

Lee still had the placard around his neck.

"Or I could sit you down and talk to you about our mutual interests. Like you want to carry on your political activities without being pestered on a daily basis."

"And you want."

"There is a crackdown in progress. This anti-Castro business has gotten out of hand. There's a group called Alpha 66 that makes hit-and-run attacks on Soviet ships in Cuban ports. People in Washington are very unhappy. It's an embarrassment to the administration, and they're determined to stop it, and the Bureau has orders to gather intelligence against these groups that are shipping arms and making raids."

It occurred to Lee that this man thought he'd performed some function for Agent Freitag in Fort Worth. He must be in the files as a cooperating Marxist, ha ha, or part-time political informer.

"There's a detective agency here in town," Bateman said. "It operates as a nerve center for the anti-Castro movement in the area. A man named Guy Banister runs the office. He is ex-FBI. Normally speaking we are on the same side. We trade information with Banister all the time. But sometimes there is the necessity of, we turn around, we turn about. I want to get inside Guy Banister Associates. I need a little opening, a crack in the wall. By the way I want to ask. Were you with the Office of Naval Intelligence, going into Russia? Because I know a communication was sent from our Fort Worth desk to ONI."

"They had a false defector program."

"Inserting people. This I'm aware of."

"There are gray areas in ONI. I'm one of those areas."

Bateman seemed to appreciate the remark. He said, "That's only fitting because in this city at this particular time, black is white is black. In other words people are playing havoc with the categories."

There was a trace of enthusiasm in his voice.

"Banister recruits students. He has students go into campus situations to monitor leftist activity. You're student-age. You're familiar with the language of left and right. You know your Cuba."

"I approach Banister for an assignment but I'm actually an informer for the Bureau."

"We use the word informant. It's not sleazy and ratty terminology. What would you say to being developed along those lines? You'd be surprised at the status of some of our informants. Off the top of my head I'd say we could stock the alumni association of a fair-size college."

They sat over their lunch plates for a moment, thinking it all out. There was a Merry Xmas sign going gray on the wall.

"Now tell me, do I keep going? Because this business implies trust. It is tricky to bring off. It requires a certain kind of individual. There is risk and chance in these things. But there's also solid trust. There is complete backing. I give that to an informant."

Lee ate his food, showing nothing.

"How it might operate goes something like this. You walk into Banister's office. It is convenient to your place of work, right around the corner. You tell them you're an ex-Marine and you mention contacts with the Bureau in the state of Texas. Make it clear you're a Castro hater. Tell them you want to pose as a leftist, to infiltrate local organizations."

"I could tell them I'm starting an organization."

"This is a thought."

"A local office, like, Fair Play for Cuba."

"This has possibilities."

"I could get pamphlets from New York in large quantities, plus application forms."

"This is promising," Bateman said. "You tell Banister you will start a chapter right here in town. This will draw pro-Castro people to your door. You'll gather names and addresses. Banister loves a good list."

"It goes round and round."

"You seem to pretend."

"But I'm not pretending."

"But you are pretending."

They ate their lunch. Bateman explained that if Guy Banister wanted to check Oswald's background, he would naturally contact the local FBI office, specifically Bateman, who would provide highly selective information. He also explained that he wasn't allowed to drink coffee. The Director had placed a ban, making the Bureau free of addictive stimulants.

"I think Banister will be interested. But don't expect funds. This would be a tiny sideline for him. I'll arrange an informant's fee of two hundred dollars a month. Out of this, you run your project. And of course you tell me what they're doing at 544 Camp Street. Because they're doing something all the time."

"I want to study politics and economics."

"You're an interesting fellow. Every agency from here to the Himalayas has something in the files on Oswald, Lee. One thing I have to be sure about. No one else shares your services. This is Bureau policy. I can't do business with an informant who has a relationship with another agency. Are we okay on that?"

"We're okay," Lee told him.

"You can carry on your politics in the open. That's the charm of the thing. And you're right around the corner from those people. Location-wise, it's perfect."

Lee took a bus down to Camp Street, the placard back in the

envelope, and walked around the building several times. Streets in deep shade. No one around but winos in Lafayette Square and a woman in a long coat and heavy white socks who seemed upset that he was walking behind her. She stopped to let him pass, muttering urgently, her hand making a motion like hurry up.

Trotsky is the pure form.

The rear seat of an automobile lay in the middle of the sidewalk. A man coated in dirt and vomit was spread out there, one arm dangling, and he looked so sick or hurt or crazy it was not possible to enjoy the picture of a car seat without a car, plunked down on a sidewalk.

Trotsky brushing roaches off the page, reading economic theory in a hovel in eastern Siberia, exiled with his wife and baby girl.

On Monday, during his ten-minute break from work, he went to 544 and got an application from a secretary. The building had two entrances, two addresses. One for who you are, one for who you say you are.

He bought a Warrior-brand rubber stamping kit for ninety-eight cents. He wrote to the Fair Play for Cuba Committee, asking for a charter, and before getting a reply he went to a printer, said his name was Osborne and got a thousand handbills printed. *Hands Off Cuba!* He stamped some with his own name, some with Hidell. Then he rented a post-office box, went to another printer, ordered application forms and membership cards. He got Marina to forge the signature A. J. Hidell in the space for chapter president and sent two honorary memberships to officials of the Central Committee, Communist Party U.S.A.

He went out in his gold shorts and thong sandals at midnight, dumping garbage in other people's cans, sometimes ranging three or four blocks before he found a can with room to spare for one more bag of bones and slop.

When he took the filled-out application back to Guy Banister Associates he saw a man at the building entrance who looked familiar. It was Captain Ferrie, the Civil Air Patrol instructor, the man who kept mice in a cage in his hotel room back about seven years ago, Lee recalled, when he and his friend Robert were tracking down a .22 for sale. Lee drew closer and saw there was something very different about the man. He seemed to have tufts of fur glued to his head, like handfuls of animal hair just pasted on. His eyebrows were high and shiny.

Ferrie seemed to be expecting him.

"You were in the office yesterday or day before. Am I right?"

"I was applying for a job part-time."

"Undercover work. I heard your voice. I said to myself I know that voice. Another lost cadet come back to Cap'n Dave."

They laughed, standing in the entranceway. A car stopped suddenly and pigeons fired up from the square across the street.

"Isn't life fantastic?" Ferrie said.

The Fair Play Committee discouraged him from opening a branch office. But they were nice and polite and made spelling mistakes and anyway the important thing was the correspondence itself. He would keep everything. These were his papers. When the time came he would be able to present Cuban officials with documentary proof that he was a friend of the revolution.

Besides he didn't need New York's backing to open an office. He had his rubber stamping kit. All he had to do was stamp the committee's initials on a handbill or piece of literature. Stamp some numbers and letters. This makes it true.

David Ferrie took him to the Habana Bar, a gloom palace near the waterfront. Open round the clock, Latin rhythms on the juke box, people with a look about them of chronic absenteeism, some failure to cohere—exiles, cargo handlers, seamen without papers, half a dozen amorphous others, mainly solitary men sitting well spaced at the long bar.

Ferrie and Oswald took a table.

"The man who runs this place is involved with the Cuban Revolutionary Council."

"Which side are they?" Lee said.

"Don't you want to take a guess?"

"The look of this place."

"Sadder than shit."

"Anti-Castro."

"The Feebees come in here to talk to him about who's who in the movement. They don't know what they're doing otherwise. They see a Mex kid with a butch haircut and think he's a Cuban warrior."

"Where did you get that word?"

"Feebees? That's my word. A long-time word of mine."

"I thought it was my word."

"You must have heard it from me," Ferrie said. "This happens all the time. People think they invent things they actually heard from me. I have a way of creeping into people's minds. I get inside people's minds."

A nasal voice, sinuously trailing the question of whether it ought to be believed.

"We have definite ESP, you and I. It probably covers years and continents. Have you ever lived outside the U.S.?"

Lee nodded.

"We probably had each other in range all that time. I want to experiment with remote hypnotism. Hypnotism over the phone or on TV. A fantastic political weapon. Some woman is after me for so-called hypnotizing her son so I could orally stimulate his genitals. I give flying lessons to boys at Lakefront."

Ferrie took him to visit a man who lived in a restored carriage house on Dauphine Street, behind a high white wall with a red door in the middle of it. His name was Clay Shaw and he was tall and middle-aged, with a sculptured head and striking white hair. He stood in the middle of the large room that occupied the entire main floor. Silk curtains, bronzework, cork floors covered with Oriental rugs. Two young men were seated, alert and bright as weathercocks.

"When is your birthday?" Shaw said first thing.

"October eighteen," Lee said.

"Libra. A Libran."

"The Scales," Ferrie said.

"The Balance," Shaw said.

It seemed to tell them everything they had to know.

Clay Shaw wore well-made casual clothes and had the easy manner of someone clearly educated to all the right things. When he smiled, a vein seemed to flash from the corner of his right eye to his hairline.

He said, "We have the positive Libran who has achieved self-mastery. He is well balanced, levelheaded, a sensible fellow respected by all. We have the negative Libran who is, let's say, somewhat unsteady and impulsive. Easily, easily, easily influenced. Poised to make the dangerous leap. Either way, balance is the key."

"I brought him here," Ferrie said, "to see your collection of whips and chains."

Everyone laughed.

"Clay has whips and chains, black hoods, black capes."

"For Mardi Gras," one of the young men said, and everyone laughed again.

Lee felt his smile floating in the air about six inches from his face. They stayed fifteen minutes and went out into the twilight.

"Do you believe in astrology?" Lee said.

"I believe in everything," Ferrie told him.

He took Lee to his apartment, dark rooms with broken furniture and religious objects. The bookshelves were covered in wood-grain

Con-Tact paper and bowed under the weight of many hundreds of medical books, law books, encyclopedias, stacks of autopsy records, books on cancer, forensic pathology, firearms.

Barbells on the floor. A framed document on the wall, a Ph.D. in psychology from Phoenix University—Bari, Italy.

Lee used the bathroom. Amber vials of pills and capsules filled the glass trays. There were loose capsules all over the floor and in the tub. Layers of sticky filament coated the washbasin and the wall next to it—whatever kind of glue he used to attach his mohair wig.

In the living room Ferrie began speaking about his condition even before Oswald emerged from the toilet.

"It's called alopecia universalis. Of mysterious etiology and without known cure. Instead of hiding it, I adorn it, I dress it up. God made me a clown, so I clown it up. When my hair started coming out, I thought it meant imminent apocalypse, the Bomb falling on Louisiana. The Bomb would seal my authenticity, make me a saint. Fallout shelters were called family rooms of tomorrow. I was ready to live in the meanest hole. The missile crisis came. This was the purest existential moment in the history of mankind. I was completely hairless by then. Let me tell you I was ready. Push the button, Jack. The only way I could forgive Kennedy for being Kennedy was if he rained destruction down on Cuba. I bought ten cartons of canned food and let my mice go free."

Ferrie looked out the window. On the wall next to him was a picture of Jesus with eyes that track the person passing by. Ferrie's voice coming in a whisper now.

"Then there's the theory about high altitudes. Hair falling out so suddenly and completely. Exposure to high altitudes. Pilots have been afflicted, men who spent too much time at ultra-high altitudes, like U-2 pilots."

"Did you ever fly a U-2?"

"I can't tell you that. It's the deepest secret in the government, the names of men who fly those planes. But let me ask *you* a question, speaking of secrets. Why do you want a job doing undercover work for the anti-Castro movement when it's clear to me that you're a Castro partisan, a soldier for Fidel?"

He turned away from the window and looked directly at Lee, who found the only way to answer was his funny little smile.

That was how it started. Lee sat many nights on the screened porch cleaning the Mannlicher, working the bolt on the Mannlicher, after midnight, formulating plans.

He'd learned from the Militant that he could get a visa to Cuba in Mexico City, evading the travel ban. He could work for the revolution as a military adviser. An old and deep ambition. They would be happy to have an ex-Marine with progressive ideas.

He collected correspondence and put it in the spare room with all his other papers, with Castro speeches and booklets on socialist theory.

He handed out leaflets on the Dumaine Street wharf and talked to a dozen sailors about Fair Play for Cuba. A port policeman came and ordered him off.

Ferrie let him play both sides. Banister gave him a small office at 544 to store material. He hardly talked to Banister. Banister gave the impression of being hard to talk to. Lee stamped the Camp Street address on some of his material. They let him come and go.

A crazy summer. Storms shaking the city almost every afternoon. Heat lightning at night. Clouds of mosquitoes blowing in from the salt marshes. As weeks passed he sensed a change around him. People at 544 began to regard him differently—the Cubans who came and went, the young men who posed as Tulane students to collect information on left-wingers and integrationists. Lee was becoming less a curiosity or puzzle. He felt he walked in a special light. They were looking at him carefully now.

Banister's secretary thought his first name was Leon. Ferrie started calling him Leon, after Trotsky. Mistakes have this way of finding a sweet meaning.

The First Lady was pregnant, just like Marina. He read somewhere that the President liked James Bond novels. He went to the branch library on Napoleon Avenue, a little one-story brick building, and took out some Bond novels. He read that the President had acquainted himself with works by Mao Tse-tung and Che Guevara. He went to the library and got a biography of Mao. He got a biography of the President which said that Kennedy had read *The White Nile*. He went to the library to get *The White Nile* but it was out. He took *The Blue Nile* instead.

John F. Kennedy was a sometime poor speller with miserable handwriting.

He sat on the porch in his basketball shorts reading science fiction recommended by Ferrie. He dry-fired the Mannlicher. He still had the textbook from his typing class in Dallas and he sat some nights with the book open to a diagram of a typewriter keyboard. He practiced fingering the letters in alphabetical order—*a* with the left pinky, *b* with the left index finger, tapping the page repeatedly without looking down, as he'd been taught in class.

Marina said, "Papa, there is garbage."

He hung out at the Crescent City garage, which was next door to the coffee company where he worked. He came in wearing his electrician's belt with grease gun, screwdriver, pliers, friction tape, etc. He stretched his ten-minute breaks to half an hour, sitting in the office reading gun magazines and talking to the guy who ran the place. There were beer mugs sitting in the window, maps on the wall. He could kill ten minutes looking at a map.

The Crescent City garage had a contract with the U.S. government to keep and maintain a certain number of vehicles for use by local agencies.

Sundays the street was empty and the garage was closed and looked like an abandoned Spanish church inside the lowered grille, with light falling through the high dusty windows. This was where he met Agent Bateman, who had a key to the office. They went through the office and sat in one of the cars set aside for the Secret Service and FBI. He told Bateman what he'd learned at 544 Camp, which wasn't a hell of a lot. He wanted to use the Minox but Bateman said no, no, no, no. He gave Lee a white envelope containing a number of well-wrinkled bills, like money saved by children.

Lee insisted on knowing the informant number he'd been assigned and Bateman told him it was S-172. Then Lee said he wanted to apply for a passport and wondered if there might be a problem, due to his record as a defector. Bateman said he'd look into it.

Mosquitoes in swarms. He saw himself typing a paper on political theory, basing it on experience no fellow student could match, a half-eaten apple at his elbow.

When Lee has a certain look on his face, eyes kind of amused, mouth small and tight, he finds himself thinking of his father. He associates the look with his father. He believes it is a look his father may have used. It *feels* like his father. A curious sensation, the look coming upon him, taking hold in an unmistakable way, and then his old man is here, eerie and forceful and whole, a meeting across worlds.

"There's something I know about you, Leon, that I find fascinating. It's something almost no one else knows. Very few people know. You're the night-rider who took a shot at General Ted Walker two and a half months ago in Dallas."

Lee's mind went blank.

"I can't tell you how I know," Ferrie said. "But there are men who are interested in you. At first I only played a hunch. I thought Leon and I, we have a psychic bond. I took your application to Banister. I had an argument all set. I would say to Guy, 'Here is a man who wants to spy on our operations. He wants to use us but we will end up using him. Not through manipulation or political conversion. He believes in his heart that he's a dedicated leftist. But he is also a Libran. He is capable of seeing the other side. He is a man who harbors contradictions.' I was ready to say to Guy, 'Here's a Marine recruit who reads Karl Marx.' I was ready to say, 'This boy is sitting on the scales, ready to be tilted either way.' "

Lee finished off his beer.

"But I didn't have to present an argument at all. All I had to do was say your name. Banister was eager to grab you and hold on. Turns out he'd been making inquiries about you on behalf of an old buddy of his. A fellow named Mackey. You were lost. Nobody knew where you went after Dallas. Guy cracked his meanest smile when I told him you were greasing coffee machines right around the corner and wanted to join our staff. He picked up the telephone. 'Look what I found.'"

Ferrie ordered two more beers and said, "You are the object of some intense scrutiny. Banister doesn't know the exact nature of the role being planned for you. But it's only a matter of time before he finds out."

Three, four, half a dozen Cubans sat around the Habana tonight in camo T-shirts and pants, boots stained with dry white mud.

"Are you afraid you'll get caught for Walker? You never mentioned Dallas to me."

"I never mention it to anyone."

"You think they'll *know*. All you have to do is say the word Dallas and everyone will *know*. Prison is terrifying. The first thing they do when they arrest a man is look up his ass."

"I found that out in the Marines."

"They look up your ass before they know your name. It's like some Pygmy ritual in the Congo."

Lee could not drink more than a single beer without feeling funny.

"Do you practice a religion? Do you go to church?"

"I'm an atheist."

"That's dumb," Ferrie told him. "How could you be so stupid?"

"Religion just holds us back. It's an arm of the state."

"Dumb. Shortsighted. You have to understand there are things that run deeper than politics. Our political skin is just the thinnest outer crust. I was brought up a Catholic in Cleveland." Ferrie's eyes went comically wide as if the remark had taken him by surprise. "Penance was the major sacrament of my adolescence. I used to haunt the confession boxes. I went from one to the other. It felt more like a sin than a way of absolving sin. There was a real sneaky pleasure there. I told my sins, I made up sins, I said my act of contrition, I went to the altar rail and said my penance and then I got back in line again. On Saturday afternoon four confessionals were going full-blast. I made the circuit. Kneeling in the dark and whispering my sins to a man in skirts. I went to seminaries, twice, to learn the trade. Even started my own church. Only a fool rejects the need to see beyond the screen."

Lee went to the men's room and stood there with a static around him, like space is crisscrossed with gray lines. He stood for two minutes in the middle of the room. When he got back to the table, Ferrie started right in.

"Didn't Kennedy know how *big* Cuba is? Didn't anyone tell him you can't invade an island that size with fifteen hundred men?"

"Cuba is little."

"Cuba is *big*. Why did he consent to an invasion if he didn't mean to follow through? Why did he promise us a military victory and then back off? Because he lost his nerve. He muted everything. He soft-pedaled it. He wanted an invasion that was *subtle*. It's a wonder Castro realized he was under attack."

"Cuba is little."

"I'll tell you what rankles," Ferrie said, "and this is something I hear every day from Guy. Guy feels strongly about this. He thinks Kennedy and Castro are talking to each other. They're writing secret letters, they're sending emissaries back and forth. Friendly overtures. There's something they aren't telling us. Something we don't know about. There's more to it. There's always more to it. This is what history consists of. It's the sum total of all the things they aren't telling us."

Lee got in a shoving match out on the street with some Latin type who had pockmarks and a dangling silver cross. He didn't know how it started. Even gripping the man's biceps and talking into his face, he couldn't remember how the thing got started. A few people stood around mainly for lack of other amusement. Then he was home in bed.

He read gun magazines in the garage office. One of the coffee heads would appear in the door and tell him he'd better get back. Back to the motors and blowers, the hoppers, grinders, conveyor belts.

His passport arrived the day after he applied.

He walked into the spare room at home and thought some things had been moved. It couldn't be Marina, who had orders to stay out. He inspected his papers, checked the closet where he kept his guns. Something was different, an invisible whispery difference, like when you know a thing deeply in a dream without knowing how or why.

A woman who looks Seminole somehow, squat-headed, whatever they look like, he doesn't really know, comes walking out of a crowd in the French market nearly scaring him with the strange flat eyes of some burning saint.

He remained the only member of the Fair Play for Cuba chapter in New Orleans. Didn't mean a thing. Summer was building toward a vision, a history. He felt he was being swept up, swept along, done with being a pitiful individual, done with isolation.

Marina pushed the stroller along their street. She tried to read the street names set into the sidewalk in light-blue tile.

Would he try to send his wife and baby to Russia or would they all go to little Cuba, where there was a purer socialism and a true joy among the people?

Last night she got up for a glass of water at 2:00 A.M. and found him sitting on the porch in his underwear with the rifle across his lap.

He had nosebleeds in the night. Once she watched his body shake for half an hour.

She made him translate magazine stories about the Kennedys. He didn't mind doing it and sometimes added details not in the stories.

In pictures taken near the sea, with the wind ruffling his hair, the President looked like her old boyfriend Anatoly, who had unruly hair and kissed her in a way that made her dizzy.

Lee didn't wash for days at a time. He wore the same clothes and told her not to mend his socks or patch the elbows of threadbare sweaters. This was a complete turnabout. Here I am, he seemed to say. Look at what the system stamps out.

She knew, she was absolutely certain that Mrs. Kennedy would give birth to a boy. It was sure to be a boy, she told Lee, and then they would have a boy themselves, soon after.

She was ashamed to confess she was a woman of moods.

She was pregnant like Mrs. Kennedy but had not been examined by a doctor yet. Lee took her to Charity Hospital, a massive gray building that looked like a place you entered only once, never to emerge. In the marble lobby were enormous portraits of doctors in robes, doctors with the sky behind them, men with more important things on their mind than the gall bladder and kidneys. The trouble started at the information booth. A woman told Lee this was a state hospital and people could be treated free only if they'd been Louisiana residents for a certain period. Marina had not been living here long enough.

All that marble. It made her feel like a refugee. Lee followed a doctor down the corridor, almost begging. He picked up another doctor coming back this way, pleading and arguing at the same time, his face twisted and pale.

They were turned away.

Lee prowled the lobby, talking to people who walked in unaware, telling them the story. It's just another business. They make a business out of pain and suffering. No one knew what to say to him and finally he just paced the floor in silence, walking off his anger.

It was an anger that Marina did not try to soothe or wish away because she believed in her heart it was correct.

She pushed the stroller past some shops with large signs out front. She sounded the words in her mind. Washateria. One-hour

Martinizing. She saw fewer people as they strayed a little north, a little east.

She wondered how many women had visions and dreams of the President. What must it be like to know you are the object of a thousand longings? It's as though he floats over the landscape at night, entering dreams and fantasies, entering the act of love between husbands and wives. He floats through television screens into bedrooms at night. He floats from the radio into Marina's bed. There were times when she waited for him, actually listened late at night for a few words of a speech or a news conference recorded earlier in the day, waited for the voice of the President, the radio on a table near the bed.

They had matching scars on the arm, Marina and Lee.

This was the basic question that didn't leave her day or night. Would he force her to go back to Russia?

She said to him, "A gloomy spirit rules the house." "I am not receiving happiness," she said.

He talked to June about little Cuba. Do you love little Cuba? Do you have sympathy for Uncle Fidel? There was a photograph of Castro on the wall that he'd clipped from a Soviet magazine. What do you think of Uncle Fidel? Do you love and support little Cuba?

She thought of the President sometimes, in pictures taken near the sea, while Lee was making love to her.

He kept after her to write to the Soviet embassy in Washington, teary-eyed letters, requesting visas, requesting travel expenses. She knew he was confused about the future.

She was a blind kitten who always returned to the person who caressed her, no matter if he also treated her cruelly.

She took Junie out of the stroller now and let her walk alongside. Junie didn't like to walk holding anyone's hand. She walked along on her own, endless joy and endless toil.

Sitting on the porch at 2:00 A.M. with the rifle across his lap.

They walked down many quiet streets. The houses were old and silent and some had cast-iron galleries and white columns.

There was no one else around. The afternoon was heavy and still. She stood on a corner and saw cars going through an intersection about seven blocks away but nothing moved nearby and she wondered if this might be an area closed to normal activity during certain times of day. One-hour Martinizing. They passed homes with carved entrances, with magnolias out front and straight-standing palms. She tried to take Junie's hand. The heat became oppressive. They passed a house with double galleries and she could see frescoes through the living-room window. She put June back in the stroller, forced her in, stuffed her back in. Then she turned in the direction she thought led home, walking quickly now, no longer looking at the graceful, old and silent homes.

She thought carefully in English, Where are all the people?

Bateman told him about a group called the Cuban Student Directorate. It was run out of a clothing store a few doors down from the Habana Bar. Confidential Source S-172 walked in one day and talked to a guy named Carlos, about thirty years old, shiny-haired, wearing dark glasses.

He brought along his old Marine Corps training manual to sort of indicate who he was and where he stood. Inside of a minute they were talking about bridges, blowing up bridges, laying powder charges, making homemade explosives, homemade guns.

Carlos, however, did not seem eager to tell him how he might enter the anti-Castro struggle. He wouldn't accept Lee's offer to join the organization, wouldn't even accept a cash contribution. He was wary of infiltrators. He said it straight out. This was a sensitive time.

They had a nice talk anyway. Lee left his training manual behind as a gesture of good will and said he'd come back soon. They shook hands at the door.

What happens? Four days later Lee is on Canal Street wearing his Viva Fidel sign and handing out pro-Castro leaflets. Along comes Carlos with two friends. Lee watches Carlos do a double-take from out of the archives.

He approached in an attitude of menace, taking off his glasses. Lee crossed his arms on his chest and smiled. He didn't want to fight with Carlos. He liked him. Carlos had that Latin quality of being easy to like.

"Okay, Carlos, if you want to hit me, hit me."

He stood there with his arms crossed, smiling nicely. A small crowd collected, backing Lee toward the entrance of a Walgreen's. One of the men with Carlos grabbed some handbills out of Lee's fist and threw them in the air. This caused some scuffling on the fringe. Then a police car rolled up and then another one and soon they were all walking across the sandy parking lot of the first-district station house on North Rampart.

Lee demanded to see Agent Bateman of the FBI.

Half an hour later Bateman walked into the interview room, hands held out, palms showing, a certain rigid set to his features.

Lee said, "They want to know how many members in my Fair Play chapter."

"What did you tell them?"

"Thirty-five."

"Fine. But why bring me into it?"

"Because what are they liable to do if I don't show I'm linked to law enforcement?"

"It is only disturbing the peace. So-called creating a scene."

"Well get me out."

"I can't get you out."

"This wasn't the deal. Getting me arrested."

"You got yourself arrested. And if I get you out, it exposes everything. Giving them my name is bad enough. Did they ask why you wanted to see me?"

"They asked about Karl Marx. I told them the real Karl Marx was a socialist, not a communist."

"I am deeply disappointed, Lee."

"Well I couldn't just let them bury me. I have a wife and baby."

"One night is all you'll lose."

"I had to show there's someone who knows who I am. A figure of authority."

"It is only disturbing the peace. Tell them as little as possible. Let them think you're just a hometown boy with political ideals."

"I told them I'm a Lutheran."

"First-rate," Bateman said, nice and nasty.

They photographed him front, profile and full figure and then took prints of his fingers and palms. They told him to drop his pants and bend over. Later he sat in a holding cell seeing himself as he would appear in the mug shots, dignified and balding. He listened to the drunks and hysterics. They brought more men in as the night progressed. A howler and a dancer. They brought in a Negro with an aluminum-foil hat, a little religious cap made of Reynolds Wrap, with trinkets dangling from the sides.

Trotsky took his name from a jailer in Odessa and carried it into the pages of a thousand books.

It was Lee who told Marina that Mrs. Kennedy's baby had died during the night. A boy, born prematurely, with respiratory problems. Marina stood by the window crying. It hit her with the force of something she'd feared all along without letting it surface. Thirty-nine hours of life for the President's son. She cried for the Kennedys and also for herself and for Lee. How could she grieve for Mrs. Kennedy's baby and not think about the child she carried in her own womb? This was the future and it was marked.

Lee went to court. The first thing he noticed was that the room was separated into white and colored. He sat square in the middle of the colored section, waiting for his case to be called. Then he pleaded guilty and paid a ten-dollar fine. He shook hands with Carlos and walked out the door.

You see, none of this really mattered. What mattered was collecting the experiences, documenting the experienes, saving it all for the eyes of Cuban officials. What is it called, dossier?

There was a camera crew from WDSU waiting outside the courtroom and they shot some footage of Lee H. Oswald for the evening news.

Four days later he was back on the street handing out leaflets in front of the International Trade Mart.

The day after that he went on the radio to talk about Cuba and the world.

Bill Stuckey, the host of *Latin Listening Post*, was expecting a folk-singer type with a beard and sooty fingernails. Oswald was neat and clean, in a white shirt and a tie, and carried a looseleaf notebook under his arm.

They sat in the studio, with an engineer to record the interview, and Stuckey began right away, introducing Oswald as the secretary of the New Orleans chapter of the Fair Play for Cuba Committee.

Lee said, "Yes, as secretary, I am responsible for the keeping of the records and the protection of the members' names so that undue publicity or attention will not be drawn to them, as they do not desire it."

He said, "Certainly it is obvious to me, having been educated in New Orleans and having been instilled with the ideals of democracy and objectiveness, that Cuba and the right of Cubans to self-determination is more or less self-evident."

He said, "You know, when our forefathers drew up the Constitution, they considered that democracy was creating an atmosphere of freedom of discussion, of argument, of finding the truth. The right, the classic right of life, liberty and the pursuit of happiness. And that is my definition of democracy, the right to be in a minority and not to be suppressed."

Stuckey listened to him talk about the United Fruit Company, the CIA, collectivization, the feudal dictatorship of Nicaragua, movements of national liberation. Thirty-seven minutes in all, which Stuckey was compelled to reduce to four and a half for his five-minute show, and this was a shame because Oswald's presentation was intelligent and clear and his way of leaping out of difficult corners extremely deft.

Stuckey invited Secretary Oswald out for a beer when the interview was over. Then he sent a copy of the tape to the FBI.

That's how it went, that's the kind of summer it was. One day he was going after roaches with a pancake flipper, mashing them flat—one of those soft plastic flippers that are always on sale. He'd lost his job. They fired him because he didn't do the work, which seemed reasonable enough. Storms shaking the city. They shot Medgar Evers dead in Jackson, Miss., a field secretary of the NAACP. Later they would dynamite the Sixteenth Street Baptist Church in Birmingham, four Negro girls killed, twenty-three injured. One day he was hunting down roaches in his kitchen, unshaved, wearing clothes he hadn't changed in a week. The next day found him in a gawky Russian suit and narrow tie, with his looseleaf notebook at his side, engaged in radio debate on *Conversation Carte Blanche*, another public-affairs show on WDSU. This time they'd checked up beforehand and had questions ready about Russia and his defection, catching him by surprise. Working the bolt on the Mannlicher. Cleaning the Mannlicher. They had plans for him, whoever they were. Heat lightning at night. It was easy to believe they'd been watching him for years, working things around him, knowing the time would come.

A man, a madman, whatever he was, shadow-boxed outside the toilets at the Habana.

Ferrie didn't seem to know sometimes whether a story was funny or sad. He told Lee about the time he tried to perfect a tiny flare device equipped with a timer. He wanted to make thousands of these devices and attach them to the bodies of mice. He wanted to parachute the mice into Cuban cane fields. He was driven by the image of fifty thousand mice scattering through the sugar cane as the timers ignited the flares. He wanted to be the Hannibal of the mouse world, he said, and seemed dejected by the failure of the plan.

"During the revolution," Lee said, "Castro made it a point to burn his own family's cane fields."

"Listen to me. This Walker business is strictly in the past. You ought to forget him. A dead General Walker means nothing to Fidel. He is old hat. He is day-old shit. No one listens to Walker anymore. Your missed bullet finished him more surely than a clean hit. It left him hanging in the twilight. He is an embarrassment. He carries the stigma of having been shot at and missed."

"How do you know I want to try again?"

"Leon, do we actually have to speak the words? Don't we know when a death is passing in the air? They're beginning to crowd you. Banister says they're serious men. They've been in your apartment."

"I know. I had a feeling."

"You *sensed* it. See? Nobody has to say anything. The scales will simply tip and then we'll know."

"What were they looking for?"

"Signs that you exist. Evidence that Lee Oswald matches the cardboard cutout they've been shaping all along. You're a quirk of history. You're a coincidence. They devise a plan, you fit it perfectly. They lose you, here you are. There's a pattern in things. Something in us has an effect on independent events. We make things happen. The conscious mind gives one side only. We're deeper than that. We extend into time. Some of us can almost predict the time and place and nature of our own death. We know it on some deeper plane. It's almost a romance, a flirtation. I look for it, Leon. I chase it discreetly."

The shadow-boxer was on another level now, making the slowest of moves, working out the mathematics. He stood in place, head down, and dragged his arms across his upper body, finding resistance, a retarding force, like someone gesturing in space.

"Your man Kennedy has a little romance of his own with the

idea of death. Men preoccupied with courage have their dark dreams. Jack's a little death-haunted all right, but not pathologically, not creepy-crawly like me. Poetic. That's your Jack."

"He's not my Jack," Lee said.

"He knows the course. He's been close to dying several times. A brother killed in action. A sister killed in a plane crash. A baby dead. A Catholic. A Catholic gets it early. Incense, organ music, ashes on the forehead, wafer on the tongue. The best things shimmer with fear. Skelly Bone Pete. We used to stay out of certain alleyways, certain dark streets. That's where he was waiting with his wino breath and stinky underwear. Specialized in kids."

One of the bar girls stood by the juke box swaying, a West Texas woman who looked sandblasted, with bleached-out hair and skin, little gold lashes. Ferrie waved her over. He took a black bow tie out of his pocket and gave it to her. She clipped it to Lee's shirt collar. They thought that was pretty cute. Her name was Linda Frenchette and she held her hands up to her face and flexed her thumbs, snapping Lee's picture.

"He doesn't like to smoke or drink," Ferrie said. "He never says dirty words. We want to be nice to him."

"Nice for a price," she said.

"You get the front end. I get the back end. Like bumper cars," Ferrie said.

They thought that was cute too.

They all got into Ferrie's Rambler and drove up Magazine. The theme of the ride was "Taking Lee Home." Linda Frenchette sat in the back seat. She had tequila in a wineglass and clapped a hand over the top of the glass every time the car stopped short. She found a TV lunchbox on the seat with cartoon figures painted on the surface and some hand-rolled cigarettes inside. Ferrie took one and lighted it while Lee steered from the passenger seat. Hashish, said Cap'n Dave. They rolled up the windows and let the heavy scent collect, strong and rooted. Ferrie passed the stick around. A pudgy little thing tapered at both ends. They were taking Lee home.

They parked in front of a nice-looking house with a two-story porch, a couple of doors up from Lee. He'd used their garbage can several times. Linda lighted up another stick. They passed it round and round. It was 3:00 A.M. and with the windows up and the smoke collecting, there was very little world out there. They gave Lee instructions on smoking the dope. They argued about it, fiercely. He was smoking just to smoke. Then Ferrie recited the history of hashish, lighting up another stick, which took forever. Everything moved through time. The heat in the car was getting hard to take and the smoke seared Lee's throat. Linda dipped her tongue in tequila and softly licked his ear. They were in a place where a heartbeat took time.

"This is one of those times I don't know if I'm doing it or remembering it," she said.

"Doing what?" Ferrie said.

"In other words am I home in bed thinking about this or is the whole thing happening right now?"

"What whole thing?" Ferrie said.

His voice was far away. He rolled down his window to let the smoke out. Lee looked straight ahead. Bright ashes tumbled down his shirtfront. He realized Linda was reaching over the seat back. She groped, is the only word, at his belt buckle and fly.

"I'm hoping dear Jesus I'm at home. Because the idea that I have to get there yet is too much razzle to imagine."

Lee let Ferrie open his pants. Then Linda had his cock jumping in her fist and was hanging way over the seat back with her mouth open wide, sounding a comic growl.

Lee looked straight ahead. He heard Linda breathing through her nose. She changed her position, hitting her head on the jutting ashtray. He tried to recall the name of a girl he wanted to date once, plaid-skirted, when he was dating age.

Then Ferrie's voice began to reach him in weighted time, moving slowly, one word, another, deeply shaped, like ads for epic movies, those 3-D letters stretched across a bible desert.

"They've been watching you a long time, Leon. Think about them. Who are they? What do they want? I'm with them but I'm also with you. There are things they aren't telling us. This is always the case. There's always more to it. Something we don't know about. Truth isn't what we know or feel. It's the thing that waits just beyond. We share a consciousness, like tonight. The hashish makes us Turks. We share a homeland and a spirit. What Linda says is true. You're at home, in bed now, remembering."

Then he reached across the dangling woman to straighten Lee's bow tie.

Marina had a standing invitation to stay with her friend Ruth Paine in Dallas. Ruth Paine would be a big help when the new baby came. She knew some of the Dallas émigrés and wanted to improve her Russian, which gave Marina a chance to return the favor.

It looked like New Orleans was over. In a way it had never begun. Lee wanted her back in Russia to free himself of responsibility. She thought he would settle for Dallas, at least for now.

Ruth Paine was passing through New Orleans from the East or the Midwest and she could take Marina back to Dallas with her. This is what Marina discussed with Lee. He would go to Mexico City to get his Cuban visa and Marina and June would go to Dallas with Ruth Paine, a Quaker and good friend.

Then they would see what came next.

They stood firing their weapons in the misty light. He was detached from the action, empty, squeezing off a round, a round, another. Strictly pouring lead. The other men had little to say to him and kept a calculated distance. This was all right with him. It was a summer of things taking shape at the edges.

David Ferrie wore earmuffs, firing at cans of tomato paste, unopened. Mass-market gore spritzed in the morning air. He didn't use the hearing protectors they wear on gun ranges. Ordinary dime-store earmuffs, but he could shoot. The Cuban could shoot. The rangy guy, Wayne, with the long wandering face, and kind of stoop-backed, fired only a couple of rounds, then drifted off.

Ferrie had to get back to New Orleans to speak to the Junior Chamber of Commerce. He said he'd be back next day to take Lee home.

The leader, T-Jay, seemed half amused by Lee. Strong-looking, a slight paunch, a tattoo bird flying out of his fist. Marlboro man, thought Lee.

T-Jay was aware of his desire to go to Cuba. Had Ferrie told him? Had Lee told Ferrie? Did Agent Bateman know? Had he told Bateman why he wanted a passport? These questions passed quickly through Lee's mind. Didn't mean a thing. Summer was building toward a vision.

T-Jay told him to train with the Mannlicher, not one of the new rifles. This was his intention all along. It was Lee who'd asked to come out to the camp. He'd insisted to Ferrie. He needed target work, serious time with his weapon.

Except that he was out of ammunition. Ammo for this type carbine was hard to find. He'd hit every gun shop in New Orleans. T-Jay seemed amused, all-knowing. He said he had an ample supply, obtained directly from the Western Cartridge Company on the basis of past dealings. See? Everything is taken care of. It's falling into place.

He curled into a sleeping bag on the floor of the long shack.

He has a lot to show the Cubans. There is correspondence from the Fair Play Committee and the Worker. He has handbills and membership cards.

He knows one thing sure. He is going to study politics and economics.

Take 'em to Missouri, Matt.

There is still this mix-up over his discharge, which they refuse to change to honorable.

Marina thinks he is in another parish looking for work in the aerospace industry.

The President reads James Bond novels.

He has proof of his subscriptions to left-wing journals. He has the court summons describing the incident that led to his arrest.

The revolution must be a school of unfettered thought.

Rain-slick streets.

Aerospace is the coming thing, with courses at night in economic theory.

He is working on a new project in his steno notebook. He has headings like Marxist, Organizer, Street Agitation, Radio Speaker and Lecturer. Under these he is writing concise descriptions of his activities, with attachments. He has the news story of his court appearance with his name spelled correctly. He has tax returns he took from the offices of the graphic-arts firm where he worked in Dallas, just to save, just to have in case of something like this, to take and keep. This would qualify as intelligence.

I am experienced in street agitation.

I have a far mean streak of independence brought on by neglect.

Aerospace.

It wasn't until they hit the gleaming traffic, the raw flash on the edges of New Orleans, that Ferrie brought up the subject.

"President Jack has been working overtime. Did you know this? To put Castro in the ground. The deepest of cover operations. Ask me how I know. I do legal research for Carmine Latta. Carmine has knowledge of this thing. The Agency has worked with crime figures to put the hit on Fidel."

The bright crush around them. Faces in side windows.

"Listen. They can't do it without Kennedy's knowledge. He has some dirty business, who does he consult? CIA is the President's toilet."

Children carried past, squinting in the hard light.

"Carmine has talked to people from Chicago, from Florida. This is amazing material, Leon, for you to think about. Think about it. On one level the government is seeking conciliation with Cuba. On another level it is sending out assassins."

The next day—it was September 9—Lee picked up the Times-Picayune and read that Castro was charging the U.S. with plotting assassinations.

"United States leaders should think that if they are aiding terrorist plans to eliminate Cuban leaders," he said, "they themselves will not be safe."

Lee read the story several times. It was as if they had control of the news, Ferrie, Banister, all of them, all-knowing. Of course it was only coincidence that Ferrie mentioned the thing one day and it appeared in the paper the next. But maybe that was even stranger than total control.

Coincidence. He learned in the bayous, from Raymo, that Castro's guerrilla name was Alex, derived from his middle name, Alejandro. Lee used to be known as Alek.

Coincidence. Banister was trying to find him, not knowing what city or state or country he was in, and he walked in the door at 544 and asked for an undercover job.

Coincidence. He ordered the revolver and the carbine six weeks apart. They arrived the same day.

Coincidence. Lee was always reading two or three books, like Kennedy. Did military service in the Pacific, like Kennedy. Poor handwriting, terrible speller, like Kennedy. Wives pregnant at the same time. Brothers named Robert.

His nosebleeds started again the second night he was home. There was blood on the pillowcase. Marina told him he'd been shaking in his sleep.

They knew all about him, even where to get cartridges for his rifle. Plus the Feebees were reading his mail. Plus Marina was almost eight months pregnant, complaining about the way they lived, sarcastic about his principles as a fighter for progress. He missed two meetings with Bateman. He didn't care about the money. They could keep their money. They didn't own or control him. He lost weight. He could feel the difference in his clothes and see it in his face in the mirror. He took a careful stance on the screened porch and aimed the rifle at a man crossing the street, holding right where the head and neck join, saying the word windage to himself. He decided to study Spanish again.

He got his tourist card from the Mexican consulate. He got his documents and clippings in order. It was all for little Cuba, so the Cubans could see who he was.

He could get his visa and have them stamp it with a future date. He could go back to Dallas and shoot the fascist Walker. Then return to Mexico City, knowing his visa was already set, a solid fact, guaranteed travel to Havana. They would welcome him there as a hero.

He'd studied Spanish once before, or twice before. It would come easy this time.

Ferrie called his rifle the Man-Licker.

He fastened the playpen and stroller to the top of Ruth Paine's station wagon, a green Chevy, a '55, with rust spots and soft tires. He jammed suitcases and boxes inside, everything they owned. It was Ruth Paine's now. He sneaked the rifle in, disassembled in an old blanket wrapped tight with kitchen string. He tied a granny knot.

He told Ruth Paine he might go to Houston to look for work, or maybe Philadelphia.

Marina's eyes were wet with worry and love. He ran his fingertips along her high white neck. He fought off the tears. He thought his face might crumple like a child's, washed in sorrow.

That night he streaked through a heavy rain with bag after bag of leftover junk, pushing old newspapers into a neighbor's garbage can, letting pop bottles crash. Was anyone watching? Did a sleepless old lady keep track of these midnight sprints? He went back to the house at a shambling trot and was out again a moment later, quick-walking down the driveway with more junk pressed to his chest, the boy who spoke to no one on the street.

The next evening he stood on the porch waiting for the bus to pull up at the stop directly across Magazine. When it did, he hurried across the street carrying two canvas bags and owing fifteen days' rent.

At the Trailways terminal he headed for the window to buy a ticket to Houston, which was the first stage of the journey to Mexico City. David Ferrie was standing by the window. He wore a rumpled plaid sport jacket with a newspaper sticking out of one pocket. He looked like a horseplayer with two days to live.

"Where to, Mexico? To pick up a visa for little Cuba?"

"That's right," Lee said.

"Without a word to Cap'n Dave? I don't like this, Leon."

"You won't tell me what it is they want me to do. I have to make my plans best I can."

"They knew you were going. They've been watching extra close. I am personally put out about this. Cuba now, Leon? We haven't done our work yet."

"I'm planning I might come back."

"You'll come back all right. You know why? They don't give visas to Americans so easy. Plus you want to come back. You want to finish our work."

"What do they want me to do?"

"We both know the answer to that by now."

"You know. I don't."

"You've known almost all along. I think you knew before I did. You came to the swamps to shoot your Man-Licker. You know what side we're on. You know we're not about to choose a target suited to your tastes. But you wanted to come. I think you picked it out of the air. I honestly believe you beat me to it."

A Negro in hip boots wandered through the terminal selling yo-yos that lit up in the dark.

Ferrie talked Lee into having a meal together. Raymo would drive him to Houston tomorrow if that's what he wanted. Save the bus fare. Enjoy the comfort of the family car.

They ate scrambled eggs in Ferrie's apartment. There were explosives stored under the kitchen table. Ferrie kept his jacket on, wagged the fork as he spoke.

"I've seen the Fair Play material you keep at 544," he said. "I've noticed something you haven't noticed. Librans never notice references to themselves. The official symbol of the Fair Play for Cuba Committee is a man's hand holding aloft a pair of scales. Two weighing pans hanging from a rigid beam. Everywhere you go. It's all around you. Which way will Leon tilt?"

"I don't know what they want me to do."

"Of course you know."

"Tell me where it happens."

"Miami."

"That means nothing to me."

"You've known for weeks."

"What happens in Miami?"

Ferrie took a while to finish chewing his food.

"Think of two parallel lines," he said. "One is the life of Lee H. Oswald. One is the conspiracy to kill the President. What bridges the space between them? What makes a connection inevitable? There is a third line. It comes out of dreams, visions, intuitions, prayers, out of the deepest levels of the self. It's not generated by cause and effect like the other two lines. It's a line that cuts across causality, cuts across time. It has no history that we can recognize or understand. But it forces a connection. It puts a man on the path of his destiny."

25 September

Lee woke up on the sofa some time after midnight. He was wide awake almost at once. The TV was on a bookshelf, picture flipping, no sound. He heard Ferrie gargling in the bathroom. The smell of hashish stuck to everything, to Lee's hair and clothes, the fabric on the sofa.

He watched Ferrie walk into the room naked. His eyebrows and toupee were gone. He was sad and pasty, decolored, moving out of the background glow into the stutter light of TV. He resembled someone in the land of *nūdo*, a shaved nude in a booth in Tokyo, a nude monk you pay to photograph, some endless variation on the factual nude, a satire for tourists. He looked unclear, half erased. Could he tell Lee's eyes were open?

He stood a moment among the books and pole lamps as if he'd forgotten something. What could he forget, naked? Lee shifted around so that his back was to the room. He shifted like someone asleep, just rolling over. He closed his eyes. He groaned like someone deep in sleep.

Ferrie sat on the edge of the sofa, reaching around to put a hand on Lee's belly over the shirt, a hand on Hidell, leaning closer now, his breath sharp with mouthwash.

"People have to be nice to each other."

He moved his hand around. Wandering hands, Lee thought. An old term, an old thing they said in junior high, what a girl said about a boy. He's got wandering hands.

"People be nice," whispered Cap'n Dave.

He seemed to be easing his body lengthwise onto the sofa, arranging himself behind Lee, the hand circling a central area, moving slowly over Lee's pants. Lee wouldn't let him undo the belt. They actually grappled for a moment. They fought over the belt buckle without changing positions on the sofa. Lee kept his eyes closed. They hand-fought and slapped at each other. Ferrie was strong. He was using one hand, gripping Lee's wrist hard. It's called an Indian burn when you put your hands around someone's wrist and twist in opposite directions. Another old term, a thing from grade school maybe.

"People be nice, be nice, be nice."

He seemed to be pressing with his body now. The hand sort of quieting down. Lee put his legs tight together. His eyes were still closed. He felt the rough fabric of the sofa on his face. Ferrie was breathing all over him, covering his head and neck with heavy breath.

Hide the *L* in Lee.

No one will see.

Then he felt it on his pants, seeping in. He tried not to take it personally. They separated themselves and Ferrie got a towel for him and then put on a robe. This was achieved mostly in the dark.

"When you get back to Dallas, there are some places you ought to know about."

"I'm going to Mexico City."

"But when you get back. There's a place called Gene's Music Bar. You ought to drop in some night. Or the Century Room, which I hear just opened."

"What for?"

"Meet people."

"What kind of people?"

"People you want to meet. I don't know Dallas bars myself. I'm passing on the word. Stay away from the Holiday. That's rough trade. Not for you, Leon."

"I don't know what you're talking about."

"Of course you do. Gene's Music Bar is number one on your list. You definitely want to catch the action. Tell me what it's like."

Out came the hashish.

David Ferrie said, "Hashish. Interesting, interesting word. Arabic. It's the source of the word assassin."

Jack Ruby liked his juice fresh-squeezed in the morning. He bought eight grapefruits at a clip, grabbing them out of the bin with a steely look, like this is the only thing that can save me. There were grapefruits wedged in every part of the fridge. He liked to slap the surface of a good grapefruit. Dependable. He liked to heft the thing in his hand. The whole business of juice was allied in his mind with swimming laps in a pool or working out with weights. He was a physical-culture nut when he had time.

When he stepped out of the kitchen, that's when the bachelor chaos began to flow. The place resembled a lost-and-found. To Jack it was okay. He hated and feared a hotel look. All he had to do was recall the time ten years ago when he became depressed over business failures, when money problems were climbing up his back and pressing on his skull. It got so bad he took a room in a cheap walk-up hotel and isolated himself for eight weeks with the shades drawn, eating only enough to stay alive. He was a nothing person. He had no desire to live. It was the one time in his life he was guilty of despair, which is the deepest misery of the spirit, the hardest to overcome.

Maybe this is why Jack had a roommate. To avoid the scariness of being alone. Or was it just his habit of taking in strays, people of untremendous means? George Senator was fifty, a postcard salesman, divorced through the mail, with an eighth-grade education. He'd been in and out of jobs for years, a short-order cook, a novelty man, a salesman of women's apparel whose territory had been reduced from the entire state of Texas to the jackrabbit wastes. He helped out at the club and cooked Jack a meal now and then, although he didn't broil things right and could never learn the organics of another person, the little niceties of diet that mean so much.

Coming out of the kitchen with the juice glass in his hand, Jack barely glanced at George, who sat bloated on the sofa in a beat-up robe, coughing into his cupped hands.

"I'm expecting a huge phone call. Stay away from the phone. Like into next week I'm referring."

"Who do I ever call?" George said.

"I don't know. The weather."

"I don't follow the weather. I don't go anywheres near it."

Jack barely heard. He had the ability to share an apartment with a roommate and just barge and rush around as if the guy wasn't there. His mind raced too fast for a guy like shapeless George to catch a ride. He didn't even know what the spare room looked like since George moved in. Maybe he painted it orange. Not that he didn't like having George around. It's a matter of once you're used to a human presence, growing up like I did with seven brothers and sisters plus two dead in infancy, you feel there's something missing in a household.

Living alone is a pressure situation. The roommates agreed on that.

Jack took a Preludin with his grapefruit juice. He walked around the living room, trying to say in his mind what he was thinking. Six weeks and no word. They were letting him dance in midair. He went into the kitchen and made more juice. He needed a scalp treatment. He was falling behind in every area of personal care.

"Who is the call?" George said.

"A guy from New Orleans I used to know."

"This is the money."

"He told me he'd be in Dallas today. Okay. I'm waiting."

"What about the other guy?" George said.

"Karlinsky? The man is purist-minded from the start. I expected no action and that's what I got."

"So you said, what, let me contact New Orleans."

"I went right through Karlinsky. I went ten feet over his head."

"This other guy leaves an opening?"

"We wait and see."

"What, you asked him straight out you needed a loan?"

"He already knew my situation. He knew from last June when we bumped into each other in the street. I was in New Orleans looking at Randi Ryder for the club."

"I never been," George said.

"It's a city where the money's not so tight and clean."

He put on his jacket and hat, got his moneybag and revolver, picked up Sheba from her chair and went down to the car. He dropped the dog on the front seat, opened the trunk and tossed the moneybag in. He drove to Commerce Street and bought a couple of newspapers at a corner stand. Back at the car he spotted his dirty laundry in the rear seat, where he'd left it six, seven, eight days ago, tied together with a pajama leg. He looked around for a glass of water. Nervous in the service. Then he drove half a block in reverse to the Carousel, checking the spelling of the girls' names on the marquee. Some tourists from Topeka were looking at the glossies on the wall out front. Jack introduced himself, shook hands, gave them his card, got the dog from the front seat and went on up the narrow stairway.

Walking into the empty club made him feel how inspirational it was to grow up quitting school in Chicago, nickname Sparky, scalping tickets outside fight arenas, selling carnations in dance halls, and now he is a club owner, a known face, with ads in the paper, as only America can turn out.

He went to his office and called the local IRS and told them he had to postpone the meeting they'd scheduled because he was unable to get his records properly compiled. A phrase his attorney had suggested. They made a new appointment and he promised to bring thirteen hundred cash to ease the matter of delinquency. Another phrase.

He went to the bar, poured a glass of water and swallowed another Preludin. To speed the day along and help him think positive. The phone rang in his office. He hurried in and picked up. It was George at the apartment. The call had come. The man was in town. Tony Astorina. Carousel at noon.

The dogs in the back room were barking to be let out. Jack went down to the car and drove a block and a half to the Ritz Delicatessen. He bought half a dozen sandwiches and beverages and drove right back.

His brother Sam called. He had some new production ideas for those plastic spinners, those twirly things that spin on high wires in front of service stations and car lots for a festive appearance.

The Times Herald called.

A stripper named Double DeLite called.

KLIF called.

Detective Russell Shively called.

His brother Earl called. He tried to talk Jack out of the twist-board idea. Jack wanted to manufacture an exercise device consisting of two fiberboards with some kind of ball-bearing disks between them and you stand on the boards and twist and shimmy, for fun and body tone both.

Tony Astorina walked in, doing a friendly little boxer's bob and weave. It looked like all the motion he was capable of. He had that expression of where's the coffee. Jack had coffee right here. They talked a little preliminaries. Tony was about forty but dressed young. His eyes were getting slitty inside the looming flesh. He said there was a place he had to be in forty-five minutes. He made it sound important. Jack did not want to hear this kind of remark. He wanted to believe Tony was involved in this conversation, not just passing by, passing time.

The barking in the back room was feeble and hoarse, like dogs in some Chinese village.

Then Tony said, "Loanshark is not our thing, Jack. There are people I can refer you. But I wouldn't be truthful if I said it could happen. These clubs, I don't know, they're shaky propositions."

"The boys know me in four cities, five cities."

"Your reputation is Jack Ruby is one tough Jew. To put it plain. He goes back to the unions."

"Scrap Iron and Junk Handlers."

"He did a lot of things you can give him credit."

"I brawl too much. It's this temperament where I lash out. I follow the theory you take the play away. You barrel in hard and fast before they even know they're in a dispute. Ten seconds later I'm a baby."

"But I'm making the point. The point isn't temperamental. It's a question of where's the money coming from to pay back."

"From business. From the clubs. Plus some ventures I'm planning in other vicinities. I'm saying you are close to Carmine."

"Carmine. I can't go to Carmine with something like this. Carmine has enormous, don't even get me started—things going on you can't believe. You think he does business all day long? He has an organization to do the business. The man is in conference. He has meets all the time. He's running a country, Jack."

"I'm saying you put a word in his ear. You plant an idea."

"There's so much stuff they put in front of him. Things from out of nowhere, I never heard of. Like I just found out about Kennedy and that woman. It went on two years. Mo talked to Carmine all the time."

"What woman?"

"You know Mo?"

"Giancana."

"Sam."

"Giancana."

"For two years Kennedy is ramming this woman that's Sam's mistress. I don't know the first thing. They do it in New York. They do it in L.A. They find like twenty minutes in Chicago, bing bang, when he's there for a fund-raising."

Jack was trying to draw himself a picture.

"And Carmine gets reports. She saw him here, she saw him there. He said this, he said that. Two years, Jack. They did it in the White House."

Jack could not conceive of a situation whereby the President of the United States would be fucking the girlfriend of Momo Giancana. There had to be a mistake somewhere. This is a guy from the Patch in Chicago, from Dago Town, four or five blocks from where Jack grew up. Jack used to be personal friends with two of Mo's enforcers. He'd been hearing Giancana's name for decades. Since the days he was called Mooney. A wheelman for the 42 Gang. Fifty or sixty arrests. Time in Joliet. Time in Leavenworth. A powerful figure today. Chicago, Las Vegas, etc. But sharing a woman with the President? Jack knew it was going to be hard to swing the conversation back to a loan for a failing business.

Tony was still in his chair but only technically. There was an air of departure, a small restlessness that Jack could trace to his hands, like a smoker who quits.

"Jack, I come by here for old time."

"We used to swim on the Capri roof."

"I'm saying. I didn't come by for the coffee."

"Tony. I appreciate."

"I come by because we go back together."

"We got laid in adjoining rooms."

"Havana, madonn'."

"Tony, I have plans I'm painting the club. A whole new scheme. I want to feature a silky type red, like an old-timey red. The convention business picks up soon. If Carmine could see his way clear to just think about this for a couple of minutes, riding in the car someday."

"I wish I could leave you some ray of light."

"I appreciate."

"I only drive the man around. In fact I'll tell you the most important thing I do for Carmine. Every morning I put him in his vest. I tie him in nice."

"What vest?"

"His vest. His body armor. He's running a fucking country."

They shook hands at the top of the stairs. Then Tony embraced Jack, who felt the emotion of the moment.

"There's something I want to do. I want to send you a twist-board. I have this twistboard I want you to try. Test model. Tony. We used to *swim*."

Jack called George Senator at the apartment.

He called his sister Eva.

He called Rabbi Hillel Silverman.

He called Lynette Batistone, Randi Ryder, to tell her she couldn't have the night off after all. Double DeLite was sick to her stomach in Grand Prairie.

Jack opened the door to the back room and the dogs shot out madcap and scrambling. There is a thing about the trust of a dog that makes up for a lot of heartache we take in this life. He plucked Sheba from the tumble of fur and went down to the car. He drove one block to the bank. He drove to the Sheraton and went into the coffee shop to tell the girl at the register a joke he knew would knock her to the floor. He drove to some stores looking for a certain food supplement for dieters. He heard police sirens and thought about following, just for a little adrenaline, but felt uninterested all of a sudden, down in the dumps.

This kind of gloom made him feel anonymous. Who was he? Why should anyone care about him?

He drove around a while, then stopped at a bakery and bought a cheesecake. He took it to the Police and Courts Building and rode the elevator to three. He stuck his head in a few offices and took the cake to the press room. Four or five clerks and detectives came in. Jack took a Preludin with a mouthful of cold coffee that was sitting in a paper cup. Somebody noticed the stub where Jack's index finger used to be. A little accident in the nature of an old-time dispute. He told two jokes that went over well. Then he went down the hall to Homicide and looked in on Russell Shively, who was at his desk reading Field and Stream, a lanky type with a sunburnt face who always made Jack feel here is my corny idea of a Texas lawman.

"Russell, how long we known each other?"

"Hell, I don't know."

"Have I ever mentioned suicide to you?"

"I don't believe so, Jack."

"Russell, if I ever mention suicide or the phrase kill myself or do away with myself, I am telling you right now it is not an empty threat to get attention. If you ever pick up the phone and hear a voice that says I'm killing myself and you think it's my voice, Jack Ruby, then I'm telling you right now I'm not bluffing."

These remarks came out of nowhere, of course, so Russell Shively just looked carefully into Jack's eyes and nodded, with no idea what to say.

Jack put his snap-brim fedora back on his head and walked out of the room. He went down to the car and drove off toward the Carousel. He thought of some calls he had to make. Bottles and jars rolled across the floor of the car. He thought of the fight that led to the stub finger. A dozen years ago he had a fight of a total animal nature with a guitar player at the Silver Spur, which Jack was running at the time. The guitarist bit off part of his left index finger. It was a single, sustained and determined head-wagging bite in the course of a stretch of wrestling and it left the top part of the finger hanging, beyond repair. This was harmful to Jack's public image because he wanted to join the Masons, the Freemasons, whatever they're called, for the business contacts and the fellowship. But the Masons would not accept a man who was missing part of his anatomy. This was an ancient bylaw that they kept in the books.

He called his attorney.

He called the Morning News about an ad for the club.

He called a stripper named Janet Alvord.

"Do I look swishy to you, Janet? What about my voice? People tell me there's a lisp. Is this the way a queer sounds to a neutral person? Do you think I'm latent or what? Could I go either way? Don't pee on my legs, Janet. I want the total truth."

The bartender was here. Jack complained that the bar glasses were not clean enough to suit him. He spotted the new waitress, who walked in wearing a low-cut ruffled blouse. He took her into a corner and told her a joke. She had a rumbling laugh. He told another quick one and walked off fast, looking back at her laughing in the corner.

He liked a woman with a freckled cleavage.

He went down to the car and drove home for an early dinner. Because what is it like to be a Jew in a place, in a state like Texas? You feel to yourself don't ever speak out, don't ever stand out. But he loved this city. It made him a living in his own way. He didn't have to hide what he was. He didn't have to listen to Jewish jokes from the MC at the club. The MC knew one Jewish joke could land him in Emergency. No complaints. It's just the little feeling you get sometimes there's some secret thing they're shielding. He grew up in the neighborhoods, the crosstown wars. What was Dallas next to that? He used to come home with blood on his clothes for sticking up for the Jewish race. He met his sisters at the streetcar stop in Dago Town to make sure nobody catcalled Jew-girl at them, or walked close behind smacking their lips, or put a hand on them. No complaints. It's just the impression of you're off to the side. But he had friends on the force. He liked to give a loan to a young cop with a new baby. Plainclothes officers came to the club. How many cities could he name where a Jew can walk into police headquarters and he hears, Hello, how are you, it's Jack. I owe my life to this town.

George said they were having spaghetti tonight.

"I thought tonight was a broiled haddock."

"Where?"

"Didn't I come home with haddock—when was it?"

"I don't know," George said.

Jack took a Preludin with some leftover juice.

"Ask me I'm unhappy."

"Meaning what?"

"Meaning with reference to what he said."

"No loan."

"They're getting ready to padlock my clubs."

"You take too many of those things, Jack."

"They're medically an obesity drug."

"Nobody's that fat."

"I need the stimuli," Jack said.

He took the newspapers he'd bought that morning and went into the toilet. All Jack's reading took place in the toilet. It was the best part of his day. He read the nightlife, the ads for the clubs, the local tidbits, the entertainment column. There were the shows around town. He checked the competition. His mind settled down when he was crapping. There was a restfulness and calm.

Later he stood in the kitchen talking to George.

He didn't want to reach the point again where he had to sleep at the club. There was a time not long ago when he didn't have a place to live. He was between apartments with not a lot of ready cash to maneuver. He slept at the club. He lived there, ate there, slept in a foldout bed in a back room next to the room with the dogs. His whole life conducted under one roof. A stink of beer and cigarettes and dog and what-have-you. That was the second-worst period after the Cotton Bowl Hotel, where he sat in the dark for eight weeks. He refused to go down to that level again. Of no place to live. Of totally outside the norm.

George said you can tell when the spaghetti's cooked by picking a strand out of the boiling water and flinging it against the wall. If it sticks, it's done.

Jack ate quickly and set out for the club in his bouncing Oldsmobile.

Guy Banister sat in his office after dark, the old lion head sunk in thought. Some bum was urinating in the street, drilling the wall of the building. The desk lamp was on. Guy picked up his file on the Red Chinese. It was the file he saved for quiet times of day, the final nightmare file, to be brooded over slowly.

Red Chinese troops are being dropped into the Baja by the fucking tens of thousands. Mobilizing, massing, growing. Little red stars on their caps.

In fact there was nothing new in the file. The same old rumors and suspicions. They are down there in the pale sands in their padded jackets, gathered in one great silent sweep, waiting for the word. It didn't need elaboration or update. There was something classic in the massing of the Chinese.

He wanted to believe it was true. He did believe it was true. But he also knew it wasn't. Ferrie told him it didn't matter, true or not. The thing that mattered was the rapture of the fear of believing. It confirmed everything. It justified everything. Every violence and lie, every time he'd cheated on his wife. It allowed him to collapse inside, to melt toward awe and dread. That's what Ferrie said. It explained his dreams. The Chinese caused his dreams. Every terror and queerness of sleep, every unspeakability—it is painted in China white.

Men floating down in white silk. He liked to think of an unmechanized mass, silent men gathering their chutes, concealed in the pale sands. This was not the missiles or the satellites, all that cocksure technology. The Chinese file contained the human swarm, in padded jackets, massing near the border. A fear to savor slowly.

The door opened and Ferrie walked in, breaking the reverie. He leaned against a wall eating french fries from a carton.

"I came to give a report. Not that you want to hear it."

"Where's Oswald?"

"Houston by now. I had Frank and Raymo take him. He'll get on a bus for Mexico City."

"Mackey says he can fix it so the Cubans won't take him. He's got Agency connections in Mexico City. Agency's bound to have someone inside the Cuban embassy. We're counting on Leon going back to Texas. We know that station wagon parked outside his house had Texas plates. His wife and kid left in that car."

"I'm pretty sure his rifle went with them."

"Is he leaning our way?" Banister said.

"This is the part you don't want to hear."

"He says no."

"That's right. But there's time."

"Does he know who we want?"

"He knows."

"Not interested."

"It needs time. He's been carrying on a struggle inside."

"He's your project, Dave."

"We had a talk this morning. To the extent that he talks. He hasn't made the leap."

"You keep saying you'll get inside his mind."

"I'm in his mind. I'm there. Like a fucking car wash."

"He shot at Walker."

"That's the point. Walker was politics. But Leon can't get worked up over Kennedy. He figures the man has made amends for past errors. He's a little dazzled by the Kennedy magic."

Banister wanted to crush something.

"Leon's a type he is willing to relinquish control at some point down the line," Ferrie said. "It just hasn't happened yet. Where's Mackey?"

"Miami. He's got two houses set up. One for Alpha people. One for his own team."

"If Leon is in?"

"If Leon is in," Banister said, "you fly him to Miami the night before."

"Then what?"

"We have to work it out."

"Once it's done I want him out of there," Ferrie said. "I don't want him abandoned or killed. He leaves his rifle behind and he gets out like the rest of them."

"That's always a possibility," Banister said.

Ferrie tossed the empty carton toward a basket.

"Do you trust Alpha 66?" he said.

"What the hell. They've been running a high fever ever since Pigs. That's two and a half years with a thermometer up their ass. They're ready. Nobody doubts their readiness."

"Do you trust Mackey?"

"I trust him completely," Banister said. "He wants a wall of shooters. Maybe eight men elevated on both sides of the street. As many as ten men. A shooting gallery."

"I thought Mackey liked a hand-knit operation."

"That's what he likes. This is what he gets. Alpha is in whether we want them or not. Best to join forces. He'll make the most of it. Once the motorcade route is public, he'll scout the area and set up positions. The hero comes riding into town. Tra-la, tra-la. We get him first crack out of the box."

They went down the stairs and paused outside the building entrance.

Banister said, "We have one more thing working. We want to leave an imprint of Oswald's activities starting today and ending when the operation is complete. A series of incidents. We want to establish Oswald as a man that people will later remember. Someone involved in suspicious business."

"What if Oswald doesn't cooperate?"

"We create our own Oswald. A second, a third, a fourth. This plan goes into effect no matter what he does after Mexico City. Mackey wants Oswalds all over Texas. He wants Alpha to supply the people. I talked to Carmine Latta about money for this thing."

"I'm the one who talks to Carmine."

"Not this time."

"I'm the contact."

"Shut up so I can tell you."

"Carmine and I have a rapport."

"There's an Alpha chapter in Dallas with headquarters in some rundown house. Carmine sent his bodyguard to Dallas earlier today. Pockets hot with cash."

In Mexico City

Postcard #6. Mexico City. Ancient and modern. Sprawling yet intimate. A city of contrasts. Leon stands in his room at the Hotel del Comercio, counting out his pesos. He has a street map with the day's destinations clearly marked. He has his documents and clippings. He has his thirty-five-cent Spanish-English dictionary with the kangaroo emblem. (New, concise. *Nuevo, conciso.*) He enjoys foreign travel, just like the President.

He walks two miles from his hotel to the Cuban embassy. He tells the woman he is going to Russia and wants to stop off in Cuba for a while. It is easier to get a transit visa because of the Cuban wariness of Americans. And anyone on his way to Russia gets the benefit of the doubt.

The woman examines his old Soviet work permit, his proof of marriage to a Soviet citizen, his proof of leadership in the Fair Play for Cuba movement, the news story of his arrest and a number of other documents.

She does not say *sí*. She does not say *no*.

She sends him off to get photographs for the visa application.

He stops in at the Soviet embassy, a couple of blocks away. The nearness is reassuring. The embassy is a large gray villa with a columned entrance and fancy dormers. There are armed sentries and a tall iron fence with a spiky top. It occurs to Leon that a concealed camera is probably taking his picture as he enters.

An official looks at his papers. It might be nice, he says, if Leon could come back with his Cuban transit visa in hand.

All right. He gets his picture taken and goes back to the Cuban embassy. The woman says he must get his Soviet entry visa before he can get his Cuban transit visa.

All right. He goes back to the villa. The man tells him a Soviet visa will take four months to arrange if he can get it at all. Leon says that when he was in Finland he got a visa in two days. The man says, "But this is Mexico City," and Leon expects him to add, "Hotbed of intrigue."

He eats the soup of the day, rice and meat. It costs forty-two cents. He checks the menu against the dictionary, then takes a bite of food, then checks again.

The next day at the Cuban embassy he demands to see the consul. He stands there shouting at the man. They have a loud and bitter exchange. He knows his rights. He is a friend of the revolution.

Then he goes to the Soviets and tells the man to check with the embassy in Washington. There are letters on file. His wife is Russian. They were married the day Castro won the Lenin Peace Prize.

It occurs to Leon that this man is KGB. So he mentions Kirilenko. Is this a good idea or not? At least it's a name, it's a link. It also occurs to Leon that he is being photographed not only by hidden Soviet cameras but probably by CIA cameras concealed in the building across the street or in a parked car or dangling, for all he knows, from a satellite in the sky.

His room number is eighteen. It is almost October and he was born on the eighteenth. David Ferrie was born on March 18. They have sat and discussed this. The year of Ferrie's birth is 1918.

On Sunday he goes to the movies in the afternoon and again in the evening.

The next day he visits the Cuban embassy, talks to the Soviet embassy on the phone and then visits the Soviet embassy. It occurs to him that the CIA probably taps the Soviet telephones.

Cuba and Russia. Russia is not totally out of the question. He could actually go back to Russia if Marina's visa comes through. He could visit or actually stay. They could be a family again.

Leon asks the Soviet official if there is any reply to the telegram sent to Washington. He tells the man he has information to offer in return for travel expenses to the USSR. He mentions Kirilenko again.

In the afternoon he consults his copy of Esta Semana, which he picked up in the hotel lobby. Events and locations in English and Spanish. Everything here happens in twos and his eyes constantly dart from one language to the other.

The next day they tell him at both embassies that there are no new developments. Once again he shows his documents, his correspondence. Documents are supposed to provide substance for a claim or a wish. A man with papers is substantial.

But this is the bureaucratic trap, in two languages, three languages, and nothing has effect. He is turned down, frozen out. It's hard to believe the representatives of the new Cuba are treating him this way. It's a deep disappointment. He feels he is living at the center of an emptiness. He wants to sense a structure that includes him, a definition clear enough to specify where he belongs. But the system floats right through him, through everything, even the revolution. He is a zero in the system.

For the third or fourth time he eats dinner in the small restaurant next to his hotel. It occurs to him that communications are flowing between agencies in the U.S. based on these wiretaps and the pictures taken by these hidden cameras.

Up to now he has been the only North American in the hotel and in the restaurant. But he realizes someone is looking at him, a man at a table near the kitchen, and Leon is fairly certain it is not a Mexican. He thinks he had a glimpse of the man coming in. But he doesn't want to look that way and see who it is. He senses something about the man that he doesn't want to know. There is music playing on a radio that sits on a shelf, maybe a fandango. He shifts in his chair, turning his back completely to the corner of the room where the man is sitting. Because the curious thing, the odd and strange and singular thing is that Leon believes the man is T. J. Mackey. He sips his water carefully. He feels the blood sort of surge up his back. He knows the man is not Latin, from the glimpse. He knows he's broad-shouldered, hair cut close. He takes the dictionary out of his pocket just for something to do, a busyness, flipping through the pages. It was just a glimpse, a blur. He drinks his water slowly, almost formally, aware of himself, holding himself in a correct and serious way, as anyone does who knows he is being watched.

Walking across the square he hears someone call, "Leon," but the name is pronounced more Spanish than English and he decides it is not meant for him.

The next day he gets on a bus at eight-thirty in the morning and sits in seat number twelve, which he has reserved in the name H. O. Lee. It is not until they approach the International Bridge, seventeen hours later, that Leon realizes he has forgotten to visit Trotsky's house, the fortified house in Mexico City where Trotsky spent his last years in exile. The sense of regret makes him feel breathless, physically weak, but he shifts out of it quickly, saying so what.

He carries two bananas in a paper bag and he takes them out and gulps them down before the bus reaches customs. He figures fruit is not allowed across the border and the last thing he wants now is another tussle with authority.

4 October

Mary Frances pushed the vacuum cleaner across the living-room floor. She was feeling bloated and hormonal. It was an effort just to exist, to put one heavy foot ahead of the other. Friday, after school, and she had to vacuum around Suzanne, who knelt on the floor watching cartoon rabbits on TV. She vacuumed over the bump between the living room and dining room. She vacuumed around the table and under the oak sideboard. There was so much drag on her body today, so many resisting forces.

Win walked past the doorway with a knife in his hand.

She pushed the vacuum cleaner back into the living room. It was a five-year-old Hoover with a receptacle unit shaped like a space satellite. Funny, she thought, how she could vacuum back and forth in front of Suzanne and the girl never complained. The girl looked right through her. The girl heard the cartoon voices through the noise of the Hoover.

After dinner Win went down to the basement to investigate a noise. He watched himself come down the plank stairs, head tilted slightly, fingers of the right hand extended. Houses make noises,

Mary Frances said. He smelled turpentine and understood how you could become hooked on the smell of turpentine, give yourself up to it, volatile, sticky, piney, your whole life centered on spirits of turpentine. Mary Frances told him that houses shift and settle all the time.

Thanks. But there is sometimes more to it.

He went back up to the living room and sat with her, listening to the radio. She liked the revivalist preachers, men of a certain creepy eloquence.

"Don't you feel well?" he said.

"I'm all right."

"I want you to be well."

"I'm all right."

"Because it would be devastating if you weren't well. That mustn't happen, understand? I actually couldn't bear it."

She had a Sears catalogue on her lap. She'd used catalogues to shop when they were posted to remote areas. ISOLATION TROPIC. He wondered what the hell had happened to Mackey.

"Don't be so solemn," she said.

"Don't you like being fussed after?"

"Not the way you do it."

"The housewife who never has time for herself. Doesn't she relish a little attention?"

"Not the way you do it. Looking so stricken. It chills my blood."

He laughed. They heard Suzanne walk through the kitchen singing a rhyme popular with local kids. Mackey had eluded all attempts by Parmenter to trace him. What did it mean? Larry said he probably just walked off. Doesn't want to do it. Wants to change careers. It's over. We tried.

> "Beans, beans, the musical fruit
> The more you eat, the more you toot."

Parmenter himself was in Buenos Aires getting a preview of his new job. This is the future of the Agency, he said to Everett.

Keeping track of world currencies. Moving and hiding money. Building reserves of money. Financing vast operations with complex networks of money.

Lancer is coming to Texas.

"Did you notice the casual tone?" Mary Frances said.

"It's a kids' jingle. What sort of tone?"

"No but the way she sort of rehearsed the casualness. So we wouldn't know we were supposed to hear."

"It was casual because it was casual."

"Where's the steak knife you were using to scrape paint? We keep losing knives."

Premonition. The story about the President's trip was in the Record-Chronicle a week ago. A brief tour of Texas in November, after his swing through Florida. Stops at Houston, San Antonio, Fort Worth and Dallas. Buried inside the paper. Three or four lines that only a person with a compelling interest in the President's whereabouts might take note of. Win thought it was eerie that President Jack would be headed in this general direction. The plot coming to the plotter. Assuming he made it past Miami. Because Parmenter might be wrong. Something might still be in force, some movement, a driving logic.

"I can't find the paint scraper," he said.

"Just leave the knives alone."

"There's something about a paint scraper. You know it's there. You're looking right at it. But you can't quite pick it out of the background. Let's face it, the background is vast and confusing."

He wanted a way out of guilt and fear. He was not strong enough to survive the damage this operation might cause if it developed a second life. He half yearned to be found out. It would be a deliverance in a way to be confronted, polygraphed, forced to tell the truth. He believed in the truth. He feared and welcomed the chance to be polygraphed. The Office of Security had models designed to fit in suitcases. You could be fluttered in your home. They would arrive with a two-suit Samsonite case. Unpack the machine, mix some control questions in with the serious stuff. His body would do the rest, yield up its unprotected data. The machine intervenes between a man and his secrets. There is something intimate about the polygraph. It measures skin conduction and hears you sweat. It allows you to give yourself away. Lies quicken the breath. They make the blood pound. It was such an old-fashioned idea, dated and quaint, but he'd seen himself how well it worked. Failed one test. Broke down at the start of another. Polygraph. A nice technical sound to it, a specialist's sound, but still traditional, decipherable, from the Greek.

"Where is she?" He called out, "Where's my little girl?"

"In her room," Mary Frances said.

He called out, "But we want her down here. We need some serious cheering up."

"Once she's in her room, the subject's closed. The day is definitely over."

"I had to share a room," he said.

"I had my own, thank God."

"I think you'll find that the great figures of history rarely had their own rooms."

"I loved my room," she said.

"Are you saying nothing ever again has been quite so nice?" He called out, "Come down and talk to us or we'll be very unhaaaap-py."

He went out to the porch to investigate a noise. He stood there smoking. He could hear the radio faintly. An old voice, a radio voice from another era can bring back everything. This was a house that nurtured memories. The curved porch. The oak posts furled in trumpet vines.

He knew all the techniques ever devised to beat the machine but he also knew he would be helpless to bring them into play. He believed in the polygraph. He wanted to cooperate, show everyone the machine was working well. Devices make us pliant. We want to please them. The machine was his only hope of deliverance after what he'd done, what he'd loosed into the crowd. A way out of death. Because in time a pity would fall across their faces. They would all see he only wanted what was right for his country. He loved his country. He loved Cuba, knew the language and the literature. He would go beyond yes and no. Tell them about the deathward-tending logic of a plot. T-Jay is out there somewhere, chewing gum and squinting in the light. They would nod and understand. A forgiveness would come to their eyes. Because they are not, after all, unmerciful men. Say what you will about the Agency. The Agency forgives.

God is alive and well in Texas.

He went inside and turned off the radio. The day wasn't half done and it was time to go to bed again. He checked the front door and turned off the porch light. He walked down the hall for the millionth time, checked the back door, checked to see that the oven was off. The last thing downstairs was the oven, except for the kitchen light. He turned off the kitchen light and began to climb the stairs.

He slipped near the top of the stairway, an ordinary misstep, no harm, no deeper meaning, but Mary Frances was out of the bedroom in a silent burst to take him by the elbow and lead him inside.

He sat at the edge of the bed taking off his shoes. She watched him, reading his face for signs.

"Just a little slip," he said.

"It sounded."

"Just an ordinary fool missing a step."

"You have a seminar tomorrow. Arts and Sciences Building. Ten A.M."

"I want you to be well," he said. "You have to be absolutely well. We can't have a situation where you're not completely yourself. I couldn't even begin to carry on if you somehow weren't well. I count on you for everything that matters."

The Agency forgives. There wasn't a man in the upper ranks of the four directorates who didn't understand the perils of clandestine work. They would be pleased by his willingness to cooperate. What's more, they would admire the complexity of his plan, incomplete as it was. It had art and memory. It had a sense of responsibility, of moral force. And it was a picture in the world of their own guilty wishes. He was never more surely an Agency man than in the first breathless days of dreaming up this plot.

He stood at the side of the bed in his pajamas. He'd forgotten to register the fact that the oven was off. He would have to go back downstairs to check the oven. Mary Frances lay in the dark, already sleep-breathing, deep and even. He has to see that the oven is off and he has to register the fact. This means they are safe for another night.

Mackey stood by the refrigerator drinking water from a pitcher. He wore a sweatsuit and baseball cap. He'd taken to running at night to keep his weight down.

He took off the cap and blew into it. Then he sat at the kitchen table and peeled an orange. The house was at the end of an unfinished street about half a mile from the heart of Little Havana.

Raymo walked in. He said, "When did you get back?"

"This afternoon."

"Did you hear there's word going around? Somebody in Chicago's planning the same thing."

"Banister called. He got a look at an FBI teletype. An attempt on the life."

"Four-man team. At least one of them might be Cuban. JFK's supposed to be in Chicago like November second."

"We have to wait our turn."

"If word leaks out there, same thing could happen to us."

"I'm counting on it," T-Jay said. "In fact I'm taking steps to make it happen. It's the only way we'll succeed. We're going in quick and tight. You keep it quiet. You don't tell Frank or Wayne."

"Forget Miami."

"That's right."

"Then we don't bring Leon here."

"That's right."

"Where is he?"

"He took a Transportes del Norte bus to Laredo. I'm betting he took a Greyhound from there to Dallas. Main thing is the Cubans didn't take him. No visa for Leon. It's beginning to take shape. Small, spur-of-the-moment, that's what we want. An everyday Texas homicide."

"JFK."

"Goes to Dallas next month. The man's a serious traveler. And wherever he goes, somebody wants a piece of him. Deep sweats of desire and rage. I don't know what it is. Maybe he's just too pretty to live."

He detached a couple of wedges from the orange and handed them to Raymo.

"Somebody keeps an eye on Leon."

"I think Leon will be hiding from us," T-Jay said. "He knows what we're up to and he doesn't necessarily approve. For the time being, we have our own model Oswald. Alpha is running people up and down the state. Eventually we'll have to pinpoint the original."

"When we took him to Houston he doesn't say ten words to me. He only talked to Frank."

"What did he say to Frank?"

"He got after Frank right away. He wanted some Spanish lessons."

Suzanne sat up in bed in the dark. She knew they were asleep. Once the radio hum withdrew from the wall by her ear, all she had to do was count to a hundred. Both sound asleep. If she was going to move the Little Figures, now was the time. She needed a safer hiding place. The closet had so much junk they would clean it any day and the Little Figures were hidden in one of the pockets on the shoe bag that hung inside the door. Once they found the Little Figures, that was the end of Suzanne. She would have no protection left in the world.

Lucky she had a good new place to keep them safe.

She got out of bed and raised the shade halfway, letting in light from the streetlamp. Then she moved softly in her nightgown that touched the floor. She took the Little Figures out of the shoe bag and sat them down on the narrow ledge behind the old bureau that used to belong to Grandma. The ledge stuck out about an inch near the bottom of the bureau. Hers was the only hand that could fit between the bureau and the wall. That was the perfect place because the Figures were already seated so they balanced just right. They were a clay man and a clay woman that her best friend, Missy, had given her as a birthday present. They were Indians who dwelt in pueblos and their hair and their clothes were painted black, with little black dots for the eyes and mouth.

She got back into bed and pulled the covers up.

The Little Figures were not toys. She never played with them. The whole reason for the Figures was to hide them until the time when she might need them. She had to keep them near and safe in case the people who called themselves her mother and father were really somebody else.

In Dallas

Four women sat around the table in Mrs. Ed Roberts's kitchen, drinking coffee and passing the time of day. A basket of folded laundry rested on the counter. Ruth Paine gestured again, calling for a pause. They all waited. Then she spoke softly in her halting Russian to Marina Oswald, who listened and smiled, a finger curled through the handle of her cup. The talk was kids, husbands, doctors, the usual yakkety-yak, but Ruth found it interesting. A chance to speak Russian. Mrs. Bill Randle, sitting next to her, nodded periodically as she translated. And Dorothy Roberts studied Marina's face to see that she was getting it. They wanted her to feel she was part of things.

The kids made a racket in the next room. Ruth Paine told her two neighbors that Marina's husband was having no luck finding work. He was living in a rooming house in Oak Cliff until he could find a job and an apartment for his family. Marina was due any day, of course.

Dorothy Roberts mentioned Manor Bakeries. They had a home-delivery service. Then there was Texas Gypsum, where somebody said they were hiring.

Ruth Paine said Marina's husband didn't drive, so that cut down the prospects.

Mrs. Bill Randle, Linnie Mae, said maybe she would have a piece of that coffee cake after all. It looked real good.

Dorothy Roberts said, "Is it warm for October or is it just me?"

A van door slammed across the street.

Then Linnie Mae Randle mentioned her brother. How he was saying the other day he thought they needed another fellow at the book warehouse where he worked, on the edge of downtown Dallas.

Ruth translated for Marina.

One of the little girls came in, wetting her finger to pick crumbs off the tabletop.

Dorothy opened the door to the carport.

"Out on Elm Street," Linnie Mae said. "Near Stemmons Freeway."

Five minutes later Ruth and Marina and June Lee and Ruth's small children, Sylvia and Chris, cut across the lawn to the Paine residence next door, a modest ranch house with an attached garage. Ruth turned at the door and watched Marina coming along slowly, vast, wide, ferrying one more soul across the darkness and into the world, or into suburban Dallas. The Oswald family was catching up to the Paines. Not that Ruth minded. She didn't even mind having Lee come out to visit once a week. She was separated from her husband and it was nice, actually, having a man to do certain jobs around the house.

Inside, Marina asked Ruth if she would telephone. Ruth looked in the phone directory for Texas School Book Depository. She talked to a man named Roy Truly about a job for a young veteran of the armed forces whose wife is expecting a child, and they already have a little girl, and he has been out of work for a while, and is desirous of employment, and is willing to work part-time or full-time, and is there a possibility of an opening?

Marina stood nearby, waiting for Ruth to translate.

It was a seven-story brick building with a Hertz sign on the roof. Lee was an order-filler. He picked up orders from the chute on the first floor and fixed them to his clipboard. Then he went up to six, usually, to find the books. Most of the order-fillers were Negroes. They had elevator races in the afternoon. Gates slamming, voices echoing down the shaft, laughter, name-calling. He took the books down to the girls on one, to the wrapping bench, where the merchandise was checked and shipped.

All these books. Books stacked ten cartons high. Cartons stamped Books. Stamped Ten Rolling Readers. Stacked higher than the tall windows. The cartons are a size you have to wrestle. When you open a fresh carton you get the fragrance of paper, of book pages and binding. It floods you with memories of school.

He liked carrying a clipboard. The clipboard made him feel this was a half-decent way to earn a dollar. He didn't have to listen to crazy-ass machines. There was no dirt or grease on the job. Just dust rising when the men ran to the elevators in the afternoon, three or four men pounding across the old wood floors to begin the race down—sunny dust forming among the books.

Lee sat in the dining room at the Paine house, wondering where the women had sneaked off to. Then Marina and Ruth walked in carrying a cake and singing "Happy Birthday." He was taken by surprise. It was a shock. He laughed and cried. Twenty-four.

He stayed over that night, a Friday, and the next evening he sat on the floor watching a double feature on TV, with Marina curled up next to him, her head in his lap.

The first movie was *Suddenly*. Frank Sinatra is a combat veteran who comes to a small town and takes over a house that overlooks the railroad depot. He is here to assassinate the President. Lee felt a stillness around him. He had an eerie sense he was being watched for his reaction. The President is scheduled to arrive by train later in the day. He is going fishing in a river in the mountains. Lee could tell the movie was made in the fifties from the cars and hairstyles, which meant the President was Eisenhower, although no one said his name. He felt connected to the events on the screen. It was like secret instructions entering the network of signals and broadcast bands, the whole busy air of transmission. Marina was asleep. They were running a message through the night into his skin. Frank Sinatra sets up a high-powered rifle in the window and waits for the train to arrive. Lee knew he would fail. It was, in the end, a movie. They had to fix it so he failed and died.

Then he watched *We Were Strangers*. John Garfield is an American revolutionary in Cuba in the 1930s. He plots to assassinate the dictator and blow up his entire Cabinet. Lee knew this was the period of the iron rule of Machado, known as the President of a Thousand Murders. The streets were dark. The house was dark except for the flickering screen. An old scratchy film that carried his dreams. Perfection of rage, perfection of control, the fantasy of night. John Garfield and his recruits dig a tunnel under a cemetery. Lee felt he was in the middle of his own movie. They were running this thing just for him. He didn't have to make the picture come and go. It happened on its own in the shaky light, with a strand of hair trembling in a corner of the frame. John Garfield dies a hero. He has to die. This is what feeds a revolution.

Lee sat there after the movie ended, with loud late-night commercials coming one after another, fast-talking men demonstrating blenders, demonstrating miracle shampoo, and Marina next to him, asleep, softly breathing.

It wasn't only the movies that made him feel a strangeness in the air. It was the time of year. October was his birthday. It was the month he enlisted in the Marines. He shot himself in the arm, in Japan, in October. October and November were times of decision and grave event. He arrived in Russia in October. It was the month he tried to kill himself. He'd last seen his mother one year ago October. October was the missile crisis. Marina left him and returned last November. November was the month he'd decided with Dupard to take a shot at General Walker. He'd last seen his brother Robert in November.

Brothers named Robert.

He got Marina settled in bed, then sat next to her and murmured serious baby talk to help her fall asleep again. He felt the power of her stillness, a woman's ardor and trust, and of the child she carried. He would start saving right away for a washing machine and car. They'd get an apartment with a balcony, their own furniture for a change, modern pieces, sleek and clean. These are standard ways to stop being lonely.

The landlady let him keep a jar of preserves and some milk in a corner of the fridge. He sat with the other roomers about half an hour a week, watching TV was all. He never spoke to them or raised his eyes to see them clearly. They were gray figures in old chairs, total nobodies. He was registered as O. H. Lee.

The rooming house was in an area of Oak Cliff that he knew well. The Gulf station where he'd rendezvoused with Dupard was across the street. The speed wash, now called Reno's, was half a block away. He went into the speed wash but Bobby didn't work there anymore. The place in daylight was home turf to half a dozen women and their scruffy kids. The children ate and played. The Coke machines sent bottles clunking into the slot.

His room was eight by twelve. Bed, dresser, clothes closet. He spent hours there reading the Militant and the Worker. One night he took the 22 bus back downtown. He walked the streets, looking into bars. He walked all the way down South Akard and stood outside Gene's Music Bar. Two men brushed past him, entering, and he followed them in. He stood near the door. The place was crowded. There were hard benches along the walls, rough-hewn benches. He could easily clear the room with an AR-15, which is what they use to guard the President, firing full auto. The idea was to stand here as long as he could without being noticed, just to watch, to see how queers work out their arrangements.

Somebody said, "It's none of my business *but.*"

He tried to pick out a person he might want to talk to, an understanding type. He drew some glances, then straight-out looks.

It was either go to the bar and order something or walk out the door. He decided this was a visit just to see. He could come back with a surer sense of things, not feeling so watchful and odd. Hidell means don't tell. He went out into the cool air, where he realized he was sweating. When he got to the rooming house he read every word of the week-old Militant. He also read between the lines. You can tell when they want you to do something on behalf of the struggle. They run a message buried in the text.

Three days after Rachel was born he went to a rally at Memorial Auditorium. The main speaker was Edwin A. Walker. Lee stood at the rear of the hall, watching people come in. The secret he carried with him made him feel untouchable. He was the one, the man who'd fired the shot that barely missed. It was a secret and a power. And he was standing right here, among them, among the Birchers and States Righters, wearing his .38 under a zipper jacket.

Crowd of about a thousand. Walker stood up there in his tall Stetson and moaned and groaned about the United Nations. Clap clap. The UN was an active element in the worldwide communist conspiracy. Clap clap. Lee slipped into a seat about midway down the aisle. He felt the smallness and rancor of these people. They needed to knock someone to the ground and stomp him for fifteen minutes. Feel better now? Walker went on about something called the Real Control Apparatus. He spoke in a clumsy way that engaged nothing, compelled nothing. There was a Lone Star standard on one side of him, a Confederate flag on the other. Lee moved farther down the aisle, stooped over so he wouldn't block anyone's view, and found a seat near the stage. Walker was a tired man. His face was like some actor's made up to show fatigue and aging. Lee saw a picture of a bright-red splotch on Walker's shirtfront just below the heart.

Outside the hall people crowded around the general, trying to touch him, show him their faces. He moved slowly to a waiting car. Lee pushed through the crowd. People thrust their faces into Walker's line of sight. They called to him and reached across bodies.

Lee caught the general's eye and smiled as if to say, Bet you don't know who I am. Untouchable. He had his hand inside the jacket, gripping the stock of the .38, just to do it, to get this close and show how simple, how strangely easy it is to make your existence felt. He saw a picture of the crowd breaking apart, crying out as they scattered, No, no, no, and Walker on the pavement, hatless now, a front-page photo in the Morning News.

He took the bus to his rooming house. He sat on the bed, holding the revolver. Shooting Walker was a dead-end now. He had no means to get to Cuba. They probably wouldn't take him even if he shot the man and managed to escape. History was closed to Edwin Walker. He put the gun in a dresser drawer. He went to the kitchen and drank some milk, standing in the dark.

What would he have to give Fidel before they let him live happily in little Cuba?

He sat at the wheel of Ruth Paine's station wagon. Dust blew across the gravel surface of the huge parking lot. It was Sunday and the lot was empty.

Ruth Paine was tall and slender, a long-jawed woman in her thirties with wavy doll's hair and librarian's glasses. She turned in her seat, looking straight back.

"Slow, slow, slow," she said. "Take it very slow."

He went in reverse for thirty yards, then hit the brake too hard, jolting them both. They sat looking out at the windswept lot.

"Did you tell him where I live?"

"I don't know where you live," she said. "It wasn't until he asked that I realized I didn't know. Even Marina doesn't know. Put it in forward and we'll do some turns."

"Did he say how he found you? How he knew Marina is staying with you?"

"He seemed a very reasonable man. I don't think he'll cause you any trouble at work. He said he wouldn't do that and I believe him."

"He knows where I work?"

"I told him. I didn't see what else I could do. They're the government, Lee."

He stared through the windshield.

"Put it in forward. Drive toward that litter basket. Then make a left around it."

He remembered now. He'd left a forwarding address at the post office in New Orleans before he went to Mexico City. Ruth Paine's address. But why are they looking for him? Because they know he visited the Soviet and Cuban embassies. They have him on film. They have recordings of his voice. What is it called, electronic eavesdropping?

"Ease up on the accelerator," Ruth said.

A broadsheet was fastened around the litter basket. THE VATICAN IS THE WHORE OF REVELATION. He made the turn nicely and straightened out.

"He wanted to know about anyone visiting or calling. I told him your social contact at the Paine house consisted mainly of dialing the number that says what time it is. He thought that was fairly funny."

If the Feebees could find him, so could Guy Banister. Whatever the Feebees knew, Banister could find out. A whole Sunday paper scattered in the wind, pages skipping past. He brought the car to a stop and stared through the windshield.

Ruth Paine said softly, "Let's try it in reverse one more time."

He saw something in the Morning News about JFK coming to Dallas. A noon luncheon. November 21 or 22. He barely scanned the story. He barely ran his eyes over the surface of the words. It was a bright cool day. He saw a shopping cart roll slowly out of an alley.

Marina slipped out of the house during the FBI man's second visit there. She walked around and around his car, trying to figure out what make it was. She couldn't read the raised metal lettering but she did memorize the license number, as Lee had ordered, and wrote it on a slip of paper when she got back to the house, getting one digit wrong.

Lee wrote a letter to the Soviet embassy in Washington, using Ruth Paine's typewriter. He had to type the letter several times and had trouble with the envelope as well, getting the address and return address mixed up and leaving out numbers and whole words. But it was worthwhile to see the sentences emerge so clear and solid with the authority his handwriting could not convey. He complained about the notorious FBI. He tried to tell the embassy between the lines that he was known to the KGB. He asked about Soviet entry visas and announced the birth of his daughter. He blamed Mexico City on the Cubans.

Then he wrote a note to the FBI man and took it on his lunch hour to the local office of the Bureau, where he handed it to a receptionist and walked out. He understood the agent's name to be Hardy and this is the single word he wrote on the envelope. He did not sign or date the note. The note said he was tired of the FBI bothering his wife and if they didn't stop he would take action. It also said he was affiliated with the New Orleans FBI, including being assigned an official code number, and that could be verified.

He practiced parking on the weekend with Ruth.

The nosebleeds started again.

He played with little Rachel, who had dimples just like Papa. It was David Ferrie who'd told him months before that dimples were a mark of the Libran.

Nicholas Branch has a sound tape made in Miami nine days before the President was due to appear in that city. The conversation on the tape was secretly recorded by one William Somersett, a police informer. The man talking to Somersett is Joseph A. Milteer, a member of the Congress of Freedom and the White Citizens Council of Atlanta.

SOMERSETT   I think Kennedy's coming here on the eighteenth, something like that, to make some kind of speech.

MILTEER   You can bet your bottom dollars he's going to have a lot to say about the Cubans. There's so many of them here.

SOMERSETT   Yeah, well, he'll have a thousand bodyguards. Don't worry about that.

MILTEER   The more bodyguards he has, the easier it is to get him.

SOMERSETT   Well how in the hell do you figure would be the best way to get him?

MILTEER   From an office building with a high-powered rifle. He knows he's a marked man.

SOMERSETT   They're really going to try to kill him?

MILTEER   Oh, yeah, it's in the working. There ain't any countdown on it. We've just got to be sitting on go. Countdown, they can move in on you, and on go they can't. Countdown is all right for a slow prepared operation. But in an emergency operation, you've got to be sitting on go.

SOMERSETT   Boy, if that Kennedy gets shot, we've got to know where we're at. Because you know that'll be a real shake if they do that.

MILTEER   They wouldn't leave any stone unturned. No way. They will pick somebody up within hours afterwards if anything like that would happen. Just to throw the public off.

When the Secret Service heard the tape, they prevailed upon the President's men to cancel the motorcade scheduled for Miami. Kennedy traveled by helicopter from the airport to a downtown hotel, where he spoke to a group of journalists.

Branch has two theories about this incident.

One, T. J. Mackey leaked news of the plot either directly to Milteer or to people in his circle. It's a fact that Mackey had connections in the intelligence unit of the Miami police and it's possible that he knew Milteer was being monitored. Milteer, a sixty-two-year-old Georgian, was known to be involved in violent resistance to integration.

Two, it was Guy Banister who told Milteer about the Miami plot and unwittingly ruined the operation.

(The Secret Service did not forward details of the taped conversation to agents responsible for the President's safety in Dallas. The FBI questioned Milteer superficially after the assassination.)

Branch also has a theory about the Oswald doubles who were active for almost two months, mainly in and around Dallas but also in other Texas cities. He thinks Mackey devised the scheme principally to occupy Alpha 66, to get them so deeply entrenched in rigid arrangements and setups that they wouldn't be able to adjust when the Miami façade folded over in the first breeze. Joseph Milteer had spoken of the difference between countdown and go. Mackey wanted to be sure that Alpha was stuck in countdown. He would be sitting on go.

The operation was crude. Someone looking like Oswald walks into an auto showroom, says his name is Lee Oswald, says he will soon be coming into money, test-drives a Comet at high speeds and makes a remark about going back to Russia. Someone who says his name is Oswald goes to a gunsmith and has a telescopic sight mounted on his rifle. Someone looking like Oswald goes to a rifle range half a dozen times in a thirteen-day period and makes a point of shooting at other people's targets.

All of these incidents took place at times when the real Oswald was known to be elsewhere.

To Nicholas Branch, more frequently of late, "Lee H. Oswald" seems a technical diagram, part of some exercise in the secret manipulation of history. A photograph taken by hidden CIA cameras of a man walking past the Soviet embassy in Mexico City bears the identifying tag "Lee H. Oswald." Oswald was in Mexico City at the time but the man in the picture is someone else—broad-chested, with a full face and cropped hair, in his late thirties or early forties. Another form of double. It's not surprising that Branch thinks of the day and month of the assassination in strictly numerical terms— 11/22.

But there's something even more curious than the misidentification. The man in the photograph matches the written physical descriptions Branch has seen of T. J. Mackey.

(The Curator has never been able to provide a photograph of Mackey labeled as such.)

Branch sits in his glove-leather chair looking at the paper hills around him. Paper is beginning to slide out of the room and across the doorway to the house proper. The floor is covered with books and papers. The closet is stuffed with material he has yet to read. He has to wedge new books into the shelves, force them in, insert them sideways, squeeze everything, keep everything. There is nothing in the room he can discard as irrelevant or out-of-date. It all matters on one level or another. This is the room of lonely facts. The stuff keeps coming.

The Curator sends thirty more volumes from CIA's one-hundred-and-forty-four-volume file on Oswald. He sends cartons of investigative reports and trial transcripts concerning people only remotely connected to the events of November 22. He sends coroners' reports on the dead.

Salvatore (Sam) Giancana, the syndicate boss who grew up near Jack Ruby in Chicago, is found dead in June 1975 in his finished basement, shot once in the back of the head, six times in a stitching pattern around the mouth. He was scheduled to testify five days later before a Senate committee looking into plots against Castro. The murder weapon is found and traced to Miami. No arrests in the case.

Walter Everett Jr., the man who conceived the plot, is found dead in May 1965 in a motel room outside Alpine, Texas, where he was assistant to the president of Sul Ross State College. Ruled a heart attack. He was registered as Thomas Stainback.

Wayne Wesley Elko, the ex-paratrooper and part-time mercenary, is found dead in January 1966 in a motel room outside Hibbing, Minnesota. Ruled acute morphine poisoning. In his pickup, police find tools and copper wiring stolen from an iron mine nearby, and a two-year-old boy asleep in a toddler's car seat.

Francis Gary Powers, the U-2 pilot, gets a job with KNBC in

Los Angeles, flying a helicopter and reporting on traffic and brush fires until one day in August 1977 when the Bell Jet Ranger evidently runs out of fuel and comes yawing down in a field where boys are playing softball, killing Powers instantly.

The crash occurs just three miles from the Skunk Works, a building with blacked-out windows at Lockheed Aircraft where the first U-2 was developed twenty-two years earlier.

Branch has become wary of these cases of cheap coincidence. He's beginning to think someone is trying to sway him toward superstition. He wants a thing to be what it is. Can't a man die without the ensuing ritual of a search for patterns and links?

The Curator sends a four-hundred-page study of the similarities between Kennedy's death and Lincoln's.

Wayne shared the back seat with Raymo's ancient shepherd dog. The idea was travel light. They'd moved out of Miami real quick, grabbing essential things, so it was hard to see the need for an animal coming along, big and sick as it was, gasping for last air.

They rode through the night.

Raymo drove and Frank sat next to him. They spoke Spanish most of the time, which Wayne didn't try to decode. His mind was still on fire with the knowledge of what they were going to do. They were going to go over the line. It was like science fiction. It carried you past the ordinary portals.

Frank drove for a while and Wayne sat up front. At least they weren't using the Bel Air. This was a '58 Merc with a pockmarked body and an engine out of the speed shop, easy-breathing, the pounce of a slingshot dragster. Wayne turned the radio full-blast. The wind shot through. They'd left all the new weapons with Alpha except for one rifle Mackey was transporting. Rock 'n' roll screamed in Wayne's face. Middle of the night near Tallahassee.

Wayne's old man used to say, "God made big people. And God made little people. But Colt made the .45 to even things up."

But this wasn't a mission to locate the social mean. They were making a crash journey over the edge. Wayne kept shaking his head to settle all the pieces. Making these shiver motions that drew a look from driver Frank. Wayne was amazed that an idea like this could even exist in America. And here he was in the middle of it, wind streaming through the car.

They stood pissing in a field in a light rain.

Wayne took the wheel with the first ruddled light breaking behind them. Radio off and windows shut now. Frank asleep in the rear seat and moaning through his crowded teeth.

"I'm still absorbing this thing," Wayne said, looking across at Raymo. "You read science fiction?"

"Fucking crazy, Wayne?"

"There's a quality I used to feel before a night jump. Like is this actually happening?"

"We're talking this is real."

"I know it's real."

"First they cancel Chicago right out. Then they do Miami without the motorcade. *They* know it's real."

Wayne kept studying Raymo, occasionally darting a look at the road. The car was tight and quiet, beautifully behaved.

"Like we're racing across the night," he said, mock-hysterical.

"They're paying some nice money. Think of you're doing a day's work."

"Like we're hand-picked men on the biggest mission of our lives."

They passed a convoy of military vehicles. After a while Raymo gestured toward the back seat and said, "There's something cross my mind."

"What?"

"I'm thinking I ought to put him down."

"What? Your dog?"

"He lost all coordination. He tries to get up, he can't keep his paws from sliding out."

"When the nervous system goes."

"I hate to take him to the box. They gas them in a box."

"You don't want gas."

"I hate the idea they use gas."

"Some things you know what has to be done."

"I had this dog since before Girón."

"But you don't have the heart."

"You hate to be the one."

"I'm stopping first chance," Wayne said.

He studied Raymo's face, which showed nothing, and five miles farther on he took an exit for a regional airport.

He had his hunting knife wrapped in a couple of sweaters in his khaki poke.

He stopped on the grassy border of a long straight road that ran alongside a chain-link fence with barbed wire canted at the top. He got out and waited while Raymo eased the big dog onto the grass. Silhouettes of hangars and small planes. Raymo got in the car and drove fifty yards and stopped. The dog stood by the side of the road. Wayne approached from the rear, standing over the animal, straddling it. Stars still out. He grabbed the dog's scruff and lifted hard. The front paws paddled air and Wayne moved his knife-hand under the dog's jaw. He growled, cutting the animal's throat. Then he let go with the left hand. The dog fell flat and hard, lying between Wayne's feet, blood running. He growled at it again and walked to the car, holding the bloody knife high. He wanted Raymo to see it, just as a sign, a gesture that had no meaning you could put into words.

He was able to sleep now. They all slept for a brief time in the late morning. Hours later in the dark they picked up the first pulse of Dallas on the radio, a scratch and rustle at the edge of the band, and they listened to an eerie voice ride across the long night.

"Tell you something, dear hearts, Big D is ner-vus tonight. Getting real close to the time. Notice how people saying scaaaary things. Feel night come rushing down. Don't y'all sense it around you? Danger in the air. You can see it in the streets. Billboards. Bumper stickers. Handbills. They're saying awful things about our leaders. I'm walking down the street this morning and there's a zigzag thing painted on a storewindow and it hits me all at once like *it's a swastika*. Do you think I'm making it up? I'm not making it up. Let me pass a thought through the ozone just to get your clock unwound. How do we know it's really *him* that's coming to town? Don't you know the rumors he travels with a dozen look-alikes when he goes into no man's land? Just to disorient the enemy. So maybe we're getting Jack Seven or Jack Ten. Or all of them at once in different locales. I can understand the need, myself. Or might be I'm just receptive to other people's fantasies. Some things are true. Some are truer than true. Oh the air is swollen. Did you ever feel a tension like right now? You know what Dallas is like, don't you, in the universal scheme? We're like everywhere. Or we're like everywhere wants to be. Dress alike, talk alike, think alike. We're a *model* for the country. I'm not making it up. But the little itchy thing is seeping out. Don't you feel it oozing to the surface? People say he's riding Caroline's tricycle into town. Not tough enough to lead us to Armageddon. All the ancient terrors of the night. We're looking right at it. We know it's here. We feel it's here. It has to happen. Something strange and dark and dreamsome. Weird Beard says, Night is rushing down over Big D."

Raymo, Wayne and Frank had never been to Dallas and they wondered what this creep could mean.

Wednesday. Lee walked out of the rooming house and went up the street to a diner where he had breakfast most mornings. He checked the license plates on cars parked along North Beckley, looking for Agent Hardy's number.

They'd get their own furniture, modern pieces, and a washing machine for Marina.

He had eggs over light. He ate with a folded-up newspaper under his left elbow. The noise and talk fell around him. He kept his head close to the page, reading the fourth or fifth story in the last week about a Yale professor of political science arrested in the Soviet Union as a spy. Arrested outside the Metropole Hotel, one of the places Lee had stayed. Arrested and then released. The story was really about him. Everything he heard and saw and read these days was really about him. They were running messages into his skin.

He walked to the bus stop, checking license plates along the way. A coppertone Mercury eased alongside and moved at Lee's pace down the street. It had those smoked-over windows. He was prepared to give his name as O. H. Lee and tell them nothing else. He knew his rights. He had his guaranteed rights. He would not stand for harassment.

The window slid down and David Ferrie rested an elbow on the door, then turned to look at him.

Lee said, "I can't be late for work."

They drove to the Book Depository. Lee interrupted the talk several times to give directions, concerned that they'd miss a turn.

"Been reading the papers?" Ferrie said. "I understand they've had a story every couple of days. First he's coming. Then he's having lunch at the Trade Mart. Then there's a motorcade looping through the downtown area. Then yesterday's papers, both papers, which I saw myself. A street-by-street outline of the motorcade route. Harwood to Main. Main to Houston. Houston to Elm. Down Elm to Stemmons Freeway. I thought to myself, Old Leon's *looking* at this. What's he feeling right now? What were you feeling, Leon? It must have been an incredible moment. Like a vision in the sky. Must have froze your blood."

"I'm only aware five cities, two days. He'll be here a couple of hours."

"They know where you live and they know where you work."

"I didn't see yesterday's paper as a matter of fact."

"Of *course* you saw it. It said the President's passing under your fucking window. The fucking building faces Elm Street, doesn't it? You spend most of the day on the sixth floor, don't you? His car is coming along Houston right straight at you. Then dipping away down Elm. Moving slowly and grandly past. The one place in the world where Lee Oswald works. The one time of day when he sits alone in a window and eats his lunch. There's no such *thing* as coincidence. We don't know what to call it, so we say coincidence. It happens because you make it happen."

Ferrie was pink-faced, nearly shouting. Lee gave a direction to turn left. Ferrie gripped the steering wheel hard.

"You see what this means. How it shows what you've got to do. We didn't arrange your job in that building or set up the motorcade route. We don't have that kind of reach or power. There's something else that's generating this event. A pattern outside experience. Something that *jerks* you out of the spin of history. I think you've had it backwards all this time. You wanted to enter history. Wrong approach, Leon. What you really want is out. Get out. Jump out. Find your place and your name on another level."

Lee directed him to Houston Street, where they parked in front of the Old Court House, facing south, their backs to the Book Depository, which was a block and a half away. Ferrie wiped spit from the corners of his mouth. He seemed out of breath. Lee sat calmly looking out the window.

"It's been waiting to happen, Leon."

"I have to be at work at eight."

"That building's been sitting there waiting for Kennedy and Oswald to converge on it."

"Just o::t of curiosity. How did you find out where I live? The Feebees don't know. They know where I work."

"They know where you work. That's how we know. We followed you from work last night. We're more interested in you than they are. Listen. I sat in the car outside your rooming house half the night. I was *afraid* to come see you. Now that it's going to happen, I'm scared half to death. I've got fear running through my system. Look at what we're doing. The chaos? The fucking anguish we'll cause? We'll give everybody cancer. I sat in the car. I was afraid to face you. I thought, What are we doing to poor Leon? I thought, Poor Leon's seen that item in the paper. Harwood to Main. Main to Houston. Houston to Elm. Like a scary nursery rhyme. He's going to kneel in that window and *do* it. And I'm one of the ones. I'm the agitator. I'm the fool that's responsible."

Lee took a stick of gum out of his pocket and broke it in half. He offered a piece to Ferrie, who slapped it out of his hand.

"Where's the rifle?"

"In a garage in a suburb, where Marina's staying."

"They drive you to Galveston when it's done. I meet you there. This way we're one city removed from the scene. There's a plane all set in Galveston. We fly to Yucatán. A place called Mérida. They drive you across the peninsula. They put you on a boat to Havana. They want you in Havana. It suits their purposes just as it suits yours. The boat's all set. They'll give you a name and documents." Ferrie looked at him sadly. "Or there's more to it. Something we don't know about. Like they kill us both in Yucatán."

Lee gave a little laugh, expelling air from his nose. Then he turned to look at the clock attached to the Hertz sign on the roof of the Book Depository. He got out of the car and walked down the street.

Just after lunch hour he went past Roy Truly's office on the first floor. Mr. Truly, the man who'd hired him, was talking to one of the textbook salesmen. Lee saw the salesman hand Mr. Truly a rifle. Two or three other men stood in the doorway commenting. Lee walked over. There were two rifles the salesman said he'd just bought. He had a .22 for his son for Christmas. And a deer rifle that Mr. Truly was inspecting. The fellows commented from the doorway. Lee watched the salesman box up the .22 and then he walked over to the elevator and hit six. He wasn't surprised to see rifles in the building. How could he be surprised? It was all about him. Everything that happened was him.

Thursday. T. J. Mackey stood in front of the County Records Building. He crossed the street to the triangle lawn between Main and Elm. He looked toward the railroad tracks above the triple underpass. Then he jogged across Elm and stood on the sloped lawn in front of the colonnade. He walked up toward the stockade fence that set off the parking lot. He stood facing Elm. He walked back toward the sign for Stemmons Freeway. Cars, everywhere, dashing. He looked at the sky and wiped his mouth.

Later he sat in a dark Ford on the downtown fringe, unwrapping a sandwich. This was an area of old packing houses with train tracks partly paved over and sides of buildings showing brick and mortar exposed by the demolition of adjacent structures. Every usable space was set aside for parking—alleyways, dusty lots, old loading zones. There was a clinging midday silence, a remoteness that Mackey found odd, a block and a half from the crowds and traffic.

He watched Oswald approach uncertainly.

He was sure Oswald wanted to be the lone gunman. This is how it is with solitaries, with men who plan eternally toward some total moment. Easy enough to make him believe it. But he would also have to make sure Oswald didn't fire until the limousine was moving away from him toward the triple underpass. T-Jay wanted a crossfire. If Oswald misses, his second shooter is in prime position; he has the car almost head-on. T-Jay did not trust Oswald to make the shot. This was the kid who missed General Walker at a hundred and twenty feet—a stationary man in a well-lighted room. And the Mannlicher is an old, crude and unreliable weapon. If he fires and misses while the car is still on Houston Street, coming at him, with no clear shot for the second gunman, then we all walk away with nothing. As a shooter, Oswald was redundant, strictly backup. His role was to provide artifacts of historical interest, a traceable weapon, all the cuttings and hoardings of his Cuban career.

T-Jay saw him spot the car, tilting his chin slightly. He walked over and got in, carrying a sandwich and a half-pint carton of milk.

"How's the new baby?"

"Fine. Doing real well."

"He's going to be coming at you for one street length, swinging out of Main and coming at you down Houston," T-Jay said. "You don't take him then. This is not the time. It's an easy shot, the easiest we could possibly expect, but they'll be looking right at you. There's a pilot car, there's about fifteen cops on motorcycles, there's a Secret Service car with eight men, four of them hanging off the running boards. They're all clustered around the President's limousine and they're all looking your way. Once the shot is off, they'll know exactly where it came from. That building will be flooded with police. I strongly recommend. I can't be too emphatic. Wait. You wait for them to turn down Elm and head toward the underpass and the freeway. It's not a hard shot. You aim at the mass, the center portion of his body or whatever part of his body is visible through the scope. Wait. You wait for him to veer away from you down Elm. Then you wait for him to clear the oak tree. He has to clear that tree. I estimate the first shot at less than two hundred feet. After that, depends on how fast the driver reacts. I figure the sound will ricochet toward the underpass. They won't be certain of the source. You're behind them now, which makes it harder for them to pick you out of the landscape. You gain extra seconds. Maybe ten extra seconds to get downstairs. It could make the difference. Wait. Be sure to wait. Don't even show yourself in that window until the car reaches the oak tree. Then wait for it to clear the tree."

The plan had one thing going for it that Win Everett's levels and refinements could not have supplied. Luck. T-Jay watched Oswald peel the lettuce off the bread and eat it separately.

"Once you're on the street, get out of the area fast. Jefferson Boulevard, not far from your rooming house. Go to West Jefferson, north side of the street, number 231. It's a movie house with a Spanish-type façade. It'll be open. They open the doors at twelve-forty-five. You go in, take a seat, watch the movie. We'll have you in Galveston by nightfall and out of the country by dawn."

Mackey crumpled the sandwich paper and threw it out the window. He took four cartridges out of his pocket. He jiggled them in his fist and let them drop into Oswald's lunch bag.

"I don't see any way you'll need more than four rounds."

"There won't be time."

"Trust your hands."

"I've worked the bolt a thousand times."

"What's the baby's name?"

"My wife named her Audrey, after Audrey Hepburn in *War and Peace*. Tolstoy. But her middle name is Rachel. We call her Rachel."

"You're going to love this operation," T-Jay said.

He watched Oswald walk out of the alleyway onto Griffin Street and then head southwest, back to work.

The main thing is Kennedy dead.

The next thing is Oswald dead.

Once Oswald's leftist sympathies are exposed, the authorities will conclude, will want to conclude, that Castro agents recruited him, used him, killed him.

Guy Banister would alert the FBI to the Hidell alias.

David Ferrie would spend a lonely night in Galveston.

Marina and Lee were in the backyard of the Paine house, pushing kids on the swings in turn, Sylvia and Chris and Junie and a neighbor's little girl and boy. It was dark but the kids didn't want to go inside. Two swings, two parents to push them.

"But you still haven't said what you're doing here on a Thursday."

"I miss my girls," he said.

"Without even calling."

"If you come to Dallas to live."

"No."

"Then I won't have to call. Everything will change. I can't live in that room too much longer."

"The children are better off here."

"Do you know the size of that room?"

"Ruth is still happy to have us stay."

"Papa thinks you don't love him."

They took two kids off the swings, put two more on. Marina was still angry at Lee for not telling her that he was using a false name. She found out when Ruth called the rooming house and asked for Lee Oswald. She wanted this foolish business to end. All these comedies. First one thing, then another.

The kids screamed, "Higher."

"I'll buy you a washing machine," he said.

"We might be better with a car."

"I'm saving the best I can. First we need to get an apartment."

"No."

"If you come to Dallas to live."

"No."

"The girls want to be with their daddy."

"Who will I talk to all day? Here I can talk to Ruth. Ruth is a big help to me."

"A balcony like Minsk," he said.

At dinner Ruth asked that the three of them hold hands around the table. She explained this was how Quakers say grace. Each person is supposed to recite a silent prayer, although it was clear to Marina that Lee's silence was not the prayerful kind.

When Marina was cleaning up in the kitchen, Ruth came in and said in a slightly puzzled way that someone had left the light on in the garage. They said it was probably Lee looking for a sweater among his belongings. Most of the things they owned were in boxes in Ruth's garage.

In the bedroom Marina took off her clothes. Lee sat in a chair, dressed except for his shoes and socks. Getting ready for bed, the same as anyone, here in this American place.

"Everything will change."

"No."

"But first we have to live together."

"I don't see any reason to hurry."

"If you come to Dallas to live."

"The children play outside here. Ruth is here."

"I have a little saved."

"I don't want my baby sucking nervous milk."

"Our own furniture for a change."

She stood naked on the far side of the bed. She reached around to the chair for her nightdress. He was watching her. She thought he was going to say something. She put the nightdress over her head and rolled back the bedcovers. Ordinary in every way, simple moments adding up, with rain falling on the lawn.

In the morning, early, he was gone. She found money in little bunches on top of the bureau and she counted it up, amazed. One hundred and seventy dollars. She was sure it was everything he had.

Three times he'd asked her to live with him in Dallas. Three times she'd said no. She stood by the bureau thinking. It was a well-known pattern, things that happen in threes. There was a certain dark power to the number three. She'd noticed all her life how it meant bad luck.

22 November

At the airport they were standing on baggage carts and clinging to light posts. They were draped over the chain-link fence, people in raincoats, waving flags, hanging off the sign for Gate 28. Skies were clear now and the 707 swung massively to a stop on the tarmac. They came running from their cars. They stood at the edge of the crowd, jumping up and down. Children rode the shoulders of gangly men. There was a mood rising from the packed bodies, an eager spirit of assent. Members of the welcoming party edged into place at the foot of the ramp, fussing with their clothes and hair. The aft door opened and the First Lady appeared in a glow of rosebud pink, suit and hat to match, followed by the President. A sound, an awe worked through the crowd, a recognition, ringing in the air. People called out together, faces caught in some stage of surprise resembling dazzled pain. "Here" or "Jack" or "Look." The President fingered his lapel, gave a little jacket-adjusting shrug and walked down the ramp. The sound was a small roar now, a wonder. They shook the fence. They came running from the terminal building, handbags and cameras bouncing. There were cameras everywhere, held aloft, a rustling of bladed shutters, with homemade signs poking through the mass.

Welcome Jack and Jackie to Big D.

After the handshakes and salutes, Jack Kennedy walked away from his security, sidestepping puddles, and went to the fence. He reached a hand into the ranks and they surged forward, looking at each other to match reactions. He moved along the fence, handsome and tanned, smiling famously into the wall of open mouths. He looked like himself, like photographs, a helmsman squinting in the sea-glare, white teeth shining. There was only a trace of the cortisone bloat that sometimes affected his face—cortisone for his Addison's disease, a back brace for his degenerating discs. They came over the fence, surrounding him, so many people and hands. The white smile brightened. He wanted everyone to know he was not afraid.

The Lincoln was deep blue, an iridescent peacock gleam, with an American flag and a presidential standard attached to the front fenders. Two Secret Service men in front, Governor Connally and his wife in the jumpseats, the Kennedys in the rear. The Lincoln moved out behind an unmarked pilot car and five motorcycles manned by white-helmeted city cops showing traditional blank faces. Stretching half a mile behind came the miscellaneous train of rented convertibles, station wagons, touring sedans, Secret Service follow-up cars, communications cars, buses, motorcycles, spare Chevys, Lyndon, Lady Bird, congressmen, aides, wives, men with Nikons, Rolliflexes, newsreel cameras, radiophones, automatic rifles, shotguns, service revolvers and the codes for launching a nuclear strike.

The Lincoln seemed to glow. Sunlight flashed from the fenders and hood, made the upholstery shine. The Governor waved his tan Stetson and the flags snapped and the First Lady held roses in the crook of her arm. The burnished surface of the car mirrored scenes along the road. Not that there was much to collect in the landscape at hand. Airport isolation. Horizontal buildings with graveled rooftops. Billboards showing sizzling steaks. Random spectators, brave-looking, waving, in these mournful spaces. And a man standing alone at the side of the road holding up a copy of the Morning

News opened to the page that had everybody talking. *Welcome Mr. Kennedy to Dallas.* An ad placed by a group called the American Fact-Finding Committee. Grievances, accusations, jingo fantasia—not so remarkable, really, even in a major newspaper, except that the text was bordered in black. Nicely ominous. Jack Kennedy had seen the ad earlier and now, with towered downtown Dallas in the visible distance, he turned and said softly to Jacqueline, "We're heading into nut country now."

Still, it was important to be seen in an open car without a bubbletop, without agents on the running boards. Here he was among them in a time of deep division, the country pulled two ways, each army raging and Jack having hold of both. Were there forebodings? For weeks he'd carried a scrap of paper with scribbled lines of some bloody Shakespearean ruin. *They whirl asunder and dismember me.* Still, it was important for the car to move very slowly, give the crowds a chance to see him. Maximum exposure as the admen say, and who wants a president with a pigeon's heart?

And there were friendly crowds ahead. The strays on the outskirts, stick figures, gave way to larger groups, to gatherings. They appeared at intersections. They stood on bumpers in stalled traffic and cried, "Jack-eeee." Signs, flags, surging numbers, people fifteen deep, crowds growing out over the curbstone, craning for a look at the brilliant limousine. The cops astride their Harleys trimmed the ragged edges. There were people backed against building walls who could not see the limousine but only figures gliding by, spirits of the bright air, dreamlike and serene. The crush was massive down near Harwood. It was a multitude, a storm force. The motorcycles rumbled constantly, an excitement in the sound, a power, and the President waved and smiled and whispered, "Thank you."

Advise keep crowds behind barricades. They are getting in the street here.

Street by street the crowd began to understand why it was here. The message jumped the open space from one press of bodies to the next. A contagion had brought them here, some mystery of common impulse, hundreds of thousands come from so many histories and systems of being, come from some experience of the night before, a convergence of dreams, to stand together shouting as the Lincoln passed. They were here to be an event, a consciousness, to astonish the old creedbound fears, the stark and wary faith of the city of get-rich-quick. Big D rising out of caution and suspicion to produce the roar of a sand column twisting. They were here to surround the brittle body of one man and claim his smile, receive some token of the bounty of his soul.

Advise approaching Main go real slow speed.

Into the noontide fires. Twelve city blocks down Main Street, some embers of the melodrama of small towns, of Hallmark and Walgreen and Thom McAn, scattered among the bank towers. The motorcycles came, a steady throttling growl, a tension that bit into the edge of every awareness. The sight of the Lincoln sent a thrill along the street. One roar devoured another. There were bodies jutting from windows, daredevil kids bolting into the open. *They're here. It's them. They're real.* It wasn't only Jack and Jackie who were riding in a fire of excitement. The crowd brought itself into heat and light. A knowledge charged the air, a self-awareness. Here was a new city, an idea that traveled at the speed of sound, pounding over the old hushed heart, a city of voices roaring. Loud and hot and throbbing. The crowd kept pushing past the ropes and barricades. Motorcycles drove a wedge and agents dropped off the running boards of the follow-up car to jog alongside the Lincoln. Was it frightening to sit in the midst of all this? Did Jack think this fervor was close to a violence? They were so damn close, nearly upon him. He looked at them and whispered, "Thank you."

The men in dark glasses were back on the running boards as the motorcade began its swing into Houston Street and the last little dip before the freeway.

They ran to the birdcage elevators, four young men in the lunch-hour race, horse laughs, jostling at the gates. Lee heard them call to each other all the way down. Dust. Faded white paint on the old brick walls. Stacks of cartons everywhere. Old sprinkler pipes and scarred columns. A layer of dust hovered at a height of three feet. Loose books on the floor. His clipboard already hidden, jammed between cartons near the west wall. Stillness on six.

He stood at the southeast window inside a barrier of cartons. The larger ones formed a wall about five feet high and carried a memory with them, a sense of a kid's snug hideout, making him feel apart and secure. Inside the barrier were four more cartons— one set lengthwise on the floor, two stacked, one small carton resting on the brick windowsill. A bench, a support, a gun rest. The wrapping paper he'd used to conceal the rifle was on the floor near his feet. Dust. Broken spider webs hanging from the ceiling. He saw a dime on the floor. He picked it up and put it in his pocket.

He looked down Houston Street as the motorcade approached, slow and vivid in the sun. There were people scattered on the lawns of Dealey Plaza, maybe a hundred and fifty, many with cameras. He held the rifle at port arms, more or less, and stood in plain view in the tall window. Everything looked so painfully clear.

The President had chestnut hair and the First Lady was radiant in a pink suit and small round hat. Lee was glad she looked so good. For her own sake. For the cameras. For the pictures that would enter the permanent record.

He spotted Governor John Connally in one of the jump seats, a Stetson in his lap. He liked Connally's face, a rugged Texas face. This was the kind of man who would take a liking to Lee if he ever got to know him. Cartons stamped Books. Ten Rolling Readers. Everyone was grateful for the weather.

The white pilot car turned, the motorcycles turned. The Lincoln passed beneath him, easing left, making the deep turn left, seeming almost to rotate on an axis. Everything was slow and clear. He got down on one knee, placed his left elbow on the stacked cartons and rested the gun barrel on the edge of the carton on the sill. He sighted on the back of the President's head. The Lincoln moved into the cover of the live oak, going about ten miles an hour. Ready on the left, ready on the right. Through the scope he saw the car metal shine.

He fired through an opening in the leaf cover.

When the car was in the clear again, the President began to react.

Lee turned up the handle, drew the bolt back.

The President reacted, arms coming up, elbows high and wide.

There were pigeons, suddenly, everywhere, cracking down from the eaves and beating west.

The report sounded over the plaza, flat and clear.

The President's fists were clenched near his throat, arms bowed out.

Lee drove the bolt forward, jerking the handle down.

The Lincoln was moving slower now. It was almost dead still. It was sitting naked in the street eighty yards from the underpass.

Ready on the firing line.

Raymo got out of the supercharged Merc in the parking lot above the grassy embankment a little more than halfway down Elm. A wooden stockade fence enclosed the parking area, with trees and shrubs set alongside. The rear bumper of the car nudged the fence. There were ten or twelve cars parked nearby, many more in the spaces to the north and west.

Raymo stood a moment, rolling his shoulders. He gave a firm hoist to his balls, three quick jogs with the left hand. The fence was about five feet high, too high for him to brace his left arm comfortably. He went to the rear of the car and stood on the bumper. He looked out over the fence and across a stretch of lawn. The pilot car approached the Elm Street turn.

Frank Vásquez got out of the car on the driver's side. He carried a Weatherby Mark V, scope-mounted, loaded with soft-point bullets that explode on impact. He stood by the rear fender until Raymo extended a hand. Frank gave him the weapon.

He went back to the driver's seat. The car bounced when he got in and Raymo glanced back sharply.

The crowd noise from Main Street was still in the air, faintly, a rustle somewhere overhead, and Frank, with his back to the action, sat at the wheel listening. His view was past the railyards to the northwest. Water towers painted white. Power pylons trailing into a flat grim distance. All light and sky. He felt like he could see to the end of Texas.

Raymo stood just west of the point where the two sections of fence form a near-right angle. From the deep shade of the trees he looked out on a sun-dazzled scene. Small groups collecting on the grass on both sides of Elm, families, cameras, like the start of a picnic. The limousine came swinging into the street. People on the north side of Elm, their backs to Raymo, shaded their eyes from the sun. Other people waving, Kennedy waving, applause, sunlight, sharp glare on the hood of the limousine. A girl ran across the grass. The dangling men. Four men dangling from the sides of the follow-up car, only a few feet behind the blue Lincoln.

Dallas One. Repeat. I didn't get all of it.

Leon fired too soon, with the car passing under the tree. The report sounded like a short charge, a little weak, a defect, not enough powder.

Kennedy reacted late, without surprise at first, his arms coming up slowly like a man on a rowing machine.

The driver slowed to half-speed. The driver sat there. The other agent sat there. They were waiting for a voice to explain it.

Pigeons flared past.

Raymo eased the gun barrel out over the fence. He set his feet firmly on the bumper. His left forearm, bracing the weapon, was wedged between the tops of two pickets. He tilted his head to the stock. He waited, sighting through the scope.

On the grass a woman saw the limousine emerge from behind a freeway sign with the President clutching at his throat. She heard a sharp noise, like a backfiring car, and realized it was the second noise she'd heard. She thought she saw a man throw a boy to the grass and fall on top of him. She didn't really hear the first noise until she heard the second. A girl ran waving toward the limousine.

The noise cracked and flattened, washing across the plaza. This wasn't making sense at all.

There was so much clarity Lee could watch himself in the huge room of stacked cartons, scattered books, old brick walls, bare light bulbs, a small figure in a corner, partly hidden. He fired off a second shot.

He saw the Governor, who was turned right, begin to look the other way, then double up suddenly. A startle reaction. He knew this was called a startle reaction, from gun magazines.

He turned up the handle, drew the bolt back, then drove it forward.

Stand by a moment please.

Okay, he fired early the first time, hitting the President below the head, near the neck area somewhere. It was a foolishness he could dismiss on a certain level. Okay, he missed the President with the second shot and hit Connally. But the car was still sitting there, barely moving. He saw the First Lady lean toward the President, who was slumped down now. A man stood applauding at the edge of the telescopic frame.

Lee jerked the handle down and aimed. He heard the second spent shell roll across the floor.

There were roses on the seat between Jack and Jackie. The car's interior was a nice light blue. The man was so close he could have spoken to them. He stood at curbside applauding. A woman called out to the car, "Hey we want to take your picture." The President looked extremely puzzled, head leaning left. The man stood applauding, already deep in chaos, looking at crumpled bodies, a sense of guns coming out.

Put me on, Bill. Put me on.

Bobby W. Hargis, riding escort, left rear, knew he was hearing gunfire. There was a woman taking a picture and another woman about twenty feet behind her taking the same picture, only with the first woman in it. He couldn't tell where the shots were coming from, two shots, but knew someone was hit in the car. A man threw his kid to the ground and fell on him. That's a vet, Hargis had time to think, with the Governor, Connally, kind of sliding down in the jump seat and his wife taking him in, gathering the man in. Hargis turned right just after noticing a girl in a pretty coat running across the lawn toward the President's car. He turned his body right, keeping the motorcycle headed west on Elm, and then the blood and matter, the unforgettable thing, the sleet of bone and blood and tissue struck him in the face. He thought he'd been shot. The stuff hit him like a spray of buckshot and he heard it ping and spatter on his helmet. People were down on the grass. He kept his mouth closed tight so the fluid would not ooze in.

In the jump seat John was crumpled up. Nellie Connally pulled him over into her arms. She put her head down over his head. She was pretending she was him. They were both alive or both dead. They could not be one and one. Then the third shot sent stuff just everywhere. Tissue, bone fragments, tissue in pale wads, watery mess, tissue, blood, brain matter all over them.

She heard Jackie say, "They've killed my husband."

It could have been Nellie's own voice, someone speaking for her. She thought John was dead. Then he moved just slightly and she thought at the same time that Jackie was out of the car, gone off the end of the car, but now was somehow back. John moved in her arms. They were one heart pumping.

We are hit. Lancer is hit. Get us to Parkland fast.

The car picked up speed and everything went rushing past. Nellie thought how terrible this must be, what a terrible sight for people watching, to see the car speeding past with these shot-up men; what a horror, what a sight.

She heard Jackie say, "I have his brains in my hand."

Everything rushing past.

The man in the white sweater, applauding, saw the stuff just erupt from the President's head. The motorcycles went by. There were guns coming out, a man in the second car with an automatic rifle. The second car went by. A motorcycle went fishtailing up the grassy slope near the concrete structure, the colonnade. Someone with a movie camera stood on an abutment over there, aiming this way, and the man in the white sweater, hands suspended now at belt level, was thinking he ought to go to the ground, he ought to fall right now. A misty light around the President's head. Two pink-white jets of tissue rising from the mist. The movie camera running.

Lee was about to squeeze off the third round, he was in the act, he was actually pressing the trigger.

The light was so clear it was heartbreaking.

There was a white burst in the middle of the frame. A terrible splash, a burst. Something came blazing off the President's head. He was slammed back, surrounded all in dust and haze. Then suddenly clear again, down and still in the seat. Oh he's dead he's dead.

Lee raised his head from the scope, looking right. There was a white concrete wall extending from the columned structure, then a wooden fence behind it. A man on the wall with a camera. The fence deep in shadow. Freight cars sitting on the tracks above the underpass.

He got to his feet, moving away from the window. He knew he'd missed with the third shot. Went wild. Missed everything. Maggie's drawers. He turned up the bolt handle.

Put me on. Put me on. Put me on.

He was already talking to someone about this. He had a picture, he saw himself telling the whole story to someone, a man with a rugged Texas face, but friendly, but understanding. Pointing out the contradictions. Telling how he was tricked into the plot. What is it called, a patsy? He saw a picture of an office with a tasseled flag, dignitaries in photos on the wall.

He drew the bolt back, then drove it forward, jerking the handle down. He walked diagonally across the floor to the northwest end, where the staircase was located. Books stacked ten cartons high. That fragrance of paper and binding.

The fender sirens opened up, the guns started coming out.

The girl stopped running toward the car. She stood and looked without expression.

A woman with a camera turned and saw that she was being photographed. A woman in a dark coat was aiming a Polaroid right at her. It was only then she realized she'd just seen someone shot in her own viewfinder. There was bloodspray on her face and arms. She thought, how strange, that the woman in the coat was her and she was the person who was shot. She felt so dazed and strange, with pale spray all over her. She sat down carefully on the grass. Just let herself down and sat there. The woman with the Polaroid didn't move. The first woman sat on the grass, put her own camera down, looked at the colorless stuff on her arms. Pigeons spinning at the treetops. If she was shot, she thought, she ought to be sitting down.

Agent Hill was off the left running board and moving fast. There was another shot. He mounted the Lincoln from the bumper step, extending his left hand to the metal grip. It was a double sound. Either two shots or a shot and the solid impact, the bullet hitting something hard. He wanted to get to the President, get close, shield the body. He saw Mrs. Kennedy coming at him. She was climbing out of the car. She was on the rear deck crawling, both hands flat, her right knee on top of the rear seat. He thought she was chasing something and he realized he'd seen something fly by, a flash somewhere, something flying off the end of the limousine.

He pushed her back toward the seat. The car surged forward, nearly knocking him off. They were in the underpass, in the shadows, and when they hit the light he saw Connally washed in blood. Spectators, kids, waving. He held tight to the handgrip. They were going damn fast. All four passengers were drenched in blood, crowded down together. He lay across the rear deck. He had this thought, this recognition. She was trying to retrieve part of her husband's skull.

He held on tight. He could see right into the President's head. They were doing eighty now.

FLASH
SSSSSSSSSS
BLOOD STAINEZAAC
KENNEDY SERIOSTY WOUNDED
SSSSSSSSSS
MAKE THAT PERHAPS PERHAPS
SERIOUSLY WOUNDED

Raymo's view was briefly obscured. He had to wait for the right side of the limousine to clear the concrete abutment. He knew Connally was hit. He had time to think, Leon's picking them off one by one. He had a sense of people ducking and scattering even though they weren't in the frame. Now the car moved clear, quartering slowly in. He held on Kennedy's head. The man was leaning left, tight-eyed in pain. A hundred and thirty feet. A hundred and twenty feet. He got off the shot. The man's hair stood up. It just rippled and flew. Raymo stepped off the bumper and got in the back seat. Frank had the car moving. He drove between rows of parked cars behind the Depository. He headed straight for three freight cars marked Hutchinson Northern. Raymo leaned forward. Watch it, man. But he didn't say a word.

See if the President will be able to appear out here. We have all these people that are waiting. I need to know whether to feed them or what to announce out here.

Frank found a lane to the street. He went one block east on Pacific Avenue. He made a left onto Record Street. Warehouses and parking lots. He felt there was someone sitting inside his body making these moves and turns. He tried not to think past the moment. Elevated highway straight ahead. He had a pestering fear about what would happen when they were past the moment of turns and traffic signs. He didn't know how he'd feel when he was back in his body again.

The guns were coming out.

Cops left their Harleys to run up the slope with pistols drawn. In the motorcade the Secret Service men had automatic weapons cocked, sidearms coming out.

Pigeons reversing flight, beating eastward now.

Mackey watched from the south colonnade, across Elm, across Main, across Commerce. There was no one on the lawns or under the trees here. It was the matching half of the plaza, less than a hundred yards from the scene but totally remote, hot and empty in the glare. He stood against a column, arms folded. He let his sunglasses dangle from his right hand.

The sirens opened up. Outside the Book Depository, policemen stood with rifles and shotguns pointing up. Men pointing. People looking up.

```
              GET OFF NXR
              BULLETIN
SSSSSSSSSS         ZA SNIPER SERIOUSLY
              WOUNDED
              OFF ALL OF YOU              STAY
   OFF AND
              KEEP OFF          GET OFF
```

A small girl stood with a hand over each ear. The motorcade was in collapse, vehicles stopped, others rushing past. Ordinary traffic moved into Elm. Many people running up the steps between the stockade fence and the colonnade. A goddamn mob of people. Figures prone on the grass. A man pounding his fist on the hood of a car. Mackey saw a man get out of another car and fall down. Ragged cries and shouts. People on their knees. Others sitting, with cameras, out of breath and unbelieving.

He saw a fire truck come down Main. It was the dumbest thing he'd seen in twenty years.

<pre>
                    SPEAKING AT THE TT
                    WILL U U PLEASE STAY OFF THIS
                    WIRE
     SSSSSSSSS
                    STAY OFF   STAY OFF
     SSSSSSSSS
                    ZA SNIPER SERIOUSLY WOUNDED
                    PRESIDENT KENNEDY
                    DOWN TOWN DAL LAS TO DAY
                              PERHAPS FAAATALLY
</pre>

From this distance Mackey wasn't sure whether the people going up the embankment steps looked like a lynch mob or men and women in raw shock, in flight, running with others. He was thirsty and depressed. Strange harsh cries kept sounding from the lawns, from the echoing underpass, a thickness of voice, all desperate effort, like speech of the deaf and dumb.

Lee hid the rifle on the floor between rows of cartons near the sign for the stairway. They'd find it easy enough. But he still had to hide it, just to do the expected thing, make them believe he didn't want to be identified. It was the same with the clipboard, already hidden, and the unfilled orders that were fixed to it. He wanted to give them something to uncover, a layer to strip away.

He liked the idea of a job that required a clipboard.

He was down the stairs fast and headed for the Coke machine on the second floor. A Coke in his hand would make him feel secure. It was a prop, a thing to carry around by way of saying he was okay. He thought he might need a prop to get him out of the building.

He heard a voice behind him like, "Come here."

It was a cop with a drawn gun rushing into the lunchroom. He had one of those plastic covers on his hat for rainy days. Lee turned and walked slowly at him. He showed a face you'd see on any public transport, anonymous and dreamy. He made it a point not to notice the pistol aimed at his chest.

Roy Truly came in then and the cop said, "Does this man work here?" And Mr. Truly said yes and they both headed out to the stairway. Lee got his Coke and wandered down one flight and out the front entrance, a hole in the elbow of his shirt.

Agent Grant stood under the canopy at the Trade Mart entrance, just off Stemmons Freeway. He was explaining to two local business leaders how to present themselves to the Kennedys. He heard sirens getting louder. He saw the pilot car, the motorcycles, the Lincoln doing maybe eighty, with somebody spread-eagle on the rear deck. Other vehicles following, high speed, the craziest damn scene, a press bus blowing past. He asked one of the businessmen what time he had. Then they all checked their watches, placing the event in a framework they could agree upon.

HE LAAAAAAAAAA

There was a man holding Mary's arm and she was crying. He had hold of her camera trying to take it with him. He said he was Featherstone of the Times Herald. Mary's friend Jean was saying, "I thought that was a dog on the seat between them. I was saying I could see Liz Taylor or the Gabors traveling with a dog but I can't see the Kennedys on tour with dogs." Mary was not listening to this. She was crying and fighting to keep her camera. This man from the paper would not let go her arm. He was dragging her away toward Houston Street. Jean wasn't able to get to her feet. She sat on the grass trying to finish her train of thought about seeing a dog in the car. She wanted to say to Mary, she did actually say, "I realized finally that little fuzzy thing. It was roses on the seat between them."

Flying down that freeway with those dying men in our arms and going to no telling where. Everything flashing by. A billboard reading, Roller Skating Time.

Lee got off the bus in stalled traffic and walked to the Greyhound terminal to catch a taxi. The traffic was stalled for pretty obvious reasons, so maybe the bus was not a good idea. He walked south on Lamar, the sirens going all around him, and spotted an empty cab. They were a little removed here from the major congestion.

He got in next to the driver and here is a nice old lady sticking her head in the window looking for a taxi. Lee started getting out. He offered the cab to the lady. But the driver rolled away and Lee gave him an address a few blocks from his rooming house. It was a five- or six-minute ride, going out over the old viaduct. The driver said something about all the squad cars running a code three—lights spinning, sirens going. He wondered what was up.

Lee got out and walked north on Beckley, hearing a jangling in the air, feeling the first nervousness.

What do I look like?

To anybody seeing me, where do I look like I'm coming from?

He checked the numbers on the license plates of parked cars.

Do I look like someone leaving the scene?

His stomach was empty and he had that feeling in the mouth where there's a rusty taste, something oozing from the gums.

That old patchy sadness of this part of Oak Cliff, the room-to-let signs and the trees going bare, the clotheslines, the bare-looking house fronts.

He was wishing he'd taken that Coke along.

The housekeeper was watching TV and it was all over the air waves. She said something but he went right by. In the toilet he pissed and pissed. It just kept coming.

Jangling in the air.

He went to his room and opened the dresser drawer for the .38. It was only common sense. He couldn't go out there without a gun. This was the day of all days when he needed protection.

They'd find the Hidell rifle. He had Hidell documents in Ruth Paine's garage. His wallet was full of Hidell. So it was only common sense to take the Hidell handgun. A dozen layers to strip away. It was everything, together, Hidell.

He scooped the loose cartridges out of the drawer. Bought off the street by Dupard. Would they even go bang?

He'd left his blue jacket at work. He took his gray one. Wherever he'd be spending the night, and the rest of his life, he might need a jacket. Plus it covered up the gun.

The room. The iron bed.

To anybody watching, what do I look like with the bulge at my hip under the jacket?

Unknown white male. Slender build.

He went out the door and down the walk. He was having a little trouble figuring what to do. All the clarity was gone. There was a nervous static in the air.

What do I look like?

Do I stand out in the street, walking?

He went down Beckley figuring there was no choice but to go to the movie house where they were supposed to pick him up. He knew he couldn't trust them but there was nowhere else to go. He had fourteen dollars and a bus transfer. They had him cold. He could be walking right into it. The lurking thought, the idea of others making the choice now. He wanted to believe it was out of his hands.

He saw a police car up ahead, coming this way, and he made a left onto Davis, knowing he'd turned too quick. The streets were nearly empty. He actually saw the cop watching him move down Davis, squeezed eyes peering, although the car was out of sight now.

Okay, he shot him once. But he didn't kill him. To the best of his knowledge he hit him in the upper back or somewhere in the neck area, nonfatally. Then he missed and hit the Governor. Then he missed completely. There are circumstances they don't know about. Are they sure it was him in that window? It could be different than they think. A setup.

Slender white male. Five feet ten.

The car came into view again, down Patton, and he walked halfway along the next block. Then he did an about-face and went back to Patton and walked south. To fake out the car. He figured if he went to where he'd seen the car, it would be somewhere else.

Do I look like a suspect fleeing?

Have they figured out who's missing from the Book Depository?

What is my name if I am asked?

He went down Patton to Ninth Street. Nobody around this time of day. The idea was to make a quick move back to Beckley, across Beckley, down to Jefferson. A dozen old hair-drying machines stood along the curbside. A mattress on a lawn.

He wanted to write short stories about contemporary American life.

At Tenth and Patton he expected to see the car, if at all, moving away from him. But it was cruising east, to his right, coming at him. He crossed the street and began walking east and by this time the car was right behind him, tagging along, going ten to twelve miles an hour, the motorcade speed, teasing.

From the corner of his eye he could see the number on the door. A number ten. The car was marked number ten and this was Tenth Street.

He wasn't sure if he stopped first or the car stopped. It was like they both had the same idea. He went over to the window on the passenger side.

They spoke at the same time. Lee said, "What's the problem, officer?" And the cop, strong-featured, looking maybe one-eighth

Indian, said something about "You live around here, buddy?"

Lee stuck his head right in the window, smelling stale cigarettes, and said, "Any reason to want to talk to me?"

"You look to me like you're taking evasive tactics."

"I'm walking in broad daylight."

"To me, you're doing every possible thing to evade being spotted."

There was a voice squawking on the radio.

"I'm just a citizen on foot."

"Then maybe you'd like to tell me where you're going to."

"I don't think I'm required to tell you that. I live in this area, which I'm telling you more than required by law."

He took the position, the attitude, that he was being singled out for harassment. Even if they had a description, from witnesses looking up at the window, how specific could it be?

"I'm saying for your own good."

"I'm only walking on the street."

One other person in sight, a woman approaching the intersection of Tenth and Patton.

"You carrying ID or not?"

"I'm a resident here."

"I'm saying for the last time."

He did not like the way cops, had never liked it when cops sat in their car and you had to approach them with documents, bending all the time, leaning toward their windows.

"I'm only asking what's the reason."

"Better show me some paper real soon."

"I hear you."

"Then do it."

"I'm a citizen on foot."

"I'm saying one last time."

They spoke at the same time again. The cop sat in his Ford getting a little testy. A voice on the radio said, *Disheveled hair*.

We're on Tenth Street and the car is number ten. All the factors are converging.

"Look. If I have to get out of this vehicle."

"Harass."

"I want to see your hands."

"This is how we have misunderstandings."

"Hands on the fucking hood."

"I hear you."

"Then fucking do it, pencil-neck."

The cop reached for the door handle on his side, not taking his eyes off Oswald. They were going to another level now.

"I'm only asking what for."

"Hands, *hands*—where I can see them."

"I have a right I'm on the street without harassment."

He began easing out the door. He said something else about "Go real slow," and Lee said, "A man taking a walk in his own city."

Talking at the same time.

The cop was on the other side of the car. A little traffic down the street. Lee pulled the .38 out of his belt and fired four times across the hood, blinking and muttering. Poor dumb cop. Opened his mouth and slid down the fender. Lee saw a woman ninety feet away and their eyes definitely met. She dropped some stuff she was carrying and put her hands in front of her face. He moved in a jog step to Patton and turned south, ejecting empty cartridges from the cylinder and reloading as he went.

Helen took her hands away from her eyes. She was all alone screaming in the street. The policeman's cap was a little ways out from the body. He was on his side and gushing blood. She picked up her purse and work shoes and went toward him, calling for help and screaming. She walked bent over, actually screaming at the body.

Then there were some people in the street and a man climbing out of a pickup. Helen approached the body screaming. The man was in the police car saying, "Hello hello hello." Helen saw the blood take oval shape in the street. She moved around the body and put her shoes on the hood of the car. She stood bent over, seeing wounds in the chest and head. She just could not believe the volume of blood.

The Mexican said into the dashboard, "Hello hello hello."

Later there was an ambulance and many police cars with red lights and sirens, cars on the sidewalks and lawns and men taking pictures of the stains in the street. Helen stood in front of a frame house halfway down the block, where she'd somehow ended up, trying to tell a detective what she'd seen. She said she waitressed at the Eat Well downtown and was on her way to the bus stop to go to work. Three or four shots, real rapid fire.

Back at the scene there were two small white canvas shoes on the hood of Patrolman Tippit's car. The men from Homicide stood around wondering. They discussed what these objects could possibly mean.

Wayne Elko sat in the last row of the Texas Theater, center section, watching a black-and-white movie called *Cry of Battle* with Van Heflin and a bunch of people he'd never seen before. It was about an hour into the movie and Van Heflin has just shot Atong, a Filipino bandit. This is taking place a little after Pearl Harbor and Wayne was pretty sure the Japanese were getting ready to pull a night raid on the Filipino guerrillas and their American friends. Under his jacket he carried a target pistol with the barrel tooled down to a nub and an eight-inch length of baffled tubing attached to it. There were seven other men scattered in the theater. The shot will sound like someone coughing.

There's a female guerrilla in skintight jeans. Wayne was thinking how Hollywood invents these women just for afternoons like this, exposed and white, men at loose ends hiding in the dark. That's when Leon appeared at the head of the aisle. He stood there a moment to accustom his eyes. His hair was messed up and his shirt was outside his pants and he looked scared and he looked wild. He took a seat three rows from the back. He was two rows in front of Wayne and four seats to the left.

Be cool, Wayne. Do not rush into this.

Wayne watched the silver faces show fear and desire. He was waiting for the noise on-screen to increase, for the Japs to swarm over the guerrilla camp with machine guns and grenades. He planned to ease out of the row, step in behind Leon, whisper a small *adiós*, then mash the grooved trigger, already walking backwards to the lobby.

But he would wait for the noise and cries.

He would let the tension build.

Because that's the way they do it in the movies.

It didn't get that far. Four or five minutes after Leon came in, an exit door opened near the stage, showing silhouetted figures. Then men appeared at the rear and there were voices in the lobby. Someone turned up the house lights and Wayne saw police sort of combing the aisles. Two cops on the stage, thumbing their gun butts and peering out.

The picture died away with a swoony sound.

They searched two men in the rows up front. They came up the aisles. Some more of them pushed through another exit. Sirens repeating in the street. A cop jumped down off the stage. Another drew his gun. Cool head, Wayne. There was a pie-face cop who approached Oswald. Leon got to his feet and said something. When the cop moved into the row, Leon took a swing at him. He hit him hard in the face. The hat spun around on the cop's head. He punched Leon, who twisted away, grinning and hurt, then showed a pistol in his hand.

They fell all over him. Cops grunting, banging their knees on the seats. The first cop and Leon were in the seats struggling for the gun. Officers cursing. Wayne heard a click and thought the hammer snapped on someone's hand. They were on Leon from the row behind him, grabbing his neck and hair. He almost ripped the nameplate off one man's shirt. It was general grappling that went on and on, awkward and intense.

They worked the gun out of his hand and were trying to get the cuffs on. The rows were bursting with police. They gave him a little roughing up.

When they had him in handcuffs they moved him into the aisle. There were cops still banging their knees on the edges of seats, picking up their caps and flashlights. They took him out to the lobby, quick-time, pressing around him.

Wayne heard Leon's voice going out the door, "Police, police brutality."

There was a moment when the patrons didn't know what to do. Then the ones who were standing returned to their seats. Somebody called, up front, "Lights." Another guy tilted his head sideways and up, saying, "Lights, lights." They all waited in their seats, hearing the sirens go into the distance. They tried clapping hands. Then Wayne spoke up, "Lights, lights." And in fifteen seconds the house lights went down and the picture shot onto the screen.

The men settled down contentedly. Wayne felt the mood close around them, the satisfied air of resumption. It wasn't just this picture to see to the end. There was a second feature coming up, called *War Is Hell*.

The prisoner stood inside the jail elevator, which was sealed to ordinary traffic. Four detectives edged in tight, rangy men in dark suits and ties, high-crowned Western hats, their faces closed to interpretation.

The media crowds collected and rocked in the corridors. They were waiting for the prisoner to come down to the interrogation room here on the third floor of the Police and Courts Building. TV cameras sat on dollies and there were cables slung over windowsills, trailing through the offices of deputy chiefs. Nobody checked credentials. Reporters took over the phones and pushed into toilets after police officials. Total unknowns walked the halls, defendants from other parts of the building, witnesses to other crimes, tourists, muttering men, drunks in torn shirts. It was a roughhouse, a confoundment. Every rumor flew. Disk jockeys arrived to fill in, blinking, flinching, wary. A reporter wrote notes on a pad he balanced on the back of the chief of police.

They set up a chant. "Let us see him, bring him down. Let us see him, bring him down."

Hours going by. Blank faces arrayed against corridor walls. Men crouched near the elevators waiting. They sensed the incompleteness out there, gaps, spaces, vacant seats, lobbies emptied out, disconnections, dark cities, stopped lives. People were lonely for news. Only news could make them whole again, restore sensation. Three hundred reporters in a compact space, all pushing to extract a word. A word is a magic wish. A word from anyone. With a word they could begin to grid the world, make an instant surface that people can see and touch together. Ringing phones, near-brawls, smoke in their eyes, a deathliness, a hanging woe. Is Connally alive? Is Johnson safe? Has SAC gone to full alert? They began to feel isolated inside this old municipal lump of Texas gray granite. They were hearing their own reports on the radios and portable TVs. But what did they really know? The news was somewhere else, at Parkland Hospital or on Air Force One, in the mind of the prisoner on the fifth floor.

Someone said he's coming. A kind of clustered stirring, like riled bees. Then formal jostling across the floor, a grab for position. When he appeared in the elevator door, a slight man in handcuffs, with a puffed eye and stubble, they went a little crazy. Stooped photographers moving backwards, hand mikes shooting out of the crowd, everybody shouting, reaching toward him. A howl, a passion washing through the corridor. Newsreel cameras floated over the heads of the men escorting him. They had to throw some elbows, working him toward the door of the interrogation room. One eye puffed, a cut over the other, his shirt hanging loose. He resembled a guy who comes out of a doorway to bum a smoke. But a protective defiance, an unyielding in his face. The flash units fired. TV floodlights cooked the nearest heads. The reporters stared and wailed. It was hard to breathe in the ruck around the prisoner. They looked at him. They all cried out.

"Why did you kill the President?"

"Why did you kill the President?"

He said he was being denied the right to take a shower. Denied his basic hygienic rights. The escorts worked him to the office door.

Questioned, arraigned, displayed in lineups. He felt the heat of the corridor mobs every time he got off the elevator, the actual roil of moist air. Assassin, assassin.

In his cell he thought about the ways he could play it. He could play it either way. It all depended on what they knew.

He had the middle cell in the maximum-security block in the jail area. They kept the cells on either side of him empty. There were two guards on constant watch in the locked corridor.

Every time they brought him back to the cell, they made him take off his clothes. He sat in the cell in his underwear. They were afraid he'd use his clothes to harm himself.

A bunk bed, a chipped sink, a sloped hole in the floor. No flush toilet. He had to use a hole.

They stared up his ass. They came and shaved some hair from his genitals, two men from the FBI, placing the samples carefully in plastic baggies.

The revolution must be a school of unfettered thought.

In the interrogation room there were Dallas police, Secret Service, FBI, Texas Rangers, county sheriffs, postal inspectors, a U.S. marshal. No tape recorder or stenographer.

No, he didn't own a rifle.

No, he hadn't shot anyone.

He was not the man in the photograph they'd found in Ruth Paine's garage—the man with a rifle, a pistol and left-wing journals. The photograph was obviously doctored. They'd taken his head and superimposed it on someone else's body. He told them he'd worked for a graphic-arts firm and had personal knowledge of these techniques. The only thing in the picture that belonged to him was the face and they'd gotten it somewhere else.

He denied knowing an A. J. Hidell.

No, he'd never been to Mexico City.

No, he wouldn't take a polygraph.

They asked him if he believed in a deity. He told them he was a Marxist. But not a Marxist-Leninist.

It was pretty clear they didn't get the distinction.

Whenever they took him down, he heard his name on the radios and TVs. Lee Harvey Oswald. It sounded extremely strange. He didn't recognize himself in the full intonation of the name. The only time he used his middle name was to write it on a form that had a space for that purpose. No one called him by that name. Now it was everywhere. He heard it coming from the walls. Reporters called it out. Lee Harvey Oswald, Lee Harvey Oswald. It sounded odd and dumb and made up. They were talking about somebody else.

The men in Stetsons took him back through the crowds to the jail elevator. He held his cuffed hands high, making a fist. Flashbulbs and hoarse cries. They kept shouting questions, shouting right over his answers. The elevator climbed to the cell block.

In the clink. Back in stir. Up the river. In the big house. Lights flicker when they pull the switch. So long, Ma.

Rain-slick streets.

Courses at night in economic theory.

He sat in the cell and waited for the next event. He knew it was late. He pictured Ruth Paine's street, the lawns and sycamores. Was Marina in bed, scared, sorry, thinking she might have shown him more respect, seen the seriousness of his ideas? He wanted to call her. He pictured her reaching for the phone, a drowsy arm warm from the sheets, and the trustful mumbled hello, her eyes still closed.

Never think it is your fault when I am the one. I am always the one.

Now they were coming to take him down again. He believed they would release him once he settled on the right story to tell them. The way the Russians released Francis Gary Powers. The way they released the Yale professor they arrested for spying. Trumped-up charges. Screw is slang for prison guard.

They took him to the assembly room in the basement. This was the fourth time today they'd brought the prisoner down. Three times for lineups. Now it was midnight and they wanted him to meet the press in a formal and controlled exchange.

Hell and bedlam. Crowds jammed clear back out to the hall. Reporters still trying to press in, just arrived from the East Coast and Europe, faces leaking sweat, ties undone. The prisoner stood on the stage in front of the one-way screen used for lineups. His hands were cuffed behind him. Photographers closed in, crab-walking beneath him. Reporters shouting out to him. A moan of obscure sounds that resembled charismatic speech. The chief of police could not get into the room. He tried to edge his way, prying people apart with his hands. He was concerned for the safety of his prisoner.

A burly man moved through the crowd introducing out-of-town reporters to Dallas cops. He handed out a brand-new card he'd printed for his club. Who could it be but Jack Ruby? It was a card he was proud of, with a line drawing of a champagne glass and a bare-ass girl in black stockings. It was a come-on to the average patron, but with class. Nobody challenged Jack's presence in the assembly room. He had the ability to carry a domineering look into a building. He was looking for a radio reporter named Joe Long because he had a dozen corned-beef sandwiches out in the car which he planned to take to the crew at KLIF working into the night to report this frantic tale to the unbelieving city. Instead he spotted Russ Knight, the Weird Beard, and even arranged an interview, clearing the way for Russ so he could tape the District Attorney for local radio. Jack was playing newsman and tipster tonight. He was in complete charge of mentally reacting. He had a pencil and pad at the ready, just in case he caught a remark he could give to NBC.

That's it, boys, take the little rat's picture.

It mulled over him that he might go to the Times Herald later and see how things were going in the composing room. He had a sample twistboard in the car and he thought he might treat the people to a demonstration, just for the frolic of the moment. It was always a popular sight, Jack doing a rolling rumba to show off the board.

The horror of the day swept over him. He began to sob, talking to a newsman by the back wall.

Ask the weasel why he did it, boys.

The reporters wouldn't stop shouting. The prisoner tried to answer a question or make a statement but no one could hear him. It was a riot in a police station. Too crowded here, a danger, and the detectives moved in to end the session before it even started.

They took him back to the cell. He stripped to his underwear and sat on the bunk, thinking, feeling the noise of the assembly room still resonating in his body. A cell is the basic state, the crude truth of the world.

He could play it either way, depending on what they could prove or couldn't prove. He wasn't on the sixth floor at all. He was in the lunchroom eating lunch. The victim of a total frame. They'd been rigging the thing for years, watching him, using him, creating a chain of evidence with the innocent facts of his life. Or he could say he was only partly guilty, set up to take the blame for the real conspirators. Okay, he fired some shots from the window. But he didn't kill anyone. He never meant to fire a fatal shot. It was never his intention to cause an actual fatality. He was only trying to make a political point. Other people were responsible for the actual killing. They fixed it so he would seem the lone gunman. They superimposed his head on someone else's body. Forged his name on documents. Made him a dupe of history.

He would name every name if he had to.

In Dallas

Dealey Plaza is symmetrical. A matching pair of colonnades, stockade fences, triangle lawns and reflecting pools—split down the middle by Main Street, which shoots straight out of the triple underpass into downtown Dallas. To one side of Main, Elm Street curves out of the underpass and proceeds at a gradual elevation past the Texas School Book Depository, where Lee Oswald stood in the sixth-floor window with a rifle in his hands. To the other side of Main, Commerce Street carries incoming traffic eastward past the Carousel Club, six blocks into the downtown core, where Jack Ruby sits in his office at 4:00 A.M. cursing the smirky bastard who killed our President.

He was alone and vomiting. He vomited the meals of the last three weeks. Crying for five minutes, vomiting for five minutes. He couldn't bear to hear the name Oswald one more time. Even off in his own mind the name was waiting at the end of every shrunken thought.

Some of the clubs stayed open Friday night. Jack closed the Carousel and Vegas. He was committed to closing for the weekend in honor of the President being shot.

He vomited into a polyethylene bag he had somebody manufacture for his twistboards. Then he picked up the phone and
called his roommate, George Senator.

"What are you doing?" he said.

"What am I doing? I'm sleeping."

"Schmuckhead. They killed our President."

"Jack, that was yesterday."

"We're going out to take pictures. Where's the Polaroid?"

"At the club."

"You know those Impeach signs? There's one around here
someplace. I'm coming to pick you up."

"I want you to know. There's this constant interference of the
time that I wake up and the time that you go to bed. Which don't
match."

"Get dressed fast," Jack told him.

He found the camera and drove out to his apartment building.
It was located over a freeway and looked like a motel that changed
its mind. The whole scene was removable. George was sitting on
the iron stairway in baggy clothes and slippers. They headed back
downtown.

Jack explained the nature of the assignment.

First there was the ad in the Morning News. It said, *Welcome
Mr. Kennedy to Dallas*. A series of lies and smears. Not that Jack
fully absorbed the points in the ad. It was the nasty tone he noticed
most. And of course the black border. And of course the fact that
the ad was signed by someone Bernard Weissman. A Jew or someone
posing as a Jew to blacken the name of the Jews. Then it just
happened that he drove past a billboard with three towering words
on it. *Impeach Earl Warren*. The ad had a post-office box number.
So did the billboard. Thinking about it in his mind, as he went
over both incidents, Jack believed the number was the same.

"So I am trying to put the two together."

"You think the same person."

"Whereby the same person or group is behind both incidents.
And since it is against the President, I am trying to take a crime
reporter's frame of mind."

They drove all over the downtown fringe trying to find the Earl Warren billboard and check out the box number. Jack was sure there was conspiracy here. The John Birch Society or the Communist Party were the suspects uppermost. He had his pad and pencil to take down particulars.

That clean but lonely feeling when there are no other cars. The traffic lights changing just for you.

He started vomiting again on the Central Expressway. The way he did it was to open the door, right hand clamped on the steering wheel, and drop his head down to vomit on the road. He could tell where they were going by his view of the white line, which was only inches away. George was screaming at him to stop the car or give up the steering to him. Jack straightened up. He said don't worry, he'd done this as a kid growing up in the toughest streets of Chicago. It was part of how you survived. Then he leaned way over to vomit some more. He vomited half his life out the car door, due to these assaults on his emotions.

They found the billboard on Hall Street. George got out of the car and took three pictures with the flash. To Jack Ruby this was hunting down a major clue and acquiring physical evidence. Now they had to find a copy of the ad so they could compare the box numbers. Jack didn't know where he'd left his newspaper. They drove to the coffee shop at the Southland Hotel just to take a break from these excitements. The place was either just closing or just opening. An old bent Negro working a mop. They sat at the counter and there's a copy of the Morning News lying right there waiting. They looked at each other. Jack ripped through the pages and found the ad. George took out the Polaroids.

The numbers didn't match.

Jack looked around for someone to get some coffee. He didn't even comment on the numbers. He had a twelve-inch stare, a dullish flat-eyed gaze. How a complete nothing, a zero person in a T-shirt, could decide out of nowhere to shoot our President.

They drove past the Carousel to take a look at the sign Jack had put up, one word only, saying CLOSED.

Then they went home. Jack got a few hours' sleep, woke up,

took a Preludin with his grapefruit juice and watched a famous New York rabbi on TV.

The man spoke in a gorgeous baritone. He went ahead and eulogized that here was an American who fought in every battle, went to every country, and he had to return to the U.S. to get shot in the back.

This, with the rabbi's beautiful phraseology, caused a roar of sorrow in Jack's head. He turned off the set and picked up the phone.

He called four people to tell them he'd closed his clubs for the weekend.

He called his sister Eileen in Chicago and sobbed.

He called KLIF and asked for the Weird Beard.

"Tell you the truth," Jack said, "I never know what you're talking about on the air but I listen in whenever. Your voice has a little quality of being reassuring in it."

"Personality radio. It's the coming thing, Jack."

"Plus when do I see a beard in Dallas?"

"I'm the only one."

"Russ, you're a good guy so I called with a question I want to ask."

"Sure, Jack."

"Who's this Earl Warren?"

"Earl Warren. Are we talking this is blues or rock 'n' roll? There was an Earlene (Big Sister) Warren sang on the West Coast for a while."

"No, Earl Warren, from the Impeachment signs. The red, white and blue signboards."

"Impeach Earl Warren."

"That's the one."

"He's the Chief Justice of the Supreme Court, Jack. Of the United States."

"The events have got me bollixed up."

"Who can blame you?"

"It's the worst thing ever in our city."

"One little man comes along and turns everything upside down. And we'll get the blame for him."

"Don't say his name," Jack said. "It has an effect of making me worse in my mind. Like I'm watching a dog playing in the dirt with my liver."

Saturday afternoon. Lee Oswald sat in a small glass enclosure with a phone on a shelf to his right. The door across the room opened. Here she came moving toward him, bandy-legged, dry-eyed, jowly, hair pure white now, long and white and shining. She sat on the other side of the partition. She looked at him carefully, taking him in, absorbing. They picked up the phones.

"Did they hurt you, honey?" she said.

She went on to tell him how she heard the news on the car radio and turned around and went home and called the Star-Telegram and asked them to take her to Dallas in a press car. Then she was interviewed by two FBI men, both named Brown. She told them for the security of the country she wanted it kept perfectly quiet that her son Lee Harvey Oswald returned to the United States from Russia with money furnished by the State Department. This was news to the Browns and they were pop-eyed.

"They're taping this, Mother."

"I know. We'll be careful what we say. I told them I haven't seen my son in a year. 'But you are the mother, Mrs. Oswald.' I told them I've been doing live-ins as a nurse and they didn't tell me where they'd moved to. 'But you are the mother, you are the mother.' I told them I didn't even know about the new grandchild. I had to endure a year of silence and now there is family news every minute on the radio."

These men, Brown, were looking for suspects in every direction. Magazine people were keeping the family in a room at the Adolphus Hotel. It was kept extremely hush hush. They were whisked from place to place with precautions. All of them. The accused mother, the brother, the Russian wife, the two little babies. Accompanied by approximately eighteen to twenty men who were suspicious of them and of each other. These were FBI, Secret Service and Life magazine. There was a man continually taking pictures. And Marguerite rolled her stockings down and he took that picture too, of the mother rolling her hose after a day that made history.

"Things were done without my consent," she told Lee. "But I'm checking every quote I make to them and if there are mistakes coming out, I'll know it is all stacked up against us, going back to Russia."

The babies had diarrhea in their hotel surroundings and there were diapers strung across the room from wall to wall. A president had to die before she could learn she was a grandmother again.

When Marina went into the room to talk to Lee she didn't know the police had found prints of the photographs she'd taken in the backyard on Neely Street. They were with Lee's belongings in Ruth Paine's garage. Marina had found two prints herself, overlooked by the police, in little June's baby book. The pictures with the fateful rifle. The gun in one hand, then the other.

She had both pictures folded inside her shoe.

"There's nothing to worry about," he said into the phone. "You have friends to help you."

It was painful seeing him in this state. Not just the bruises and scratches. This was a man who appears in a dream, a distorted figure in some darkness outside ordinary night.

She thought of the mild face of the boy she'd married, the unexpected American who asked her to dance. The face was almost plump then, rosy with cold, and the hair neatly parted, the clothes pressed. He was even cleaner than she was, very clean coming to bed, clean in every habit.

Then the worker in Texas and Louisiana, sometimes grease-spattered, losing weight, losing hair, dog-weary, suffering nosebleeds in his sleep, refusing to change his clothes.

Now this vision, this man with a beak nose and dark eyes, one brow swollen, clothes too big for him. This specter with gray skin. She looked at the lumpy Adam's apple, the prominent nose. His cheeks were sunk under the bones, leaving this nose, this bird beak.

He had to be guilty, she thought, to look so bad.

He told her not to cry. His voice was gentle and sad. He told her they were taping every word.

So she could not tell him about the pictures in her shoe. Or about the other thing she'd discovered after the police had left last night. This was his wedding ring in a demitasse cup on the bedroom bureau. He'd left it behind with the money, early Friday morning.

The money, the photographs, the wedding ring.

Three times he'd asked her to live with him in Dallas. She said no, no, no.

He told her now to buy shoes for June. Don't worry, he said. And kiss the babies for me.

The guards got him out of the chair and he walked backwards to the door, watching her until he was gone.

Home, Aunt Valya would be putting up sauerkraut, polishing copper, busy with the usual things, going with Uncle Ilya to visit the Andrianovs, a life without sudden turns and interruptions, and waiting for the first heavy snows.

She didn't even know about the policeman. She didn't know about Governor Connally. No one told her until later in the day that Lee was accused of wounding one of them and cold-bloodedly killing the other.

They led him back to the cell. He took off his clothes and gave them to the guard. He ate a lunch of beans, boiled potatoes and some kind of meat.

Nothing about this place bewildered him or set him to wondering what would happen next. The reporters did not surprise him, uproar in the halls. The lawmen asked the obvious questions and even when he failed to anticipate what they'd ask, it was still everyday obvious stuff. The cell was the same room he'd known all his life. Sitting in his underwear on a wooden bunk. A sink with a dripping tap. Nothing new here. He was ready to take it day by day, growing into the role as it developed. He didn't fear a thing. There was strength for him here. Everything about this place and situation was set up to make him stronger.

Even his appetite was back. This was the first meal he could really dig into. There was coffee in a mug. He drank it slowly. He thought. He listened to the guards talk softly in the narrow hall.

There was a third way he could play it. He could tell them he was the lone gunman. He did it on his own, the only one. It was the culmination of a life of struggle. He did it to protest the anti-Castro aims of the government, to advance the Marxist cause into the heart of the American empire. He had no help. It was his plan, his weapon. Three shots. All struck home. He was an expert shot with a rifle.

Saturday night. David Ferrie was driving in circles through the city of Galveston, Texas. His monkey fur was askew on his head. His mind had reached the stage of hysteroid extremes.

When the President was shot he was in a federal courtroom in New Orleans, where Carmine Latta's tax evasion case was being decided in the old man's favor.

When Leon was picked up by the police he was in his apartment packing for the trip to Galveston. He had his old Eastern captain's hat, gold-braided, that he was putting in an overnight bag. He heard the capture on the radio.

This was cause for panic. He gave in to it at once. Ferrie believed panic was an animal action of the body to ensure that the species survives. It was far older than logic. He kept on packing, only faster, and hurried down to his car.

He drove in circles around New Orleans for hours, listening to news reports. Then he filled the tank and headed west through a black storm, one of those sky bursts full of slanting coastal fury, and seven hours later he was in Houston.

He drove in circles around Houston. At 4:30 A.M. he checked into a place called the Alamotel. He was in no mood for patriotic puns. He spoke Spanish to the desk clerk, went to his room and made a series of calls to people in New Orleans, friends, lovers, clergy. He sought comfort in these calls and spoke Spanish even to those who didn't know a word.

He was afraid Leon would give the police his name.

He was afraid Leon would be killed.

He was afraid Leon, alive or dead, had his library card in his wallet. He seemed to recall letting Leon use his card once.

In the morning he bought newspapers and coffee and sat in the car listening to the radio. He felt his life trembling on the edge of the news reporter's tongue. He drove to a skating rink and made more calls. Banister wouldn't talk to him. Latta was at a sit-down. He called teenage boys he'd taught to fly. The skating-rink organ produced a sound that made him think of total death. He went out to the car.

Something about the time of year depressed him deeply. Overcast skies and cutting wind, leaves falling, dusk falling, dark too soon, night flying down before you're ready. It's a terror. It's a bareness of the soul. He hears the rustle of nuns. Here comes winter in the bone. We've set it loose on the land. There must be some song or poem, some folk magic we can use to ease this fear. Skelly Bone Pete. Here it is in the landscape and sky. We've set it loose. We've opened up the ground and here it is. He took Interstate 45 south. He didn't want them to kill Leon. He felt a saturating sense of death, a dread in the soft filling of his bones, the suckable part, approaching Galveston now.

He drove in circles around Galveston. The plane was probably still at the airport. He thought he might fly it out of here, a Piper Aztec, and make the escape to Mexico without the assassin. It didn't seem the least bit crazy. It seemed a ritual suited to the event.

The event was total death. Only a ritual could save him from succumbing.

He checked into a place called the Driftwood Motel. He spoke Spanish on the phone.

What was he doing in Galveston? Wasn't he here to fly the plane? The idea of flight had drawn him. He was a flyer, a master of the element of air. He was prepared to submit to death if it came at the end of a flight across the shining gulf, on some scoured brown flat in Mexico, remote, in fierce heat, with mountains trembling in the haze. These were the rules he insisted on. Mexico is a place where they understand the dignity of rules for dying.

He reached Banister on the phone. Guy told him something was in the works, a chancy plan, a long shot. David Ferrie decided to get a good night's sleep and head back to New Orleans in the morning.

There were wreaths and flower clusters arrayed on the lawns of Dealey Plaza, marks of sadness and farewell, and Jack Ruby drove through the streets at midnight, soaking up atmosphere and emotion. He looped through the plaza half a dozen times. He drove past seven or eight clubs to see who was open. It made him angry in that patriotic way of clenching your jaw tight when you see your fellow citizens profiteering from the heartbreak of others, conniving to be the only ones open on a weekend of national pain. All day he'd watched TV at various points in his circuit of downtown Dallas. This death was everywhere. Pictures of the grieving family. Reenactments at the scene of the murder. This was an event that had the possibility of being bigger in history than Jesus, he thought. So much impact and reaction. It was almost as though they were re-enacting the crucifixion of Jesus. God help the Jews. Empty soda bottles rolled around his feet.

He drove home and started pulling things out of the refrigerator to eat. He felt a compulsion to stuff the body against despair. He wanted to handle food, to cook it and smell it, watch animal blood spurting in the pan. Take back muscle and blood. Take back gristle. He needed chewy meat and seltzer water fizzing in his teeth. It adds a little reserve to my strength of will.

He spent ten minutes making a sandwich but didn't have the

heart to eat it. He went into the living room and picked up a newspaper to make sure his ads looked okay—the notices that his clubs were closed. George was hulked on the sofa in Jack's old robe, a beer can sweating in his hand.

Jack called his brother Earl in Detroit.

He called his sister Eva here in Dallas to talk for the third or fourth time about what happened. Eva began to weep. She was totally broken up. He handed the phone to George because he wanted his roommate to hear his sister weep. It was a broken hacking sob. Authentic. Jack and Eva wept and George stood with the phone planted on the left side of his head, looking impressed.

Jack went to bed. He stared at the ceiling in the dark. Every time a truck passed on Thornton Freeway it made a noise like paper ripping. The phone rang and he went into the living room and picked it up. He listened about twenty seconds. Then he put on his clothes and drove to the Carousel.

He went up the narrow stairs and turned on the lights. The dogs started barking in the back room. He sat in his office running his hand through his hair. He needed a scalp treatment fast.

He heard the footsteps. Then Jack Karlinsky walked into the office. He looked a little tired. He wore an open-collar shirt and his neck was stretched and ridged. He looked old at this hour, unprepared. He brushed some dog hair off the sofa and sat down.

"It's terrible, what's happening to this city, Jack. Every hour brings new words of grief abroad and wonderment how this could happen. Already the Europeans are talking this is conspiracy. What do we expect? They have their centuries of daggers in the back, frame-ups and poisons. This is adverse thinking. It builds up a pressure which is bad for the city, bad for us all."

"When I think of my father coming out of some Polish village."

"Polish village, exactly."

"To the carpenters' union in Chicago."

"To raise a boy who grows up owning a business, Jack. This is what we want to defend. What is the first thing people say about this tragedy? What does my mother say, eighty-eight years old, in a nursing home? She calls me on the phone. Do I have to tell you what she says? 'Thank God this Oswald isn't a Jew.' "

"Thank God."

"Am I right? How many people are saying the exact same thing these last two days? 'Thank God this Oswald isn't a Jew.' "

" 'Whatever he is, at least we know he's not a Jew.' "

"Am I right? These are the things people say."

"When I think of my father," Jack Ruby said.

"Of course. This is what I say."

"Always drinking, drinking. Out of work for years. My mother talked Yiddish to the day she died. She couldn't write her name in English."

"This is exactly the situation we find ourselves today. I'm saying there are things that need protection."

"I'm a great believer in you have to stand up for your natural values."

"Don't hide who you are."

"Don't hide. Don't run."

"This is a subject I talked to Carmine only today. I've been talking to Carmine direct. He made reference to he was anxious about Oswald. It makes the whole country look bad, all this talk on a level of conspiracy. I'll tell you what people want. They want this Oswald to vanish. That's how you close the book on loose talk. People want him off the map, Jack. He's a nuisance to behold."

"It's a tide of emotion where anything can happen."

"It's a wave. You feel it in the streets. It carries everyone along. We're involved one way or another whether we like it or not. Look at the ad that ran in the paper with a thick black border. Signed with a Jewish name. People notice things like that. They file it away. There's a lot of extreme feelings that attach themselves to Jews."

"I personally feel I've been dropped in a pool of shit."

Jack Karlinsky nodded.

"Let me tell you something right straight out. The man who gets Oswald, people will say that's the bravest man in America. And it's just a matter of time before somebody clips him. They're saying reports of mob action any time. The people want a blank space where he's standing. This act, they'll build a monument, whoever does it. It's the shortest road to hero I ever saw."

"You talk to Carmine."

"Carmine mentioned your name. From Tony Push. They know about you, Jack, in New Orleans."

"I did some things in the Cuba days."

"In other words this Oswald is an aggravation. He knows some little iffy things. He has some names he's playing around in his mind. Carmine wants to clear the air."

"I was over at headquarters, dropping in this afternoon. There's talk they're moving him to the county jail."

"I was about to say. It's a procedure they have to follow in a felony case. This city, it's screwy, the way certain affairs are handled in the legal arena. Commit a violent crime and there's a good chance you'll walk. This is a feature of the local climate. You know as well as I. Murder is easier to get exonerated than breaking and entering, Jack."

"It's considered how people behave."

"Am I right? It's considered settling things Old West–style. They have it ingrained in the way they think. You get a shvartzer kills another shvartzer in a gunfight, the case won't even go to trial."

"Nobody cares enough to try a case like that."

"This is what I say. I'm saying. Popping a guy like Oswald, this is the same approach. Can you project a heavy sentence to take this guy out?"

"People want to lose him."

"You'll see total rejoice. As things now stand, Jack, what are you worth to the city of Dallas? You're a Chicago guy to them. You're an operator from the North. Worse, a Jew. You're a Jew in the heart of the gentile machine. Who are we kidding here? You're a strip-joint owner. Asses and tits. That's what you mean to Dallas."

"Who are we kidding?"

"Who are we kidding here?"

"When I think of my mother."

"Exactly what I'm saying."

"My mother went crazy in a big way. I can't describe the horror. I used to look in her eyes and there was nothing there that you could call a person. She screamed and raged. That was her life. My father hit her. He hit us. She hit us. She thought we were all shtupping each other. Brothers and sisters having constant sex. I never went to school. I fought. I delivered envelopes for Al Capone."

"I'm saying. This is my point. It builds up a pressure that's bad for us all."

There was a short heavy silence.

" 'Thank God he's not a Jew.' "

" 'Thank God whatever he is, at least he's not a Jew.' "

"Jack, I'm sure you hear the same thing in the street I've been hearing for almost two days. The man who kills that communist bastard is saving the city of Dallas from world shame. This is what they're saying in the streets."

"What is Carmine saying?"

"Good point. Because here you have an ally. Here you have protection and support. Carmine himself brought up the subject of the loan. I think you'll be delighted with the terms."

"And for this?"

"For this you undertake to rid the city."

"In other words."

"Jack, you're a floater all your life. This is a chance you put your fist around something solid. You want to end your life selling potato peelers in Plano, Texas? Build something. Make a name."

"So what you're saying, Jack."

"Take him off the calendar."

"Clip him."

"Turn him into a crowd," Karlinsky said sadly.

He unwrapped a cigar but didn't light it. He looked old and drawn. He sat like a patient in a waiting room, preoccupied and tense, hunched forward on the sofa.

"Carmine is offering that we completely forgive the loan. We make the loan, then we cancel the debt forever. Forty thousand dollars. Deliverable at the first convenience. It's just a question how soon. We expect very soon. We don't expect a major delay here."

"What about my clubs?"

"We look after them in the meantime. I have every confidence you'll see a rebirth. Think of the people who'll want to say they paid a visit to the Carousel. Jack Ruby's club, who took out Oswald."

"To see what kind of atmosphere."

"Out-of-towners in total droves. You own a gun, Jack?"

"What do you think?"

"Carmine is getting full cooperation from the boys in Dallas. They have people they render assistance in the police. The police are going to move Oswald out of the building via the basement. It is for some time after ten A.M. There are two ramps to the street."

"Main Street and Commerce."

"I'm saying, Jack. The ramps will be heavily guarded. The building entrances closed off. The accordion gate between the two parts of the building will be locked. The power will be off in the elevators except for the jail elevator, which they'll use to bring Oswald down."

"I can probably walk right down a ramp."

"Wait. I'm saying."

"I'm a known face in the building."

"Not tomorrow you can't walk down a ramp. They are letting in reporters with press cards and that's it. A limited number, mainly picture-taking. This transfer is very delicate. They have extra men coming in. They're determined it goes off without a hitch."

"Then how do I get in?"

"I'm saying, Jack. There's an alley that runs along the east side of the building. You're inconspicuous here. Halfway down there's a door to the new part of the building, the municipal annex. This door is always locked except tomorrow we arrange it's open. There is no guard on the door. You go in the building. Once you're inside you see elevators and stairs. You take the stairs down. They're fire stairs. This is how you get in the basement."

"How do they bring him out?"

"Handcuffed to a detective. Another detective on the other side. What kind of gun do you have?"

"Snub-nose .38. Fits in a pants pocket."

"You'll have the heaviest hard-on in America."

Karlinsky laughed bleakly, a growl down in the throat. Jack sat behind the desk, looking blank. The conversation ended here.

Jack was alone for an hour figuring out how to meet recent wages and bills without the weekend receipts. This kind of petty arithmetic tightened his skull.

He looked in his address book for a number. Then he called Russell Shively, his detective friend, at home. It was after 3:00 A.M. Jack listened to the lonely phone ringing.

"Yes. Who's this?"

"Hello Russell."

"Who the hell is this?"

Jack paused.

"They are going to kill that bastard Oswald in the police basement tomorrow during the transfer to the county jail."

He paused again, then put down the phone.

Lee Harvey Oswald was awake in his cell. It was beginning to occur to him that he'd found his life's work. After the crime comes the reconstruction. He will have motives to analyze, the whole rich question of truth and guilt. Time to reflect, time to turn this thing in his mind. Here is a crime that clearly yields material for deep interpretation. He will be able to bend the light of that heightened moment, shadows fixed on the lawn, the limousine shimmering and still. Time to grow in self-knowledge, to explore the meaning of what he's done. He will vary the act a hundred ways, speed it up and slow it down, shift emphasis, find shadings, see his whole life change.

This was the true beginning.

They will give him writing paper and books. He will fill his cell with books about the case. He will have time to educate himself in criminal law, ballistics, acoustics, photography. Whatever pertains to the case he will examine and consume. People will come to see him, the lawyers first, then psychologists, historians, biographers. His life had a single clear subject now, called Lee Harvey Oswald.

He and Kennedy were partners. The figure of the gunman in the window was inextricable from the victim and his history. This sustained Oswald in his cell. It gave him what he needed to live.

The more time he spent in a cell, the stronger he would get. Everybody knew who he was now. This charged him with strength. There was clearly a better time beginning, a time of deep reading in the case, of self-analysis and reconstruction. He no longer saw confinement as a lifetime curse. He'd found the truth about a room. He could easily live in a cell half this size.

Sunday morning. Jack did the normal shuffling, getting the day going. It took him a certain time to beam in on things. He drank some grapefruit juice and paced the living room. George was on the sofa reading a newspaper and Jack kept going by with that stare of his that reached only a foot into the world.

"Jack, for me to express a facial nature, you know it's hard with words, but I don't think you look so good."

Jack turned on TV. He washed and shaved, using a Wilkinson sword blade for the name appeal and smacking on aftershave so it hurt. He made scrambled eggs and coffee and looked at the first section of the Times Herald, still in his shorts, while he ate. There was an open letter to Caroline Kennedy that was so emotional it choked off his ability to swallow. In his mind he rehashed the tragedy of the President and his lovely family.

The telephone rang. It was Brenda Jean Sensibaugh, Baby LeGrand, calling from her apartment in Fort Worth.

"Jack, the rent is due. There is nothing to eat in the house for me and the kids."

"I barely pick up the phone."

"I'm coming to the point so we don't waste time. Last night was supposed to be pay night."

"You know damn well why we closed."

"I'm not stating it was wrong to close. Just tell me how I get from one week to the next without a pay night."

"You already drew some on your salary."

"Don't be hateful or short with me, Jack. I'm asking a small advance so my children will have a meal before the day is over. I am one of your dependables and you know it. I'm only asking what I need to get through the day food-wise and place a little sum in my landlord's fist to keep him quiet."

"How much, bitch?"

"Twenty-five dollars. I can't get all the way to Dallas but if you could telegraph a money order or however they do it, I can go downtown and pick it up."

Jack realized there was a Western Union only half a block from the Police and Courts Building. Lucky for her. If he hurried he could wire twenty-five dollars to Brenda and then go shoot that bastard Oswald.

He took a Preludin with his coffee dregs and got dressed. Dark suit, gray fedora, Windsor knot in his silk tie. He picked up Sheba and told George he was going to the club. Downstairs he dropped the dog in the front seat and started up the car.

He was running late. If I don't get there in time, it's decreed I wasn't meant to do it. He drove through Dealey Plaza, slightly out of the way, to look at the wreaths again. He talked to Sheba about was she hungry, did she want her Alpo. He parked in a lot across the street from the Western Union office. He opened the trunk, got out the dog food and a can opener and fixed the dog her meal, which he left on the front seat. He took two thousand dollars out of the moneybag and stuffed it in his pockets because this is how a club owner walks into a room. He put the gun in his right hip pocket. His name was stamped in gold inside his hat.

He went across the street and filled out the form to send the money. The clerk time-stamped the receipt 11:17. Jack was even later than he thought. For the first time he put a little hurry in his day and in less than four minutes he stood in the dark garage below police headquarters.

If I get in this easy, it means they want me to do it.

He walked across the deserted parking area toward a pair of unmarked Fords waiting in the space between the ramps. He heard voices saying, "Here he comes, here he comes," and at first he thought they meant him. He walked up a slight incline and stood at the edge of a group of reporters. Vault noises, voices, hollow bouncing sounds filled the areaway, car engines, clanking equipment. There were plainclothes cops and white-hatted brass everywhere. Detectives lined the walls leading from the jail office to the ramps. Russell was standing right there but Jack didn't have time to catch his eye. Most of the newsmen and three TV cameras were clustered on the ramp to Jack's right, leading to Main Street. An armored bank truck waited at the top of the other ramp.

"Here he comes."

"Here he comes."

"Here he comes."

The timing was split-second, the location was pinpoint. Spotlights came on. Everything was black and white, highlights and heavy shadows. He saw a cluster of police come out of the jail office escorting the prisoner, who wore a dark sweater and looked like nobody from nowhere.

There was a movement of reporters. Then flashbulbs, shouts echoing off the walls, and it all seemed strange to Jack, already seen, and he stood in the artificial glare in the dank basement with the ramps stained by exhaust smoke and a charge of octane in the air.

Here he comes.

Jack came out of the crowd, seeing everything happen in advance. He took the revolver out of his pocket, bootlegging it, palming it on his hip. A path opened up. There was no one between him and Oswald. Jack showed the gun. He took a last long stride and fired once, a mid-body shot from inches away. Oswald's arms crossed on his body and his eyes went tight. He made a sound, a deep grunt, heavy and desolate. He began his fall through the world of hurt.

A tumble of bodies over the gunman, all these men in Stetsons heavy-breathing, struggling for the weapon, someone's knee emplaced in Jack's gut. He was at a loss to understand their attitude. None of this was necessary if they knew him. He felt even worse, hearing Russell Shively's voice pitch above a dozen other noises, saying, "Jack, *Jack*, you son of a bitch."

A shot.
There's a shot.
Oswald has been shot.
Oswald has been shot.
A shot rang out.
Mass confusion here.
All the doors have been locked.
Holy mackerel.
A shot rang out as he was led to the car.
A shot.
Mass confusion here.
Rolling and fighting.
As he was being led out.
Now he's being led back.
Oswald shot.
The police have the entire area blocked off.
Everybody stay back is the yell, is the yell.
A stocky man with a hat on.
Oswald doubled over.
One of the wildest scenes.
Screaming red lights.
A man in a gray hat.
Somehow he got in.
The police protection and the police cordons.

People. Policemen.
Here is young Oswald now.
He is being hustled out.
He is lying flat.
There is a gunshot wound in his lower abdomen.
He is white.
Oswald white.
Lying in the ambulance.
His head is back.
He is unconscious.
Dangling.
His hand is dangling over the edge of the stretcher.
And now the ambulance is moving out.
Flashing red lights.
Young Oswald rushed out.
He is white, white.

Remember the ambulance in Atsugi, camouflage-green, wavering in the heat haze on the tarmac, and the pilot climbing out?

Lee didn't feel real good. First they shot him, then they tried to give him artificial respiration. He learned in Marine training this is the last thing you do for a man with abdominal injuries.

He could see himself shot as the camera caught it. Through the pain he watched TV. The siren made that panicky sound of high speed in the streets, although he had no sense of movement. A man spoke close to him, saying if he had anything he wanted to say he was going to have to say it now. Through the pain, through the losing of sensation except where it hurt, Lee watched himself react to the augering heat of the bullet.

Remember how the pilot looked, a spaceman in a helmet and rubber suit?

Everything was leaving him, all sensation at the edges breaking up in space. He knew he was still in the ambulance but couldn't hear the siren any longer or the voice of the man who wanted him to speak, a friendly type Texan by the sound of him. The only thing left was the mocking pain, the picture of the twisted face on TV. Die and hell in Hidell. He watched in a darkish room, someone's TV den.

The falling away of things we carry around with us, twilight and chimney smoke. What is metal doing in his body?

He was in pain. He knew what it meant to be in pain. All you had to do was see TV. Arm over his chest, mouth in a knowing oh. The pain obliterated words, then thought. There was nothing left to him but the pathway of the bullet. Penetration of the spleen, stomach, aorta, kidney, liver and diaphragm. There was nothing left but the barest consciousness of bullet. Then the bullet itself, the copper, lead and antimony. They'd introduced metal into his body. This is what caused the pain.

But remember the men watching the jet take off? Could hardly believe how quick it lost itself in mist.

They logged him in at Parkland at 11:42. Chief complaint, gunshot wound.

The heart was seen to be flabby and not beating at all. No effective heartbeat could be instituted. The pupils were fixed and dilated. There was no retinal blood flow. There was no respiratory effort. No effective pulse could be maintained. Expired: 13:07. Two sponges missing when body closed.

Aerospace.

It is the white nightmare of noon, high in the sky over Russia. Me-too and you-too. He is a stranger, in a mask, falling.

If we are on the outside, we assume a conspiracy is the perfect working of a scheme. Silent nameless men with unadorned hearts. A conspiracy is everything that ordinary life is not. It's the inside game, cold, sure, undistracted, forever closed off to us. We are the flawed ones, the innocents, trying to make some rough sense of the daily jostle. Conspirators have a logic and a daring beyond our reach. All conspiracies are the same taut story of men who find coherence in some criminal act.

But maybe not. Nicholas Branch thinks he knows better. He has learned enough about the days and months preceding November 22, and enough about the twenty-second itself, to reach a determination that the conspiracy against the President was a rambling affair that succeeded in the short term due mainly to chance. Deft men and fools, ambivalence and fixed will and what the weather was like. Branch not only has material resulting from the Agency's internal investigations—Everett and Parmenter cooperated to varying degrees—but he also has key information about the last stages of the plot derived from sources inside Alpha 66.

The stuff keeps coming. The Curator sends FBI surveillance logs. He sends a thirty-five-hour film chronology of unedited network footage shot during the weekend of November 22. He sends a computer-enhanced version of the Zapruder film, the 8mm home movie made by a dress manufacturer who stood on a concrete abutment above Elm Street as the shots were fired. Experts have scrutinized every murky nuance of the Zapruder film. It is the basic timing device of the assassination and a major emblem of uncertainty and chaos. There is the powerful moment of death, the surrounding blurs, patches and shadows.

(Branch's analysis of the film and other evidence leads him to believe the first shot came much sooner than most theories would allow, probably at Zapruder frame 186. Governor Connally was hit two point six seconds later, at Zapruder 234. The shot that killed the President, crushingly, came four point three seconds after that. Even though he has reached firm conclusions in this area, Branch will study the computerized version of Zapruder. He is in too deep to stop now.)

The Curator sends a special FBI report that includes detailed descriptions of the *dreams* of eyewitnesses following the assassination of Kennedy and the murder of Oswald.

The Curator sends material on Bobby Dupard. Branch knows about Dupard only through the Curator. But how does the Curator know? Did Dupard tell someone about his role in the attempt on Walker? Did Oswald let his name slip to someone in New Orleans?

There are worrisome omissions, occasional gaps in the record. Of course Branch understands that the Agency is a closed system. He knows they will not reveal what they've learned to other agencies, much less the public. This is why the history he has contracted to write is a secret one, meant for CIA's own closed collection. But why are they withholding material from him as well? There's something they aren't telling him. The Curator delays, lately, in filling certain requests for information, seems to ignore other requests completely. What are they holding back? How much more is there? Branch wonders if there is some limit inherent in the yielding of information gathered in secret. They can't give it *all* away, even to one of their own, someone pledged to confidentiality. Before his retirement, Branch analyzed intelligence, sought patterns in random scads of data. He believed secrets were childish things. He was not generally impressed by the accomplishments of men in the clandestine service, the spy handlers, the covert-action staff. He thought they'd built a vast theology, a formal coded body of knowledge that was basically play material, secret-keeping, one of the keener pleasures and conflicts of childhood. Now he wonders if the Agency is protecting something very much like its identity—protecting its own truth, its theology of secrets.

The Curator begins to send fiction, twenty-five years of novels and plays about the assassination. He sends feature films and documentaries. He sends transcripts of panel discussions and radio debates. Branch has no choice but to study this material. There are important things he has yet to learn. There are lives he must examine. It is essential to master the data.

Ramón Benítez, the man on the grassy knoll, is seen in a photograph taken in April 1971 at the dedication of the eternal flame in Cuban Memorial Plaza on Southwest Eighth Street in Miami. An urn containing the flame rests on a twelve-foot column. Five plaques list the names of the fallen—*los mártires de la brigada de asalto*. The Curator forwards vague reports that Benítez, using another name, drove a taxi for some years in Union City, New Jersey. Otherwise, nothing.

Also present in the crowd that day, caught in photographs, is Antonio Veciana, the founder of Alpha 66. Eight and a half years later he will be shot and wounded in Miami. This will happen after publication of the House select committee's report on assassinations—a report that includes Veciana's allegation that Lee Oswald met with a member of U.S. intelligence in Dallas some time before November 22. No arrests in the case.

Brenda Jean Sensibaugh, the stripper to whom Jack Ruby wired money, is found hanging by her toreador pants in a holding cell in Oklahoma City, June 1965, after an arrest on charges of soliciting for the purpose of prostitution. Ruled a suicide.

Two days later, Bobby Renaldo Dupard is shot to death during a holdup at Ray's Hardware in West Dallas, where he was employed as assistant manager. Branch immediately connects the name of the store with one of those useless clinging facts that keep him awake at night. This is where Jack Ruby, in 1960, bought the gun he used to kill Oswald.

Jack Leon Ruby dies of cancer in January 1967 while awaiting retrial for the murder of Oswald. In his time in prison he attempts suicide by ramming the cell wall with his head and by trying to jam his finger in a light socket while standing in a puddle of water.

He tells Chief Justice Earl Warren at the commission hearings that he has been used for a purpose, that he wants to tell the truth and then leave this world. But first they have to take him to Washington. He will tell the truth to President Johnson.

He lives in a cell in an isolated area of the county jail, a small square room with a toilet bowl and a mattress on the floor. A guard reads the Bible to him. Jack believes this man has a listening device in his clothes. They safely store away all his incriminating remarks and then erase all the remarks that prove his crime was unpremeditated, a spasm of personal conscience.

When he is feeling totally morose, a nothing person, he rereads the telegrams he received in the first days after the shooting. HOORAY FOR YOU JACK. YOU ARE A HERO MR. RUBY. WE LOVE YOUR GUTS AND COURAGE. YOU KILLED THE

SNAKE. YOU DESERVE A MEDAL NOT A JAIL CELL. I KISS YOUR FEET BORN IN HUNGARY LOVE. Then he remembers the guilty verdict, the death penalty, the reversal on flimsy technicalities. He knows that Dallas wants him dead and gone just like Oswald. He knows that people regard all the shootings of that weekend as flashes of a single incandescent homicide and this is the crime they are saying Jack has committed. He is worried that he has been miscast. He runs across the room and butts his head.

He wears white jail coveralls and scribbles notes when his lawyers come to the interview room, where the walls are bugged. He insists on taking a lie-detector test because the sincerity and authenticity of the truth are precious qualities to Americans. "It seems as you get further into something," he scribbles on a pad, "even though you know what you did, it operates against you somehow, brainwashes you, that you are weak in what you want to tell the truth about." Authorities arrange a polygraph exam in July 1964. Results are inconclusive.

He begins to hear voices. He hears one of his brothers screaming as people set him on fire outside the county jail.

He believes all his brothers and sisters will be killed because of what he did.

He believes people are distorting his words even as he speaks them. There is a process that takes place between the saying of a word and when they pretend to hear it correctly but actually change it to mean what they want.

He believes the Jews of America are being put in kill machines and slaughtered in enormous numbers.

He is miscast, or cast as someone else, as Oswald. They are part of the same crime now. They are in it together and forever and together.

The lawyers leave, the doctors come waltzing in. The cancer is spreading. He can smell it on the hands of his examiners. Jack Ruby reads his telegrams.

Does anyone understand the full measure of his despair, the long slow torment of a life in chaos, going back to Fanny Rubenstein toothless on Roosevelt Road, screaming in the night, going back in time to the earliest incomprehension he can remember, a truant, a ward of the state, living in foster homes, going back to the first blow, the shock of what it means to be nothing, to know you are nothing, to be fed the message of your nothingness every day for all your days, down and down the years?

You have lost me, Chief Justice Warren.

He begins to merge with Oswald. He can't tell the difference between them. All he knows for sure is that there is a missing element here, a word that they have canceled completely. Jack Ruby has stopped being the man who killed the President's assassin. He is the man who killed the President.

This is why Jews are being stuffed in machines. It is all because of him. It is the power and momentum of mass feelings.

Oswald is inside him now. How can he fight the knowledge of what he is? The truth of the world is exhausting. He lowers his head and runs into the concrete wall.

And Nicholas Branch studies the psychiatric reports. He reads into the night. He sleeps in the armchair. There are times when he thinks he can't go on. He feels disheartened, almost immobilized by his sense of the dead. The dead are in the room. And photographs of the dead work a mournful power on his mind. An old man's mind. But he persists, he works on, he jots his notes. He knows he can't get out. The case will haunt him to the end. Of course they've known it all along. That's why they built this room for him, the room of growing old, the room of history and dreams.

Sunday night. Beryl Parmenter sat watching TV in her little house in Georgetown. They were showing reruns of the shooting.

Over and over. The screen is full of broad-shouldered men in hats, all around Oswald, who is bare-headed, his features whited out by glare except for his left eye, shining darkly. Jack Ruby comes into the frame, bulky and hunched. His hand is bright static around the gun. The picture jumps. The surprise and pain in Oswald's face remove him from the company around him. He is alone, already far away, the only one not wondering what has happened. A cold moment of stillness after the shot. Then everything flies apart.

She didn't want these people in her house.

The camera doesn't catch all of it. There seem to be missing frames, lost levels of information. Brief and simple as the shooting is, it is too much to take in, too mingled in jumped-up energies. Each new showing reveals a detail. This time she sees that Ruby carries dark-rimmed glasses folded in his breast pocket. Oswald dies unchanged.

Why do they keep running it, over and over? Will it make Oswald go away forever if they show it a thousand times? She knew exactly what Ruby was thinking. He wanted to erase that little man. He wanted him out of here. He didn't want to see him or hear him or think about him. Just like the rest of us, Jack. We want him out of here too. And now he's gone but it isn't helping at all.

Beryl had admired President Kennedy. She'd even felt a small personal involvement in his rise, a sort of landed interest, inasmuch as the Kennedys had lived for a time in a brick house on N Street, practically around the corner, when Jack was a senator. She wanted to feel a satisfaction in the death of Oswald, some measure of recompense. But this footage only deepened and prolonged the horror. It was horror on horror.

She didn't want these people here. But she felt morally bound to watch. They kept on showing it and she kept watching. She had the sound turned down because the voices of reporters made her cry.

She'd been crying all weekend, crying and watching. She couldn't shake the feeling she'd been found out. These men were in her house with their hats and guns. Pictures from the other world. They'd located her, forced her to look, and it was not at all like the news items she clipped and mailed to friends. She felt this violence spilling in, over and over, men in dark hats, in gray hats with dark bands, in tan Stetsons, in white caps with shiny visors and badges pinned to the crowns. The little hatless man said "Oh" or "No."

After some hours the horror became mechanical. They kept racking film, running shadows through the machine. It was a process that drained life from the men in the picture, sealed them in the frame. They began to seem timeless to her, identically dead.

Larry was in the cellar cataloguing wines.

She began to cry again. She wanted to crawl out of the room. But something held her there. It was probably Oswald. There was something in Oswald's face, a glance at the camera before he was shot, that put him here in the audience, among the rest of us, sleepless in our homes—a glance, a way of telling us that he knows who we are and how we feel, that he has brought our perceptions and interpretations into his sense of the crime. Something in the look, some sly intelligence, exceedingly brief but far-reaching, a connection all but bleached away by glare, tells us that he is outside the moment, watching with the rest of us. This is what kept Beryl in the room, this and the feeling that it was cowardly to hide.

He is commenting on the documentary footage even as it is being shot. Then he himself is shot, and shot, and shot, and the look becomes another kind of knowledge. But he has made us part of his dying.

They replayed the sequence into early morning. Beryl stayed in the room and watched. The telephone rang for the twentieth time. She didn't move. The pain entered Oswald's face. She wasn't taking any calls this particular wintry weekend.

25 November

The road curved uphill through the burial ground, past jack oaks and Chinese elms, above grassy swales tracked with grave markers, and two dusty police cars moved slowly along, unaccompanied, an incongruous stately pace. At the top of the rise they stopped outside a pretty sandstone chapel to release the mourners to their organized grief. But it seemed at once that something was wrong. The family climbed out of the cars and there were Secret Service men and cemetery staff gathered in the archway, showing the grim pride that low officials take in a despised duty. The wind began to sing in the east, sweeping out of the reaches of industrial prairie between Dallas and Fort Worth, and Marguerite Oswald stood outside the chapel in a black dress and black-rimmed glasses, holding the new baby in her arms, the granddaughter whose birth they had kept from her, and her face wore a look of helpless pain. Because somebody canceled the service. Somebody ordered the body removed from the chapel. Because the chapel was empty. The body was not there.

They called many ministers, Lutheran men of God, but no

one wanted to pray over Lee Harvey Oswald. This is the reason, your honor, they were in the utmost sheepish hurry to put my boy in the earth. Robert was crying bitterly, trying to get them to return Lee's body to the chapel for a brief service, an appearance in a holy place. So then I intervened and said, "Well if Lee is a lost sheep and that is why you don't want him in church, it escapes the purpose of a church. The good people do not need to go to church. Let's say he is called a murderer. It is the murderers who need a church. Isn't this what Jesus teaches?" They were in such a hurry to bury Lee Harvey Oswald they forgot to notify the men who carry the coffin to the graveside, so news reporters teamed up to move the body. I have many stories, your honor. I have stories I am sure you do not know. I am the mother in the case.

Hurrying clouds now. The wooden coffin rested on a bier above the open grave, with a massive concrete vault below, vandal-proof, a thousand years of peace. The family sat in dented metal folding chairs under a faded canopy. Robert Oswald was between the widow and the mother, each woman holding one of the little girls. Reporters were restricted to the far fringes. No friends or well-wishers allowed, not that any were clamoring to attend. Secret Service men and uniformed police stood around the canopy, many with hands folded in front of them, dipping their knees in turn, and there were armed guards stationed along the cemetery fence. The joke among reporters was that Fort Worth was taking better care of Oswald dead than Dallas did when he was alive. Robert was trying not to break down again. He was a man of earnest bearing, dark-browed, with neatly trimmed hair, a sales coordinator, a hard worker, looking older and more responsible than any twenty-nine-year-old from here to Texarkana, as if young Lee's truancy, the defection, the undesirable discharge, the lost jobs, all of it, had planted him in a stiff shirt for life.

Your honor, I cannot state the truth of this case with simple yes and no. I have to tell a story. This is a boy the other children teased. It was torn, torn shirts and a bloody nose. Listen to me. I will write books about the life of Lee Harvey Oswald. I have information pertinent to the case. I am all over the world. I have struggled to raise my boys on mingy sums of money and today I am everywhere, newsreel and foreign press, but where are the funds for a decent burial? There are stories inside stories, judge. Lee collected stamps in a book and practiced chess alone at the kitchen table and they sent him to Russia to infiltrate. I will wear a camera and make a photographic record of Lee's life, getting houses and rooms on the record. I will tell how I worked at many jobs to raise my boys, leading up to practical nurse. I know what sickness looks like. I know low pay. I have worked for nine dollars a day, live-in, twenty-four hours' duty. I wore my nurse's uniform three days, sneaking from hotels with the secret police of different branches, with Life magazine running alongside, and a translator, and a photographer, and the Russian daughter-in-law, and the two sick babies. Marina stands and smokes a cigarette plain as day. I am in my uniform and they bring clothes for her. There are diapers hanging everywhere. TV gave the cue and Lee was shot. They kept it from us, being women, and then in the car to the next hotel something came over the radio and the agent said, "Do not repeat, do not repeat." And I said, "Is that my son?" And he didn't answer. So then I said, "My son is shot, isn't he?" And he said into the mike, "Do not repeat, do not repeat." So then I said, "Answer me, I want to know." "Do not repeat, do not repeat." So then they showed it on television in the room but Marina and I were not shown the sequence. They made us sit behind the television and the agents all crowded around in front and watched. And the back of the television was to us. And fifteen to eighteen men crowded in to watch on the other side. They gave us coffee and they watched.

I am going through a death and it is hard.

I intend to research this case and present my findings. But I cannot pin it down to a simple statement. I came home to find red welts on his legs at the age of two, where Mrs. Roach whipped him on Pauline Street, and then I placed him in a home and he slept with his brothers in a big long dormitory, one hundred little boys in rows and rows of cots. He attended six schools by the age of ten.

They will search out the environmental factors, that we moved from home to home. Judge, I have lived in many places but never filthy dirty, never not neat, never without the personal loving touch, the decorator item. We have moved to be a family. This is the theme of my research.

I am smiling, judge, as the accused mother who must read the falsehoods they are writing about my boy. Lee was a happy baby. Lee had a dog. This is the boy who spent only one month in attendance at Arlington Heights High School before he entered the Marines when we were living on Collinwood Avenue and there are three pictures of this boy in the school yearbook. Now, why do you pick out this one boy who is in school so briefly, of all the boys and girls there, and make him the subject of three photographs? People say, "Mrs. Oswald, I don't get the point." You don't get the point? The point is how it goes on and on and on and on. That's the point. The point is how far back have they been using him? He used to climb the tops of roofs with binoculars, looking at the stars, and they sent him to Russia on a mission. Lee Harvey Oswald is more than meets the eye. Already there are documents stolen from me. There are newspaper clippings stolen from my home by one of the branches of secret police. I am all over the world and they are rifling my files.

A minister showed up, willing to say a few words at the grave. He was an executive of the Council of Churches and hadn't conducted a service in eight years. But he wanted to help, although he'd left his Bible in the car. The undertaker opened the coffin and Marina Oswald approached and kissed her husband and placed two rings on his fingers. She wore a dark dress and pale cloth coat and she was sobbing now, and the babies were crying, and the security men dipped their knees and gazed vaguely skyward. Marina found herself thinking, how odd, that when Khrushchev visited Minsk while she was living there with Lee, there were strong rumors of an assassination attempt. If that had been Lee, if Lee had been picked up for that, they would have taken better care of him. At least say this for Russians; they can guard a suspect. These grudging minutes at the grave completed her abandonment, except for dreams. Her dreams would be incomplete for years, deprived of Alek in his early sweetness, the way he loved to play with June Lee, could sit and look at her for hours. The minister said, "O God of the open sky and of the infinite universe." She was alone with two small children under these blowing clouds, an outcast, bent in grief and loss, living in a motel with a dozen armed men. She tried to understand how this could happen.

Now, about Marina as Russian or French. It is amazing how her English improved right after Lee is killed. It is amazing how she suddenly has a cigarette in her hand, which I never witnessed when Lee was alive. I will research the picture of Marina to learn if it is true. I have a sixth sense, judge. People have remarked on my ESP. If Lee Harvey Oswald shot the President, why didn't I know it at the time? It is a prevalent feeling every mother has when the phone rings and she knows it is her son. Why didn't I sense he was in a window with a gun when the shots rang out? Even being his gun doesn't mean he did the shooting. I will wear a camera. I will time his movements on the fatal day. I am ready to go round and round on this because there are stories inside stories, that the press is unaware. Marina knows English, Marina knows French. This foreign girl is trained. They brought clothes for Marina. They showed me a story in the paper where a woman has offered her a home. They want Marina to admit to his guilt and they will find her a home. Robert sides constantly with the secret police. Our dispositions do not jell. This is the heartbreak of blood relations. I am forgetting many things, your honor. Lee had a bicycle. Lee had a dog. This boy was shot handcuffed to an officer of the law. Somebody paid to have him shot on cue. TV gave directions and down he went. We have a moral issue all through this that I am fighting for. My mail is opened. There are three letters missing from my desk. Lee wrote to me from Russia, "I am lonesome to read." In this letter he is thanking me for sending books. He is saying please. He asks for news of his homeland. This is a letter that is missing. Our government has been watching him for years.

Did Lee even know he was being used? This is a question I will research. Listen to me. I have to tell a story. I have to work into this, living in the French part of town. He knew Robert's manual by heart. He liked histories and maps. The recruiting officer said, "Mrs. Oswald, there is less delinquency in Japan and those places than we have here." He sold a bill. He was willing to sneak Lee in at age sixteen, before the legal limit. They were preparing him. They were using him already. Three photos in the yearbook and he was only there a month. People say, "Mrs. Oswald, what is the point?" The point is how far back did it go? When did they start watching him? Did he belong to them for life? The point is what about the boy in the casket? Lee in a suit and nice tie looking completely different from the scarecrow son in the newspapers and TV, a sturdy boy, broad-faced, like a Russian. Is the person they buried the same as the person they killed? Did they really kill him? Is the person who came back from Russia the same as the person who went? I have a right to ask these questions. How tall is Lee? What are his scars? I will bring these questions out in books and appearances.

I wrote to Mr. Khrushchev July 19, 1960, when my boy was lost in Russia. I received no reply. I went to Washington January 21, 1961, to petition President Kennedy to find my boy and bring him home. So—wait now, this is good—they write I am neglectful. I left my boys to shift for themselves. I drove all the way to New York in that old junky Dodge. I pulled up stakes in our Western slang too many times. When the truth is that the mother is neglected. If you research the life of Jesus, you see that Mary mother of Jesus disappears from the record once he is crucified and risen. Where is the mother who raised the boy? When the boy is dead, do they build a box around the mother? I played piano by ear. I was a popular child. I can't give facts point-blank. It takes stories to fill out a life. Only think of Mr. Ekdahl, who cheated me out of a decent divorce and abandoned me to a life of scaring up dimes. Mr. Ekdahl is a story. Marina is a story where the details are lax. I strictly believe in my suspicions. Her statements, her way of life, she smokes, she does not nurse her baby. Marina has a manager. She has offers coming in and where is the mother? I am pictured in Life magazine in my uniform with hose rolled down. I have suffered like my son. We have the same construction.

It was near dusk now, stormlight forming at the edges of low-sailing clouds, dark and mobbed, and there was urgency, a wildness in the sky, everything electric. The minister finished reciting a psalm and the funeral director prepared to lower the coffin. Policemen adjusted their gun belts shyly. The family stood and watched. Robert and Marina had similar looks, soft, lost, pleading. Make it different, make it not happen, give him another chance, another life. Marguerite, holding little Rachel across her folded arms, showed a desolation so total it could be taken as the only thing left, all she had and was, all she'd given returned to her in a suit in a box, all fall and smash, a soul struck by ruin. She passed the baby to the minister and put her hands to her face, not touching but enclosing only, keeping the moment safe from every woe outside her own.

They lowered her youngest son to the red clay of Texas, burying him for security reasons under another name, the last alias of Lee Harvey Oswald. It was William Bobo.

Now Marina came forward and picked up a handful of dirt. She made the sign of the cross, then extended her arm over the grave, letting the dirt fall. Marguerite and Robert had never seen anything like this. The beauty of the gesture was compelling. It was strange and eloquent and somehow correct. They'd agreed on nothing since Robert was a boy but now they leaned together to the mound of earth and took some dirt and blessed themselves, then held their fists upright over the grave and let the dirt spill out, running through their hands like sand hurrying in an hourglass, lightly falling on the pinewood box.

I stand here on this brokenhearted earth and I look at the stones of the dead, a rolling field of dead, and the chapel on the hill, and the cedar trees leaning in the wind, and I know a funeral is supposed to console the family with the quality of the ceremony and the setting. But I am not consoled.

And this is from oldentimes, that the men will kill each other and the women will be left to stand at the grave. But I am not content to stand, your honor.

I will time his movements on the fatal day. I will interview every witness. I am not speaking just to be speaking. I know as the accused mother I must have facts. Listen to me. Do you know I took Russian classes at the library? I went and studied once a week on my one day off, hoping in my heart that Lee would contact me someday, that I could talk to Marina in a normal way. Listen to me. Listen. I cannot live on donation dribs and drabs. Marina has a contract and a ghostwriter. She refused to wear the shorts I bought. And this boy on a Sunday in Fort Worth was not packed to go anywhere and the next day was gone with his wife and baby to a job in Dallas, overnight, without notice to his former employer or his mother. A job in photography where the details are not known. You have to wonder. Who arranged the life of Lee Harvey Oswald? It goes on and on and on. Lee had a stamp collection. Lee swam at the Y. I used to see him on Ewing Street with his hair all wet. Hurry home dear heart or you will catch your death. I am not letter-perfect but I have managed, judge. I have worked in many homes for fine families. I have seen a gentleman strike a wife in front of me. There is killing in fine homes on occasion. This boy and his Russian wife did not have a telephone or television in America. So that is another myth cut down. Listen to me. I cannot enumerate cold. I have to tell a story. He came home with a birdcage that had a stand with a planter. It had ivy in the planter, it had the cage, it had the parakeet, it had a complete set of food for the parakeet. This boy bought gifts for his mother. He was lonesome to read.

My only education is my heart. I have to work into this in my own way, starting with the day I took him home from the Old French Hospital in New Orleans. I am reciting a life and I need time.

Her hair was bright and strange in the painted glare. The first drops fell. For these final moments at the grave she was still a family. But she knew the minute they moved toward the cars, the Secret

Service would separate her from the others. Think of the emptiness of going home alone. Think of not ever seeing the babies again. She was certain there was a campaign of permanent isolation. The funeral director took her arm and murmured something. She shook him off. The family clustered under umbrellas held by their protectors, moving to the cars now, slowly. Marguerite stayed with the diggers. They wanted to fill the hole before the rain got heavy and they worked in earnest, three men pitching dirt methodically. A couple of local policemen came near. The Secret Service came near with those faces made of slate. Still she did not leave. The mistake she'd made was handing over the baby. As long as she held the baby, she was still a family. They'd taken her youngest son and now they were taking the daughter-in-law and the two little girls. Marguerite felt a weakness in her legs. The wind made the canopy snap. She felt hollow in her body and heart. But even as they led her from the grave she heard the name Lee Harvey Oswald spoken by two boys standing fifty feet away, here to grab some clods of souvenir earth. Lee Harvey Oswald. Saying it like a secret they'd keep forever. She saw the first dusty car drive off, just silhouetted heads in windows. She walked with the policemen up to the second car, where the funeral director stood under a black umbrella, holding open the door. Lee Harvey Oswald. No matter what happened, how hard they schemed against her, this was the one thing they could not take away—the true and lasting power of his name. It belonged to her now, and to history.

AUTHOR'S NOTE

This is a work of imagination. While drawing from the historical record, I've made no attempt to furnish factual answers to any
questions raised by the assassination.

Any novel about a major unresolved event would aspire to
fill some of the blank spaces in the known record. To do this,
I've altered and embellished reality, extended real people into
imagined space and time, invented incidents, dialogues, and
characters.